THE

BAY-PATH;

A Tale of New England Colonial Life.

BY

J. G. HOLLAND,

AUTHOR OF "LETTERS TO THE YOUNG," "LESSONS IN LIFE," ETC.

NEW YORK:
CHARLES SCRIBNER, 124 GRAND STREET.

1862.

TO

SAMUEL BOWLES,

MY

Friend and Associate.

PUBLISHER'S PREFACE.

A SMALL edition of this work, published in 1857, having been for some time entirely out of print, a constant and increasing demand for it has led to its republication.

The very great popularity of the author's subsequent works, which have, in the aggregate, nearly reached the sale of one hundred thousand volumes, would, of itself, give unusual interest to this volume; but it is with special reliance on its own merits that it is again offered to the public.

April, 1862.

PREFACE.

Fiction, though much abused by those who write it, and persistently traduced by those who do not comprehend its true mission, has always been a favorite mode of communicating truth, and has, for its support, the highest sanctions of Christianity. The Author of the Christian system spake evermore in parables in the illustration of important practical truth. In fact (let it be reverently uttered), the great principle in human nature which called Him into the world, is identical with that on which the claims and power of legitimate fiction rest. He came to embody abstract truth in human relations, and the naked, incomprehensible idea of God, in the human form. He came to exhibit in human development the true nature of the divine life, and to demonstrate, in human experience, under the influence of legitimate human motives, the beauty of holiness. It was upon this principle that his wonderful parables were based. The necessity was to exhibit truth in its relations to the feeling, thinking, acting soul; and, in order to meet that necessity at that day, it was requisite that the case should be imagined and the relations created. In the birth of new questions, in the revolution of opinions, and in the shifting aspect of affairs, this great necessity becomes perpetual, and the requisites for its satisfaction remain the same.

With this view of the legitimate aim and high office of fiction, the following pages were written. They were written for New England people at home and abroad, and with the conviction that the basis of New England character is essentially religious. They were written, also, with the belief that the early colonial life of New England, though cramped in its creeds, rigid in its governmental policy, formal in its society, and homely in its details, was neither without its romantic aspects nor its heroes, in high and humble position, with whose full hearts, independent wills, and manly struggles, the largest spirit of this age may fully sympathize. The colonial age of New England was its true age of romance. It was in that age that its institutions were born, its habits established, and its principles planted; and it is to that age that we must look for those exaggerated forms of social, religious, and political life, whose remote or direct relations with the present illuminate them with an interest which everywhere and in all ages informs the childhood of a nation.

For whatever of plot there may be in the following tale, history must, in a general way, be held responsible. The names, localities, characters, and leading incidents are historical. The tale is, in reality, a section or segment of history, withdrawn from its location and relations, and endowed with a life and spirit which aim to be consistent and harmonicus with the body of facts with which they are brought into association. Had the writer felt at liberty to develop his plot entirely at his will, or, rather, had he not felt that history was a more reliable guide to the ends sought to be attained than imagination, some portions of the work, which may not be deemed artistic, would have been differently constructed.

In the title of the book, the reader is at liberty to see more than the simple designation of the channel of travel and transportation between the colonial centre and the distant settlement; for, along its pages, the writer has endeavored to trace, through dim forests of superstition, by the side of life-giving streams of thought, over barren hills of bigotry, among rocks of passion, and across mountain-tops of high resolution and noble action, the path over which those influences passed which shaped the policy of the governing power and moulded the destiny of the governed.

It is not necessary, perhaps, to say that, in the execution of this work, the writer is conscious of having fallen not only below his own ideal, but below the high claims of his subject; yet the extremely kind and cordial treatment which the public have already extended to it, in another and less permanent form, emboldens him to hope for many readers, and for their considerate indulgence.

REPUBLICAN OFFICE, SPRINGFIELD,
January, 1857.

THE BAY-PATH.

CHAPTER I.

It snowed incessantly. Far up in the fathomless grey the shooting flakes mingled in dim confusion, or crossed each other's lines in momentary angles, or came calmly down for a brief space, and then fled traceless into the tempest; and all, as they met the breath of the blast, became its burden, and were swept in blinding and spiteful clouds to the earth. All around, the storm was vocal. The pines hissed like serpents, and the old oak, catching the wild roar of his children in the far north-east, as it came on and on, over writhing and bowing forests, took up the same strong strain, and, struggling like a giant, sent it off triumphantly to the south-western hills.

But the storm was skilful as well as strong. It wove a wreath in the hair of the splintered stump; it chiselled fair capitals upon rude gate-posts; it crowned stone chimneys with layers of marble; it veneered rough house walls with ivory; it made soft pillows and spotless shrouds for dead old trees; it wrought fair cornices for rough cabins; it clothed with ermine unsheltered beasts, and sought fantastic shapes around every corner and in every nook where there was sufficient quiet for the quest.

It had snowed thus all day, and the wind had roared thus, and the new-born shapes had piled, and shifted, and changed thus; and the storm had its witnesses. From the windows of a row of humble cabins, scattered at wide distances from each other, impatient eyes looked out, from time to time, and, occasionally, a muffled form issued forth to the unprotected wood-pile, to gather materials for keeping the storm out of doors.

From the glazed window of the only framed house in the settlement, peered out a wonderful pair of eyes. They were dark, clear and bright, and mild and meaningless. Their owner was a deer, a pet of the house, who stood through long passages of the storm, and watched the falling snow and the driving clouds of sleet, and winked as the arrowy needles struck the window pane. Then, turning his head without stirring a foot, he gazed intently upon the inmates of the room, seated round the roaring fire. Or, his hoofs tapping sharply upon the floor, he retreated from the window, and looked closely and calmly into the faces of those who loved him best, or rubbed his sprouting antlers upon kind shoulders, or begged for bread at the hand—the fairest hand in the settlement—of her who fed him.

The other occupants of this room were a man who had reached nearly fifty years of age, and who, undisturbed by the storm without, was busily engaged in examining papers, and in writing; a prim, silent lady of the same age, who sat quietly in the corner, mending some rough article of male apparel; and a maid of twenty years, who was employed in teaching a boy of twelve.

It was a singular group. The old man, with his large, pleasant eye, looked up amid the pauses of his labor, and regarded his children with affectionate interest; the grave dame pursued her labor in reverence and silence; while the dumb companion, walking from one to the other of the group, or passing between the window and the fire, and attracting the eyes of the maiden and the boy, formed a pic ture of wild and civilized life, beautifully representative of the mixed materials and strange combinations and companionships of a new settlement.

The scene thus opened is in the Agawam of 1638. The family thus introduced is that of William Pynchon, the founder of the settlement, and one of the principal men of the colony of the Massachusetts Bay. He emigrated from England in 1630, was one of the patentees of the colony named in the charter of 1628, and originally settled at Roxbury, of which town he was the principal founder. Soon after landing in New England, he lost his wife, a woman dearly loved and much lamented,—the mother of children who needed her guidance, comfort, and counsel.

A few years passed away, amidst the scenes of the new settlement, and the pressure of new and heavy public responsibilities, when Mr. Pynchon, with a memory still true to the mother of his children, married Mrs. Frances Samford, "a grave matron of the church of Dorchester," to whom he had been attracted by an event in his family with which she was intimately associated. Henry Smith was her son by a former husband, and he had married Ann, the oldest daughter of Mr. Pynchon. Thus connected, they had all removed, in 1636, to Agawam (the Springfield of the present); and two years, with their hardships and changes, had passed over the family at the date of their introduction to the reader.

Incessantly fell the snow, until, as the short day drew to a close, the wind lulled, the sun shone through a golden rift in the west, and the storm had passed. And, everywhere, deep, and white, and soft, lay the snow. Once more the village was astir. The axe that had hung idle all day swung lustily at each cabin door; boys whose confinement had been torture burst forth into the air with a wild whoop and halloo; and before the sun had set, the few cattle and horses of the settlement were yoked to a sled which held a full freight of joyous boyhood, and with shouts the motley procession passed through the street. Paths were shovelled from each door to this, thus made, and the arteries for the circulation of the social life-blood were again established.

Through all the shouting, and all the boisterous demonstrations of freedom that reached his ear from without, the boy John Pynchon sat unmoved, or only lifted his head from his book with a smile, as the chattering throng passed by.

"John," said his father, "why do you not go out, and enjoy yourself with the rest of the boys?"

"Because I do not wish to, sir," was the dignified and respectful reply.

"But why do you not wish to?" inquired the father.

"I don't know, sir,—I can't tell you exactly," hesitated John.

"I think, with all respect to you, sir," said Mrs. Pynchon, bowing to her husband, "that John is afraid of tearing his clothes, which is very good and very proper in him, I'm sure."

Mr. Pynchon looked at John with a quiet smile, and John looked at Mary, his sister and teacher, and the two latter laughed good-naturedly and heartily at the profound solution. The old lady bent on them a not unkind look of inquiry, and subsided to the patch and the needle.

The question remained unanswered, save in the mind of him who proposed it. He had no difficulty in tracing, in the memory of his own youth, the reason of the change which had passed over his son. In high natures the transition from boyhood to manhood is instantaneous, even if not recognised in the consciousness. Under some deep impression, or by some strange inspiration, the young spirit catches a glimpse of its own depth and destiny, and, immediately, the sports and toys of boyhood have lost their power to charm. Or, perhaps, the eye comprehends the grace of some fair form, and the heart, older than the head, traces the outlines of a relation more beautiful and blissful than all other relations, and throws a flood of light upon a future, by the side of which all the present, and all the past, become tame and tasteless.

John Pynchon had grown up by the side, and under the influence of one who was to him mother and instructor, as well as sister. Mary Pynchon! The light of a father's heart, the light of a wilderness home, the light of every eye that beheld her—beautiful, lovely, noble Mary Pynchon! She had lived with this young brother, and had become a portion of his experience. They had walked through the dim old woods together, and she had told him of England, and of his mother, and the long voyage across the ocean, which he remembered as a dream; and she had patiently assisted him in the acquisition of the elements of education, and had been his comforter and companion, in sickness and health, in joy and sorrow, while his father was absorbed in the affairs of the plantation or his constant studies, and while Mrs. Pynchon busied herself in the congenial pursuits of a thrifty housewife. It was not strange that with such culture the boy ripened early, and preferred the society of his sister to that of the noisy rabble whose shouts had filled the air.

The room in which this family were sitting was not devoid of articles that gave even to its rough walls an air of elegance. Gov. Winthrop's "blessing of the Bay" had brought from Roxbury many articles of furniture, in keeping with the wealth and position of their owner. An elegantly mounted hunting-piece stood in one corner, while a pair of well wrought snow-shoes hung by its side. A tall case of drawers and a small oak secretaire occupied opposite ends of the apartment; while a bed, shielded by curtains, was lifted against the wall that opposed the huge fire-place.

The shadows of evening fell around the house, as the family partook of their homely supper, and the meal had but just been cleared away, and the candle-wood set blazing upon the hearth, when a strong rap resounded at the door. John answered the summons and admitted a large, muffled figure—a man who stamped his boots furiously, but who said not a word until he had fairly reached the middle of the room, when, as Mr. Pynchon entered from the other side, he effected a most obsequious bow, with a burly head of bristling hair. The eyes of the new comer were small organs that had an uncertain, vacillating way of looking at everything, and his voice, as he saluted the master of the house, was mild and nervously—querulously—musical, although the growl of a bear would have been more in consonance with his size and appearance.

"Ah! Mr. Moxon," said Mr. Pynchon, courteously, "I am glad to see you. We have both had a day pretty much at our own disposal, I imagine, and we can afford to spend the evening together. I hope you are very well to-night."

"I am well, sir—well in body—better, perhaps, than is well for me. Madam, I beg your pardon (bowing to Mrs. Pynchon, of whose presence he had thus far been oblivious). Yes, sir—better than is well for me. I feel as if greater trials were necessary to me—necessary to my peace. This poor weak heart of mine needs to be driven to its faith—Ah! Mary! John! (an accidental recognition of two faces hitherto unobserved)—driven to it, or else I relapse into doubt, and especially here, where I am so much alone."

During this brief and disconnected address, Mrs. Pynchon had dropped her work, and sat drinking in the words without a very perfect comprehension of their import. It was enough to know that the speaker was her minister, and his subject religion, and she had no doubt that he was dropping pearls; and so, while he removed his muffler and cloak, she said, "how true!"—an unguarded expression, as she had not heard her husband's opinion, which she gracefully sought to cover by brushing up the hearth with a turkey's wing.

Mr. Pynchon sat down, and gazed for some moments into the fire, and then, in his calm way, said—" Mr. Moxon, unbelief never troubles me here. It never troubles me when I am alone. Here, in these solitudes, I live with God. I know, and constantly realize that He is above me, and around me. It is only in crowds that I tremble. When I see a throng—an innumerable multitude—suggestive, as it is, of the number of a nation, and that, in turn, of the number of a generation, and that, again, of all the generations that have come and gone in the world's history, I stagger at the thought of their immortality, and doubt whether there is room for them, even in their destiny."

" Mr. Pynchon, you and I have been frank with each other," replied the minister, shifting uneasily in his chair, and looking suspiciously around the room, " and I confess to you that my great want is faith—faith. Sometimes I feel as if I had it—as if I had grasped it—as if (and he looked up excitedly)—as if my arm were thrown around a pillar of God's throne,—and then it goes from me—vanishes—and leaves me weak and miserable. Sir, where you are the strongest, I am the weakest. Here, alone, with nothing but the wilderness and wild men around me, I feel as if I were astray in God's universe; as if I were lost to His care, and forgotten in His knowledge. I want more support, more companionship of belief, so that my faith shall be able to fall in no direction without striking a firmer faith that shall throw it back to its position. I am comforted here to-night, with you, and strengthened by being near you, and yet"—(and he abruptly and hurriedly arose, and crossed the room)—" I am the spiritual teacher of this settlement!" The last sentence was uttered in a tone of deep self-abasement and condemnation.

This exhibition had no novelty with Mr. Pynchon, but

it was new in a great measure to the family, who sat in silence and deep interest during its continuance. Mrs. Pynchon was bewildered, while Mary listened, both to her father and to Mr. Moxon, with the most intense interest. Her bright countenance caught the eye of her father, and, turning kindly to her, he said, "Come, my good child, my Christian philosopher, tell your minister and your father what the trouble is with them."

Mary's cheek became suffused with a modest blush, and her blue eye bright with the truth and intelligence within it, as she replied:

"Father, I cannot explain the difference between you and Mr. Moxon, or, perhaps, I should say, the difference in your views and feelings under the same circumstances, but it seems to me that the great differences in religious experience grow out of the fact that there is a great difference between our being in religion, and religion being within us. There are many, too many, it seems to me, who are simply in religion. They move in a religious atmosphere, and handle religious things, and eat religious food, for their daily necessities or occasional emergencies, and are thus at the mercy of their temperaments and the sport of circumstances. There are others whose spirits religion occupies and possesses, and it seems to me that with such God is present, both in the crowd and in the wilderness, and that they have no need to seek for faith anywhere, for faith possesses them everywhere."

"Well done! my daughter. We are both reproved," replied Mr. Pynchon, placing his hand upon her earnestly up-turned forehead; but Mr. Moxon, who had stood listening to her without looking at her, remained silent, and in motionless reflection. A new light seemed to open upon him, and severe self-questionings were in almost unconscious progress within his troubled and uncertain nature. Was that the solution of his struggle? Was he in religion or religion in him? The voice of an angel could not have aroused him more powerfully than the maiden's simple but positive revelations. The assurance of a firmly poised reason, and the confidence of a steadfast heart, were rocks against which his bark could not dash without instantaneous wreck. Its timbers were too loosely joined—too poorly fitted. This child of his flock, this girl, with her fine instincts and her well instructed heart, had thrown his soul into entire confusion, and he certainly seemed likely to have all the trials which he felt that his happiness and security demanded.

Mary became instantly conscious of the effect she had produced on her minister's mind, and would have erased it, if possible; for she believed that his eccentricities were more attributable to a defective mental and physical organization than to a lack of genuine religious experience; but, just as she had opened her lips to speak, Mr. Moxon started, turned his head suddenly, and, snuffing the air nervously, exclaimed, "musk!"

"Ah! Commuk! Commuk!" shouted John, breaking a silence he had maintained since the advent of the minister, and leaping, at one bound, half way to the uncurtained window.

All turned their eyes in that direction, and there, staring steadily in upon the group, the fitful light of the burning candle-wood flashing full in his tawny face, stood a tall Indian, holding up to view a package of beaver skins, whose proximity Mr. Moxon had so readily detected.

"Tell him to come in, John," said Mr. Pynchon. John was at the door in a moment, and, releasing Commuk from his burden of peltry, brought it in, and laid it upon the hearth. The Indian, with whom John was a favorite, and who was no less a favorite of the boy, followed the latter with a brace of partridges, which he insisted upon putting into no hands but those of Mary, who received them with a smile of acknowledgment, and passed them into an adjoining apartment.

This strange interruption broke up the whole current of thought and conversation. Mrs. Pynchon, to whom the singular appearance of the minister had become extremely oppressive, was immediately alive to the new order of things She had seen the partridges, and given expression to her gratification in an exclamation that hung upon the letter *m* with a singing tone, as if her imagination were already feasting on the broiled and buttered birds. The prospect of the trade which was wrapped up in that valuable package of beaver skins had also tended to enliven the good old lady. It looked like living. It looked like business.

Commuk had said nothing. Nothing but grunts, of greater or less significance, had escaped him, in response to the various remarks that had been addressed to him. Mrs. Pynchon gave up to him her corner, and John, who seemed to anticipate the Indian's wants more readily than the rest, soon deposited a pewter plate in his lap, charged with bountiful slices of corn bread and cold venison.

Meanwhile, Mr. Moxon had busied himself with a readjustment of his muffler, had replied to Mary's kind inquiries concerning his wife and children, and was hurrying on his cloak, apparently holding his breath, so far as possible, when the family gathered respectfully around him and responded pleasantly to his hurried "good evening." The beaver skins and the Indian were too much for his fastidious sensibilities, and the cold, clear air outside was as grateful to him as balm. Commuk had watched him through the process of leave-taking without tasting his food, but when the door closed he gave a satisfied grunt and settled back to silence and his supper.

While the new comer is thus engaged, and the family carry on their conversation in a quiet tone, watching John as he unties and holds up, one by one, the beaver skins that are to be transferred in sale to Mr. Pynchon, it will be well to give a brief history of the gentleman who has just engaged our attention.

The Rev. George Moxon received Episcopal ordination in England, and sought within the regular forms and lofty sanctions of the established church that peace of mind and stability of belief for which he had longed and prayed; but he sought in vain. He then studied the Puritans, and the vitality of their sturdy virtues became attractive by degrees, as it was developed in fixedness of purpose, determination of will, devotion to duty, and steadfastness of faith, until he lost his hold of the mother's hand, and passed over to the non-conformists. At this time he was serving as chaplain to Sir William Brereton, and preaching in St. Helen's Chapel, near Warrington, in Lancashire, from which place he was obliged to flee in disguise, a citation for his appearance having been placed upon the door of his chapel. He embarked at Bristol, crossed the Atlantic, became a freeman at Boston in 1637, and, during the same year, commenced his labors as the first minister of the church in Agawam.

In Mr. Pynchon he had found a mind self-poised, a clear judgment, a steady friendship, and a true Christian charity. To such a nature as his, Mr. Pynchon was a fountain of strength, and light, and encouragement; and, as that gentleman was his patron in a certain sense, and a man who was his equal in education, and eminently his superior in social and political position, he felt no humiliation in revealing to him his trials, and throwing himself upon his counsels and sympathies.

Commuk, the Indian, who sat devouring his supper in the corner, was altogether less civilized than his dress indicated, for that was, at least, half English. He was one of the thirteen Indians who conveyed by deed the territory of Agawam to Mr. Pynchon and his associates, and at this time had upon his back one of the "eighteen coats" received as the principal consideration named in the conveyance. The deer-skin leggings and moccasins that appeared below it, and the long hair and nondescript head-gear exhibited above, produced a figure hardly less ludicrous than wild and picturesque.

The effect of the warm fire and of the supper upon Com muk was such as to interfere entirely with the progress of the trade, for he had no sooner completed his meal than, securing his peltry, he stretched himself upon the floor near the fire, and went to sleep. This was a step beyond Mrs. Pynchon's calculations. It interfered with all her ideas of good housekeeping. Besides, he might, if allowed to remain there, set the house on fire. She had no special fear of the Indian, but she would not consent to sleep in the room with him; so she and Mary retired together, and left John and his father to occupy the apartment with the Indian. The fire was replenished with heavy logs, and, at an early hour, silence and sleep had settled upon the household.

CHAPTER II.

AT the time Mr. Moxon issued from the house of Mr. Pynchon, the stars were sparkling brightly in the heavens, and the deep snow lay still and white beneath them. His own house was not far off, but the night was so still that he walked past it, wrapped in his thoughts, and unmindful of the biting cold. He walked on until a fox, out upon a marauding excursion, crossed the path but a few feet in advance of him, when he paused, and followed with his eye the suspicious prowler, as, with a quickened bound, he fled to the woods upon the eastern hill.

Still pausing, he looked upward and around. There, from above, looked down the stars, glowing and flashing upon him by thousands, and yet those stars were worlds—parts of great systems, freighted with wonderful life and stupendous destinies! There they wheeled in their calm cycles, and filled the abysses with light and order, and the music of their endless song! There was no clash, no jar, no rebellion there! There they hung, and swung, as if they were the lamps that lighted the passage between the two eternities.

He looked at them long, and then dropped his eyes upon the dim outline of cabins, scattered along the distance, revealing from an occasional glazed aperture the light that gleamed from blazing hearths; and they seemed so lonely and so small, that it appeared almost blasphemy to think that they should come within the cognizance and care of the infinite God of an infinite universe. And then he came back to himself, a poor unit, a weak atom, at war with itself, and inharmonious with its accidents; and he sank down, down, into depths of conscious insignificance, so fearfully profound, that death and despair could hardly have been darker.

He started from his reverie with a pang, and began to retrace his steps. He had walked but a few rods when, in passing a cabin, he heard a boisterous laugh, and loud voices in merry conversation. He knew the inmate, and disliked him. He was a new comer in the plantation, and he had already had an altercation with him. The minister stood irresolutely before the door, qnestioning whether it were his duty to enter or pass on. He felt sure that there were apprentices in the house who had stolen from their homes to listen to John Woodcock's stories.

At length, the half sarcastic, half good-natured voice of the occupant broke out with—"Come, gal, aint it about time you was climbin' them 'ere wooden notches?"

The reply came in the voice of a petulant, ill-trained girl —"No, dad, I know what you want. I know what you're goin' to do—you're goin' to play cards."

"Well, little one, we wont trouble you to keep tally. 'Twould be oncommon perlite in you to do it, but we're gentlemen—we cant 'low it."

"I won't go up-stairs to-night, in the snow, any way," replied the girl determinedly. "I know what you want."

"You're an oncommon smart child," responded the father, growing bitter in tone. "Didn't you never hear of a little gal, about your size, that went up stairs one night, and went to bed, and while she was sound asleep the booggers come, and carried off her poor old father, and several particular friends, and didn't touch the little gal, 'cause they had such long toe-nails they couldn't get up stairs?"

An impatient, disdainful ejaculation from the girl, and a loud, coarse laugh from the company present, were the response to this flight of the father's fancy.

"Mary, gal," pursued the father, "do you see that picter? That's a beautiful picter, ain't it? 'Seems to me that picter looks considerable like your great-grandmother. Now if you'll come here, you'll find them features will put you in mind of somethin'."

This characteristic allusion to a rod that hung upon the wall was complimented with another coarse laugh from the speaker's companions. The girl was still determined and silent.

The minister, who had overheard all, and had become deeply interested, approached the door, and through a small window, looked into the room. There sat the girl, staring into the fire, with her thin lips pressed firmly together, and her eyes strong with anger.

At length feeling that the storm of her father's wrath was about to burst upon her in a form more dreadful than that of mockery, she burst into a fit of uncontrollable crying. Then her tongue was loosed, and she poured out upon her father her insane wrath in one voluble stream, which at last subsided into a hysterical alternation of sobbing and scolding. The scene seemed rather to amuse her father, who sat looking at her coolly during its continuance, and then asked her what she was going to do about it.

"I'll tell Mr. Pynchon, and Mr. Moxon, too," spitefully replied the child.

The matter had at last proceeded too far to be decidedly pleasant, even to Woodcock, for it had produced a painful silence in his company, and he dared not then lay a finger on his child. So, referring to her threat, he said, "Do tell em:—happy to have you go up and invite the gentlemen down here. Give 'em John Woodcock's respects—happy to see 'em at eight o'clock—business of importance—messenger jest in from the Bay—arrival of the Church of England on wheels—Oh! (arising and going over the mock ceremony of receiving the gentlemen alluded to), Mr. Pynchon! I trust your worship is well to-night. Sit down, sir; how's the old woman, and what's the price of beaver? I expect Mr. Moxon here soon, and then we'll have a quiet game of cards, and something hot, p'raps."

"I wish Mr. Moxon *would* come," exclaimed the girl, rising and looking intently at the door.

There was something in her action and manner that attracted every eye, and even her father paused, and looked with the company at the door.

They had been in that position but a moment, when the wooden latch was slowly raised, the door was opened, and Mr. Moxon stood, at his full height and broad dimensions, in the room. There were three lads there, who did not belong there. Pale with fright, they slunk back from the light, and pulling their caps down over their faces, endeavored to pass behind him out of the door. He turned, and recognised each as he passed, and closed the door after them as they retired. Then turning to Woodcock, he addressed him in a voice in which sadness and sternness were equal ingredients:

"Goodman Woodcock, those apprentices have been seduced here by you, and it becomes my duty, as the minister of this place, to reprimand you for your great sin in this thing. You have also abused that child, who, without a mother, is as much your slave as your daughter."

Woodcock was no coward, but he was taken by surprise, and a moment's reflection restored him to himself. Looking the minister doggedly in the face, he replied, "If I was somebody else, and somebody else was John Woodcock, and a gentleman had walked into his house, and no questions asked, and stepped between him and his friends, sayin' nothin' about his own flesh and blood, and given him cold sass and what's tantamount to a Pope's bull, I should say to John Woodcock, 'My friend, when you skin your own skunks, in your own cabin, and a neighbor who comes snuffin' round the latch-string, says the smell is onpleasant, say to that gentleman you presume there's roses in the next house, and people dyin' to have him come and smell on 'em.' "

"I understand you, John, and am not to be offended by your uncharitable, not to say impertinent, remarks. You will very probably hear of this again. In the meantime, I beg that you will treat this child kindly and cease to sacrifice her comfort, and everything good in her character to—to—"

"Oh, don't be bashful, Mr. Moxon; now you're here, you might as well finish up the business, and do your duty—in season and out of season, you know," said the cool, hard-faced man, with a sneer.

"To your recklessness of religion, and your depraved tastes," continued the minister.

"Yes, that's it—there's where it comes. I don't know what would become of religion in this colony if it wasn't for John Woodcock. There's been a great many saints made, improvin' their gifts on me, sir. It sort o' polishes 'em up, and finishes 'em off, to practise on me. I've had people come forty or fifty miles sometimes to see a real sinner—one of the genuine article. You see they're rare in this country. There's so many Christians here that people have to depend on their neighbors for sins enough to talk about."

The minister looked at the speaker sadly, as he went on in his tone of biting sarcasm, and seeing that he could effect nothing further, withdrew, and, closing the door after him, sought his home.

The evening had been an eventful one to him. The cabin of Woodcock and the incidents there had transformed him. He had performed what he believed to be Christian duty, and though it had not produced a single good result towards him who had engaged it, so far as he could see, he felt like a new man. He was refreshed and invigorated. Turning from the great things of God to the small things of duty; from infinite spheres of motion, to the modest circle of his own responsibilities, from the passive reception of humbling thoughts, to the active exertion of humble power upon objects morally and intellectually inferior to himself, he had grown in stature and in strength, measured by his own emotions, until he had come near to God, by a faith that satisfied, and that bathed his heart in perfect peace.

After he left Woodcock's cabin, that individual sat before his fire, for some time, in silence. At length, turning towards his daughter, who sat looking into the fire, and preparing her mind for whatever turn affairs might take, he said, in softened tones, "Mary, gal, get into my bunk, and go to sleep. I'll manage somehow."

The girl started to her feet, and seemed, at first, as if she were about to rush into her father's arms, but she passed by him, and commenced gathering a bed upon the floor, composed of blankets and skins. As soon as this task was completed, she hastily prepared herself for the night, and lying down upon her rude bed, was soon asleep. The father waited until the bonds of unconsciousness were sufficiently strong upon her, and then, lifting her gently from the floor, he laid her upon his own rough couch, and covering her warmly, resumed his seat before the fire.

"Well," exclaimed he at last, commencing a rambling soliloquy, "the gate's h'isted, the floom's full o' water, and John Woodcock's the grist. I wonder if the gentleman that's jest took toll likes the grain. It don't make no difference whether he does or not. What business had he to come in, and disturb my hen-roost, and scare my chickens? But that's the way here—jest so in Roxbury. Ministers and magistrates always nosin' round, 'tendin' to their duties. Duties! who made 'em duties? This 'ere cabin's mine, and I'm myself—John Woodcock. I don't look like a baby. I hav'n't asked anybody to come and watch over me, and be my guardeen. Here they've been to work, makin' a devil of me ever since I landed, tryin' to make me a saint—getting me mad so's to make me better. And there's them boys. I've got 'em into a scrape, I s'pose, but I couldn't help it. I've got to fellowship with somebody, and so have they, but we aint any of us pious enough for the parson, nor perlite enough for the Square, and that's enough to drive the saints out of sight and hearin'. Wonder if they think it's natur to live here all alone, and say nothin' to nobody.

"Arter all, the Square is a pretty good man. He thinks I don't know what he come here from Roxbury for, but I'll bet my head agin a pewter mug that his reason for comin' here and mine look enough alike to be twins. I see it plain enough long ago. The Bay folks was too stiff for him. He didn't like bein' crowded better'n I do."

Here he was disturbed by words from his child, who, dreaming, was deprecating some punishment from his hand. "Poor gal," continued he, "I haven't but just found you out. You're just like me, too, and I've been crowdin' you just as other folks crowd me. I've been too hard on you, Mary. But you're strange—strange. I guess we'll get along better, after this—I guess we will."

Woodcock then added a huge log to his fire, took a few economical whiffs from a short pipe, and committed himself to rest.

John Woodcock has introduced himself to the reader with sufficient detail, perhaps, but it will be proper to give a brief sketch of his more recent history. He, with John Cabel, was the first white man who erected a house in the Connecticut Valley. In 1635, he was sent from Roxbury, in advance, by William Pynchon and his associates, to prepare a dwelling and plant corn. He was just the man to undertake the task. At the distance of many miles from any white settlement, Windsor and Hartford being the nearest, he had sufficient room and felt no restraint. With a strong, original nature, he spurned all control, and only asked for the privilege of minding his own business, or of doing his business in his own time and way. He was not ill-natured, but he had grown wilful by being badgered by church and police, until he was sensitive in the extreme.

His daughter Mary was his only child, the only child of a wife who had been dead for some years. Her father's peculiarities had debarred her from the associations so necessary to the development of soft and childlike traits, and she had grown to the age of twelve with passions unchecked, and with a character whose affinities were coarse, even to masculineness. It was the first time that he had ever caught a glimpse of the secret of her singular development of character. He had thought her wilful and stubborn, and so she was; but as soon as he began to trace in her a likeness to himself, his heart softened with a kindly sympathy, and he resolved to treat her more tenderly.

CHAPTER III.

On the morning following the events that have been recorded, the first person moving in the house of Mr. Pynchon was Commuk, the Indian, who, long before daylight, had exhausted sleep, and newly fed the expiring fire. The earliest beams of the morning found the family again assembled, and while the thick smoke of the kindling pine was ascending from each cabin chimney in the settlement, through the still, icy air, Commuk made his way to the principal village of his tribe, but a short distance southward. The price of his beaver skins—a hatchet and a balance of wampum—hung in his belt, while a few trinkets, presents from John and Mary, found a less exposed receptacle in the honest English pockets of his coat.

Soon after the morning devotions were concluded, Mary, who was standing at the window, exclaimed, "I wonder where Mr. Moxon can be going at so early an hour this morning!"

Mr. Pynchon joined his daughter at the window, but neither attracted the attention of the reverend gentleman, as he made his way past the dwelling, apparently very much absorbed in thought, and bent upon the attainment of an immediate object. At length he passed beyond the range of the window, and disappeared, but, in a short time, again came in sight, on his way back, and directed his steps towards Mr. Pynchon's house.

Mary met him at the door with a cordial grasp of the hand, but he had hardly crossed the threshold when he drew back, as if suddenly recollecting himself, and inquired whether the Indian had gone. On being assured that that individual and his offensive burden were both out of the way, he came forward, and, without removing his coat and muffler, related to Mr. Pynchon the events of the previous evening, in connexion with his visit to the cabin of Woodcock; and stated that he had started out that morning to inform the masters of the three apprentices he had found there of their delinquency, and its cause and probable consequences, in order that they might take such steps with Woodcock and the boys as they might deem proper. After arriving at the house of the first of these masters, he had changed his mind, and come back to ask Mr. Pynchon's advice in the premises.

Mr. Moxon watched that gentleman as he received the narrative, and when, as it closed, he perceived that his hearer hesitated, his own positiveness of mind, or whatever amount of that quality he possessed, entirely left him, and he sat down irresolute, and with the old symptoms of dejection.

At length Mr. Pynchon said: "I know John Woodcock very well. I have known him for several years, and I have seen the effect upon him of the efforts that have been made to curb his naturally independent spirit. I think the best thing to be done is to get him to come here, and have a quiet talk with us upon the subject, and to treat him in a friendly way. It is the thing to be done first, I am certain."

As Mr. Moxon made no objection to this arrangement, a messenger was sent to Woodcock, requesting him to call, as soon as convenient, at Mr. Pynchon's house, and, at the desire of Mary, to bring his child.

The temporary suspension of this matter gave to both of the gentlemen an opportunity to recur to the subject always uppermost in their thoughts when together—religion; and in this they engaged until the return of the messenger, who reported that he had found Woodcock waiting for him, and quite impatient that he had not come before, as he declared he had been expecting him for half an hour. The only thing to delay him was the bringing of his daughter, a matter for which he had not calculated. While they were talking, Woodcock came in sight, bearing his child upon his back, his burden being completely covered by a wolf skin that dangled downward to his heels.

The poorly suppressed mirth excited by his appearance was a good preparation for his reception, and, when he appeared at the door, there was not a frown in the room to throw a cloud upon his coming. Even the grave lady of the house, softened by the influences around her, looked up kindly at the old culprit, as he entered. Woodcock paused, and without letting go his grasp of the child's hands, held her still suspended upon his shoulders, as he bowed to one and another of the group; and then, after the most convulsive workings of his features, he burst into a hearty, boisterous fit of laughter.

This, of course, changed the aspect of things at once. The dignity of the house and the presence had been violated, and with such an effect as to assist him very much in regaining control of his emotions. In the meantime, Mary Pynchon had relieved him of his burden, and had led the poorly clad, haggard-looking child from the room.

As soon as he could speak, Woodcock commenced an apology. "Mr. Pynchon, I beg pardon—I meant no offence to your honor, or your house, but I took a consait just as I come in, that this 'ere old wolf skin is a very remarkable strip of luther. It took twenty men two days to get this skin, sir. They chased the critter that wore it one day, and dug for him another, and when they brung him home, it struck me that the animal was a mighty sight too small for so big a fuss. So, says I to myself, here's the old skin agin, and a miserable critter inside of it, and a big onreasonable fuss outside. I meant no offence to you, sir, but the consait was a little too much for me, and I couldn't hold in."

Having concluded what he honestly meant should be a satisfactory apology for his rudeness, Woodcock threw his wolf skin over a chair, sat down, and looked at Mr. Pynchon in a way to indicate that he was ready for business.

That gentleman regarded him gravely for a moment, and then said, "Goodman Woodcock, I am informed by Mr. Moxon that you are pursuing disorderly practices in the plantation by enticing apprentices to your house, and harboring them at unseasonable hours; and that, when reprimanded by him, you gave him disrespectful replies, to his great grief and scandal. He proposed, at first, to bring the matter before me as a magistrate, but I thought we had better see you, and talk it over first, and ascertain what you had to say about it."

A bitter smile passed over the face of the old woodman, as he replied, "I thank you, Square, for considerin' me, but I'm afraid it's too late to do me any good this way. I've been thinking how this man pushed into my cabin last night, and I know 'twant right; and for me to set down here to be labored with, and him to set there with his pious face a lookin' on, as if he'd done nothin' wrong, goes agin my grain and makes me wicked."

Mr. Moxon sat very uneasily during this speech, and, turning to Mr. Pynchon at its close, remarked, "I think, sir, that you will conclude with me that my first impulse was the true one, for I doubt not that the man is given over to a reprobate mind, and utter hardness of heart."

This was sufficient to throw Woodcock back upon his old ground of mockery; and, turning sharply upon the minister, and giving him his characteristically dogged look of defiance, he replied, "When a man tells me in a sermon that I have got a precious soul, and that his heart is runnin' over with love for me, and that the Lord above loves me, too, and then comes into my house to get me to tread on his toes, and calls me names for hurtin' his corns, I'm thankful I got hold of the name of John Woodcock before such a one as George Moxon was mixed up and baked."

"Woodcock," said Mr. Pynchon, sternly, "I insist on no such language towards your minister, and shall not allow it in this house."

"Well, there it is, sir; you turn agin me as soon as I touch the minister. It's jest so down t' the Bay. Magistrates and ministers all hang together. They seem to think the colony was made for them; but who does the work? They have all the honors, and the rest on us have to stand back. It's 'Mister,' and 'Goodman;' and it's 'set here,' and 'stand there;' and it's the top o' the milk to one, and skim milk to the other. Here you are a rulin' on us, and I don't see the justice on it. P'raps my memory is unsartin, but it seems to me I have read somewhere that it's the business of them that wants to be great to serve them that aint so particular about it."

Both gentlemen sat somewhat uneasily during this criticism of the spirit of the institutions of the day, and the homely but pointed reproofs connected with it. Mr. Pynchon responded briefly, to the effect that he did not propose a discussion of questions of theology or state. Woodcock had been invited there as a man who had honorable feelings, to settle a matter in which he was evidently at fault, in a manner which should neither injure his pride nor be a subject of scandal in the plantation. He hoped no more trouble would arise in relation to this affair, and that Woodcock would cease to give occasion for complaint. As for Mr. Moxon, he had done simply what he deemed it his duty to do, and in the execution of his duty had not transcended the sphere warranted by the usages of the colony or the opinion of the church.

Woodcock heard him through, and then inquired if they were done with him.

"I am done," said Mr. Pynchon, with a bow to Mr. Moxon, intimating that the man was at his disposal.

"I wish," said Mr. Moxon, with an earnest, solemn air, "to say a few words of warning, and then I shall feel as if my duty had been discharged. Goodman Woodcock, you are placing your soul in peril by your course of life, and even now there is reason to fear that it is given over to destruction. Your heart, which should be humble and penitent, is stubborn and rebellious. In your foolish pride, you speak evil of dignities, despise the religion of Christ and its ministers, and meet the reproof due to your course of life and conduct with mockery. I warn you of the terrible end of all this, and may God have mercy on you, and, in his infinite grace, save your soul!"

All this was uttered with genuine feeling, and under the dictates of a sense of duty that even Woodcock did not fail to recognise, but he looked at the minister sadly and bitterly, and replied, "'Taint no use for you to talk to me that way. You can't do me no good. You're too far up, and I'm too low down. Your words come down jest like rain spatterin' on a rock. They don't soak in any. You ain't the 'pothecary to give me physic, and that ain't the right kind of stuff if you was. It only raises the devil in me, and riles me all up. What's the use trying to drive a man, and running agin his pluck, if he's got any, when you might be kind o' human with him? No, sir, you've made up your mind agin me, I know that—and when I know you don't understand how I feel, and what I'm talking to you about, it's no use for you and me to make any more words."

The minister drew a long sigh, and Mr. Pynchon turned to his writing-desk, as if to hint to Mr. Moxon that the quicker the interview was terminated the better.

"Where's the gal?" inquired Woodcock, rising.

Mr. Pynchon stepped to the door opening into the apartment occupied by the remainder of the family, and told Mary that the child's father was about to depart. The door was closed for a moment, then it was re-opened, and in bounded Mary Woodcock, wild with delight, clothed anew with articles from Mary Pynchon's stores of the well preserved garments of her childhood, a snug pair of moccasins on her feet, and a warm hood upon her head.

"Oh, father! father!" exclaimed the delighted child; and unable to express her own feelings, or give direction to his, she stood on tiptoe before him, and stretched up first one arm for his inspection, then the other, then turned around, put her hand upon her head, lifted, one after the other, her feet, and exhausted every childish ingenuity to exhibit the extent and beauty of her newly gotten treasures; and then, as she could do no more, she threw her head upon his lap, and burst into tears.

In the meantime, Mary Pynchon and the pet deer had entered the room. Tom (the name of the pet), went from one to the other of the company, lifting his slender neck towards their faces, and making himself generally, though inoffensively inquisitive, until he came to Mary Woodcock, when he put his cool nose down to her cheek, and brought her once more to her feet. Seeing the eyes of all bent upon her, she moved off with Tom to the window, as if deeply chagrined at having made herself so conspicuous.

Woodcock sat still for a few moments, his lips quivering with an emotion that he could not suppress, and then, rising, he approached Mary Pynchon, and said, "Miss Pynchon, I hav'n't no words for such as you, and you don't need 'em. You've got plenty of better ones made a purpose for you. That old Bible up there is full on 'em, and when you find some in it that are jest as thankful and jest as humble as they can be, I want you should remember John Wood cock, and think he's sayin' 'em to you."

Mary was touched by his emotion, and, taking his rough hand, said, "I am very glad if I have done anything tc make you and your little girl happy. I hope you will be very kind to Mary, for she has no mother, and must be very much alone. Do let her come and see me sometimes."

"Do you understand that, sir?" said Woodcock, turning to Mr. Moxon. "That's what I call preachin'. I haint been much used to such preachin' as that, but I know it's genuine. It's the only kind for my case. Do you s'pose I'd lay a finger on that gal of mine with a heart like Mary Pynchon's lovin' her? Do you 'spose I wouldn't work for her, and bear with her, strange and offish as she is sometimes, when I see such a woman fussin' over her, and makin' her comfortable and happy? I feel as if my gal had just been baptized, which she never was, and I couldn't feel much better myself, if I'd been took into the church, which I ain't fit for, the Lord knows. That's the kind o' preachin' that does me good."

So saying, he walked up to his little girl, and was about to lift her upon his back, but she begged to be allowed to go by herself. He then threw the wolf skin over his shoulders, bade a homely good morning to the silent family, and, preceded by his child, who, elated with her new possessions, went bounding through the snow before him, sought his own cabin.

"God hath chosen the foolish things of the world to confound the wise, and God hath chosen the weak things of the world to confound the things which are mighty," said Mr. Pynchon, looking with a smile at his daughter, as Woodcock closed the door.

"I am afraid," returned Mary, archly, "that we shall quarrel in dividing that quotation satisfactorily among ourselves, and it is pity John Woodcock had not remained a little longer, as he might have assisted us."

"What portion of it do you suppose he would wish to appropriate to himself?" inquired Mr. Moxon, looking up.

"He would claim for himself neither wisdom nor might, I presume," replied Mary.

"Hum! No—that belongs to the confounded party, of course," replied the minister, slightly nettled. "I do not approve of playing with texts of Scripture, but it seems to me that, with this application, the quotation should have been extended. 'And the base things of the world, and things which are despised,' would more fully complete the description of the man, in my opinion."

Mary did not like the tone in which these remarks were uttered, and playfully sought to divert the course of conversation by saying that she thought they were complimenting Woodcock too highly. She claimed a little credit for herself, and even Woodcock had accorded to her the merit of being a good preacher; though for her part, she could not see as her sermon had more than one head, and that had a hood on it, or that its application consisted of more than an old frock and a pair of moccasins. She would prefer that those articles of apparel receive the compliments bestowed on Woodcock rather than he should have them all to himself.

Mrs. Pynchon, who abounded especially in the grace of silence, and who really had excellent traits of character, springing from a basis of practical common sense, was accustomed, in the course of any family scene or social interview, to make some remark which, with a fatal perversity, rarely failed to be one that amused its hearers with its utter innocence of pertinency and point. This seemed to spring from the fact that she did not remember the conversation and events out of which grew the peculiar aspect of the subject upon which she might happen to remark; and it was for this reason, doubtless, that her choice speeches were irrelevant by rule, and rarely failed to excite a smile, even among those who respected her most and loved her best. Her reverence for her husband was thoroughly sincere, and as formal as sincere, and, with many of the matrons of her day, she believed that her special duties pertained to the good ordering of the house, the economical administration of the kitchen and the wardrobe, and that when this was done, and well done, there was little time for anything else.

In regard to the frock that Mary had just given away so readily, she felt some sensitiveness, as it was only through her own considerate economy that it had been brought from the Bay. So the frock became the prominent object in her thoughts, and the one around which all the events and associations of the morning clustered; and when she felt moved to speak, she stated that the frock was really a very good one, and she was sorry it had made so much trouble. She had taken care of it, thinking that perhaps by and by Mary might get married, when she was sure she would find it very handy.

"Mother!" exclaimed the girl, blushing to her temples, and then turning quickly to the pet she said, "Come, Tom, let us go," and retired from the room. But the blush retired with her, as well as Tom, and her thoughts wandered off and away, along the Bay Path, through the thick, dark woods, and over the streams, and across the hills—the weary path over which she had travelled nearly two years before—and there came up to her mind the form of one who had moved with grace and majesty in her dreams, and whose bright, bold face, and mild, resolute eye, had been to her through all the months of her lonely dwelling at Agawam, a charming presence and a kindly power.

Mr. Pynchon, Mr. Moxon, and Woodcock, were not improper representatives of three prominent classes of men in the early days of the Massachusetts Bay colony. The first represented the highest and noblest class in the colony. He was as intelligently orthodox in faith as any of his contemporaries, but much less bigoted and intolerant than most of them. He had the sense to see that the rigid policy of the government of the colony, intimately connected, as it was, not only with the government of the church, but with its type of religious faith and life, had the double tendency of dwarfing and perverting the development of those who came willingly and conscientiously under its yoke, and of driving into recklessness and desperation those free and strong spirits who felt the yoke to be an intolerable, if not an ignominious, burden. To the last class Woodcock belonged. The spirit which he manifested in his interview with Mr. Moxon was the legitimate result of the treatment to which he had been subjected. He had grown morose and quarrelsome under it, until he had come to regard a minister with hatred and contempt, and to look upon the leading men in the colony as in league with the ministers to do him evil. He seemed, however, to appreciate the difference that existed between Mr. Pynchon and most of his class, and to regard him with a sympathetic respect that betrayed a nature still, in many respects, true to itself.

It was with the more rigid class of political religionists that Mr. Moxon sympathized; and that class was in power, and maintained their position for many years, until at last the church became separate from the government, and more liberal and enlightened counsels prevailed in both bodies.

Consequently it was that, as the minister left the house of Mr. Pynchon, he left it poorly satisfied with the result of the morning's operations. He thought too lenient a course had been pursued with Woodcock—one calculated to make him regard his sin as of little account—one, even, that seemed to reward him for his obstinacy.

CHAPTER IV.

The Sabbath morning following these occurrences was still, clear, and frosty; not a soul was stirring, and it seemed almost as if the lonely cows of the settlement had forgotten to call to each other from their scattered sheds.

At length, when the morning had well advanced, a window in the house of Mr. Pynchon was raised, and a small white signal hung out—an announcement of the hour, by the only timepiece in the settlement. Immediately, from a house within sight, a sturdy figure came forth, bearing a very singular looking Sabbath burden. It was a drum, on which the bearer proceeded to beat a brisk tattoo, which he continued from one end of the street to the other, with such interruptions in his rhythm as occasional snow-drifts and unavoidable missteps would naturally produce.

The drum-beat changed the aspect of the village immediately. Men, women, and children poured out of their humble dwellings, and bent their steps towards Mr. Pynchon's house, no meeting-house having been built, and that being the largest house in the settlement,—large enough, too, to hold all the white inhabitants without discomfort.

The first individuals who arrived were those the least interested in the occasion—the apprentice boys. Among them were those already introduced to the reader under somewhat suspicious circumstances. The leader of this little company was one Peter Trimble. It was he who opened the door, put his head in to see if everything was right, put it out again to assure his friends that the survey was satisfactory, walked in, beckoned the others to follow walked across the floor, took his seat upon a rough-board, temporary bench, motioned to the others to do the same, and then winked significantly at John Pynchon. John looked at him with gravity, but when he saw Peter thrust his hand into his pocket, and change his little mass of features into a physiognomical interjection, and give two or three emphatic forward dodges of his head, as if he would have said, "Oh! John Pynchon, you haven't the smallest possible idea what I've got in my pocket—I'm dying to show it to you," John could not withstand the temptation, and, passing quietly across the room, he took his seat near the mysterious Peter.

Peter's object was accomplished, and so, without making any further allusion to the contents of a pocket that never had a presentable occupant, except in chestnut time, he proceeded to unroll, with slyly rustling whispers, the budget of his gossip.

"Seen old Woodcock lately, John?"

"Yes."

"What did he say?"

John looked around the room to see if he was observed, but made no answer. As soon as the stamping at the door gave opportunity, however, Peter resumed:

"When have you seen old Moxon?"

"I saw *Mr.* Moxon yesterday," replied John, a little indignant, as he knew that his father was liable to similar familiar treatment.

"Oh! *Mr.* Moxon—yes! well—what did he say?"

"Said a good many things," replied John, with his eyes on his father.

"Anything about me?"

"I didn't hear anything; why?"

"Oh! the greatest row you ever see."

"What was it?" inquired John.

"Oh! the darndest row—you've no idea."

"Anybody hurt?"

"Well, no—not exactly hurt, but 'twas an old row, now."

"Don't talk quite so loud—tell me about it," said John cautiously, his curiosity having been considerably excited.

"Well," said Peter—"down to old Woodcock's on a time t'other night—game o' cards on the board—pipes all round—in come old Moxon, and pitched into us;—old Woodcock drew off, and let him have—doubled him up—these two fellows left—scat to death—we locked the door, and I made the parson promise not to tell."

"Peter," said John, "I believe you are lying to me. I'll ask the other boys to-morrow."

"Well—'twas a great row, waan't it? Oh! you ought to 'a been there."

"I don't believe a word of it," said John, his curiosity having sunk into solemn disappointment and vexation at being so heartlessly betrayed. Then rising, he took his seat in another part of the room.

Peter had only made a commencement of his business. His next care was to cover up his tracks. So, turning to his companions, he informed them in broken whispers of the story he had told John, and how John had swallowed the whole thing, and only wished he had been one of the company at Woodcock's.

"Now mind," said Peter to the boys, "if John says anything about this to you, you just back me up, and we'll have the greatest kind of sport out of it." This last assurance was eked out with various animated nods and expressive winks, tending to impress upon their minds the infinite degree of satisfaction in store for them, if they would but follow his instructions.

Peter was not exactly satisfied with the kind of assent he had obtained to his propositions, and as soon as opportunity was offered, by the noise occasioned by a new arrival, he turned to his companions, and, assuming a threatening aspect of countenance, and executing several fierce diagonal nods, said, "You do just as I tell you, now; if you don't you'll catch it. I'll duck you—I'll rub your face in the snow till you can't see. You just try that once—I'll take it out of your hide."

How much further the redoubtable Peter would have proceeded, had it not been for a slight interruption that occurred at this moment, it is impossible to tell, but, as adverse fortune would have it, he had become so much absorbed in his own proceedings as to forget to keep an eye out for those in progress around him, and just as he was about to launch another thunderbolt at the heads of his dumb and fearful friends, he felt a sharp rap upon his own head, and, looking up hurriedly, he saw above him a long stick, while at the other end of it stood Henry Smith, looking at him in solemn reproof. Peter immediately appeared to have a vision of an infinitely attenuated cobweb, swinging somewhere in infinite space, and to have brought to mind some favorite passage of scripture which, through the almost unconscious machinery of his lips, he endeavored to render *verbatim* to his inmost soul. When the bearer of the rod became satisfied with the impression he had made, he withdrew it, and gave it a convenient standing place near his seat.

The assembly had become, during the few brief minutes occupied by this side scene, an interesting and impressive one. The most striking figure of the group—made so by his age, intellectual appearance, and dress—was Mr. Pynchon. Draped in a long, silver-buttoned coat that nearly concealed his deer skin small-clothes, and the puffs and rosettes that marked the junction of the latter with his hose, with a broad collar or band of linen lying flat upon his shoulders, and a closely fitting cap upon his head, he was the impersonation of quiet dignity and patriarchal grace.

Near him sat his family—Mrs. Pynchon with her stiffly starched and formidable ruff, that cast into comparative insignificance the quiet face above and the prim form below; Mary and John, side by side; and Henry Smith and his wife, already introduced as the children, respectively, of Mr. and Mrs. Pynchon. Henry Smith was, as an ancient record of him declares, "a godly, wise young man," and both he and his wife bore that expression of earnest seriousness that marked them as the possessors of a religion that to them was an all-comprehending, all-informing reality. There, too, was Jehu Burr, the carpenter, a short, pompous man, who had within a few months become greatly important in his own eyes for having been sent, in company with Mr. Moxon, a deputy to Hartford; and by the side of him his family. Others, whose names need not be called, filled up the large room; and in each corner, near their owners, stood the faithful muskets, which were the companions of the colonists, alike in the field, the forest, and the house of God.

It was not until after all these were seated that Mr. Moxon appeared, with his wife and one little child following him. Mrs. Moxon was a small, nervous-looking woman, with a sad expression of countenance, and a wild, wan look about her dark eyes that indicated poor health, and a familiar acquaintance with suffering. While the minister took a central seat reserved for him, his wife and child found an unobtrusive location among the audience, and sat down.

Then all was still for a moment, when the door was again opened, and John Woodcock walked in, attended by his daughter. He looked around upon the group, and the cold looks which he met in return performed their usual office upon him. His heart hardened as he stood, and he sat down, steeled against every appropriate influence of the time and place. Taking his seat near the door, and drawing his girl between his knees, he gave himself up to his old rebellious thoughts and bitter reflections.

All was silence again. The minister sat turning over a book of the Psalms, and giving occasional utterance to an ejaculation intended to prepare his throat for speaking, each time recovering from the effort by an inhalation through his nose, that gave forth a peculiar whistling sound which had become familiar to the boys, and ludicrous through Peter Trimble's attempts to imitate it. The ejaculation and the whistle were given, at last, with unusual power, when Peter, who sat with his arms folded very circumspectly, managed to give a sly thrust with his finger into the ribs of his next neighbor, when that individual, already fully charged, gave utterance to an explosive snicker that brought the long stick again into use, and smartly down upon his hard little head.

Peter's vision of the infinitely attenuated cobweb, swinging somewhere in infinite space, was renewed.

The space of time between the whistle and the laugh was so small, that they assumed, in every mind, the relation of cause and effect,—so much so, in fact, that Mr. Moxon was sensibly irritated and discomposed, and, perhaps, without a thought of what he was doing, he looked around and caught Woodcock's eye. The expression that he met there did not tend to re-assure him, but he arose and offered the opening prayer, and then gave out, to be sung, the first Psalm

"That man hath perfect blessedness,
who walketh not astray
In counsel of ungodly men,
nor stands in sinners' way;
Nor sitteth in the scorner's chair;
but placeth his delight
Upon God's law, and meditates
on his law day and night.

"He shall be like a tree that grows,
near planted by a river,
Which in his season yields his fruit,
and his leaf fadeth never;
And all he doth shall prosper well.
The wicked are not so,

But like they are unto the chaff,
  which wind drives to and fro.

"In judgment therefore shall not stand
  such as ungodly are;
Nor in th' assembly of the just
  shall wicked men appear.
For why? the way of godly men
  unto the Lord is known:
Whereas the way of wicked men
  shall quite be overthrown."

Woodcock listened to the reading of the psalm, and grew angry until it closed. He felt it to be, in effect, a public reprimand, as well as a means of private revenge. So far had he become incensed towards Mr. Moxon, by dwelling on his supposed wrongs, that he believed him incapable of a Christian feeling,—incapable of any feeling, in fact, in which he had, or by possibility could have, any sympathy. But when the singing was commenced, and the full, clear voice of Mary Pynchon—rich in its revelations of hope and trust and peace—interfused itself with, and rose above the harmony of the simple choral, Woodcock closed his eyes, and bowed his head upon his child's shoulder in deep emotion. The huge logs were steaming on the hearth, and the sound, mingling with the solemn song, brought back a vision of his boyhood. Through the gathering mists of the past he caught a glimpse of his mother singing at her distaff, and of himself, sitting at the door, looking out into the sweet summer rain.

And still the voice sang on, and the old logs hissed on the hearth.

And then came up before him a calm, patient face—courageous and resolute in its calmness and patience—the face of one so true to him, so loving and so loyal, that at last, travelling willingly in the hard path over which he had called her to walk with him, she had fainted, lain down, and died.

And still the voice sang on, and the old logs hissed on the hearth.

And then came to him a realization—vague, perhaps, but genuine—of the waywardness of his own heart, and its utter perverseness under the influences which rested upon it, and, as he apprehended the softening effect of the music of that only voice that he heard or cared to hear, he wished that the old logs would hiss on and the voice sing on for years, and that at last he might arise a changed and happy man. He felt that he was far from the possession of that perfect blessedness attributed to the subject of the psalm whose serious lesson was falling upon his ears; and yet he needed it and longed for it, and felt that if circumstances were different with him, he might have it yet, and be able at last to lie down in the grave, wrapped in the confidence of a blessed hope.

The singing ceased, and still the head of the father was bowed upon the shoulder of his child. Another prayer—long, fervent, and full of the heartfelt expression of Christian aspiration—was pronounced, and Woodcock, softened, and longing for a peace which his heart told him was somewhere, in something, waiting for him, joined in the supplication—feebly and imperfectly, as a man unused to prayer—and laid the burden of his soul upon the utterance of one whose words, but a few brief moments before, had come to him only with malevolent suggestions. When the prayer was closed, he longed to hear the Bible read. He wished for no words from man; but the reading of the Great Book in the public exercises of the Sabbath, at that day, was a forbidden service. So, lifting his eyes to Mr. Moxon, with a stern resolution to keep out his bad thoughts, if possible, he listened for the announcement of his text.

"*But after thy hardness and impenitent heart, treasurest up unto thyself wrath against the day of wrath, and revelation of the righteous judgment of God.*"

Woodcock shook his head, arose from his seat, placed his girl upon the bench, and then, taking his gun, opened the door and retired from the house. The charm was broken—the hallowed and hallowing influence dissipated. The transition to his old feeling of hardness and half-regretful defiance was accompanied by a sigh as painful as it was profound, and by the characteristic exclamation, "It's no use."

Mr. Moxon waited, before proceeding, for the restoration of silence, but order and attention were not secured for some minutes. Both Mr. Pynchon and Mary understood and appreciated the cause of Woodcock's withdrawal, and felt disturbed. Peter Trimble's curiosity was very much aroused. Bending down in a mock effort to fix his shoe, he exclaimed to the victim at his side, in a low whisper, "Indians!"

The boy was instantaneously and involuntarily on his feet, his neck stretched up, looking out of the window. Down came the long stick of Henry Smith upon his head, and down came the boy. The stick was so near to Peter that his glimpse of the cobweb was this time extremely brief and uncertain.

As soon as the sermon had begun to attract serious attention, Peter made another errand to his shoe, and whispered, "What did you see?"

"Stars," replied the boy, unconscious of anything but his last impression.

This reply came near proving too much for Peter's gravity, and it was a long time before he could command himself with sufficient confidence to raise his head.

At the termination of the services of the morning, little Mary Woodcock, who had sat with her eyes fixed upon Mary Pynchon through the greater portion of the time they had occupied, rose, and stood by the door, while the congregation passed her in retiring. The look of recogni tion and the smile for which she waited were at last secured, and she turned half reluctantly to leave the house.

During all this time, Peter Trimble, with a respectfulness for which he was not notorious, had lingered behind the congregation, and allowed them to precede him in the way homeward. As the little girl left the door, he was at her side.

Slightly touching her arm, as if he imagined that he was touching the most costly fabric, he said, in his most impertinent and sly way, "Some folks wear good clothes, and some folks wear poor clothes. Some people's fathers are rich—and some ain't. You don't remember what that hood cost, do you? It's beautiful, it's—"

"I wish you'd go 'long off, and go home," exclaimed Mary, turning upon him, her eyes flashing with anger.

"But, Molly, where d'you get your new clothes?" persisted Peter, in his bantering way.

"None of your business, you plague," replied Mary, in the same angry voice.

"Well, do you know there's been several things missed from the clothes lines lately, round here?" insinuated the remorseless Peter. "Some people lays it to Injuns, and some don't."

"If you don't let me alone, I'll go back and tell Mr. Pynchon," said Mary, stopping firmly in the path, and looking Peter fiercely in the face.

"Tell him of what?" inquired Peter, coolly. "What have I said? Won't you have the goodness to tell me what I've said? I hav'n't said anything. I only said some people lays it to Injuns and some don't. I think it's wild cats."

There was something so tormentingly insulting in the last insinuation, that Mary involuntarily, and as quick as lightning, struck him a stinging blow in his face. Peter, for the moment, lost his temper, and, taking the girl by the shoulder, he pitched her into the snow. The scream which she gave as she fell brought the family to the window at Mr. Pynchon's house, and a beckoning hand called Peter back, while Mary ran, crying at the top of her lungs, towards home. Peter arrived at Mr. Pynchon's, and was called in, as he expected to be. His cheek was still red with the effect of Mary's blow, which he assured the family was given him by the girl in return for his politeness in endeavoring to assist her to rise, after she had accidentally fallen in the snow.

"I am afraid that girl has a temper too much like that of her father," remarked Henry Smith, who, with his wife, had remained in the house.

"I believe," said Mary, earnestly, "that this boy has not told the truth. I think Mary Woodcock would never have struck him had she not been seriously provoked."

Peter protested his innocence in a tone of voice that showed that his tender spirit had been wounded to the quick by so terrible an accusation. At this moment, the frugal Sabbath dinner was declared to be in readiness, and he was told to remain until its conclusion, that the matter of his difficulty with the little girl might have a further examination.

"What do you suppose Woodcock retired for to-day?" inquired Ann Smith of her father, as they sat down to dinner.

"I suppose that he did not like the text which Mr. Moxon selected for his discourse," replied Mr. Pynchon.

"The carnal mind is enmity against God," said Henry Smith, solemnly. "How little the man understands that the degree of offensiveness which God's truth possesses for him is the measure of his own iniquity, and of his need to have that truth enforced upon him. How little he understands that the more the medicine displeases him, the more he needs it."

"This may all be very true," replied Mr. Pynchon, "but it seems to me that a little wisdom is necessary in choosing that class of Bible truths for Sabbath themes which will not drive men beyond the reach of any truth."

"All Scripture is profitable," replied the son. "The Word of God, in all its purity, is to be preached, whether they will bear, or whether they will forbear. I see not how a man of God can consult expediency in the slightest degree. His duty is plain, and he may only go on and do it, and leave the result with God."

Mr. Pynchon had been somewhat in the habit of masking his real opinions and sentiments in relation to many important subjects while in the presence of his family, because they came in collision with the prevailing opinions and sentiments around him. He felt perhaps, that were his family to think as freely as himself, they might get into difficulty by a too frank expression of their thoughts, and he possibly shrank from the responsibility of inflicting upon them the doubts and disquietude that spring from conscious differences with a prevalent faith. But this occasion was too important, and the lesson too necessary, to be neglected. Accordingly, he very fully gave his opinions upon the subject that had been introduced.

"The office of the Christian minister," said Mr. Pynchon, "I regard as the highest and the noblest which a man can be called upon to assume. The minister is the man who stands in Christ's stead, beseeching his fellow men to be reconciled to God. He is also, in the fullest sense, a servant of Christ—bound to adopt his policy, to be filled with his spirit, to be informed and inspired with his life, and to overflow, in every word and action, with that love to all mankind that shall lead him in his daily social intercourse, and in his public religious duties, to choose his means of grace with a wisdom and an unfailing perception of adaptedness that shall render impossible all serious offence. The minister who dwells upon some favorite dogma, as if its establishment were of more consequence than the salvation of a soul; who cares more for the maintenance of some point of opinion, in which his personal pride is involved, than the maintenance of faith in some trembling believer; who does not study every heart with which he comes in contact, to see precisely the kind of spiritual food it requires; who deals out his store of threatenings and promises indiscriminately; or worse—deals out threatenings where promises were better, is a man not thoroughly furnished for his position, and not fitted for his work. My opinion is that a minister, perfectly fitted for his office, never offends, and that, if he have any positiveness of character, the number of his offensive applications of truth will indicate the measure of his unfitness for his office. Men with the common share of human reason, respect earnestness, honesty, and self-devotion, wherever they see it; and when those qualities are united with an all-comprehending love of those for whom Christ died, that shines in every smile, is manifest in every action, and modulates the tone of every utterance, sin receives its rebuke in respectful silence, malice melts in meekness, and error, pride, and even bigotry's self, bow, for the moment at least, to an influence which they have neither the power to resist nor the motive to resent."

"I believe it—every word of it," responded Mary, modestly, but firmly.

"I would not dispute with my father, certainly," said Henry Smith, who recognised parental respect as a Christian duty, "but it seems to me that he virtually apologizes for John Woodcock, and blames Mr. Moxon."

"And I will not dispute with my son," said Mr. Pynchon, with a meaning smile. "It is barely possible that John Woodcock is not naturally so bad a man as he is thought to be, and that Mr. Moxon has made a mistake in his treatment of him."

"Still," replied the son, with a deferential bow, "I think it is our duty to yield our assent to the teachings of our ministers. They are placed in the church to watch over us in matters of doctrine and duty, and while it is their duty to be faithful, it is ours to yield to them the respect due their high office."

"You do not mean, brother," said Mary, laughing, "that you would cheat so innocent a thing as an office, of so valuable a thing as respect, by paying its due to its occupant, do you?"

"I do not chop logic on Sunday," replied the brother, with a faint smile.

During the progress of this conversation, Mrs. Pynchon had been exercised in a somewhat singular manner. She reverenced her husband, but loved her son, and she saw and very thoroughly apprehended the nature of their difference. Therefore with a wish to reconcile their views, and strike a fair balance between them, she had arranged her ideas for a remark or two, but, by a perverse misfortune, they became confused before she had fairly commenced their utterance. "I think," said the old lady, "that anybody who gets offended with a good gospel sermon, is not worth minding anything about. I don't say anything against Goodman Woodcock, but I do say that when we've got a good minister, we ought to—to make the most of him" (slightly breaking down) "especially—especially"—(losing the thread entirely) "as we pay him a better salary than we can afford, and have settled the ministry lands on him."

This resolution of the discussion was conclusive, if not satisfactory, and as the family drew back from the table, John pointed his finger to the window and exclaimed, somewhat excitedly, "There comes John Woodcock, father!"

All turned their eyes in the direction indicated. He came towards the house with a lowering brow, bearing in his hand a small bundle tied up in a cotton handkerchief. He knocked at the door, and was admitted.

During all this time, Peter Trimble had stood, waiting in the room the conclusion of the meal, and had not only taken observation of everything within the reach of his active vision, but had carefully noted and remembered the nature and bearing of the conversation. No sooner was John Woodcock's coming announced, however, than he turned extremely pale in the face, and trembled in every limb. Flight was not feasible, or he would have fled.

As Woodcock entered the room, he walked up to the lad, planted his huge hand upon his trembling head, and, gathering his stiffly curling hair within the grasp of his fingers, turned his face back in order to bring it to a proper angle of observation. The tears began to ooze from the boy's eyes as if Woodcock were wringing water from his hair, or had the fountain of tears directly under pressure.

"You beautiful feller, you," said Woodcock, "how glad you be to see me! Don't know when I've met anybody in some time that was so overcome. You darlin' boy! You musn't let your feelin's get the start of you in this 'ere way. You're too delicate for this country. P'raps you never heerd of a little roastin' pig that went squealin' and squealin' round, and stickin' his nose into children's porringers, and rootin' up people's garden patches, till the butcher thought he was too tender for this world, and accidentally run a knife into him, did you? It's awful to be tender. I've known people to lose all the hair they had that way."

The boy had withstood the torture as long as he could, without absolutely bellowing with pain, and as the premonitions of an unpleasant outcry made themselves manifest, Woodcock relaxed his grasp upon the hair, and, looking him in the face a moment longer, removed his hand, and apologetically expressed the hope that he had not detained him from dinner, or interrupted any important business. The lad needed no hint from any quarter to induce him to retire, and the moment he was released he left the house.

John Pynchon watched him with a not ungratified air, as he walked homewards jerking his head with a half-rotary nod, which might have been taken as an expression of impotent anger, or a wish to ascertain whether that organ was still in location.

As he retired, Woodcock turned to the family, and, with an earnest and respectful look, which was somehow tinged with his late anger, he said, "I beg pardon for skinning my eels here, but I thought I'd 'tend to it, 'fore they slipped out of my fingers. I didn't come here to do it, cause I didn't know the boy was here, but I'm glad it's done and over with, and I guess he is. I come here to do a harder job. I've been thinkin', since I went out this mornin', that savin' me won't hardly pay, when you come to take it all round—the trouble it's costin' others—and the trouble it's costin' me. It's so natural for me to hate a mean man, and a narrer man, that I know I never'd learn to like one without gettin' mean and narrer myself. Mr. Moxon and I can't hitch hosses together. Come to tie to the same post, there'll be bitin' and kickin'."

Mr. Pynchon suggested that perhaps Woodcock had better sleep upon his anger, or at least defer what he might have to say until another day.

"No, Square," said Woodcock, "you musn't choke me off—let me go through this time, and I won't bother you again. I know it ain't proper Sunday business, but I want to get it off my mind. As I was sayin', savin' me won't pay. There aint but one way to do it, and it seems 's 'ough that would spile me. I can't give up hatin' men that it aint nater to love, and if I did get so I could kind o' stand 'em, I couldn't foller their halter nor work in their harness."

The family listened to this singular demonstration in silence. Henry Smith sat uneasily, as if he would like to argue the point, and as if he deemed it the duty of some one to do it; but as his father made no reply, he said nothing. No one except the favorite daughter, Mary, had the slightest apprehension of the impression that Woodcock made upon Mr. Pynchon. This apprehension was vague, as it must have been, with no more definite communication between them than that borne along the lines of a magnetic sympathy, but it was none the less real for lacking expression.

The truth was, that Mr. Pynchon was hardly able to speak. He saw in the rough man before him, himself—the form dwarfed, the face distorted, and the features dimly defined, perhaps, as if the mirror were an agitated pool oi turbid water—but still true to the essence of his constitution, and the outline of his moral conformation. He despised Woodcock's vices, he lamented his perversity of temper, and was saddened in the view of his unchastened will; but he honored the frankness of his nature, and that unbending freedom of his spirit, which led him to feel the touch of a shackle as he would the sting of a viper, and to spurn the one with his hand as he would the other with his heel.

Woodcock waited for a moment, for some one to speak, but as every one remained silent, he walked up to where Mary Pynchon was sitting, and untying, tremblingly and in silence, the little bundle he still retained in his hand, he placed, one after another, in her lap, the articles she had given to his daughter. During this movement he had not looked in her face, but as he concluded it, and placed his handkerchief in his pocket, he caught a vision of her sad eyes, brimming with tears.

"God bless you, Miss Pynchon! Don't cry, and don't think I ain't human to fetch back these things, but I couldn't keep 'em. It's kind to the gal to fetch 'em. Everybody knows where they come from, and I've just had to pay off one little runt for twittin' her about it."

"You pain me very much," replied Mary. "I am sure

you are over sensitive in this matter. Besides, your daughter really needs the clothes."

"Well, I don't dispute it, but if you wont say anything about it, the gal shall be took care of. She shall be took care of for you. I can't take these duds away with me, so it's no use talkin', but I'm just as thankful to you as I ever was, and love your good heart just as much."

"But," said Mr. Pynchon, pleasantly, "it seems to me that your excuse for depriving your daughter of comfortable clothes does not amount to much."

"Well, Square, if I must tell the whole on't," said Woodcock, straightening up desperately, and extending his brawny arm for an emphatic gesture, "I don't feel in fightin' trim with them clothes on that gal. I feel as if an angel had got a mortgage on me, and I'm afeared she'll foreclose some time when it ain't convenient."

No one could withhold a smile at this abrupt and characteristic conceit, and under the cover of the smile Woodcock retreated, and bent his steps homeward, leaving Mary gazing downwards upon her present, thus strangely returned, and busy in revolving the motive that bore it companionship.

CHAPTER V.

Woodcock's allusions to the strangeness of his child, it will have been seen, were not infrequent, in his conversations with others concerning her; and it has already been hinted that her eccentricities were attributable in a great degree to her early loss of a mother's guidance, and her almost exclusive association with her father and his usually coarse companions. Some weeks had passed after Woodcock returned to Mary Pynchon the clothes she had given to his daughter, when, one morning, as he was cutting wood at the door, he heard a very singular noise in his cabin. He paused, with a curious, puzzled air, and said to himself, in a low tone, "What in Natur's that? Well! she *has* broke out in a new place, now!" As he stood, waiting for a repetition of the strange sound, his ears were greeted with a well executed imitation of the crow of a strong-lunged cock.

"What has got into that critter now!" exclaimed Woodcock, and then, dropping his axe, he assumed an unsuspicious face, and walked into his cabin. He found Mary busy in clearing away, and, in her poor manner, washing the rude table furniture they had used for breakfast. He looked at her a moment, and, in a kind tone of voice, said, "What are you thinkin' about this mornin', Mary?"

"Peter Trimble," replied the girl, without pausing in her operations.

"What have you been thinkin' about that little—little—nimshi?" inquired the father, with the softest appellation of contempt he could call to mind.

"I was thinkin'," said Mary, "how he run a race with Tim Bristol yesterday, and when he'd clipped it clean by him, how he jumped on to a stump, and crowed."

"And so you tried to crow, just as Peter Trimble crowed, did you?" said the father.

"I? no!—I didn't crow," replied Mary, pausing in her work, and looking up with surprise.

"Not then, but jest now, gal. Jest now you crowed didn't you?" And Woodcock looked at her encouragingly, as if he would have said, "Own up now, my child, I won't hurt you."

"I wish you wouldn't talk so to me," said the girl, growing impatient.

"Now don't go into tantrums, Mary," said Woodcock deprecatingly; "I heerd somebody crow, here, in this 'ere cabin, and thinks I to myself that's the gal, a tryin' to see what she can do."

"I wish you'd stop tryin' to fool me," said the girl in a sharp tone, her temper rapidly rising.

"Well, go 'long, Mary, go 'long, I guess I didn't hear anything," said Woodcock, "only I didn't know but when you was thinkin' how Peter Trimble crowed, you jest kind o' tried to see if you couldn't do jest so—eh, now? Didn't you do it, little tinker?" and Woodcock smiled, with an anxious, distressed smile, that was meant for a demonstration of persuasive tenderness and amiability.

At this moment, Mary was holding a vessel of hot water in her hands, and her first impulse was to dash it, with all the force in her power, upon the cabin floor; but she finally set it down, and then went to her corner at the fireplace, and, throwing herself into her chair, hid her face in her lap, and burst into her usual fit of crying and scolding.

Woodcock watched her for a few minutes with emotions of unmingled pain. He did not know what to do with her. She seemed at times to be insane, and to say and do things of which she was unconscious. He had no doubt that she had been in a waking dream,—moving in past scenes, and amusing herself in the fields of memory, while engaged in the performance of the light household duties intrusted to her hands. And he had, within a few weeks, come .. regard the condition of her mind as, in some manner, con sequent upon his former treatment of her, and the hard, un-childlike lot that had been her experience. He never had forgotten how she looked when she came from the sweet presence of Mary Pynchon, with the new clothes upon her, and the new and altogether unwonted delight on her face, and the joy that animated every motion of her limbs. She was then a new child to him, and he would have given anything in his power to make that transformation permanent.

Woodcock sat for some minutes in silence, and allowed the paroxysm of the poor child to subside, and then said, "Mary, gal, come here to your poor old father."

Mary looked up, and, through her tears, recognised a look of thorough kindness bent upon her, which accorded with the strangely sympathetic tone that had arrested her attention. Instantly rising, she walked to her father's side, when, taking hold of her, he tried to lift her to his knee. The fatherly act was so unusual that the girl shrank from his grasp, and stood away from him, to see what he meant.

"Oh, Mary, for God's sake don't!" exclaimed her father. "Come to me, and set with me, and forget all those old ugly things that plague you so."

Mary was assured, and was soon folded tenderly in the rough arms of her father.

"I want to talk," said Woodcock, in a low tone, and with his head bowed kindly down, "about one that's gone. Do you remember your mother, Mary?"

The little girl shook her head, and sat with her eyes fixed upon the floor.

"Your mother," continued Woodcock," was a clean,

sweet, han'some lookin' woman, and she had as good a heart as ever was; and if you could only jest think how her eyes looked,—'t seems 's if you could remember 'em if you ever see 'em,—so soft and lovin', I've got a consait that it would bring you all right. Don't you see them eyes a-lookin' on you sometimes, Mary? Can't you kind o' play you're little, and remember how your head used to lay on her arm, with them eyes—them beautiful eyes—shinin' on you?"

Mary's eyes were still on the floor, and she shook her head slowly and seriously.

"I'd give all I've got, or ever goin' to have, if my little gal could only think on it. Seems 's if it would start her all right ag'in, and kind o' put her in her mother's shoes, and make her grow up good and han'some.

"Mary, it don't seem but a little spell ago when I come home one night—it was twelve long years ago, but it don't seem more'n one, and 'twas 'way off in the old country—and I found this little gal in bed with her mother. You was a leetle thing then, as soft and simple as a young robin, but byme-by you begun to grow, and turn up your black eyes to her'n, and laugh in her sweet face till she cried in your'n. And then you'd go to sleep, with your cheek right up agin her soft breast, and she with her arms round you, lovin' you all the time. And when you got older, Mary, and could toddle round, and we begun to feed you on the nanny-goat's milk, and you got all tuckered out, playin' and runnin' out doors, and would come in with your eyes lookin' as heavy as lead, she used to take you up in her lap, and put your little head—littler and softer'n 'tis now—in her bosom; and there you lay, half laughin' in your sleep, and she lovin' you all the time."

Woodcock looked down to see whether his child was interested, and, as she appeared to be in deep thought, he proceeded.

"And so we all lived together for a spell, and then we

got into a ship, and come to this country. 'Twas a cruel time for all on us, but she took a cold, or a fever, or somethin', that she never worked clear off; and she kind o' pined and pined away, workin' all the time for you and me, till all at once she give it up, and telled me, jest as patient and pleasant, she was goin' to die. And there was you runnin' round, not knowin' what you was losin', and her big, shiny eyes a-follerin' you round the room, and her heart misgivin' her about how you would be brung up. And when her breath begun to come short, and she said she felt as if she was goin' away, she wanted I should fetch you, and I picked you up off'm the floor, and laid you in her arms, and put 'em round you, and your mother died, Mary, with her arms round you—so—and her heart lovin' you all the time."

Woodcock's last utterances were difficult with a depth of emotion that he had not anticipated, and could not control; and, as he paused, the big drops were falling from the eyes of his daughter, who still sat with her gaze upon the floor. The whole scene was a new experience to the child, and her feeling of embarrassment almost equalled in strength her interest in the narrative.

The father sat for some minutes in silence, and then resumed. "I thought that if I telled my little gal of all this, and she could only make it seem as if a dear, good woman had loved her, and 'tended her, and that she'd been the sweetest thing that woman had in the world, p'raps she could kind o' go back, and make a new start, and grow up soft and gentle, like other little gals. And I thought, besides, if she could only see them eyes, that used to look on her so sweet and lovin', and could get the consait that they was lookin' on her all the time, and could kind o' feel them soft, warm arms round her, night and day, that she'd get gentle, and wouldn't go to be round with Peter Trimble and the other boys, but would be a nice, modest little gal. Now, Mary, don't them eyes never come to you any ?"

The girl looked up in her father's face with a half wild, half serious expression, and said, "Father, I know them eyes; I've seen 'em."

"That's right, Mary. Do you seem to see 'em now ?" and Woodcock regarded her with an encouraging smile.

"No, I don't see 'em now. I never see 'em only nights, when I'm asleep."

Woodcock's lip quivered as he inquired, "Why can't you see 'em now ?"

"'Cause they don't come now," replied the child, with perfect simplicity.

"Do they come, as you say, always when you are asleep ?" inquired Woodcock, beginning to feel distressed.

"No," replied the girl, "they don't come always, but only when you've been whippin' me, and then they always come."

Woodcock started with a pang of terrible keenness, and heaved a sigh that was the expression of the profoundest pain.

"Then you haven't seen 'em lately," said he.

"No, I haven't seen 'em since you took away the clothes Miss Pynchon gave me. I see 'em then all night."

This declaration caused another pang, for Woodcock had not failed to recognise a certain degree of selfishness and unnecessary sensitiveness of will on his own part, in that transaction, although he had indulged himself, so far as possible, in the idea that he was justified by his motives.

"Well, Mary, I ain't never goin' to whip you ag'in," said Woodcock; "and I want to have you try to get them eyes back without the whippin', and when you see 'em, no matter if you're sleepin' or wakin', ask 'em to stay with you, and perhaps after a while we'll both be better, and we can keep the consait that she's always in the cabin with us—and"—and here Woodcock, whose original design had been seriously interfered with by the little girl's revelations, went off into a disconnected reverie, during which Mary slid from his arms, and resumed the occupation from which he had diverted her.

At length, half muttering to himself, he said, "I can't do nothin' with her, as I see. When she's wakin' she's sleepin', and when she's sleepin' she's wakin'—dreamin' when she's thinkin', and thinkin' when she's dreamin'. Everything's botched, somehow, 't I've anything to do with,—all mixed up and twisted. I can't do nothin' right, and I can't fix nothin' when't's wrong. But the gal's growin' up, and I must look after her, or she'll grow up to be no comfort to herself, nor me neither."

Then, giving expression to the idea that the world was a very unsatisfactory place to live in, he rose from his seat, and was about to open his door for the purpose of resuming his work at the wood-pile, when a hesitating rap came upon the outside. Immediately Woodcock stood confronting with John Cabel, the constable of the settlement, with whom he had had a quarrel and a suit at law, growing out of their joint agency in the erection of the first house in Agawam in 1635.

"Well, John Cabel," said Woodcock, standing in his doorway, without giving him an opportunity to enter, "you didn't come here to see me this mornin' 'cause you love me, so out with it, and no mincin'."

Cabel looked into the face of his old companion, now his enemy, and inwardly rejoiced in the opportunity of paying off a long score of revenges. He was a small man, with a small mind and infinite resource of language, sometimes spreading little turfs of thought into prairies of expression, and capable of running through all the latitudes of diplomacy in so simple a mission as that of borrowing a peck of corn.

In a tone in which pity was intended to be insultingly

predominant, Cabel commenced: "I'm sorry, John, it has come to this, but my duty as an officer of the *law* (the last word brought out strong, and enforced with six confluent little nods) compels me to do that which, considering you and I used to be hand and glove (emphasis and confluent nods), that is to say, on terms of intimacy (and John Cabel coughed, with the fore-finger of his left hand on the right aspect of his upper lip and the thumb on the left, and with a softness that showed that it was a cherished cough, and not intended to injure his lungs)—" compels me to do, as I was remarking, that which, under other—that is to say (emphasis and confluent nods) less peculiar circumstances, might not be attended with the degree of pain which I experience on this occasion."

And John Cabel coughed again, with his left thumb and fore-finger in position, and the palm of his hand so spread, to shield his mouth, that the man whom he addressed could not have inhaled from his breath any fatal effects, with which, by an imaginary possibility, it might have been charged.

"Cabel, now what's the use of your makin' a fool of yourself?" said Woodcock, regarding him with a look of supreme contempt. "If you're sick to the stomach, why don't you throw up, and get shet o' your slobberin'?"

Cabel smiled, coughed, and replied, "You have not forgotten how to joke, John, and it reminds me of other days (emphasis and confluent nods)—days when our relations were different; that is to say, when they were not unpleasant. They have been somewhat disturbed, it is true, but never with my consent, and now, to be obliged, as an officer of the law (emphasis, &c.), to visit your house, gives me more pain than I can conceal, and—"

"Look a-here, Cabel," said Woodcock, "if you don't empty your pail, and stop spillin' over this way, I'll give you the door to look at, and you may call me when you're all ready."

"Very well, John," said Cabel, changing his manner at once, "I've got a writ for ye, which tells ye to come before the magistrate to answer to a charge of slander made by Mr. George Moxon. What have ye got to say to that, eh?"

"Did you say I'd got to answer to the magistrate?" inquired Woodcock.

"The magistrate, of course."

"Well, mind your own business then, you beetle-head," said Woodcock. "I'll say what I've got to say when the time comes."

Cabel enjoyed extremely the tone of irritation with which Woodcock uttered his last reply, and gave himself gently over to the most luxurious cough of the whole series.

As for Woodcock, this new annoyance had taken him at a decided disadvantage. He was weak with the softening influences of the morning, and "never felt so little up to a gruff," as he afterwards expressed it, as he did at the time he met Cabel. He had begun to apprehend more and more, that Mary was suffering from his own reputation, and, for the moment, he felt as if he would rather die than engage in another quarrel which would tend to make him, and the one being associated with him, subjects of renewed unpleasant comment in the plantation.

It was, therefore, with something like dejection in his air and feelings that he threw the accustomed wolf skin over his shoulders, and prepared to accompany Cabel to the house of the magistrate.

In the early days of the plantation, and for many years, all cases tried before Mr. Pynchon were tried by a jury of six men, and were but irregularly managed at the best. Owing to the peculiar circumstances of the place—the lack of a prison, and the ordinary means of enforcing law—legal processes frequently exhibited a mixed character and were at the same time, and in the same case, civil, ecclesiastical, and criminal.

When Woodcock arrived at the house, he found that Mr. Moxon and the constable had arranged matters so as not to delay the course of justice by the escape of an unnecessary minute, for the six jurymen were in the house, as well as in their seats. As he walked into the house, he bowed stiffly to Mr. Pynchon, and fixed a surly gaze upon Mr. Moxon, who, on not obtaining any motion of obeisance, turned his eyes in another direction.

"I'm all ready, Square," said Woodcook; "shall I set down or stand up?"

"You will stand," replied Mr. Pynchon, "until you have heard the charge read on which you have been summoned before me."

Mr. Pynchon then read the charge, which (without going into its formalities) represented that Mr. Moxon, having been called upon while in Hartford to testify in regard to the moral and business character of Woodcock, had felt obliged, from what he knew of him, to testify against him; and that, in consequence, Woodcock had charged him with taking a false oath, in repeated conversations with different members of the plantation. After he had concluded, he asked him whether he pleaded "guilty" or "not guilty" to the charge of slander, in connexion with these representations.

"Well, Square, I aint *guilty* of anything, as I know of," said Woodcock. "I don't consider it's guilty—"

"Prevarication," said Mr. Moxon, with a nod at Mr. Pynchon.

"No, 'tisn't prevarication, neither," said Woodcock, turning to Mr. Moxon. "It'll be time enough for me to borry your jack-knife when I've got whittlin' on hand I can't do with my own."

The mistake which Woodcock's ignorance of language

had led him into was sufficiently ludicrous to draw a smile upon the faces of all present, and he thus escaped a reprimand. The smile, however, weak as it was, was sufficiently strong to restore him to himself, and to harden him for the time into the man he had long been in reality and reputation.

"What do I understand your plea to be?" inquired Mr. Pynchon.

"Not guilty!" exclaimed Woodcock, in a stiff, stern voice, and then, tossing his wolf skin over a chair, he sat down.

When the names of the witnesses were called, three of those on the jury of six arose and were sworn with the rest.

"Will your Honor 'low me to say a word?" said Woodcock, rising.

"Certainly, if relating to the case," replied the magistrate.

"Well, I was thinkin' that if you'd jest let these men that don't seem to know anything about the case go, and put the rest of the witnesses in their seats, you'd save time, and wouldn't have to pump any of 'em, 'cause they'd know all they could tell, and could tell all they know to one another. I thought I'd jest hint it to you, Square," continued Woodcock, preparing to sit down, "for it's all the same to me who's on the jury."*

* The following is an extract from the record of this trial in the Pynchon Record Book.

"George Moxon complained against Jo. Woodcock in an action of slander, in that he saith that Jo. Woodcock doth report that he took a false oath against him at Hartford, and he demands of Jo. Woodcock for the said slander £9, 19s.

"*The Jury.* Henry Smith, Jeheu Burr, Robert Ashley, Thomas Merik, Jo. Searle, Samuel Hubbard.

"Mr. Moxon produced these witnesses: Tho. Horton, Jo. Cable, Robert Ashley, Henry Smith, Samuel Hubbard."

"Goodman Woodcock," said Mr. Pynchon, in a firm but pleasant tone, "it is apparent from this remark that you intend to complain of injustice in connexion with your trial I had hoped to find you this morning in a more candid and penitent frame of mind,—one which should lead you to doubt neither our charity for you nor the honesty of our judgments in establishing justice between you and Mr Moxon. You are accused of a grave offence. You are charged with having proclaimed your minister to be guilty of the heinous sin of perjury. If the charge shall not be sustained, it will give me great pleasure to congratulate you on having freed yourself from an accusation that, to my mind, involves one of the most heartless and cruel crimes of which a man can be guilty; for there is hardly a crime that I consider so foul as that which tampers with a good man's good name. It is a crime that is the basis of nearly all the troubles in this and the other plantations of the colony, and one which I am determined shall be punished, so far as my power and influence go, in the manner it deserves."

Woodcock sat regarding the magistrate's words and manner most intently, and when he closed, he rose respectfully, and, fixing his eye fully on the eye of Mr. Pynchon, said, "I don't misdoubt, Square, but what you mean all you say, and I don't say but what it's all right, take it by and large, but I was wonderin' whether you'd a' said it if I'd been in the minister's boots, and he in mine."

Mr. Moxon was instantly on his feet, and pointing his finger at Woodcock, he exclaimed, in a tone of authoritative menace, "Take heed! take heed!"

"And I wonder," said Woodcock, shifting his eyes from the magistrate to the minister, without changing his voice, "if you'd a' stood my p'intin' to that man, and hollerin' out as he done jest now."

Mr. Pynchon reddened in the face, and replied, "I have

no words to bandy with you, Woodcock. The trial will proceed."

The witnesses were examined, one after another, by Mr. Moxon and the magistrate, and the evidence was conclusive against the accused. He had charged Mr. Moxon openly and boldly, with taking a false oath against him; and not a doubt remained on the mind of any one, in relation to the fact.

At the close of the testimony, Mr. Pynchon addressed Woodcock, telling him that he had heard the evidence which had been placed before the jury, and could not but be aware of its character; and that if he had anything to say before they should bring in their verdict, and would say it with proper respect to the court and the reverend plaintiff, he could now have the opportunity.

Woodcock sat a few moments in silence and study, and then, rising, said: "You know, Square, my tongue aint a smooth one, and I don't know how I should make out, tryin' to foller the marks, but I'll say what I think's right, and you can stop me when I get off'm the trail. I'm satisfied with what these folks have said, and I could a' saved 'em the trouble of sayin' anything, but I kind o' wanted to see how straight they'd tell their stories. They've gone through 'em pretty well, and now I'd like to tell what I meant when I was talkin' about bein' guilty, just as the minister run into me. 'Tain't very comfortable for a feller to think he haint got a good character; and when he catches another feller swearin' it away, it's natur to hang on to it. I didn't consider it guilty to hang on to mine, and that was what I was tryin' to get off. In this 'ere case, I've tried to show proper respect to the minister. I've only said he shot too far to the left to hit the truth, when if he'd been John Cabel that had done it, or any other thin strip of a man, I should a' laid him down, and stomped on him."

Here Woodcock was interrupted by an excited motion on the part of Mr. Moxon, who half rose from his seat, and who, failing to command the eye of Mr. Pynchon, settled uneasily back into his chair again. As for Cabel, he relapsed into a cough, as satisfactory to himself as it was full of provocation to Woodcock, who, seeing that he might proceed, resumed his remarks.

"As I was sayin', Square, I've tried to show respect to the minister, but I don't see what it's all for. I've been in the colony half-a-dozen years, more or less, and done as much work as any other man of my size. I marked the trees clean from Roxbury to this plantation, and put up the fust cabin here, with a little help from a poor feller (looking at Cabel) that's now bad with the heaves; and I've been crowded and knocked round, and I've paid rates and been made to walk the colony crack; and all the time I couldn't be a freeman and vote, 'cause I wan't a member of the church. I hain't been anything, 'cause the ministers wouldn't let me. I have to help support 'em, and live under their laws, and when they take a notion to swear away my character, I mustn't kick; if I do, the constable grabs my foot, and ties it up to the jury-box.

"P'raps I ain't talkin' very close to the mark," continued Woodcock, recalling himself, "and I'll come back, and take the track agin. Mr. Moxon thinks I've damaged him nine pound, nineteen shillin', which 't seems to me don't tally with his swearin' down to Hartford. I'm better'n he swore I was, or else his character's weaker'n he thinks 'tis, or else I hav'n't damaged him so much as he's tried to make out. If my character wan't good for anything, I couldn't hurt him, and if his character's weak enough to be hurt by such a man as he says I be, then he's no business to growl, and talk about money. It's a good brew that bursts the barrel, and a broken egg that spiles easy."

"I protest," exclaimed Mr. Moxon, suddenly and excitedly rising—"I protest against being made the butt of this fellow's vulgar jests. I have as much respect, may it please your Honor, as any one can have, for the rights of a man on trial for a grave offence against the laws, but I am not called upon to submit to the inflictions of his revengeful spleen. I claim the protection of the court."

"Woodcock," said Mr. Pynchon gravely, "you have forfeited your promise, and spoken disrespectfully towards the court and the plaintiff."

"I beg pardon," interrupted Woodcock, afraid that Mr. Pynchon was about to silence him, "but I meant no offence. The j'int fitted middlin' well, but the stick wan't hewed smooth. I hope you won't set me down till I've had it out, and can feel easy. This 'ere jury's goin' to say whether I owe Mr. Moxon anything or not. I've paid my part, since I've been in the settlement, to give Mr. Moxon porridge, and salt to put into it. My rates are all square, if I *have* had a hard time here; and what did I ever get for't? Nothin' but blowin's—sometimes right afore my child, sometimes right afore a whole meetin'; and then he goes to Hartford, and swears away my character, and 'cause I don't knuckle, and 'low him to tread me down, he brings me here to get money out on me, over and above the rates that bring me nothin' but cusses. I don't owe him—"

"I protest," said Mr. Moxon.

"Sit down, Woodcock," said the magistrate.

Woodcock very reluctantly undertook obedience to the command, but before he touched his seat, he rallied doubtfully, and said, "Square, if you'll give me three words more, I won't 'fend you, my word for't. I jest wanted to say that there's been considerable fuss made, fust and last, about makin' me a better man, and I thought if the jury was goin' out, and was good in figures, I sh'd like to have 'em find how long it would take to make a Christian of me in this way, and about what it'll cost."

Having finished to his satisfaction, Woodcock wiped his forehead with a dirty handkerchief, threw his coat open as if he had made a hard physical effort, and sat down.

"This case," said Mr. Pynchon, "might be safely left to the jury without any remarks from me, but it involves important consequences, and demands a few words, especially as the magistracy of this settlement has but recently been established. The plaintiff in this case is the minister of the church in our own plantation, one whom you know as a godly man, and an approved teacher of the truth in Christ. His is a holy office, a mighty responsibility, an unspeakably sacred work; and it is necessary to his usefulness that his name be preserved free from reproach. I do not decide, nor is it necessary for you to decide, whether Mr. Moxon had sufficient ground for the testimony which he gave at Hartford against Goodman Woodcock. I do not propose to say whether I think that he has treated Woodcock in all points as he should have done. In these matters, to his own master he standeth or falleth, and neither you nor I have aught to question or affirm touching them. The testimony establishes the fact that Woodcock has circulated among the people of the settlement the story that their minister has foully perjured himself. Of this you can have no doubt, independently of the confession of the defendant himself. In this thing, he has sinned against the ministry as well as the minister, wounded the cause of Christ, and done violence to that order and that dignity of office which are essential to the maintenance of Christian society. In assessing the damages, you will have reference as well to their effect upon the defendant as upon the plaintiff, and be guided by the pecuniary circumstances of the defendant to a certain extent. Large damages could not be collected, and if they could be, the effect upon him would be what no one wishes for, while I am sure the plaintiff would regret the possession of money that would place the soul of any man in jeopardy. You will now retire—"

"Square," said Woodcock, rising hurriedly from his chair, "afore the jury go, I sh'd like to put a question or two, to some of the witnesses that's been up."

"This is a very unusual, not to say disorderly request," said the magistrate.

"I know't's off'm the trail, but the fact is, this case has swum a pond since you begun talkin'. I didn't think you'd go agin me so hard, though I don't think the other side's anything to brag on."

"Whom do you wish to call again?" inquired the magistrate.

"John Cabel, and p'raps some of the jury, if you'll be so kind," replied Woodcock, "though I ain't goin' to dodge, if you do hit without hearin'."

Mr. Moxon had not exactly liked certain portions of Mr. Pynchon's remarks, but he felt sure of his case, and so did not interfere with the proceedings. Mr. Pynchon called Henry Smith to his side, and after a few minutes' indistinct conversation, told Woodcock that he could have liberty to question Cabel.

"Get up, Cabel," said Woodcock, turning sharply to that official.

Cabel turned a mute look of appeal to the magistrate, who said, "You will rise, Cabel, and the defendant will address you respectfully."

"John Cabel," said Woodcock, "who telled me that Mr. Moxon swore agin me in Hartford? Now none o' your dodgin' nor spreadin'."

"It seems to me," said Cabel, indulging in a short cough, "that that is a remarkable, that is to say, a very singular question for one to ask, who should know without asking. You are aware that I have had very little association with you of late (a long quiet cough), and that I could not have a very thorough knowledge of your sources, that is to say, your means of information."

"You're a sweet nut anyway," said Woodcock, with a smile that was half scowl. "Don't you know, as well as you want to know, that *you* told me yourself?"

Cabel looked at Mr. Pynchon, and that gentleman settled the matter by saying very peremptorily, "*Yes*, or *No*, to that question, Cabel."

"Yes."

"All right," said Woodcock. "Now, did you ax me what I'd got to say to it?"

"Yes, or no," said Mr. Pynchon.

"Yes."

"Well, what did I say?"

"You said," replied Cabel, without any urging, "that Mr. Moxon had sworn to a lie." (Emphasis, &c.)

"That's true," said Woodcock, "and now you may set down, and if we wa'nt here, afore these gentlemen, and you was a brother of mine, which I'm thankful you ain't, I sh'd say, if you sleep on marish hay, you'd better shift your bed, for it's bad for your pipes."

"Mr. Smith," said Woodcock, immediately turning to Henry Smith, at the head of the jury, "who telled you that I said Mr. Moxon took a false oath agin me?"

"John Cabel," replied Mr. Smith.

"What made me tell you jest the same thing over agin?" inquired Woodcock.

"The occasion, I believe," said Mr. Smith, rubbing his chin to help his memory, "was my inquiry of you whether Cabel had represented the truth."

"That's all," said Woodcock, rising; "I jest wanted Mr. Pynchon to see how I come to say what I did, and to ax him whether he thinks it would 'a been natur' for me to own up that my character was bad, or keep mum, which was tantamount to the same thing; and I wanted to show him how the story got to me, and got spread up and down the plantation. Mind, I don't take nothin' back, but I wanted to fetch out who planted the corn, and how I come to hoe it."

"There can be no doubt in your minds," said Mr. Pynchon, turning to the jury, "that these are mitigating circumstances, and you will give the defendant the benefit of them in your assessment of damages."

The jury retired to an adjoining apartment, and occupied but a short time in coming to their decision, which was arrived at by a vote to award Mr. Moxon, as damages, the mean average of the individual estimates of the jury.

As they returned and resumed their seats, Mr. Pynchon pronounced the inquiry, "What do the jury find?"

Henry Smith arose, and replied, "The jury find for the plaintiff, damages, £6 13*s.* 4*d.*"

"Well," said Woodcock, rising, with a mingled expression of anger and disgust upon his rough features, "I'm glad you've found the damages and found the money with 'em, for you've done a smart thing, and saved me considerable elbow grease besides."

"What do you mean by that remark?" said Mr. Pynchon sternly.

"I mean," said Woodcock, with a scowl of contempt and defiance, "that when Mr. Moxon's broth tastes like Woodcock, it won't be till after I've died game, and he's lame and lost his eyesight."

"And what do you mean by that, sir," inquired the magistrate again.

"Well, Square, my meanin' don't lay very fur under the skin, but I s'pose I can fetch it out, if you say so. I don't mean nothin' more nor less than that I don't owe the minister any money, and I shan't pay him no money."

Having very emphatically pronounced his decision, and conveyed a look of menace to John Cabel, who gave expression to a sudden sense of discretion in a cough which conveyed him, by easy stages, into semi-unconsciousness, Woodcock, whose last movements had tended towards the door, lifted the latch, and passed unmolested on his way homewards.

His departure was followed by a long consultation. Mr. Pynchon felt that his authority had been slighted, and with good reason; Mr. Moxon was dissatisfied with the amount of damages awarded him, and incensed at Woodcock's repeated insults and insolent defiance; the jury were offended that Woodcock had spurned their judgment; and Cabel, who insisted at great length that he knew John Woodcock through and through, declared that the monster had as good as threatened his life.

"There is no way," said Mr. Moxon, at last, "but to drive him from the settlement. No order can be maintained with such a man amongst us. He must leave the plantation, or he will destroy it."

And the majority, as they separated, were of his opinion.

CHAPTER VI.

The winter during which these events occurred was long and severe—so severe as to give rise, among all the settlements on the Connecticut, to serious apprehensions of scarcity of food. As a consequence, the opening of spring was hailed with unusual joy. To augment this joy the people of Agawam had received advices from the Bay that a few more families had decided to adventure their fortunes among them.

The principal communication with the Eastern settlements was by a path marked by trees a portion of the distance, and by slight clearings of brush and thicket for the remainder. No stream was bridged, no hill graded, and no marsh drained. The path led through woods which bore the marks of the centuries, over barren hills that had been licked by the Indians' hounds of fire, and along the banks of streams that the seine had never dragged. This path was known as "the Bay Path," or the path to the Bay, and received its name in the same manner as the multitudinous "old Bay roads" that lead to Boston from every quarter of Massachusetts.

It was wonderful what a powerful interest was attached to the Bay Path. It was the channel through which laws were communicated, through which flowed news from distant friends, and through which came long, loving letters and messages. It was the vaulted passage along which echoed the voices that called from across the ocean, and through which, like low-toned thunder, rolled the din of the great world. That rough thread of soil, chopped by the blades of a hundred streams, was a bond that radiated at each terminus into a thousand fibres of love and interest, and hope and memory. It was the one way left open through which the sweet tide of sympathy might flow. Every rod had been prayed over, by friends on the journey and friends at home. If every traveller had raised his Ebenezer, as the morning dawned upon his trusting sleep, the monuments would have risen and stood like milestones.

But it was also associated with fears, and the imagination often clothed it with terrors of which experience and observation had furnished only sparsely-scattered hints. The boy, as he heard the stories of the Path, went slowly to bed, and dreamed of lithe wildcats, squatted stealthily on overhanging limbs, of the long leap through the air upon the doomed horseman, and the terrible death in the woods. Or, in the midnight camp, he heard through the low forest arches—crushed down by the weight of the darkness—the long drawn howl of the hungry wolf. Or, sleeping in his tent or by his fire, he was awakened by the crackling sticks, and, lying breathless, heard a lonely bear, as he snuffed and grunted about his ears. Or, riding along blithely, and thinking of no danger, a band of straying Pequots arose, with swift arrows, to avenge the massacre of their kindred.

The Bay Path was charmed ground—a precious passage—and during the spring, the summer, and the early autumn, hardly a settler at Agawam went out of doors, or changed his position in the fields, or looked up from his labor, or rested on his oars upon the bosom of the river, without turning his eyes to the point at which that Path opened from the brow of the wooded hill upon the east, where now the bell of the huge arsenal tells hourly of the coming of a stranger along the path of time. And when some worn and weary man came in sight, upon his half starved horse, or two or three pedestrians, bending beneath their packs, and swinging their sturdy staves, were seen approaching, the village was astir from one end to the other. Whoever the comer might be, he was welcomed with a cordiality and universality that was not so much an evidence of hospitality, perhaps, as of the wish to hear of the welfare of those who were loved, or to feel the kiss of one more wave from the great ocean of the world. And when one of the settlers started forth upon the journey to the Bay, with his burden of letters and messages, and his numberless commissions for petty purchases, the event was one well known to every individual, and the adventurer received the benefit of public prayers for the prosperity of his passage and the safety of his return.

It was upon one of the sweetest mornings of May that Mary Pynchon and her brother John walked forth to enjoy the air, and refresh themselves with the beauty of the spring-touched scenery. Tom, the pet, was their companion, and as Mary heard the stroke of axes in the woods upon the Hill, she deemed it safe to walk in that direction. Her steps naturally sought the Bay Path,—not, perhaps, because it led to the most charming view, or was the easiest of access. She could not tell why she chose it. Her feet almost by force took the path which her thoughts had travelled so long, and led her towards hopes that might, for aught she knew, be on the wings of realization to meet her, and lead her back to her home, crowned with peace and garlanded with gladness.

Arriving at the summit of the hill, Mary and her brother selected a favorable spot, and sat down. Far to the North, Mount Holyoke and Mount Tom stood with slightly lifted brows, waiting for their names. Before them, on the West, the Connecticut, like a silver scarf, floated upon the bosom of the valley. Beyond it, the dark green hills climbed slowly and by soft gradations heavenward, until the sky joined their upturned lips in a kiss from which it has forgotten to awake. And all was green—fresh with new life, and bright with the dawn of the year's golden season.

There, too, were the dwellings of the settlers, some of them surrounded by palisades, for protection against a possible foe, and all of them humble and homely. Near where they were sitting still swung the axes of the woodmen, and off, upon the meadow, on the western side of the river, the planters were cultivating their corn. The scene was one of loneliness, but it was one of deep beauty and perfect peace.

Mary Pynchon would have been no unattractive feature in the scene, to one who could have observed her, as she sat with her sun-bonnet in her hand, and her features inspired by the beauty around her. A form of medium size and faultless mould was but indifferently draped and ungracefully defined by the economical fashions of the place and period; but her face was one whose beauty nothing but an impenetrable veil could hide. The spirited lip, full blue eye, well arched and finely pencilled eyebrow, and intellectual forehead, gave to her face a queenliness of expression that, to one who did not know her, might have conveyed the idea of haughtiness; but the depth of the blue eye, and the soft oval outline of the face, as it shaded off into masses of rich brown hair above, and stood relieved from a snowy neck below, produced a combination of the more delicate with the stronger constituents of beauty, as rare as it was attractive.

She had arrived at that stage in the development of her nature, when, unconsciously to herself, and unobserved by those around her, she was waiting for a mate. A true womanly nature grows to a certain point of development, and then makes a pause, and looks around for its companion. If that companion is prepared already, or appears at the convenient moment, it goes on, passes through maternity to maturity, and if then its work is done, it sits down, and waits for the angels.

There is a period in the early life of every true woman when moral and intellectual growth seems, for the time, to cease. The vacant heart seeks for an occupant. The intellect, having appropriated such aliment as was requisite to the growth of the uncrowned feminine nature, feels the necessity of more intimate companionship with the masculine mind, to start it upon its second period of development. Here, at this point, some stand for years, without making a step in advance. Others marry, and astonish, in a few brief years, by their sweet temper, their new beauty, their high accomplishments, and their noble womanhood, those whose blindness led them to suppose they were among the incurably heartless and frivolous.

It was among the vague shadows of this epoch in her life that Mary Pynchon had many of her meditations. She loved her father, and knew that her father loved her with entire devotion. She loved her brother, and felt that the noble boy returned to her his whole heart. She exercised love and sympathy for all around her, and rejoiced in the consciousness that she was a favorite with all. But that was not enough; and as she sat there, on that sweet May morning, gazing out upon the landscape, or watching Tom as he browsed among the shrubs, or playfully chiding her brother as he insisted on decking her hair with the sweet arbutus and the early shad blossoms, her heart went off again over the Bay Path, through the thick, dark woods, and over the streams, and across the hills—the weary path over which she had travelled just two years before, and there came up to her mind the form of one who had moved with grace and majesty in her dreams; and whose bright, bold face, and mild, resolute eye, had been to her, through all the months of her lonely dwelling at Agawam, a charming presence and a kindly power.

An hour or two, charmed by the influences of the sweet scene below, and the kindly sun above, had passed over the brother and sister, when they began to talk of returning. At length, they heard a long drawn call. They listened for its repetition, and the call shaped itself to the name of "Peter," and came from the quarter from which the sound of the axes had proceeded.

"Peter Trimble has run away from his chopping," said John to his sister.

At this instant, a sharp, peculiar bark, not unlike that of a fox, was heard proceeding from an evergreen thicket near by. Neither Mary nor John suspected the nature of the animal that gave it utterance; and, as it continued, the deer, whose ears it had arrested at first, and whose attention it held, started off with a bound into the Bay Path, and ran away.

The bark then ceased, and Mary and John listened to the retreating footsteps of their pet, until, at last, the trampling seemed to mingle with similar sounds, which were soon broken in upon by the crack of a gun that rang through the forest, and came at last faintly echoing back from the Western hills. Both seemed to be conscious of what had been done, and as they sat in breathless silence awaiting further developments, they heard the short, nervous leaps of the deer approaching. As Tom came in sight, and turned from the path to reach the spot from which fear had driven him, the hot blood spurted from his side at every bound. Almost sinking, he had just strength to reach the spot where Mary was sitting, and laying his pale nose in her lap, and looking in her face with his glazing eyes, settled prone upon the ground, as if his slender limbs had changed at once from springing steel to lifeless flesh.

"My poor, poor pet!" exclaimed Mary, in deep distress. "Who could have been so cruel?" Then instantaneously flashed upon her the singular combination of circumstances attending the slaughter of her favorite, and her sudden grief was merged in an apprehension for her own personal safety.

Just as she was disengaging herself from the head of Tom, so that she could rise, she heard the gallop of approaching horses. Soon the foremost rider arrived at the point opposite to where she was sitting, and, examining the bushes, exclaimed to those behind him—"Here are his marks—in here"—and, spurring his horse excitedly, he started directly towards the little group, but failed to see them until within a few feet of them. The first tone of his voice arrested Mary's attention, and, as he caught sight of her, she had half risen, and still held the head of the deer in her hands, while John had grasped her arm, as if fearful that some harm were about to fall upon her.

"Mary Pynchon! by the immortal gods!" exclaimed the stranger, and, dropping his rein, he leaped from his horse, and, as she let fall the lifeless head of Tom, grasped both her hands, and stood for a long minute gazing mutely and with passionate affection and admiration in her face. When at last he released his grasp, she pointed to the dead pet in silence, with a finger that trembled with varied emotions.

"Ah! well," said he, with a gentle, playful voice, "is it not fitting that we should offer a sacrifice of thanksgiving on the occasion of meeting thus happily? Was not the deer provided for this very purpose? Tell me that, Mary Pynchon?"

"I think it would have been gallant in you, at least, to provide the sacrifice, particularly as you do not appear to suffer much pain on account of it," replied Mary.

"Well, I am not in a state of extreme suffering, that is true," said the stranger, laughing, "and between you and me, and that suspicious-looking brother of yours, I doubt whether you are."

The allusion to her brother made her aware that the scene must be a strange one to him, and, taking John by the hand, she said, "This is Mr. Holyoke, John, of whom you have heard your father speak so frequently." Then, addressing that gentleman, she added, "I suppose John thinks that your sacrifice of Tom was a very unwarrantable affair, and regards it rather as an omen than an offering."

"Omens, my boy," said Holyoke, looking at him with a half-sportive, half-earnest expression, "are never omens unless you kiss them. A kick will kill an omen as certainly as it will a hare."

"Poor Tom!" said Mary, looking down sorrowfully upon the lifeless pet, "I have a strong disposition to make an omen of you."

"Dear lady," exclaimed Holyoke with a hearty laugh, "if we should all follow the bent of our dispositions, omens would multiply to a fearful extent."

"I should hesitate to become one so long as you are near, at least," replied Mary, with perfect self-possession, "particularly as you dislike them so much, and understand so well the manner of slaying them."

While this interview was in progress, the two companions of Holyoke sat upon their horses at a distance, curious spectators of the scene.

"By the way," said one, looking at Holyoke and his companions, "does it not strike you forcibly that boy's nose is pretty essentially broken? I never saw a more jealous-looking little scoundrel in my life. By all the nymphs of Agawam, if I were in Elizur's place I'd give him a penny, and tell him to take my horse home."

"And if the boy is the one I think he is," responded the other, "he would toss your penny in your face, and bid you do your own grooming."

The companions jested until tired of the sport, and then, as Holyoke did not seem disposed to close his interview with Mary, they looked off upon the country, and remarked upon its features. When they had grown quite impatient with the delay, and were about proposing to leave Holyoke to follow at his leisure, they discovered a commotion far down the path before them, which soon took the form of a small company of armed men. In order to account for their appearance, it will be necessary to bring upon the stage an actor with whom the reader has already formed an acquaintance.

CHAPTER VII.

Peter Trimble, who had grown tired of his chopping upon the hill, left it, on the pretence of quenching his thirst at a spring, a short distance from the location of his labors. Arriving there, he heard the voices of the brother and sister, and, secreting himself, watched them, and listened to catch such words as might reach his quick ear. This occupation proving unsatisfactory, his love of mischief took another form, and, drawing upon his faculty of imitation, he produced the bark that became so wonderfully productive in the results which have already been recounted.

Peter only paused to see the dying deer come rushing in from the Bay Path, the swift plunge of the horseman who followed him, and his meeting with Mary, when he left his hiding-place, and, reaching the path by a circuit that hid him from observation, he ran as fast as his slender legs could carry him for the village. Before reaching the first cabin, he had examined to see if there were any signs of life around it, and, catching sight of a head with an old woman's cap on it, he beckoned furiously with his hand; and the wearer, full of greedy curiosity, came out to meet him.

"What *is* the matter now?" exclaimed the old woman, with her palms deprecatingly spread towards the boy.

"Oh! there's the greatest row up on the hill you ever see," replied Peter.

"What is it?"

"Oh! it's the darndest row 't ever happened in this old plantation."

"Why! you scare me, Peter. Do tell me about it!"

"Well, you see—you know Tom, don't you—Mary Pynchon's deer? Oh! you've no idea anything about it. I can't stop—I've got to go to Old Pynchon's, and rout 'im out. It's the greatest kind of a row."

"Now you *must* tell me, Peter; I shall die—I know I shall, if you don't," exclaimed the old woman, with one hand on her hip and the other on her heart.

"Well! Tom's doubled up—shot dead. Mary's fainted away, and I guess she's wounded; and John's crazy as a loon. Indians all over the hill—oh! I can't stay no longer —don't stop me—my! what a row!"

This programme was repeated, with suitable variations during each performance, at the cabins intermediate between this and the house of Mr. Pynchon. In approaching the latter house, he met Mr. Pynchon, and began his talk in his usual style.

"Now stop, Peter," said Mr. Pynchon. "If I find that you tell me one lie, I will have you whipped."

The real facts in the case had already been buried in such a crowd of lies that Peter was obliged to stop, and carefully recall the scene, before he could safely venture to describe it. Mr. Pynchon gathered from his statement that the deer had been shot, and that a stranger was with his daughter, who, at the departure of the messenger, was grasping her hand in a very ferocious manner. He had already become alarmed at her long absence, and had set out with his gun to meet her, when he encountered Peter. Keeping on his course, he was joined by half a dozen planters who had heard Peter's story.

As for Peter, his mission was not yet complete. He had no disposition to return with the men to the scene of the terrific "row" which he had so graphically described, but he wanted some dinner, and proposed to employ what little capital he had left in procuring it. Seeing Mrs. Pynchon at the door, whither she had been called by seeing the little company of men in the distance, he approached her.

"Do you know where those men are going, Peter?" inquired the old lady, with a trusting look of inquisitiveness.

"They're going after John and Mary," replied the boy, and then added, "Oh my! How I have run!"

"What is the matter with John and Mary? Where are they?"

"They've got into a terrible row," said Peter, pathetically. "Oh, how faint I feel! I wish I was at home, so's't I could have something to eat." And he threw himself upon the ground as heavily and lifelessly as if universal paralysis had seized him.

"Poor boy!" said the old lady, "you *shall* have something, right there on the grass, and then you must tell me all about it."

This was just as Peter had calculated, and when the loaded plate was placed by his side, and his food and his batch of lies were all before him, he was very much in his element, and was really in the occupation of some of the happiest moments of his life. On being pressed for his disclosures, he disposed of a huge mouthful, and commenced.

"You see I was up in the woods choppin'. By'me-bye I heerd something a howling, and a screeching, and thinks, says I, *what's that?* (Interruption of several seconds for mastication.) Thinks, says I, is that a bear, or a catamount? Well! I hearked as much as five minutes, I s'h'd think, when all at once I heerd a tremenduous running, and I struck for the noise so's to see what the row was. I was a little scat, you know, for I couldn't tell exactly what was coming; and I fell down three or four times and that hendered me, but when I got most out to the Bay Path, what do you think I see!"

Upon the statement of this inquiry, the imaginative boy turned his impassive face up to meet an expression upon that of Mrs. Pynchon, of unmingled pain and apprehension.

"Oh! pray don't mention it!" exclaimed the old lady, holding up both hands, and waiting for the announcement, under the impression that she had urged the boy to proceed.

"Well, ma'am! as I was saying (a large mouthful and a protracted mastication)—when I got most out of the Bay Path, I see a woman and a boy, a sitting on a log. Well, pretty soon I heerd a gun go off. Didn't you hear it down here? I sh'd think you might. O! 'twas a tremenduous loud gun; it liked to spit my head; and then pretty quick I heerd something a r'r'running—r'r'running—r'r'running—l'l'lipitalip—l'l'lipitalip—l'l'lipitalip—l'lipitalip—lickitabang—ripitasmash—thunder-and-guns—up the path, and right towards the woman and the boy a sitting on the log. Well, the critter was Tom. He was shot deader'n a flounder; and he squashed right down on t' the ground."

"Poor fellow!" exclaimed the old woman, "you didn't skin him, did you?"

"Well, no, ma'am, I didn't git time," replied Peter, with a slight chuckle, which he endeavored to suppress by filling his mouth anew. "I didn't git time, for the deer hadn't more'n fell, when a man come riding in after him, on a big horse all of a lather, and says he, 'cahoot, cahoy! hullabaloo! who the devil's here!' Oh! 'twas awful! You never heerd a feller swear so in your life. When he got to where the woman was, he dropped his bridle, and jumped off'm his horse, as if he'd been catched in a twitch-up, and run right up to her, and grabbed hold of her hands, and squeezed 'em, and looked as savage as a meat-axe, till she began to cry, and take on, and—"

"Well, do tell me, Peter," said the old lady, whose patience had well nigh broken down, "where Mary and John were all this time."

"Mary and John?" inquired Peter, putting the last morsel into his mouth, and wiping his lips with his shirt-sleeve. "Mary and John! ye-e-e-s! where were they! sure enough!"

And then it occurred to him that the indefinite manner in which he had spoken of those individuals as "a woman and a boy," in order to heighten the interest of his narrative, had blinded the direct old lady who had been his listener; and he saw that his failure, any further than the achievement of his dinner, was complete.

At length, rising from the ground, and brushing his greasy jacket, he remarked in a very quiet tone, "I guess it's all right with Mary and John." Then turning his eye over his shoulder, and catching the first view of the returning villagers, he said, "You'll have folks to dinner to-day, so I guess I'll leave."

Suiting the action to the word, he started off at a brisk run, and was soon, through the aid of a kind of magic that Mrs. Pynchon did not understand, but in which he was materially assisted by a convenient stump, out of sight.

"Well! I *should* think that boy was crazy, if he didn't eat so," said Mrs. Pynchon, picking up her plate, and walking into the house.

When Mr. Pynchon, with his companions, had arrived at the scene of the morning's adventures, and found there, radiant with health, and strong with the richest pulses of manhood, Elizur Holyoke, "the sonne of Mrs. Hollioke of Linn, Mr. Pinchon's ancient friend," and one whom he had long hoped to call his own son, he embraced him with a warmth that startled the spectators, broke down John's jealousy in a moment, and brought tears of the sweetest pleasure to the eyes of Mary.

"My boy," said Mr. Pynchon, giving him the tenth shake of the hand, "so you must announce yourself to the lonely settlers of Agawam by slaughtering their cossets, eh? Well, well! Your mother shall hear of this, sir."

"Something must die," returned Holyoke, with his merry voice and sparkling smile, "to give room for the new life which I feel in being here—here by the side of your daughter."

Mr. Pynchon looked at Mary, expecting to see her face blossoming with blushes, but there she stood, self-possessed, calm, and happy, like a queen newly crowned. To her, the past was gone. The fear, the bashfulness, and the blush, that had walked hand in hand with every thought of Holyoke, were among the things forgotten, and never more to be. In the few rapturous minutes she had spent with her lover, although other hearts than his were beating near her, and other eyes gazing upon her, she had taken counsel of assurance. Her heart had moved to a higher plane of emotion, and her spirit was transferred to a sphere of purer light and stronger faith. As in a dissolving view, a scene of spring, bright with the dews of rosy morning, and wonderfully silent with its laughing waters, melts with strange identities into broad trees, sunny rocks, calmly basking landscapes, and heaven-reflecting lakes—so, in the light of assured love, and from canvas painted over with new hopes, new emotions, and new spiritual revelations, looked Mary Pynchon still, but it was Mary Pynchon transfigured. The angel of life had slipped the golden clasp of his book, and turned for her another leaf. She hardly knew it—nay, she but dimly mistrusted it. There was nothing unnatural in the new phase of her feelings—nothing that seemed unwonted in her new experience. In fact, she had never felt more unembarrassed or content. Her heart had found its home—its satisfaction—and, as she stood there, in the presence of her father and her lover, there went up from the depths of that heart an unuttered, "Oh! God! I thank Thee for this hour!"

Some minutes before Mr. Pynchon concluded his interview, the villagers and the two companions of Holyoke had started on their way down the hill. Holyoke insisted that Mr. Pynchon should mount his horse, which proposition John had no sooner heard than he started off upon a run, to overtake those who had gone before. Mr. Pynchon vaulted to the saddle, and then playfully said, "I hardly know whether to drive you in or leave you to follow."

"I never allow myself to be driven," said Holyoke. "But have no fears that I shall fail to follow, for by the shadows it is noon, and by my appetite long after."

"Very well, I leave you," said Mr. Pynchon, and starting off at a brisk pace, he was soon out of sight. The lovers, hand in hand, followed. It was mid-day, and the tender, half-diaphanous chestnut-leaves, and the maple boughs still rosy with their birth-blush, and the pine-buds, whose crystalline needles waited new dippings in the dew and dryings in the day, spread all their fans and fingers in vain to keep the warm rays from the brows of those who walked beneath them.

"Mary," said Holyoke at length, after a minute's silence, "I think you are very beautiful."

"I have no doubt of it," replied Mary quietly.

"How shall I understand that?" inquired Holyoke, with a half mischievous smile. "Do you intend to endorse my judgment or my sincerity?"

"Both, in a measure. I neither doubt your sincerity nor despise your judgment. I ought to seem very beautiful to you—the most beautiful of anything in the world."

"Why, Mary?"

"Because you love me."

"How do you know I love you?"

"I have not inquired of myself how I know," replied Mary, "but I know, nevertheless. I believe that a woman need never be left in doubt in regard to the real sentiments of her professed lover."

"Well!" exclaimed Holyoke, laughing, "I see that I have nothing to say, and, in fact, that I have not the slightest opportunity of making myself interesting, by making you jealous."

"It would be impossible, Elizur, for you to make me jealous."

Holyoke was amused, but not altogether pleased. He loved Mary with his whole heart, and his great anxiety for months had been to assure himself that she loved him; but this unquestioning faith assumed the shape and some of the attributes of dominion. There was a conscious possession of power on the part of Mary that touched a weak point of vanity in his manhood, and made him feel uneasy.

"But, Mary," said he, at length, "do you know that you have taken a very precious task out of my hands? I have come all the way from the Bay to tell you that I love you—rather to tell you how much I love you—and to tell you the same story a great many times; but you shut my mouth by coolly telling me that my errand is unnecessary."

This was intended to be uttered in a playful tone, but the quick heart of the girl recognised a shadow, as if an evil angel had crossed the path of the sunbeams that were falling upon her brow.

She stopped, lifted one hand to the shoulder of her lover, and her eyes filled with tears. "Oh! how little, how little do you know me!" she exclaimed, with a fervently affectionate utterance. "How poorly have you learned a woman's heart! I should take no pleasure in having you tell me that you love me, if I were not sure of the fact. But now I would have you tell me of it every day and every hour of my life. I would drink in the assurance in words; I would inhale it with the fragrance of flowers; I would read it on their petals; I would have the dear words, '*I love you*,' come to me, from you, through every form of utterance, and every ingenuity of expression. They can never tire and never satisfy. It is because I know that I am loved that I would hear you say so, and not because I hear you say so that I know I am loved."

Holyoke looked down into her earnest eyes, and drank in her earnest utterances, with an affectionate admiration that rendered his plea for pardon entirely needless. The kiss that he impressed upon her forehead he justified by a course of reasoning based upon the declarations that had just fallen from the girl's lips, and it was doubtless satisfactory to her.

When the happy pair arrived at Mr. Pynchon's house, they found Mrs. Pynchon in the possession of much clearer ideas of the nature of the morning's business than those which Peter Trimble had imparted to her. Holyoke received a most cordial greeting at her hands, and, in return, he answered all her questions in regard to her old friends of the Bay, and told her every particle of news that he thought would interest her.

After taking their seats at the dinner-table, Mrs. Pynchon led off the conversation by expressing her regrets that she had nothing better to set before her visitors, and wondered why somebody did not think to bring along some steaks from Tom, seeing he was bled so nicely.

"Do you suppose we would eat Tom, mother?" exclaimed Mary in perfect astonishment, laying down her knife.

"Why—wasn't he very fat, Mary?" inquired the old lady, with a puzzled expression of countenance.

"Why, mother, just think of eating the dear creature that we have fed and petted all winter!" said Mary. "I should as soon think of eating John."

This aspect of the case had not appeared to the good old

lady, but she was a little piqued by Mary's vehemence, and so, bent on maintaining her point, she said, "Well, my dear, what is the difference between a deer and a chicken? I've known you feed and pet chickens till they were fat, and then eat them rationally with the rest of us."

The laugh that followed was at Mary's expense, and the old lady urged her point no further, upon learning from Mr. Pynchon that he had sent a man to give the slaughtered pet a decent burial.

CHAPTER VIII.

THE presence of Mary Pynchon's lover at Agawam was no less the subject of common gossip than common knowledge. He had not been within the plantation a day when Mr. and Mrs. Pynchon had received business or friendly calls from nearly all who dared to call upon them, some of whom achieved their object, and won a sight of, and perhaps a word with, the interesting gentleman, while others only had the pleasure of bemoaning the "prospect of our losing Mary," or of expressing the wish that "things might turn out so that there might be an addition to the settlement."

Agawam had never had such a visitant before, and the effect of his presence upon the girls and young women particularly, was very noticeable. Before he came, they usually had enough of labor to occupy their time, but from their morning walks and afternoon rambles, which invariably led by Mr. Pynchon's house, one would have supposed that they had all become suddenly impressed with the necessity of seeking health at a common fountain, to which there was but a single safe and direct route. There was a general experience of attraction to the building that contained the new man, among the gentler sex of every age,—a kind of indefinite out-reaching of sympathy, some of which found its highest satisfaction in simply going towards its object, without the hope of coming near it, just as a score of the fresh tendrils of a grape vine will reach their delicate fingers towards a new, though distant object, each with an incipient curl of sympathy at its trembling terminus, while only one is near enough to clasp the object in a coil that knows no release but in death, or by a rupture more cruel than death.

Doubtless his relations to Mr. Pynchon and his daughter had their influence in this matter, but there was something above and beyond these,—something above and beyond anything apparent to the eye, or comprehended in the reason. He was a man who impressed every one, and received impressions from every one,—taking something from every individual with whom he might be brought into personal relation, and filling the void with himself, so that many found themselves talking as he talked, with an unwonted elegance and facility, or walking as he walked, with an unusual grace of motion.

Holyoke was no less charming to the simple-hearted Mrs. Pynchon than to her beautiful step-daughter, and became as early the confidant of the grave and reserved father as of the young and noble-hearted son. He was authority in matters of fashion, and intelligent in questions of theology, —equally at home in politics and polemics. His sojourn at Agawam was a precious episode in the life of the Pynchon family, and friendship nearly monopolized the time that love could poorly spare.

To Mrs. Pynchon he was a fountain of intelligence concerning places and persons associated with the past. To Mr. Pynchon he was a fresh, free spirit, full of vitality and strength, able by the subtle powers of intuition to solve questions that his own reason had grappled with in vain. To John he became an idol—a man—by the side of whom all the men he had seen were pigmies—mere shows of men.

On the morning following Holyoke's arrival at Agawam, he walked out with Mr. Pynchon, while John and some of the neighbors joined his companions from the Bay in a fishing excursion. Mr. Pynchon communicated to him his plans concerning the plantation, gave the character and position of each settler as passed his cabin, and soon introduced his visitor into all the interests of the place, and his own policy in their management and development. Holyoke was unreserved in his comment upon each subject as it was presented, found a practical solution of every difficulty that might be involved in it, and offered his free and natural suggestions in a manner that entirely confirmed him in the good opinion of his host. This outside survey of the plantation, and this introduction of Holyoke to its acquaintance, did not satisfy Mr. Pynchon. With the exception of Mary, he had long felt that there was no one in the plantation who was a proper receptacle of his confidence, in matters touching his religious opinions and experience; and from her he had hidden much, as has before been intimated, through the fear of disturbing her faith in Christian doctrine as generally accepted by the Puritan churches, or of loosening her confidence in himself.

Approaching the house on their return home, the old gentleman and his guest sought a convenient location in the pleasant morning sun, and sat down.

"It seems to me that you must be happy here, Mr. Pynchon," said Holyoke, breaking a silence that had lasted for some minutes.

"Why?" inquired Mr. Pynchon, looking upon the young man with a smile.

"First, because you are in a pleasant spot; second, because every one reveres you; and, third, because you may do very much as you please here," replied Holyoke.

"Are those all the reasons you can give?" inquired Mr. Pynchon.

"They are all I thought necessary to give, because the absolute essentials of happiness are things which a man generally carries with him,—which are, to a very great extent, independent of circumstances. Religion and family affection, for instance, are, or should be, unaffected by location and associations"

"So far as religion is concerned, the case, with me, is the opposite of this," rejoined Mr. Pynchon; and looking at Holyoke with a smile of peculiar meaning, he added, "and one of my best friends is engaged in breaking up my home."

"I understand the latter clause of your statement," returned Holyoke, with an answering smile, "and do not have it in my heart to blame your friend for undertaking the enterprise, but the first part I do not understand."

"I will explain," replied Mr. Pynchon, "if you have the desire or the patience to hear. You say that religion is, or should be, unaffected by location and associations, but I have no possession so seriously affected by those accidents as my religion. My relations with God have been less disturbed by them than my relations with men, since I have been here in the colony; and oftentimes I have even felt that the influences around me aided me in spiritual enjoyment and development; but I have a lack of sympathy with some of the prevalent views of religious doctrine, that does much to destroy my peace, and that sometimes fills me with emotions that would be akin to remorse, if they proceeded from anything akin to guilt."

"Where lies the trouble?" inquired Holyoke. "Has any difficulty sprung from your difference with the views of which you speak?"

"No: I have never differed openly, and there lies my trouble. I listen, on Sabbath and on lecture days, to doctrines that in my heart I believe to be full of error. Some of them disgust me by their absurdity, and others distress me by their detraction from the dignity of the divine character; and yet I feel bound to make a show of believing them, or perhaps feel it a duty to refrain from dissent and controversy. I have pursued this course because I was afraid of weakening the influence of the minister among his flock, of arousing doubts in the minds of some, of throwing others off their balance, and, in short, of injuring the cause of Christ which, if I have true knowledge of my own heart, I am most anxious to serve."

"You should be satisfied with your motives, at least," responded Holyoke thoughtfully.

"That I am not," returned Mr. Pynchon. "While I have no doubt of my sincerity in the wish to advance the cause of religion, I am led to feel that perhaps a wish to preserve my influence and position in the colony has not been altogether without power in determining my course thus far. It is this distrust of my motives, to some extent, that gives me uneasiness, but the greater part of it arises from a distrust of my own judgment in regard to duty. Is it manly, is it christianly, tacitly to approve doctrines which my judgment rejects and my conscience condemns? Am I not endangering truth by these compromises with error for its sake? Am I not doing for truth the work of an enemy, in the name of a friend? These are questions that trouble me constantly, and you can thus very readily see why location and associations have very much to do with my religion."

"Do you regard these errors of which you speak as fatal errors, Mr. Pynchon?" inquired Holyoke.

"I think a man may be saved, and still believe them, if that is a reply to your question," said Mr. Pynchon.

"And you are perfectly settled in, and satisfied with, your own views of doctrine?" continued Holyoke interrogatively.

"As well settled, perhaps, as imperfect man may be. My trials involve a question of practical duty rather than of doctrinal belief."

"What if I were to quote to you from Romans the words, 'Hast thou faith? Have it to thyself, before God,'" suggested Holyoke.

"You would not help me at all," replied Mr. Pynchon, "for I should quote from the context, 'for, whatsoever is not of faith, is sin!'"

"Well," said Holyoke, "your position is a hard one, and the question of duty is one which you only can decide. I cannot place myself in your position, but were I living on this plantation, as I do live in a settlement where, doubtless, the same errors are taught, I should not have the slightest trouble in regard to them, although my opinions might not differ from yours. Unimportant errors wear out, and drop away from truth of themselves, if they are let alone. If they are controverted, they often grow so as to hide the truth, and frequently live on the pledges of controversial pride, until they have rendered the truth with which they may have been associated a loathing and a byword. If I were certain that the ministers of the colony were against me, in a point of doctrine which I believed involved no fatal error, I should certainly save my strength and my influence for advancing essential truth, rather than expend both in a vain attempt to destroy any unimportant errors with which it might for the moment be associated. Martyrdom is never pleasant, and can hardly be called respectable when suffered at a stake which the martyr is obliged to hold up to keep it from falling."

"Just as I expected!" exclaimed a musical voice behind the gentlemen, as Holyoke uttered his last words. "I have been looking at you from the window for the last half hour, and I had no doubt that you had both shut your eyes to all these beautiful things around you, and the staple duties of life, and were discussing some dry chip of a doctrine."

Both turned, and looked into the healthful, smiling face of Mary Pynchon. Her father saw that she was dressed for a morning ramble, and guessed in what direction, without his late companion, she wished him to move; but he could not give up the conversation so readily, and addressing her, he said, "Mary, you mistake in regard to the nature of our conversation, but why do you speak so contemptuously of doctrine? It seems to me that some of the dryest chips are the staple duties of life which you so readily associate with beautiful things."

"Because that doctrine is good for nothing save as a definition of our relations, and relations are good for nothing unless they are practical," replied Mary, at once becoming serious and animated.

"The Oracle of Agawam!" exclaimed Holyoke, half sportively.

"Giving her responses in enigmas," added Mr. Pynchon.

"And consulted by idolatrous and deluded men," rejoined Mary, her flexible features in harmony with the pleasantry.

"But seriously," said Holyoke, "did you mean anything in particular by that little speech of yours?"

"Seriously, I did," replied Mary. "I meant that God is the ordainer of doctrine, and that men are the performers of duty; and that any further than doctrine involves to us a question of practical duty we have no use for it, and no business with it. I am very tired, if it is proper for me to say so (and Mary's cheeks kindled, and her eyes flashed with strong feeling), of these everlasting discussions of, and quarrels over, doctrine, and their accompanying lamentations over neglect of duty. Men will talk of nothing but doctrine from morning till night, and have nothing to bemoan in their prayers but their neglect of duty; while, if they had but done their duty they would have found out the doctrine, as well as won honor to religion, and saved remorse to themselves."

"That may all be true, and I am inclined to think that a part of it is," said Holyoke, "but I do not exactly see how a man can find out one doctrine by performing the duties issuing from relations defined by another."

"Just over the bank, there, flows the Connecticut," said Mary, raising her hand, and blushing at her own earnestness, "and its waters come from hills and valleys very far North. Now if you were wishing to find the sources of the stream, you would not wander indefinitely over the whole northern region after them. You would begin here, and trace the river upwards, and thus find them infallibly. Now in God are the sources of duty, and they flow out from Him through streamlets of relationship, until they combine in one large river which, if we follow it, will not only bring us to Him, but will show us the location, size, and character of each tributary as we advance upwards. At this end it is duty, and God is at the other, and as we can only find our way to God through duty, so we cannot fail to discover all necessary doctrine, for it must lie directly on the way. The remark of the Saviour that 'if a man will do His will he shall know of the doctrine,' is doubtless a gracious promise, but it is no less the statement of a philosophical truth."

When Mary had finished her simple and beautiful lesson, there were tears in Holyoke's eyes, called there by various agencies. In the first place, it was eloquent, and touched his sensibilities, and in the second, the beautiful speaker was his own dear betrothed; and the love that had swelled in his bosom for her brimmed with new fulness as he comprehended with new appreciation the intelligence that informed her Christian character, and the preciousness of the prize he held in the possession of her love.

Mr. Pynchon, as he turned to bid the lovers a good morning and a pleasant ramble, was a gratified witness of the emotion apparent in Holyoke, and yet his gratification was not untouched with sadness, for he could not but feel that what was the young man's gain, was to a certain extent his own loss. But as he walked slowly homewards, and turned to observe his children as they passed down the street in loving converse, and felt how precious they were to each other, and how precious a thing was love, his selfishness vanished, and a prayer for their constancy and happiness found utterance at his trembling lips.

While he was meditating, the lovers had left the street, and, striking into the Bay Path, had passed beyond his vision. They sought, by a common impulse, the spot where they had met on the previous day, and there found the fresh mound that marked the resting-place of the unfortunate pet. Mary proceeded to a neighboring shrub, and broke off a twig, white with shad blossoms, and laid it upon the mound, with such a degree of tenderness and respect that Holyoke, half amused, stepped to her side, and looking in her demure face with a merrily twinkling eye, exclaimed, "In memory of the deer—departed!"

Mary could not entirely maintain her gravity, although she endeavored to do so, and half sportively, half sadly she replied, in his own vein, "Flowers are a proper offering, for here lies a hart that loved me."

"Good! I am relieved!" exclaimed Holyoke. "I never knew a woman with a broken heart who kept her wit."

"And I never knew a man with very much wit who kept a heart to break," rejoined Mary, with an insinuating tone and a roguish smile.

"Have you any acquaintances that happen to be heartless?" inquired Holyoke with a jocular look of concern.

"Oh! no!" replied Mary, merrily laughing; "there are none among them who possess the conditions."

"A truce! a truce!" exclaimed Holyoke. "Let us have a suspension of hostilities, while I repair damages."

Holyoke's efforts to repair damages were of the usual character under such circumstances. No music had so charmed him, in his whole life, as the words of repartee that had closed his mouth. He would have been willing to be the victim of Mary's sharp words to any extent, for somehow (and there lay the mystery) her utterances seemed to be *his* property, for other reasons than that they were at his expense. To be beaten in an argument by Mary would have been a boon almost worth praying for, while to be fairly down in an encounter of wits was a bliss that he felt sure of re-achieving at every convenient opportunity. In short, the sweetest pride he had ever tasted was that which came to his lips on the same breath that asserted in language the most appropriate the equality of the pure mind with which he was matched.

Seeking still higher ground, the lovers paused and looked off upon the valley.

"When shall you be ready to leave your Arcadia?" inquired Holyoke tenderly.

"When love and duty agree in permitting me to leave it," replied the girl.

"I believe you profess to find your duty in your relations," said Holyoke, with an allusion to a portion of the religious conversation of the morning.

"And what then?" inquired Mary.

"Does it not follow that your highest duty will flow from your tenderest relations?"

"Let us speak plainly," said Mary. "Do you wish me to leave this place? Do you wish me to leave my father, my sister, my brother?"

The question was asked with evident emotion and anxious earnestness, and Holyoke could only reply by inquiring what kind of an answer she wished for or expected.

"I have thought," said Mary, "or more properly, perhaps, dreamed, that when your eyes should comprehend the beauty of that river and the valley through which it passes, and these pleasant hills, and should learn how large the harvests are, and how full the woods are of game and the streams of fish, it would seem to you a place where you would love to live,—where you would love to expend the force of your enterprise and the influence of your life. I have become strangely attached to the people here, and to the enterprise in which they are engaged. My father is happier here than he would be elsewhere in the colony, and here is my young brother, who, I am sure, could hardly get along without me. I know you cannot attribute the feeling to anything that makes me unworthy of you or your love, but I confess that the thought of leaving the settlement fills me with sadness."

Mary uttered these words with anxious misgivings, and Holyoke heard them with his eyes upon the ground.

"I know," continued Mary, taking one of his hands in her own, "that your associations are all at the Bay, that your mother is there and all your mates, but there are others there to take care of and comfort those who are dear to you. I know you would lose much by coming here, but would you not gain much? It seems hard to me to relinquish the privilege of helping to mould the character of this settlement, and give life to influences which shall be active when all the valley, up to and beyond those mountains, shall be full of people, rejoicing in happy homes and overflowing harvests. If I feel thus, who am a woman, a man with talent and power and superior position would, it seems to me, look upon such a privilege as more precious than comfort, and more valuable than riches."

She paused for a reply, and paused with anxiety, for she felt a chilling influence in the half offended look that Holyoke still cast upon the ground, but dared not lift to her honest face.

There is nothing in the world so unreasonable as a man's love, because it is so largely mingled with personal pride. A woman is simply grieved if she have not the whole of her lover's or her husband's heart. A man is offended if he even mistrust that his will, his claims, and his love are not supreme in the mind and heart of his mistress or his wife. And so, while Holyoke was listening to the beautiful words of one who had honored him by her love, and by associating him with schemes of noble social and Christian enterprise, a jealous feeling touched his heart,—a feeling springing from the idea that she had planned without reference to his will, and acknowledged claims paramount to his. He knew that the feeling was a mean one, and yet, while fully ashamed of it, he would not shake it off, but stood there, like a man as he was, with a kind of dogged determination to give pain to the woman whom he loved, and whom he would not have seen misused by another without a thorough vindication of his claim to be her protector.

"Then you do not love me well enough to go with me wherever it is for my interest to go, or where my interests already are?" said Holyoke, with a half averted gaze and reddening face.

"And can *you* say that to *me?*" exclaimed Mary, half deprecatingly, half reproachfully.

Holyoke looked at her, and had the selfish satisfaction of seeing all he wished to see, and was then ready for forgiveness. He saw a pair of eyes brimming with tears. He saw upon beautiful features an expression of wounded love and injured sensibilities. He saw what he had unworthily craved—a demonstration of his own power and her devotion. He stooped to kiss a tear that was falling from her cheek—an act which she received half unconsciously, with eyes still fixed upon him. At last, as he tried, half laughing, to rally her upon her sadness, the sense of shame came over him, and his poor pride gave way before an honest indignation against himself, which found vent in strong language.

"Mary," said Holyoke, taking her hands in his own, "it is my deliberate opinion that I am a heartless, contemptible man. I have been as mean and unmanly as Judas. I yield myself to your reproaches, and will submit to any penalty you may inflict. I'm a fool—an utter fool!"

"You cannot expect me to marry such a man as you describe yourself to be," said Mary, with a smile that rose to her face unbidden.

"If you really knew how I have abused you, and how heartlessly I have led you into this trap, I am not sure that you would not reconsider your pledge of truth to me."

"Well, confession will go further towards securing mercy for you than anything else, so you had better make a clean breast of it, and tell the worst."

"This morning, Mary," said Holyoke, leading her to a seat, "your good father walked with me all over the settlement, and pointed out the beautiful lands on both sides of the river, informing me of allotments still to be made, and lots that were for sale, and I knew the secret wish that actuated him in this survey; but I said nothing, and let him talk, accepting no hint, and blind to every anxious suggestion. And then you came, and here, after pouring frankly into my ears your noble words and wishes, that might have come from an angel, and did come from motives as pure as words were ever born in, I trampled on your feelings and your suggestions, and selfishly, and with perverse intention, injured you by doubting a love that I knew to be true. And now, with these facts before you, what should you judge I came to Agawam for?"

"You could not have come to do this."

"Very well—I did not, but what do you suppose I came here for?"

"I have had the impression," said Mary, slightly puzzled by his manner, "that you came to see me."

"I did, my love, and I came also to find a place to live in—to plant here my home, my fortunes, and my name."

"May God bless you!" exclaimed Mary, and hid her face upon his breast.

"Your prayer is answered," responded Holyoke tenderly, "even while you are speaking."

When, at length, she lifted her head, Holyoke said in a low voice, "Are my crimes forgiven?"

"No," replied Mary, "they are forgotten."

The lovers sat for some minutes in silence, which was at last broken by Holyoke. "Mary," said he, "I have just conceived an idea that seems strange to me as well as rational."

"What is it?"

"That I have become a new being in a new world."

"Explain," said Mary.

"Do you ever think of your childhood without having a vision of your childhood's home? *Can* you think of yourself as a little child, without seeing all that surrounded you when a child?"

"Granted that I cannot," replied Mary: "What then?"

"Would it not seem to you that the scene was thus a part of the soul—that the soul, by receiving impressions from it and passing into it in the realization of life, had become fitted to it, and bore the stamp of all its features?"

"I think I understand you," said Mary, "and now for your new idea."

"I felt as I was sitting here, that my soul had flowed out upon, and fitted itself to a new scene,—as if all that I saw around me had become a part of me; and certainly no thought of love for you can ever visit me, without bringing this picture with it."

"Yours should be a great love to be worthy of a casting in such a mould," said Mary, smiling at the fancy, "and I take it as a pledge that your soul can never fit itself to any other."

"Mary, you are inclined to joke me—I see it in your eye, but the truth is, I feel just now intensely poetical."

"By the way," continued Mary, with a look of well disguised concern, "you are not going to set up a claim to the proprietorship of these lands, based on the fact that they have become a part of you, are you?"

"When you become a part of me, I calculate I shall set up a claim of proprietorship," responded Holyoke, reluctantly drawn away from his pet conceit, "and why should woodland differ from wife?"

"There is one difference, at least: the wife takes your name and the woodland does not."

"Honestly, Mary," said Holyoke, "it would be a very great happiness to give my name to a scene like this, to be linked with it for ever, to have it spoken from a mountain top or sung by a waterfall."

"If you wish it," said Mary, entering into his enthusiasm, "let it be so. Do you see that blue mountain top at the North, just lifting itself above the intervening forests?"

"Yes."

"Let that be MT. HOLYOKE for ever!" said Mary, stretching out her hand.

"Amen!" responded Holyoke, "and I shall see that your authority in bestowing the name is fully honored. But what shall be done with the lonely mountain westward of mine? It would be unkind to leave that nameless."

"Let it be named in honor of the poor pet that lies yonder," said Mary, pointing to the grave of Tom.

"Let it be MT. TOM for ever!" said Holyoke, in sportive imitation of Mary, and the lovers simultaneously rose, and bent their steps homewards.

CHAPTER IX.

The reader has not yet received a proper introduction to the family of Mr. George Moxon, but there have been good reasons for the delay. The family had its peculiarities, and they were peculiarities so essentially idiocratic that the most favorable circumstances were necessary to be in conjunction, for their thorough exhibitic

For several days succeeding the events recorded in the last chapter, the weather was hot and sultry; and, on the evening which has been chosen for the introduction of this family, it had cleared, and cooled, and refreshed itself, and everything and everybody else, by the first thunder-shower of the season. A big black cloud had risen slowly and gloomily in the West; silver-headed giants had come up behind it, and peeped over one another's shoulders into the valley, slowly changing their places and climbing higher and higher, until at last a broad grey screen hid them and the sky above them, and spread over the heavens. And then there was much hurrying to and fro, in the advance battalions of the storm; and the roar of the chariot wheels and the tramp and rush of the on-coming legions filled the air. At last, the scattering shot of the first distant discharge fell pattering upon the forest leaves and on the cabin roofs; while nearer, and with still increasing vividness, flashed the magnificent artillery.

There was a great scene between the giants of the clouds and the giants of the forests. At first, the former came down on the wind in a hand-to-hand encounter. They grappled, they wrestled, they writhed, they groaned, they roared; but the forest giants were the victors, and, in the first lull of the storm, their antagonists retreated, and took up their position behind the clouds, from whence they kept up a scattering fire upon the lower hosts, who, after the heat of the conflict, stood bathing their brows in the sweeping rain. Many an old oak—a soldier of the centuries—was cleft through the helmet, and many a wounded veteran pine smoked in the sweat of his agony.

The shower came on just before sunset, and continued until the dusk of evening had almost deepened into night. There was stillness and solemnity in all the cabins. To their inhabitants, the storm was an exhibition of the power of God; and it was no less a natural impulse than a recognised Christian duty to keep reverently silent when His voice was uttering itself in tones that had once echoed from the sides of Sinai.

The house of the Moxons was peculiarly a solemn place. It was in the presence of such an exhibition of power as the storm presented that Mr. Moxon betrayed the weakest points of his character. There was something so terribly positive about the descent of a thunderbolt, the roar of the wind, and the down-coming of the rain,—something so seemingly regardless of him or his feelings,—something so levelling in its effect upon social and all other distinctions, that it took away his strength, made him forget his position, and drove him to promises and prayer. He and his wife, and two children, both girls, were gathered in their principal room, and not a word was uttered.

Mr. Moxon sat leaning back in his chair,—his lips moving in silent prayer, or his form cringing before the sharp lightning; and only stirred his limbs to change their position, which, in his nervous state, became painful after having been sustained for very brief spaces of time. Mrs. Moxon sat in another chair, holding in her arms her youngest daughter, Rebekah, and divided her attention between her, her husband, the window, and the bed near it, where lay her oldest daughter, Martha, a convalescent from a somewhat protracted illness.

Martha was the only one who had not been terrified by the shower. She had lain upon her bed in such a position as to witness through the window the progress of the storm, and she had enjoyed it very keenly.

After the rain had mostly passed over, and nothing remained to tell of the shower but the wet earth and the flashing of the lightning, whose thunder came but feebly back to the ear from the East, Mrs. Moxon rose from her chair and sat down upon the bed. Taking the little invalid's hand in her own, she said, "How does my little daughter feel this evening?"

"Pretty well," replied the child, giving her a look with her large dark eyes.

"Do you know, Martha, who has cured you? You have been very sick."

"No! Who has?"

"God has cured you, my child, and you should be very thankful to Him for it. I hope my little girl, when she says her prayers to-night, will not forget to thank her heavenly Father for his kindness to her, in making her well again."

The little girl lay reflecting upon the information conveyed by her mother, and was evidently inclined to doubt its correctness. At length, to settle a preliminary question, she said, "Mamma, who made me vomit?"

Mrs. Moxon turned and looked at her husband, who heard the reply, and who, being unable to answer the question satisfactorily to himself or the child, said nothing. The mother was saved from the necessity of continuing the conversation in that direction by a sudden exclamation of the child, whose eyes had reverted to the window.

"Oh, mamma! mamma!" exclaimed the little girl; "I saw God light a star then!"

"I guess not, my child," said the mother.

"Yes, I did, mamma, and I saw him throw down the coal, clear down by the clouds there, till it fell into the water, and went out."

The father and mother were both confounded, but their condition was not unusual, when in conversation with this child. Neither parent had been able to pursue a train of thought with her for any considerable, or at least any satisfactory distance, without being overwhelmed by some unanswerable question, shocked by some strange remark, or startled by some wild revelation. Yet both felt that they must not stop talking with her and to her, and while the mother, in particular, trembled to hear her speak, she could not refrain from the endeavor to train her wild fancies and regulate her imagination. In this endeavor, religion was her only means; but religion, by some strange though by no means unusual fatality, was just the subject, of all others, to set her imagination running upon its wildest freaks.

The mother still sat upon the bed. She wondered what she should say next. At last she thought she would try, if possible, to resume the thread of conversation she had originally commenced. "Martha," said she, "you must not only be thankful to God for taking care of you while you have been sick, and for curing you, but you must try, when you get well, to be a very good little girl, and do all you can to please Him and glorify Him."

Martha turned her large eyes towards her, and said, "Mamma, how do you do when you glorify God?"

Mrs. Moxon was puzzled at this question, straightforward and natural as it was, but she tried to answer it. "We must glorify God," said she, "by doing all He wishes to have us, and by praising Him, and loving Him, and trying to have everybody else love and praise Him." She was not exactly satisfied with her own exposition, but she deemed it correct, so far as it went, and paused.

"What does God love to be praised so for?' 'inquired the child.

Unfortunately the mother could think of nothing better in reply than to ask her why *she* loved to be praised.

Martha looked at her mother, with her wonderful eyes big with a new and strange apprehension, and said, "God isn't proud, is He, mamma?"

The poor mother rose despairingly from the bed, and resumed her seat in the chair.

"You must try to go to sleep now, Martha," said Mr. Moxon, breaking a silence that he had maintained since the commencement of the storm.

"I wish you would go to sleep with me, papa," replied the child, "for then you could go to my brick house, and see everything I've got there."

"Your brick house? What do you mean by your brick house?"

"I've got a brick house, and a blue cat in it," said the child, "just as blue as the sky, and it has got red rings round its eyes, and a whole parcel of little red kittens, all made out of bricks. Just think, papa! All made out of bricks! And I've got a beautiful doll in it, with wings—I guess her wings are green—I guess they are. Her name is Martha Brick, and she can say all her letters, and spell Nebuchadnezzar both ways; and I've got some beautiful birds! Oh! they're just as beautiful! that fly right through the window when it's down, and then one of them 'lights on the blue cat's head, and they keep 'lighting on one another, till they pile clear up to the plastering; and pretty soon I step on the blue cat's tail, and she screams, and runs up the chimney, and that tips all the birds over, and they laugh just as loud as they can laugh, and fly and get on to the backs of the little brick kittens, and drive them round the rooms and round the rooms; and pretty soon a great black man comes into the room and blows his nose, and the birds all fly out of the window again, and—"

"Martha! Martha! my dear child, you will tire yourself, so that you will not sleep to-night, if you do not stop talking in this way," exclaimed her father.

"I can go to sleep on my bed in the brick house," said the little girl, looking through the window up to the stars, "for oh! there's a beautiful angel, just as big as he can be, comes every night and sits on my bed, and tells me the prettiest stories, and sings the prettiest songs; oh! they're just as pretty! and sometimes there's two angels, and one stands on the head-board and the other stands on the foot-board, and they reach over, and take hold of hands, and kiss one another, and jump over one another's shoulders, and the blue cat and all her little kittens get into bed with me, and we sleep just as warm as can be, till the great black man comes in and blows his nose, and then the angels fly away, and the blue cat goes up chimney, and the little kittens all cuddle up into a pile."

"Why, Martha," exclaimed the mother, "where do you get such notions?"

"At the brick house," replied Martha, "and I've got a great many more of them. I wish papa would go to the brick house with me and see them."

Mr. Moxon drew his chair to the bedside of his child, and took her worn little hand in his own, hoping to quiet her nervousness and to induce her to go to sleep. The room was dark, and the younger child was already sleeping in the arms of her mother. The silence of the group seemed to grow deeper and deeper, until sleep would almost have claimed possession of them all, but there were two who were wakeful still.

Mr. Moxon knew that Martha was not asleep, and Martha knew that he was not. At last both father and daughter were seized with an involuntary shudder at the same moment.

"He went by then," whispered the child.

"Who went by?" inquired the father.

"The black man. Didn't you see him, papa?"

"I felt something—something like a shadow," replied the father. "Do you smell anything, Martha?"

The little child snuffed the air with her thin and sensitive nostrils, and said "Yes."

"What is it?"

"I don't know," replied the child, "but I've smelled *that* a great many times at the brick house."

"You don't mean, Martha, that you smell that when you see *him* at the brick house, do you?"

When the utterance of this question was completed, the father found, to his surprise, that, by one of those strange transitions incident to a highly nervous organization, the child had passed into the realm of sleep, as though an angel had shut the door of the senses with a noiseless push; and the little dreamer's "brick house" had opened of itself, and given her sudden entrance.

Mr. Moxon still held the little hand within his own, and busied his mind with the strange revelations of his child. The coincidence of the shudder that visited her and himself, at the same moment, was called up. There was an influence that affected him and his child alike—that was certain. She saw what she called a black man, and he felt that something had passed his window that had cast a shadow upon him—a shadow felt, not seen. They had both been affected by a peculiar perfume also. What was it all? Were they alone touched by these strange influences? Were those influences the offspring of disease? If not, were they—but no, they could not be! So, carefully rising, and relinquishing the hand that had grown soft, warm, and moist within his own, the minister made a place for the repose of the other child, where the mother silently laid her. The parents then withdrew together, and sought the only other room they possessed, that they might, without disturbing the children, unite in their evening devotions.

The prayer uttered by Mr. Moxon that evening was one that his wife did not entirely understand. He prayed for the forgiveness of sins that had possibly been committed unwittingly. This was something that she did not comprehend, especially as the prayer was uttered with remarkable fervor and deep solemnity. Then he prayed mysteriously with reference to the presence, the wiles, and the power of the great adversary of souls, and seemed burdened with some vague and overshadowing apprehension of evil. The prayer was long, and Mrs. Moxon, wearied with long watchings, and the new and strange influences within and around her, was glad when it was concluded, and immediately sought her bed.

The father, however, went to Martha's bedside, and drawing a chair near to it, leaned over to listen to her breathing, and to catch any dream-born whisper that might find utterance. There the poor man sat for hours in the darkness, sometimes looking through the window heavenward, then out into the night, upon shapes that formed themselves of, and clothed themselves with, the darkness, and then moved and melted into nothingness. Then he came back to the child, and at last her peaceful breathing began to have a soothing influence upon him, and, leaving her, he retired to rest.

CHAPTER X.

For many years after the settlement of Agawam, a religious meeting was held every Wednesday, at which the minister pronounced what was denominated a "lecture." On these lecture days, all the people were expected to be in attendance, precisely the same as on Sabbath days, though the day was treated in no respect as holy time. The orders of the General Court were all published on lecture days, for the benefit of the people; and all those public announcements were made which were of interest to the plantation. A portion of the day was regarded by the apprentices and children as their own, for the purposes of play. Thus the term "lecture day" early became the synonym for holiday, and Wednesday was called by its real name hardly once in a twelvemonth.

Lecture day was a great day for Peter Trimble. A multitude of the plans concocted in his fertile little brain had reference to that day. During the week of Holyoke's stay in the plantation, the people were so far diverted from observing the operations of this young mischief maker, that he was enabled to arrange the preliminaries for a grand game of fun that so excited his imagination that he could hardly sleep meantime; and when at last lecture day came, and the lecture was over, he was observed giving sly whispers to such boys as were in the secret, and all moved off towards their homes.

Peter, as soon as he had arrived at his home, went back of it, and, under the cover of trees and shrubbery, proceeded down the river bank, until he had arrived opposite to the house of Woodcock, when he approached and entered it. He knew that Woodcock was absent, at work in the fields, for he had not been at the lecture, and his canoe was not at the river's bank.

He found Mary Woodcock alone, and amusing herself by jumping over a stick, with which she had bridged the chasm between two benches. The joy that lighted her features, as Peter made his appearance, and her quick forgetfulness of all his insults, showed how much she had suffered in her loneliness, and how thoroughly sympathetic with the boy nature she had become.

Peter came into the house, taking steps that defined long, stealthy curves, as they rose and fell, from tip-toe to tip-toe, and with a countenance that indicated the highest possible degree of pleasurable excitement.

"What is't now?" inquired Mary, eagerly.

"You know Tim Bristol, Mary?"

"Yes."

"Well, you know what a regular brag he is, don't you?"

"He don't brag any more'n you do, Peter Trimble—not a single bit."

"Well, you know he thinks lots of you, any way, Mary, and he's always bragging about you."

"I don't b'lieve you ever heard him say anything 'bout me in the world," said Mary, sharply.

"*Well! Now!*" exclaimed Peter, cramming two whole sentences and two powerful interjections into two words; "if I have heard Tim Bristol brag how smart you are, and how handsome you are, and how he likes you, once, I've heard him do it—oh! lots and lots of times!" And Peter clinched his well driven lie with a violent nod of his head.

"Well, that's none of your business," said Mary, beginning to feel an entirely new partiality for Tim.

"Well, I know that," responded Peter in a candid tone,

"but he carries it too fur. Oh! you ought to hear him brag."

"I don't b'lieve he brags—what does he brag about?"

"Well, you ought to hear him once; you've no idea! Brag? He don't do anything but brag, and he brags about such droll things. What do you s'pose he said t'other day? Says he to me, 'I'll bet three shillings that Mary Woodcock can run faster than you can;' and says I to him, 'I'll bet three shillings she can't.' Says he, 'I'll bet she can;' says I, 'I'll bet she can't.' Says he, 'I know she can;' says I, 'I know she can't.' Says he, 'you darsn't bet;' says I, 'I darst.' Says he, 'put up your money;' says I, 'Mary Woodcock won't run with me, and you can't make her run.' Says he, 'you darsn't run, and you darsn't bet;' says I, 'if you'll get her to run, I'll take the bet, and give her a rod the start.'"

"What did he say?" asked Mary eagerly.

"Well, I kind a' backed him down, I thought, but I see him jest now, and he said I could ask you if I was a' mind to, but I told him you wouldn't run with me, and you wouldn't dare to run."

"Pho! Sho!" exclaimed the girl contemptuously, "I hope I ain't afeared o' you. Did Tim say he knew I could run faster'n you could?"

"Yes, he did, and he stuck to it like a nailer, too," said Peter, with one of his half rotary nods of emphasis.

"You *must* be smart, to think I'm afeared o' you," said the girl.

"Well! I don't s'pose you're afeared of me, but you darsn't run with me," said Peter, with one of his most confident nods.

"I darst, too," responded Mary, getting excited.

"You darsn't run this afternoon, any way," said Peter.

"I will, if you'll go where dad can't see me, nor nobody else," said Mary, decidedly.

At the upper end of the settlement there was a mound-like elevation, that rose on all sides from the level of the meadow, and spread to the extent of several acres into a beautiful plateau. This eminence, which is now popularly known by the inappropriate name of Round Hill, was, from the peculiarity of its position, a favorite resort for the mischief-making boys of the settlement. It was elevated above the fields, so that no one in the vicinity could see the actors, especially as their operations were carried on near the middle of the plateau. At, and near this point, a careful observer would have discovered various mysterious excavations, booths, corn-cobs, egg shells, partridge feathers, &c., which showed that it was a favorite resort for a class of boys that enter into the constitution of every community, in whom the passions for mischief and wild housekeeping are predominant.

The race for which Peter had made his arrangements was appointed for this place, and the adroit manner in which he had surmounted all difficulties may be imagined from the means by which he secured the attendance of Mary Woodcock. It did not occur to her, for an instant, that there was any actual impropriety in her engaging in the race, and her vanity and her love of exciting play settled the question, in precisely the manner which Peter had calculated upon. Accordingly, Peter told her where they could go, and promised that no one should be present, save perhaps a few of the boys, "to see that it was done all fair."

Peter led his victim nearly to the river's bank, and then pushed northward, under such covers as the land afforded, and, after a brisk walk of about a mile, reached the point of assignation. There were half a dozen boys in waiting to receive them, drawn up in a line, with Tim Bristol a few paces in front.

"Lungolunt!" challenged the half snickering Tim.

"Lungoloit!" responded Peter.

"Linkumlilligo!" said Tim.

"Lillikumdaddles!" responded Peter.

"Them's the countersigns," said Peter to Mary, in a side explanation.

"How goes the war?" interrupted Tim.

"Three to the right, and three to the left, and three to the chap I took you for," responded Peter, clapping his hands three times, and giving a long, shrill whistle, with an instrument composed of two lips, two rows of teeth, and a brace of dirty fingers.

This cabalistic exercise was one of the proudest products of Peter's genius. It had cost him infinite invention to contrive the words, and give to them the mysterious music that should insure their success with his companions. The words were only known to a select few, who became, to all intents and purposes, a secret society. When any of the privileged number met, especially if small boys or girls were within hearing, the charmed signals were exchanged with the utmost gravity, and with an effect on juvenile imaginations that was quite bewildering. Two or three sharp little fellows had caught the words, and would go back and forth among themselves, solemnly delivering them in challenge and response.

These interesting ceremonials over, all formality was dropped, and the boys gathered around the new comers.

"She's jest about tuckered me out, coming up here," said Peter, wiping his forehead on his shirt sleeve. "You've no idea how she puts."

"You're a' goin' to back out now, are you?" said Tim, with a wink.

"When you catch me backing out," said Peter indignantly, "you'll catch your great-grandmother ridin' a trottin' ridge pole; now you'd better b'lieve that;" and, as the alternative seemed extremely improbable, it was admitted on all hands that Peter would not back out.

"Dad'll get back 'fore I do, if I don't get through pretty soon," said Mary, half whispering to Peter.

"Well—here's the ground," said Peter. "I start *here*, and you start *there* (measuring off five paces and drawing a mark through the leaves with his bare heel). That's jest a rod the start. Now when Tim Bristol says 'ratta-*ban*, ratta-*ban*, ratta-*ban*, ratta-*biddle* slap!'—you start when he gets to 'biddle—slap!' "

"Yes," said Tim, "and run jest as tight as you can cut."

Mary had already taken her place, and her eye was wild with excitement, while a bright red spot burnt on either cheek.

"Hold my cap, now," said Peter to the boys, spitting on his hands, and winking in a very comical way.

"Are you all ready?" inquired Tim.

"All ready!" said Peter, spitting on his hands again, but Mary was silent, and showed by her position that she was only waiting the word for starting.

"Now!" exclaimed Tim, "Ratta-*ban*, ratta-*ban*, ratta-*ban*, ratta-*biddle* slap!"

Off flew the little girl with every muscle strained to the highest tension. She bounded over the leaves like a deer, her long hair flying wildly back from her head, and her scanty skirt fairly curbing the reach of her steps. Peter gained upon her, and the other boys kept well alongside, cheering at the top of their lungs. "Lean!" cried Tim; "cut!" shouted another, and the girl impulsively grasped the skirt of her frock and raised it to give her feet more freedom of motion.

The first sight that Peter caught of her lithe little limbs threw him into convulsions. He dashed himself upon the ground, and gave himself up to laughter the most excessive. He rolled, and screamed, and beat his head against a tree, as if he were a ram and the tree his foe. In a moment the other boys were on the ground near him, as crazy with laughter as himself.

This was the culminating point of the fun of the occasion. Peter had witnessed her habit, when running with fear, or any other excitement, and the whole affair was arranged by him in order to give the boys a chance, as he said, "to see the smartest pair of drumsticks that ever come over."

Mary ran but a few rods before she became conscious that the race was relinquished; and, turning on her heel, she stood silent as a statue, regarding the insane group. She still held her skirt in her hand, and first suspected the cause of the uproar when she let it fall. Then the hot blood mounted to her face, and, burning there a moment, retired and left her ashy pale. In an instant the whole plot had opened upon her, and shame, rage, and all the fiercest impulses of passion, took possession of her. She looked down before her, and saw a staff that some walker of the woods had cut and trimmed, and, seizing it, she started back, and Peter had but just time to escape the hard blow that she intended for him by a dexterous dodge.

The next moment he was on his feet, with the infuriated child in full pursuit, and then commenced the real race of the day. No dodges and no rate of speed availed the betrayer. The girl seemed clothed with wings, and fairly flew down upon him, beating him mercilessly. All his artifices availed him nothing. He dodged, and tripped her heels, and threw himself down for her to tumble over him, in vain. At length she drove him from the abrupt bank of the hill, and, as she was upon him in an instant, he had no choice but to start in the direction of his home. He had run but a few rods when a man leaped into the path before him, and seized him by the arm.

Peter really felt a sense of relief upon finding himself in the hands of Elizur Holyoke, who, while holding him with one hand, seized Mary's descending weapon with the other, and wrenched it from her grasp.

Mary Pynchon and her brother had both joined the group meantime; and the moment Mary Woodcock caught sight of the former she ran to her, threw her arms around her, and burying her face in her dress burst into a distressing paroxysm of tears.

Mary took the trembling little girl by the hand, led her aside, and seated her upon a bank that she might rest, and be able to tell the story of the afternoon's adventures. This she did at last, with many sobs and much shame; and while Holyoke led Peter by an unnecessary expansive ear to the house of Mr. Pynchon, Mary conducted the little girl to her father's lonely cabin, talking to her quietly and soothingly as she went, and giving her such counsel as her circumstances required.

The latter pair had been in the cabin but a few minutes when Woodcock came in. He knew by the appearance of his daughter that something serious had occurred, and, with evident trepidation, asked Mary Pynchon what it was. She sat down, and related the story, giving the blame to whom it belonged, and exculpating his daughter as far as possible.

"My God! Mary, you'll kill me!" exclaimed Woodcock, and, sinking upon a seat, he buried his face in his hands and groaned heavily.

This started the child's tears again. She was already hysterical, and the spectacle presented by both father and daughter was very painful to its only witness. Woodcock started up at last, and said, "I guess I'll go and finish off that boy."

"I beg you'll not touch the boy," said Mary Pynchon. "He shall be taken care of."

"Miss Pynchon," said Woodcock, "do you r'ally mean that?"

"I do," replied Mary, firmly.

"Do you know how I feel?" inquired Woodcock.

"I have no doubt that you feel very indignant, and I certainly do not blame you for it."

"Do you know that I'd rather starve for three days than lose a grip into that boy's top-knot?"

"I do not doubt it," replied Mary, smiling at his rude earnestness.

"And you don't want me to touch him?"

"I do not want you to touch him."

"I'm glad on't!" exclaimed Woodcock, brightening up, "'cause now, Miss Pynchon, I can jest show you how John Woodcock remembers a good turn. My hand aches to get hold of that boy (and he shook his big fist mightily), but I shan't touch him, 'cause you don't want to have me." And he smiled grimly, as if he had by a mighty effort achieved a great moral triumph, that brought him pleasure, pain, and pride in equal proportions.

Mary thanked him for his promise in regard to the boy, but she did not feel entirely easy as to his child. She thought it might be assuming too much to dictate in what manner a father should treat his daughter, and, as she could think of no better way to effect her wishes, she stooped and kissed the child, and leaving with her a whispered exhortation, bade the pair a good evening.

Woodcock followed her to the door, and arrested her departure by a slight touch upon her arm. She turned, and saw a pair of eyes suffused with emotion, and their owner making futile attempts to speak.

"Miss Pynchon," said he at length, "you needn't 'a done *that*. I shouldn't 'a touched her."

Mary pressed his rough hand in silence, and walked hastily homewards. When she arrived there, she found quite a concourse of those who had collected to learn what the trouble was; and Peter stood trembling in the midst.

Mr. Pynchon was engaged in the examination of one of the rogue's accomplices, who, as he was rather a victim than an accomplice, was telling the whole story of Peter's operations with entire correctness. Mary heard enough to learn that the truth was coming fairly out, and then left the room.

"You say," said Mr. Pynchon to the boy, "that the bet that you tell of was all flax."

"Nothin' but flax," answered the witness.

"What do you mean by that?" inquired the magistrate.

"I mean it was just vamped up for fun," answered the boy.

"Peter Trimble," said the magistrate, addressing that distinguished lad, "I think I understand your case pretty well. You are evidently in want of a course of strong discipline. The lies you have told within the past week are enough alone to call for ten lashes, and the operations of to-day call for punishment more serious than that. As you are of no particular use to your master, and are inclined to bet without money, I think you should be made to work out your bet for the benefit of those you have injured. You will work for John Woodcock, and be under his control for one month. If you behave well, and drop your lying, your betting, and your tricks, during your punishment, you will then be released. Otherwise, you will have another month of the same treatment."

Poor Peter received his sentence with a sad heart. A month with John Woodcock! It was a cloud that hung between him and all the mischief of life. He could not look at it, and so stood amidst the joking crowd, and screwed his fists into his eyes strongly and persistently, as if the fountain of tears lay very far back, and he were boring for water.

CHAPTER XI.

GREAT was the joy in the settlement at Agawam when it became known that Holyoke had determined to unite himself to the fortunes of the plantation, as well as to its fairest flower.

He had only allowed himself a week for his visit, and had made his promise to the two gentlemen who accompanied him to return with them at the close of that period. They had accomplished their object, in seeing the country, and had had the good fortune to be able, during their stay, to furnish nearly all the tables in the settlement with game and fish. They had become tired of the sport, and were ready to return; but Holyoke found it a more difficult task to leave the spot associated with the objects of his love and hope than he had anticipated, and circumstances conspired in favor of his wishes, and kindly lengthened a communion that had come to be inexpressibly sweet to him.

Holyoke and Mary, in their closing interviews, realized again, in its endless repetition, that enigma of love propounded by nearly every pair in the prospect of marriage. He loved her no better than she loved him, and yet he looked forward to their temporary separation with a degree of pain of which she had no conception. His whole being was bathed in a dream of bliss. It was a dream that enervated him,—that undermined his strengh, and sapped his firmest and noblest purposes. It shut out the future, and the great practical world around him. His existence became purely emotional, and his emotions were all sublimated by the purity and power of his passion.

He met her, at first, gaily, and with the ready gallantry of his nature; but each succeeding day found him more and more silent, until, at last, he would have been content to sit speechless for hours with Mary's hand in his own, or her head upon his shoulder. She became to him an angel, so pure and perfect, so noble and so good, so elevated above all earthly contaminations and associations, that he thought of her only as an angel—a spirit of light and joy, of beauty and goodness. She was the subject of his last thought as he closed his eyes in sleep, and of the first that sprang into resurrection with his waking consciousness. His whole being was full of her. She walked in bright beatitude through all his dreams, and shaped his thoughts to forms of beauty and words of music. She had wrought upon him the highest sanctification of an earthly love. A coarse or ribald phrase, a tainted jest, or an unchaste suggestion, as now and then one reached his ear, was pointed with a sting of the most painful offence. Bright, beautiful dream! Fair flower of paradise! Sweet glimpse of Eden! Ineffably precious experience! conceived in illusion, wrought into form by frailty, and condemned by reason, yet enthroned as the central object in memory's gallery for ever!

Mary, who had done all her dreaming previously, had now become intensely practical. She was rather anxious, on the whole, to have Holyoke depart. The plans of her life were settled, and she desired to engage in their execution. While Holyoke delayed his departure, and controlled her movements and occupied her time by his presence, she could not take a step towards preparing a home for him, an institution of which he had become entirely careless, even to forgetfulness. The business of life had begun with her. The garment of care was already put on, and she waited only for her lover to leave her, to adjust and fasten it, and in it to go about the fulfilment of her mission. Sometimes she shocked him by some homely or excessively practical suggestion, or rallied him upon his drowsiness, and not unfrequently dissipated a heaven of emotion by inquiring very tenderly whether he were sick or in pain. So that the dearer she became to him, the more incomprehensible she appeared, and the more she shocked him by the utterance of common-places, and titbits of worldly wisdom and small maxims of economy, that showed that her thoughts had, for the time, become in a degree released from him, and absorbed in plans for his future comfort and happiness.

Upon Holyoke love had the effect of intoxication, while Mary felt that her spirit had been strengthened in its temper and tone by the same power, and fitted by it, in some reliable degree, to perform the duties and overcome the difficulties of life. They had sat side by side, and respectively drank strength and weakness from the same fountain. He had grown forgetful of his manhood, his high resolutions and his noble enterprises, wrapped in the rosy folds of a present as delirious as it was delicious, while she, loving no less, had grown more thoughtful, more provident, and more womanly, in her comprehension of the duties that lay before her, and the destiny to which she had devoted herself.

The circumstances that conspired to lengthen Holyoke's stay in the plantation were connected with Mr. Pynchon's departure for the Bay, in order to discharge there his duties as a member of the Board of Assistants in the colonial legislature. While this was the leading object of his visit, the visit itself was an opportunity for him to carry forward the furs that had been collected during the season; and messages had been sent to all the Indians in the region to bring in their stock, that all might be transported together. Accordingly, for several days before Holyoke's departure, Mr. Pynchon's house was the constant scene of trade, and large quantities of peltry were accumulated. The house, and the whole settlement, in fact, exhibited, during these days, an appearance which now finds its only examples in the new villages of the retiring West. Savages—men, women, and children—came in, in throngs. The novelty of the settlement had not yet passed away, and those who did not come to sell came to see.

The last man who visited Mr. Pynchon, previous to his departure, was John Woodcock. Taking him a considerable distance aside, he said, "Square Pynchon, what did you send that boy to work with me for?"

"To cure him of his tricks," replied Mr. Pynchon.

"Well, I felt worse worked up 'bout that, than anything that's happened to me in some time," continued Woodcock, with a mortified air, "and I wouldn't 'a stood it if it hadn't been for your Mary."

"I thought you would be pleased with the disposal I made of him, and that it would be the best thing I could do for Peter."

"What do I want to do a good thing for Peter for—a little scaliwag that ought to be ketched in a trap like a musquash, and have his head stove in with a boot-heel? Be I the jail, or the stocks, or the whippin'-post?"

"I am not responsible for your choosing to misunderstand me, Woodcock; and if you do not wish to have the boy work for you, I will assign him to some one else, or change his punishment to whipping," responded Mr. Pynchon.

"I guess I understand you, Square," said Woodcock. "I don't s'pose you meant to say it in so many words that John Woodcock's a hard nut, and'll put that boy through purgatory, but that's what it amounts to. Now I haint any notion of givin' the boy up, but I wanted to show you that I've got feelin's, and can read most kinds of writin'."

"Well, John, you're a strange man. It is very hard suiting you, and it is very hard for you to suit us. By the way, have you satisfied Mr. Moxon's claim for damages yet?"

"No, Square, you know I hav'n't, you know I never will."

"Very well, you must not complain at the consequences. You know that I feel friendly towards you, and you know that the law will be executed in this plantation, if there are men enough here to execute it."

"There ain't enough men here to execute *that* thing on *me*," replied Woodcock, with a nod of decision at every second word, and a strong scowl of contempt.

"Go your way, Woodcock—you seem determined to make trouble for yourself and everybody else." Thus saying, Mr. Pynchon bade him good-bye, and entered the house to take leave of his family.

Already the weaker animals, loaded down with their packs, were filing along the street, and turning into the Bay Path, to get a start of those possessing better speed and bottom. Each rider had his own friends to take leave of, and convey messages for, and a very lively morning it was on every hand. At last, Mr. Pynchon took his horse's rein upon his arm, and, with John at his side, moved off, while Holyoke and Mary followed in the same manner—John to receive some final directions in the management of affairs at home, and to be Mary's company back, and Mary to part with her lover.

The lovers walked for some time in silence, for many eyes were upon them. As soon as the limits of the neighborhood were passed, Holyoke exclaimed with a sigh, "The Autumn! It seems a very long time till then!"

"A very short time it seems to me," responded Mary, looking into his face with a cheerful smile.

"How can you say that, and love me as you say you love me?" inquired Holyoke, incredulously.

"Do you wish to have me talk very plainly with you, Elizur?" and Mary laid her hand on his shoulder, and looked into his eyes with an earnestness and a simplicity that art never simulated and may never simulate.

"Always, my love."

"Well, then, I am very glad you are going to leave me, and I hope you will change very much before you get back again."

"Enigmas again!" and Holyoke smiled in a very sickly manner.

"No enigmas at all," replied Mary. "When you first came here, you were the man I loved, and you acted like him; now you are the same man in disguise, and it is my fault. Then you were all life and ambition, and grace and gallantry; now, you speak to no one but me, and mope all day."

"Then you are sick of me!"

For this speech Holyoke received a look that he understood. It had been repeated several times during his visit, whenever he had given utterance to an unworthy suspicion. Begging her pardon at once, he asked her to explain the ideas she intended to convey.

"You men," said Mary, "lead a busy, rough life. Your minds are occupied by great enterprises that engross your time, your strength, and your best ingenuity. When you are thus engaged in business, love is an intruder or, perhaps, a favored guest, who sits at your table, and takes your hand at morning and evening, and sees you no more. But let love find your minds vacant, and you give yourselves over to it until it possesses you, and you forget every other relation in the one that is sweetest. There is nothing natural or healthy in such a condition. You think I am cold—that I do not even appreciate the intensity of your love. I have shocked you often, and always with the best intentions, when I have had any definite intentions at all. I might have become just as insane—I pray you forgive the word—as you, had I not possessed a corrective of the natural tendencies, in my household cares and daily duties; and I bless the circumstances that kept me from forgetting myself and all around me in an all-absorbing passion. I have been to blame for not insisting that you should go out with your companions, and divide your thoughts in active pursuits."

Poor Holyoke did not know what to say to such a dissection of his love. It humbled him, and half vexed him—the more, doubtless, because he knew that Mary was right.

As he said nothing, Mary continued, more playfully, "It is well enough for a lover in doubt of the good will of the object of his suit, to be timid and without words, but for one who knows he possesses the heart of his mistress to lose his tongue is very reliable evidence that he has, temporarily at least, lost his reason."

"Well, Mary," said Holyoke, with a sigh that would have seemed painful if it had not been ludicrous, "I hope I shall recover from this in time, but cold water makes rather a serious bath for a man in a fever."

"I see," exclaimed Mary, "the crisis is past! That last speech is decidedly a symptom of amendment."

And then both, with a sense of the ludicrousness of the scene, and a realization of a hundred sillinesses in the past, laughed until Holyoke's horse, apparently astonished, turned his head around and looked them in the face. The remainder of the distance to the summit of the hill was occupied with practical Christian conversation, with promises of daily remembrance in prayer, and with a conference upon matters connected with an event which it had been decided should take place in the following autumn. At length they saw John returning, and Holyoke, pausing, took Mary's hand within his own, and kissing her tenderly, exclaimed, "May God have you in his holy keeping!" Then mounting his horse with a leap that showed him again in possession of his strength and his resolution, he rode briskly away, and left Mary, (oh! inconsistency of human nature!) lonely, weak, and weeping, to walk silently back to the almost forsaken plantation.

CHAPTER XII.

The freight of furs had hardly retired from sight, and the last Indian stragglers departed, when Mr. Moxon appeared at his door, and walked briskly towards the residence of the newly elected constable, John Searles. Calling Searles to the door, he inquired in regard to the disposition that had been made of Peter Trimble. He had heard of it before, but from the constable he learned all the particulars.

"It seems to me that it was extremely unwise in Mr. Pynchon to place that boy with so vile a man as Woodcock," said Mr. Moxon.

The new constable was a man of few words, large frame, and a practical turn of mind; and, instead of enlarging upon the fact, or joining in any discussion in regard to it, he simply said, "I know my duty, Mr. Moxon, and I do it,"—having reference to his agency as an instrument of the law in placing Peter with his temporary master.

"I am blaming no one," said Mr. Moxon, blandly—"it is a question of wisdom and policy."

"I didn't ask it—I never ask it—it's none of my business," responded Searles, without moving a muscle of his body.

Mr. Moxon saw that Searles half suspected the nature of his errand, and that conciliation was out of the question in general, and out of that question in particular. There was, therefore, no way for him but to come directly to the point, and he did this the more readily as he knew his man, and had entire confidence in his courage and efficiency. Turning slowly on his heel, and walking off a few steps, as if in thought, he came back and said, "I believe, John, you have a warrant from Mr. Pynchon to attach the body of John Woodcock, who has failed to pay the damages in the slander case."

"I have, sir," replied Searles, drawing the document from his pocket, and reading a sentence from it: "and that you keep the body of John Woodcock in prison of irons until he shall take some course to satisfy the said George Moxon."

"You may execute that as soon as you choose."

"No sooner?"

"You will execute that to-day, sir."

"Very well, sir; just as you say."

"And in regard to Peter Trimble?"

"I know my duty, sir."

"I leave you to do it," said the minister drily, and turned and walked away.

John Searles walked into his house, and read over the warrant again, sentence by sentence. "In prison of irons," said he to himself. "I hav'n't any prison of irons except a log chain, and I shall have to use a rope," and the constable busied himself for half an hour in finding and properly splicing a rope. This, after coiling it into the smallest possible space, he thrust into his coat pocket, in company with the warrant, and shouldering his carefully loaded gun, he walked coolly to the bank of the river.

Nearly all the planters had crossed the river immediately after Mr. Pynchon's departure, to labor in their corn-fields, and Woodcock was among them. Stepping into his canoe the constable pushed from the shore, and transported himself across the river. Fastening his boat, and taking his gun, he ascended the bank, and sought the field where Woodcock and his new apprentice were at work; and before the former could fairly look up, he felt a light tap on his shoulder, and heard the words, "You are my prisoner."

"How do you make out that figur'?" inquired Woodcock.

"In black and white," replied the constable, drawing the warrant from his pocket. "Do you want me to read it to you?"

Peter Trimble was all eyes and ears, until suddenly reminded of his duty by a side cut from Woodcock's hoe-handle. Searles looked through the document, and then read as follows:

"To John Searles, constable of Sprmgfield. These are in his majesty's name to require you presently uppon the recite hereof that you attach the body of John Woodcock uppon an execution granted to Mr George Moxon by the Jury against the said John Woodcock for an action of slander: and that you keepe his body in prison of irons until he shall take some course to satisfie the said George Moxon: or else if he neglect or refuse to take a ready course to satisfie the said execution of £6 13s 4d granted by the jury that then you use what means you can to put him out to service and labor till he make satisfaction to the said Mr George Moxon for the said £6 13s 4d, and also to satisfie yourself for such charges as you shall be at for the keeping of his person: And when Mr Moxon and yourself are satisfied, then you are to discharge his person out of prison. Fail not at your peril.*

"William Pynchon."

"John Searles," said Woodcock (hitting Peter an entirely incidental rap, that brought both of the boy's hands to his legs as if he had caught a weasel running up his trousers), "you and I never had a gruff, but I don't stand any o' that sort o' nonsense; so you'd better scull your dug-out over the drink again, and go to splittin' oven wood."

"Woodcock, you don't know much about me, or you

* Copied from the Record of the original Document.

know I shan't cross the river without you as my prisoner."

"Well, you don't know much about me or you'd know there wasn't boats enough on this side to take me over agin my will, 'cept in small slices."

The constable was puzzled. He had calculated upon intimidating Woodcock, but he saw at once that the man was determined, and that he would never submit until compelled by brute force.

"Don't you think you'd better go over t'other side," inquired Woodcock, "and stand on your head and read that thing back'ards?"

Searles made him no reply, and shouldering his gun walked off towards a group of planters on a neighboring field. He found there Henry Smith, Jehu Burr, John Cabel, and several others, to whom he explained his errand, and upon whom he called for assistance.

It may be readily guessed that he did not call in vain. All dropped their implements, and taking their guns, accompanied the constable to assist him in making the arrest. Woodcock saw them coming, and taking his gun, he carefully examined the priming, rubbed the flint, and, cocking his piece, threw his hat upon the ground and assumed the defensive.

"If any of you fellers want to know jest how a sieve feels," said Woodcock, as they approached him, "you'd better undertake to feel of me. I'll show you the samp you had for breakfast. You can't scare me. You darsn't fire, any one on you."

The constable and his force huddled together for a consultation, but had hardly closed their circle when Woodcock's gun was discharged into the air, and turning suddenly, they saw him wheel upon his foot and fall at his whole length upon the ground. The first impression was that he had shot himself, but, upon seeing Peter Trimble extricating himself from his feet, the constable comprehended the whole trick, and dropping his gun he leaped upon Woodcock before he could rise, and by having immediate assistance was enabled to secure his capture. Peter, who imagined he saw in this arrest his own release, had, while Woodcock's attention was entirely engaged, stepped slyly behind him, and reaching around pulled the trigger of his gun. He then dropped directly upon the ground, so that when Woodcock impulsively turned to strike or pursue him, he tumbled over him instead.

The rage and mortification of the poor victim of circumstances was intense. He had never been thus humiliated before, and he felt that death would have been far better. As he lay in the dust, and heard the sly boasts of Peter, and the cough of John Cabel, and the coarse jokes of others who had gathered around, he raved and gnashed his teeth, in his torture.

The next question was in regard to taking him over the river. Woodcock had determined within himself that he would never be taken bound to the village. He was desperate, and cared nothing for life; and he knew that the canoes in use were of such form that even when bound he could upset one of them with perfect ease. His hands were tied behind him, and his feet were allowed only play sufficient for a limping and laborious locomotion. The constable took him by his arms and assisted him to rise. He looked at no one—spoke to no one—and made no reply to petty insults, but allowed himself to be conducted to a canoe.

The constable was no coward, and though he had but little confidence in Woodcock's silence and apparent submission, he determined to undertake the task of rowing him over the river alone. The prisoner took his seat in the boat with considerable difficulty, and while Searles assumed the oar, a friend pushed the frail vessel from the beach, and with a single sweep of the oar it shot into the stream.

The transport had proceeded but a third of the way across, when Woodcock, by a sudden movement of his body, turned the boat upside down, and leaving the constable blowing lustily, and holding to the boat that persevered in lying bottom upwards, he pushed easily off upon his back and floated down the river towards the Indian village.

The movement was observed from the shore, and every man dashed into his canoe and struck for the swimmer. The chase was an animated one, but the advantage was altogether with the pursuers, and their object was speedily overtaken. The first canoe that approached was waited for by Woodcock, who managed to give it a kick with both feet and upset it, but the effort came near to drowning him, as it sent his head under the water and he came up half-strangled. While the other boats were taking care of those who had thus been treated to a bath, Woodcock managed to get under headway again, but he was at last overhauled, and, notwithstanding his struggles, a rope was passed under his shoulders and secured across his chest. They were then in the middle of the river and rapidly floating downwards.

As they were consulting upon the proper method to be pursued, a canoe pushed rapidly out from the Eastern shore, and approached them. It contained a solitary Indian, who swept a rapid circuit around the group of boats, comprehended at a glance the position of affairs, and, without uttering a word, moved as quickly back to the point from whence he had issued, and disappeared among the bushes upon the bank.

"Well," said John Cabel, pulling up after Woodcock was fairly hooked, and graciously assuming a share in the sport when it had been safely completed, "we have caught the fish, and now how shall we cook it?"

"That's the question," replied the constable.

"That's the question," responded Burr.

"Rather a serious question," said Henry Smith, gravely.

"I know what I should do," said Peter Trimble, squirting a mouthful of water through his teeth that he had just taken from a canteen.

"Out with it, boy," said the constable.

"I should stick this canteen under his neck, and tow him ashore," answered Peter.

The expedient was adopted at once. The canteen was emptied and stopped, and by its own strap it was so fastened to the captive's neck that it easily kept his face out of the water. The canoes were then fastened together, and each man bent to his oar. The tow was soon under full headway up the stream, and a rapid passage brought the fleet to the land.

It was well for Woodcock that he had escaped thus easily, for he had become very much chilled in the water, and was nearly exhausted. He was dragged up on the shore almost unconscious, but the heated sand beneath, and the kind sun above, lent him their warmth, and he had become so far restored to himself as to feel the indignity inflicted upon him as he was loaded upon a rough sled or hurdle, and drawn by a yoke of cattle to the house of the constable.

Peter Trimble, who had done more than any other one to effect the arrest, was the first to leap on shore when the canoes landed, and half a dozen steps placed him beyond the sight of his companions. Mounting the bank, he made directly for the house of Mr. Pynchon. Mary was glad to see his face, for she had heard shouts in the distance, and did not doubt that Peter knew the whole story, though she was not prepared for so terrific a "row" as he represented had taken place.

Unfortunately for Peter's reputation as a liar, the incidents which formed the basis of his story were quite equal to any he could manufacture, and he found himself in a state of perfect helplessness, telling a correct story. She questioned him closely, and was confirmed in her apprehensions of the correctness of his narrative, by seeing from her window the poor man drawn along the street, amid rude jests and swaggering boasts, like a slaughtered bear.

Mary watched the rude crowd as it retired, and felt more lonely for the moment than ever, but her resolution was quickly taken, and, throwing a handkerchief upon her head, she half walked, half ran to Woodcock's cabin, and found his daughter at the door, hacking a stick of pine, which she was endeavoring to reduce to kindling-wood.

The girl dropped her axe, and looked up brightly and affectionately as her friend approached. Mary Pynchon had started from home with no definite intentions in regard to her. It was simply an impulse to a good deed which she had neither conceived nor planned, so that when she came fairly upon the child, she had nothing to say, and could only exclaim, "poor child!" and burst into tears.

"Is *he* dead?" said Mary Woodcock, with a strange suspicion that something must have befallen the man she had recently seen so frequently with her benefactress, and with an idea that nothing less than that should so distress her.

"No, I trust not," replied Mary, recovering herself, and then she led the girl into the cabin. Peter had told her of the nature of the warrant on which Woodcock was arrested, and she saw that some one would be obliged to assume the charge of his daughter; so, sitting down in the cabin, with the girl before her, she told her very plainly of her father's situation. The child did not weep—she did not speak. A strange perception of propriety deterred her from the expression of feelings which mingled joy and grief in equal proportions. She felt that to be near Mary Pynchon, to live in the light of her smile, to feel her soft hand upon her face, to hear the rustle of her garments as they brushed past her, to listen to her speech, and do her bidding, was the greatest joy earth could bestow; and poor Woodcock would have felt a new pang could he have seen with what willingness and alacrity his daughter brought out her clothes, tied them up, and fastened the cabin, preparatory to a removal to the house of the Pynchons.

Woodcock, still bound, was, when he had arrived at the house of the constable, thrown upon a bed of loose straw, in the shed, and left alone. He had no more a tongue for contempt or bravado. He had been beaten, conquered, humiliated. He had suffered torture the most terrible he had ever known. He had been enraged and outraged, and he had been impotent in evasion and defence. Exhausted in body by his long submersion in the river, and by the excitement through which he had passed, and half-stupefied and crazed by the harsh reaction of his mental excitement, he lay all day, taking no food, replying to no question, and apparently conscious of no one's presence.

A river, bright in the sunlight, was rolling through his dreams, and phantom boats were chasing each other over its surface. For long, long hours, he lay upon the air above them, floating on the wings of his own will, listening to the clatter of their oars, and the confused shouts of those who swung them, and looking far up into the sky, and seeing the clouds as they changed into cornfields, and the cornfields as they changed back to clouds, and catching glimpses of huge wheels that rolled singly and noiselessly across the heavens, and hid their glitter in a cloud with a faint crash, like that which splashes the ears in a nightmare.

And then a whirlwind caught him in its folds, and rolled him furiously in black darkness, until strange lights flashed upon him, and fiery faces met his eyes at every turn. Then the whirlwind lifted him swiftly up, up far above the clouds, and held him there, as if in a grasp of iron, through a long hour of unrelieved breathlessness, until, in an instant, the grasp was relaxed, and he fell with terrific rapidity through the air, every nerve in his body becoming charged with an awful sense of imminent violence, only half relieved, at last, by coming softly down, and, on a breathless curve, floating far off, and striking noiselessly upon the bosom of the river. There upon the river he lay, borne by the current through the remainder of the day and into the night.

Sometimes the waves leaped up, as if to cover his face, and then parted and retired with hollow laughter. And the ripples came up, one after another, and whispered and snickered in his ears, and red-eyed fishes nibbled at his feet, but he had no power to move—and could only lie pulseless, breathless, and passive, on the strange cold water, floating somewhither, anywhither, like a forsaken hulk on a wide unknown sea.

At times, he almost extricated himself from this dream, and thought he saw standing above him a huge form like that of the minister, and heard the words, "the way of transgressors is hard." Then he subsided again to the river, and the waves grew brighter, and fair trees waved their arms from the banks, and a sweet warmth spread through his limbs. A soft hand touched his temples and grasped his wrist, and the fancy that Mary Pynchon was over him was so precious as to half waken him with a suspicion that it was an illusion. But he would not open his eyes and dissipate it.

The day wore away thus, and the night came on. For a long time confused voices mingled with his dream, and they at last died away. When all was silent, he began for the first time to come fairly into the possession of consciousness, and became immediately aware that he was not alone. He felt some one at work upon his hands, and they were then pulled out from under his back, so stiff and helpless that he could not move them. His legs were then loosed from their fastenings, and a pair of strong arms lifted him to his feet. He only knew it was a friend, and leaning upon his shoulder hobbled off with him through the street, and beyond the limits of the village.

Early upon the following morning the constable sought for his prisoner where he had left him the night previous. He was gone. The news of his disappearance flew rapidly over the village, and while some were disappointed at his escape, others, and among them the Pynchons, experienced only joy. Mary had been shocked at the brutal manner in which he had been treated, and was thankful for his release.

Many were the speculations indulged in, in regard to his disappearance. He was not known to have a friend in the plantation, and yet the constable declared it impossible for him to have been released without assistance. The minister had his own opinions upon the subject, which he kept to himself. He had heard at midnight a scream from the bed where his children lay, and had hurriedly risen only to find them both sleeping quietly in each other's arms.

CHAPTER XIII.

WOODCOCK'S disappearance was a nine days' wonder among the settlers of Agawam. The first impression was that he had fled to Hartford, or, perhaps, to either Wethersfield or Windsor, the other southern settlements; but a traveller who arrived at the plantation from Wethersfield reported that he had neither seen nor heard of him.

A fortnight passed away, and at its close a portion of the members of the expedition to the Bay came wearily in, their beasts laden with merchandise, and their heads and hearts full of news, but they brought no news of Woodcock. There was no little complaint, now that Woodcock had really disappeared, concerning the rigorous manner in which he had been treated. Some even went so far as to intimate that he had met with foul play, and privately exchanged the suspicion that he would turn up some day very much blackened and swollen on the river's bank.

The visits of Commuk to the house of the Pynchons during the absence of the expedition were much more frequent than usual, and as he left quantities of game for which he would receive no payment, his actions were remarked upon by the members of the family. He looked always for Mary Woodcock, and always asked her, in a manner which she had learned to understand, whether she had heard from her father. Her reply in the negative was received with a grunt and a shake of the head, and his singular interest in the child was set down to the credit of his well known good-nature.

Mary Woodcock's life had begun anew. She never tired of watching her benefactress, and when near her became inconveniently forgetful of her duties, for a woman was to her a new revelation. If Mary Pynchon were dressing her hair, the child would be obliged to stop and wonder at its glossy length, and watch the progress of the miracle by which it was at last separated, and disposed in puffs and plaits upon her head. It was a wonder with her for many hours how the lady came to have little holes in her ears, so as to receive and hold the modest rings that hung there. She could find no such holes in her own, having felt for them often, and evermore with disappointment.

Then she wondered whether the holes would come there of themselves when she had grown up to be a woman, or whether real ladies were born with them, while poor girls were denied such a distinction. To see her new mistress eat was a great privilege, and the source of long rivulets of thought. She measured the dimensions of every mouthful as it disappeared, marked the peculiar turn which the lady gave to her knife (for forks were not), and thought she discovered two modes of swallowing—one upwards and the other downwards. This was the theme of infinite speculation, and the basis of patient and varied experiment. Perhaps, thought the little girl, she swallows some of her food into her head, and that is what makes her hair grow so long, and opens the holes in her ears. And then, practising on the suggestion, she swallowed all the food given her with a pressure upwards that, so far as the illusion was concerned, displaced a skull full of brains with bread and milk every day.

Then she noticed that Mary Pynchon turned out her toes and moved her feet with a peculiar grace, and in her almost unconscious efforts at imitation, behaved so unaccountably as to puzzle that lady very much. But there was one exercise that had a greater effect upon her mind than any other. It became Mary Pynchon's custom to take the little girl to the most secret part of the house, and pray with her daily, holding her by the hand meanwhile. At these times, and after them each day, the child's mind was occupied with the strangest fancies. The lady spoke so sweetly, and asked God for everything that she wanted for herself or her protegé in such a tone of love and confidence, that the child did not doubt that she saw God all the time.

And then she wondered whether, when her own hair should grow long and glossy, and the little holes come in her ears, she should also obtain a vision of God's face, and be able to talk to him so pleasantly. She even went so far as to try the experiment with her arm around a little girl, composed of an ingeniously folded blanket, whose mouth commenced at the forehead and divided the face downwards.

The returning fur-carriers brought to Mary Pynchon much to interest her. First and foremost was a letter from Holyoke, whose spirit and vivacity had returned, and whose language had become restored to its old hearty and healthful tone. This was a very precious missive, enjoyed much in out-of-the-way places—an ever-abounding spring of tender suggestions and dear associations. It came as the spice of a huge dish of duties, and the sweetener of an overflowing cup of labors. A large number of plump packages were consigned to her on the arrival of the carriers—linens whose destiny lay in long lines of sheets and pillow-biers; shining specimens of latten and pewter ware, for the adornment of a hypothetical dresser, and the service of a table that lived only in an order; a string of gold beads for the neck of a bride unwed, and stuffs for drapery which in the age of honest manufacture and economical use might inclose the form of the virgin, the wife, and the mother, and perhaps even enter the grave with her, or, living still, be shown to little girls by brisk young matrons, with the words, "these were your grandmother's." All these had to be remarked upon, and overhauled and shown to neighbors, who knew of the arrival of the goods before they were fairly unloaded.

Mary answered all questions patiently, exhibited her treasures freely, and, when the task was finished, sat down with her mother and her sister Ann, and had one of those long, discursive, and unsatisfactory talks that invariably precede the laying out of that great work described in the words "getting ready to be married." And when the work was laid out, she, of course, did not know where to begin, and so began, as all with similar purposes, plans, and prospects invariably do, to grow thin, a process which she persistently continued throughout the summer.

During Mr. Pynchon's absence from home, Mr. Moxon was in the habit of calling at the house almost daily, to inquire for the health of the family, and to pass a few minutes in chat with Mrs. Pynchon and Mary.

On these occasions Mary Woodcock was nearly always present, or came in to ask some question, or was within hearing near the window, and (whether from this cause, or some other less apparent) several interviews had been passed without the name of Woodcock being mentioned. On one occasion, the little girl was absent, when the minister addressed Mrs. Pynchon with, "I see you have Woodcock's unfortunate little daughter with you." This was uttered with a kind of interrogative inflection which was equivalent to asking how it came about.

"Yes," said Mrs. Pynchon, replying to his words, and looking at Mary anxiously for a reply to his wishes.

"The sense of duty must have been very strong to induce you to add another member to your family," pursued the minister.

"Very strong," echoed Mrs. Pynchon, again looking at Mary, whose eyes were still on her work.

"I suppose," continued the minister, "that you had no

idea when you brought her here that her father would leave the plantation."

Mrs. Pynchon knew that it was Mary's business to answer these questions, if it was anybody's, so this time she looked at Mary and said nothing. Mary, who knew that it was none of Mr. Moxon's business what was done in the family, had not said anything, hoping that the embarrassment of her mother and her own silence would show that any conversation on the subject would be unpleasant. But she would not be rude, and so replied, "I did not stop to ask whether he was to be absent from his cabin a longer or a shorter time. I knew the child was unprovided for, and so took care of her."

"As I remarked," persisted the minister, "the sense of duty must have been very strong."

"I cannot take the credit of acting under even the slightest sense of duty," replied Mary.

"You surprise me," said the minister.

"By not being as good as you supposed I was?" inquired Mary, the old kind smile lighting up her face, despite her vexation.

"No, but really, what else could have induced you to undertake such a charge?"

"Self-gratification, if you please, or impulse, or sympathy, or all together," replied Mary.

"Those," and the minister assumed a bland tone, "those may be the highest motives of a carnal heart, and doubtless are, but Christ's disciples should have a higher one."

It is not a matter of surprise that Mary wondered what his motives were in pursuing Woodcock with such rigor, but her reflections upon this point could, of course, have no expression, so she simply replied that she regarded a sense of duty as being quite as far removed from being the highest Christian motive as those which she had assumed as the basis of her action in regard to Mary Woodcock.

"What can be higher as a motive of action than a sense of duty to God?" inquired the minister, with a kind of dogmatic earnestness.

"Love to God, and love to man," replied Mary, quietly.

"Our sense of duty, you will remember, grows out of this love," said Mr. Moxon.

"To make a practical matter of it," said Mary, "my sense of duty does not, so far as I know, grow out of my love, at all."

"What do you understand by the word duty?" inquired Mr. Moxon, with an apprehension that she might differ with him upon its definition.

"Duty involves obligation—indebtedness. What I understand by a sense of duty is a sense of indebtedness or obligation. What I do from a sense of duty is done in discharge of an obligation or a debt; and it seems to me that when a kind act is performed *only* from a sense of duty, it may be—I will not say must be—essentially a mean act. Further than this, I believe that many acts are done from a sense of duty which a pure love to God and man forbids."

"These are new notions, Mary," said the minister, shaking his head sternly.

"None the worse for that, if they are true, I suppose?" said Mary, and then added, "but perhaps I am not understood. I regard duty, and a sense of duty, as entirely different things. I believe that all good and just and praiseworthy deeds are performed in the realm, and under the sanctions, though not necessarily by the commands of duty. Thus, I may, from my love to God and love to man, do a good deed which I perfectly understand to be in the line of duty, without being moved to that act in the slightest measure by a sense of duty. My motive is a higher and better one."

No sooner had Mary concluded her explanation than she perceived that she had produced a marked effect upon the minister, and recognised on his face a look of mingled anxiety and distress, like that which she had produced on the occasion which introduced him to the reader. He sat in entire silence, absorbed in his thoughts, until the silence became painful to both his companions. Mary did not dare to add more, for fear of further embarrassing him, and Mrs. Pynchon, who was afraid Mary had been too bold, prepared herself for a speech of reconciliation.

"Of course," remarked the old lady, "Mary does not mean to say that she is right, and you are wrong, Mr. Moxon; I presume she never thought of such a thing as that. She only says what she thinks; it's you who ought to know."

"It never occurs to me to say more or less than what I believe," said Mary, "though it is always with diffidence that I differ with my superiors, and always, I trust, with becoming deference to their opinions."

Now, during all this discussion, there had been a practical question that stood like a standard in the heart of every individual of the group, and around this every argument, suggestion, and word rallied as naturally as if it had no meaning or power detached from it.

The relations between Mr. Moxon and Woodcock were somehow intermingled with the thoughts of all, and Mrs. Pynchon had become so painfully self-conscious as not to have the slightest doubt that her minister could see the burden of her mind with as much distinctness as he could her eyes.

Thus it happened that the only method of extrication from the embarrassment of the moment which presented itself to her was connected with this affair, and so, to set the minister on his feet, in esteem, as well as argument, she undertook to lift him out, and said, "Now, for instance, Mary,—you don't suppose that anything in the world but a sense of duty would have made Mr. Moxon deal as he has with Goodman Woodcock, do you? Don't you see that, when you come to apply it, it's a very different thing."

Mary said nothing, but her face became flushed and hot. Mr. Moxon rose hurriedly, walked to the door, and had nearly reached the street, when he turned, came back, and bade the ladies a good morning, after which, alternately looking up and down, he moved homewards. Up to this moment, he had not suffered himself to have a doubt in regard to his course with Woodcock. Mary Pynchon's words had led him to ask himself the question whether love to God and love to man, considered as the basis of action, would have resulted in the same treatment of Woodcock that had flowed from his notions of duty. His uncertainty upon this point, and his uncertainty in regard to the fate of Woodcock, fairly unsettled him, and a wish that he had been more lenient towards his victim dawned upon his mind, rose there, and burned like a star.

CHAPTER XIV.

It was not till among the last days of June that Mr. Pynchon returned from the Bay. The more important news had already reached him, in letters which he had received by occasional travellers, from Mr. Moxon and Mary.

He was entirely informed of the events that had occurred in connexion with the capture and disappearance of Woodcock, and despite that individual's contempt of his authority, regretted the whole affair very thoroughly. He had arrived somewhat late in the evening, and, after sending out the letters he had brought from the Bay to different individuals in the plantation, and distributing trifling purchases among the members of his family, he partook of a hasty supper, and prepared to retire. At this moment, he heard a light rap upon the window-pane, which was repeated upon his turning his eyes in that direction.

"Who's there?" demanded Mr. Pynchon.

"Well, 'tain't a saint, but it's nobody 'at'll damage you any," replied the unmistakable voice of Woodcock.

"Woodcock, is that you?"

"Yes, it's me, Square, and, if you're not too tired, I sh'd like about five minutes' parley with you, out here on the door-stone."

Woodcock's disappearance had been a cloud upon the magistrate, overshadowing the joy of his return, and, singular as it may seem, the rough words that met his ear were the sweetest music he had heard for many days. He immediately obeyed the summons, and shook the hand of the fugitive from justice with a heartiness entirely unbecoming a magistrate.

"Well, Square," exclaimed Woodcock, standing off, and looking at him through the dusky twilight, "I shouldn't know but what you was glad to see me, by the way you take on."

"I am very glad to know that you are safe and well, however much I may regret your conduct and its results to yourself."

"Well, Square, that's neither here nor there. What I come here to-night for is to find out whether there's anything agin my coming back to the plantation, and bein' peaceable."

"I know of no way by which you can escape the operation of the law," replied Mr. Pynchon, "and yet I do not know how Mr. Moxon might feel. I can see him and ascertain."

"There was a time, and 'twant a great while ago nuther, when I wouldn't 'a took a favor from that man; and I wouldn't now, for myself, but I don't want that gal of mine to be a tax on anybody—leastways on you, Square; and if there's any way for me to 'arn her living, without kickin' up a dust in the plantation and being a pull-back to her, I want to get my foot into it and foller it."

"Suppose there is no way?"

"Then you'll never see me agin. I ain't comin' back here to be snaked round like a beef critter."

"Will you promise to give no further trouble, provided the past is forgiven?" inquired the magistrate.

"No, I can't promise that, 'cause I don't know what 'll turn up, but 'twont be natur for me to be jest what I have been, for a man that's been in the mud don't get clean easy, and I can't forget that my back's dirty."

"You speak as if you were beyond the power of the plantation, as well as the colony,—responsible to no one."

"Do I? Well, it's so, Square, and it always 'll be so. If I can't have the right kind o' dealin's here, I sh'll go where I can get 'em."

Mr. Pynchon was silent in thought for several minutes, and then, approaching Woodcock, he laid his hand upon his shoulder, and said with much feeling and vehemence—"Woodcock, what is there to hinder your being one of the best, happiest, and most useful men in this settlement? You have strength to labor, a good natural disposition, and power to win a good name. You have a daughter to live for—one who will make you happy in the proportion that you make her respectable. The strongest desire that I now have upon my mind is that you may come back here, and become one of us, peaceably and respectably."

"Don't make a chicken of me," said Woodcock, brushing his nose, "for it gives me an onhandy bill for nothin', considerin' there couldn't anybody eat me."

"Do not jest, Woodcock, but tell me frankly what the trouble is," earnestly continued Mr. Pynchon.

"There's two men in this plantation," said Woodcock, pulling off his shoe, and shaking out a pebble, "by the name of Pynchon. One of 'em is Mr. Pynchon, and t'other is Square Pynchon. I know both on 'em middlin' well, and they never'd be took for twins. It's Mr. Pynchon that's talkin' with me now, and 'twas Square Pynchon who got me fined for tellin' the truth about the minister, and then, 'cause I wouldn't stan' it, give him a warrant to keelhaul me, and treat me like a beast. The Square thinks it's law, and the minister think's it's gospel, but, if it is, it's shabby law and worse gospel; and it's a thing that'll come round byme-bye, for a man that straightens hoops can't work ten years at the business without flippin' his own nose."

"You have certainly been very frank, Woodcock," responded Mr. Pynchon, "but you have made your usual mistake of attributing all your troubles to the circumstances under which you live, without assuming any blame yourself."

"I never shirked anything that belonged to me to shoulder," said Woodcock, "and it may be a slim thing for me to say, but I've got a notion that if my betters had been as much men as they had been somethin' smaller and less becomin', they never'd had any trouble with me, nor I with them. Magistrates forget they're men, and ministers take a consait that they're angels, and so they think it's for them to boss everything, and kick round the rest on us. I don't want to be hard on anybody, Square, but if the woman we read about that was catched makin' herself shameful, and was told by the Master on us all to go and do better, had undertook to cut up here in Agawam, you'd 'a said twenty lashes, and she'd got 'em, and Mr. Moxon would 'a said twenty Amens on the end on 'em for a snapper."

Why is it that Mr. Pynchon does not venture a direct reply to this? Does dignity or self-respect forbid? Does he feel that Woodcock is so immeasurably beneath him that it is a matter of indifference whether a reply be made or not? There he stands, face to face with a criminal,—one upon whom he had endeavored to execute the sentence of the law. Why does he not call for help, and re-arrest the caitiff? Why does he take Woodcock's hand, and say, "I'm very much fatigued, John, take care of yourself, and come again to-morrow night?" The answer to all these queries may be found in his own words, as he closes the door and enters his cabin: "The man is right, in the main—right in the main." As he hangs his coat upon a chair, he repeats the words, "right in the main;" and he stops while winding his watch, and nods very firmly, but with a mere jar of the muscles, as if it were a nod of the soul and not of the head, and reiterates "right in the main."

Woodcock left the house, and had gone but a short distance when half-a-dozen dark forms issued from the cover of a tree, and joined him, as he took his way southward out of the village.

On the following morning, Mr. Moxon was the first to call on Mr. Pynchon. The minister looked haggard and worn, as if he had passed a sleepless night; and appeared more nervous and unsettled than ever before.

"You are not so feeble as your appearance indicates, I trust," said Mr. Pynchon, grasping his hand warmly.

"The Lord is dealing very strangely with me," said the minister. "Within the past few days, thick clouds have been upon me. I only pray that I may have grace sufficient for all my trials, and that in His own good time God will deliver me out of all my distresses."

"Have you any new tribulations?" inquired Mr. Pynchon.

"None that I feel at liberty to reveal," replied the minister, "but I beg of you, my Christian father and brother, that you will remember me in your prayers, and beseech God that, if it be possible, the cup may pass from me."

Mr. Pynchon was seriously pained as well as puzzled by this language, and particularly by the deep solemnity with which it was uttered. Still retaining his hold of the minister's hand, he said, "You know, Mr. Moxon, how entirely you have my sympathy, and how gladly I would do anything in my power to relieve you."

The minister shook his head, and, releasing his hand, paced up and down the room, giving utterance to deep sighs that lacked none of the wretchedness even if wanting the resonance of groans. At length, pausing before Mr. Pynchon, he said, "The time may come when the load will be too heavy for me to bear—when my poor nature will cry out in its pain, and then I shall come to you; but pray for me, oh! pray! pray! that I may be delivered from the power of the adversary, and that the divine wrath may be stayed."

This was all enigmatical to Mr. Pynchon, and his curiosity was somewhat aroused, but the case was too painful to tamper with, and so, with the design of changing the subject, he spoke of Woodcock. The name had no sooner been pronounced, than Mr. Moxon paused, looked earnestly at the speaker, and waited with sharp attention, as if ready to snap at, and devour every word.

Mr. Pynchon saw that in some manner the subject was a key to the minister's secret, and kept quietly on. He alluded to the peculiar temperament of the man, his natural impatience of restraint, his strong native powers of mind and good qualities of heart, and the possibility that he had not received exactly that treatment from all that a thorough Christian charity and a sound policy would dictate. He was ready to assume so much for himself, and doubted not that others would, upon reflection, do the same. Furthermore, he was inclined to think that if Woodcock might be allowed to come back, and to go unmolested about his business, he would do better, and eventually become a good and useful citizen.

"Do you know where he is?" inquired Mr. Moxon, with an eye that almost burned with its earnestness.

"No! But I think I know where he will be."

"Then he's alive?" said the minister interrogatively, and added, as if in reply to his own question, "Oh! yes! he's alive; I knew he was alive."

"I have seen him," said Mr. Pynchon.

"When and where?" inquired the minister, eagerly.

"Last night, and here."

"Was there any one with him?"

"No one that I saw."

"Did you—that is—do you remember anything peculiar—that struck you—was there anything unusual connected with his appearance?" inquired the minister, brokenly and with great embarrassment.

"Nothing," replied Mr. Pynchon. "He acted entirely like himself, and looked like himself."

"Does he wish to return to the plantation?" inquired the minister.

"I think he would do so at once provided you should see fit to release him from all obligations in the slander case. He appears anxious to support his child, and he confessed to having been humbled by the treatment he has been subjected to."

"I will release him," said the minister, "on these conditions;" but without stating the conditions, he commenced pacing up and down the room again.

"On what conditions?" inquired Mr. Pynchon, after watching him for some minutes.

"I—I cannot state them," said the minister, "and it is not necessary. Tell him that I know all, and that he cannot deceive me. Tell him that I forgive everything, if he has not concluded the contract. If he has concluded it, and will break it, he may always count on me as a friend. Tell him I love my children better than I love my own life, and to kill me rather than—than—persevere in his present course. He'll know what I mean. Tell him that hell is deep and eternity long, and that no temporary advantages can compensate for the loss of the soul. Tell him that the devil was a liar from the beginning, and that brick houses will not stand in the day of judgment."

"I beg you to pause," exclaimed Mr. Pynchon, hurriedly rising from his chair. "You are surely unwell, Mr. Moxon. You have overtasked your mind, or body, or both, and cannot be aware of the strangeness of your language. Were I to tell Woodcock just what you have directed me to tell him, he would call you mad. You are certainly very unwell, sir; I beg you to be seated;" and Mr. Pynchon fairly pressed the minister into the seat he had vacated, where he sat for some minutes in silence, with his hands over his eyes, and his nerves in an agitation that was half hysterical.

At length, without uncovering his eyes, he exclaimed, as if deciding a question he had been revolving, "I must bear it alone for the present." Then rising, he said, "I leave this matter with you, and will be guided by your judgment. If you think it best for Woodcock to return, I shall interpose neither obstacle nor objection." Then, seeing other neighbors approaching the house, he bade the magistrate a good morning, and passed homewards.

On the following evening, Woodcock appeared at the appointed hour, and received the decision that had been made in his behalf. He listened with patience and respectfulness to Mr. Pynchon's counsel, and was preparing to depart, the interview having been held, as on the previous evening, outside the house, when the slender form of his child, in her white night dress, leaped from an adjoining window, and rushed into his arms. She had been disturbed by the conversation, and the voice of her father had become so real in her dreams as to awaken her to the reality of his presence; and her leap from the window was the offspring of her first impulse.

Woodcock sat down upon the doorstep, and strained the child to his heart, while she clung to his neck with the nervous vehemence of her nature. The embrace was silent, but full of love's eloquence.

"Square," said Woodcock, at last, with difficulty breaking the spell, "why can't I die now? I never shall feel so good as this ag'in. It can't be brung round ag'in any way."

"I see nothing to hinder your having many happy days, if you are well disposed," said Mr. Pynchon.

"I hain't any faith," said Woodcock, shaking his head; "I never did have good luck long 't a time nor a great while in a place, and I don't expect to." Then turning to his child he said, in a mild, kind voice, "I'm comin' back to the plantation to-morrow, gal."

The child sprang from his arms, as if he had struck her.

"What did I tell you, Square?" said Woodcock, whimpering and smiling together, at the sudden fulfilment of his prophecy.

"I don't want to go back to the cabin to live," said Mary.

"I hope you don't want to live here, and be a little beggar," said her father.

Here Mr. Pynchon interposed, and told him of Mary's singular usefulness in the house, and related a conversation he had had with her mistress during the day, in which the latter interposed the most decided objections against parting with the child, unless Woodcock should insist upon it.

"And I'll come down and fix up the cabin every day," said Mary, eagerly, taking courage from having an advocate at her side.

"I couldn't 'a fixed it to suit myself any better," said Woodcock, "but I didn't want to be beholden; and if the gal can make herself of any account, she's better off with Mary Pynchon than she could be anywhere else in the world."

Thus saying, he took the girl in his arms, walked to the window from which she had leaped, and, with a whispered word of kindness, lifted her in.

Upon the following morning, the people of the plantation were surprised to see Woodcock walk forth from his cabin, take his canoe, and go quietly to work upon his fields on the other side of the river, without attracting the notice of the magistrate, or meeting with any objections from the minister or the constable.

Arriving at his fields, he found that they had been well taken care of, through the faithfulness of the constable, whose gratitude to Peter Trimble had not hindered him from tasking that individual to the extent of his strength, in working out the magistrate's sentence. An explanation of the whole matter was publicly made on the succeeding lecture day, and the affair blew quietly over.

CHAPTER XV.

How like a troubled, feverish dream is summer to the husbandman! How early, and yellow, and hot, comes up the brazen sun! How are the tunes of the first birds and all the fresh sounds of the early day overpowered by the jar and bustle of toil! How the days fly past!—some hot and breathless, some bright and sparkling; some full of rain, wind, and thunder; others hemmed about on the western and southern horizon with bald-headed clouds, that stand and sleep all the afternoon in the sun; some so clear that they mark black shadows on the hill-sides, by trees that look so clumpy and green, so thick, dark, and downy, that one might dream of jumping from a cloud into them, and being softly caught in their cool depths; and others so sultry that the robin drags her wings by the brook side, or sucks the lifeless air with an open bill and a spasmodic inspiration!

To those who have passed through this season, exposed to its toils and debilitating influences, how welcome is the first cool breath of Autumn! How, when the crickets begin to sing through the drowsy twilight, and the dried mullein holds stiffly up its tall rack of seed-cups, and the fresh green silk of the serried corn dries and darkens into matted tufts of brown, and the foliage of the forests and the grasses of the pasture show that the freshness of their life has departed, the heart becomes calm and glad! And when the Frost King descends from his crystal home while all the world is sleeping, and breathes upon the forests, and tramples on the flowers that they may not be contemptible in the light of his radiant miracles; when the maples turn to gigantic roses, and the oaks to colossal peonies, when the meadow wears a gay bouquet upon its bosom, and the river runs the gauntlet of an army clothed in crimson and purple, and every sight and sound prophesies of relaxing toil and speedy fruition, how the heart grows strong, and the beauty and majesty of Autumn, and its golden promises and great fulfilments, touch us with gladness and gratitude!

And when, later, the leaves drop, one by one, upon the ground, carpeting the solitudes for the dances of the fairies; and the nuts open their brown portals to the curious squirrel, and great congregations of crows spend whole days in meaningless vociferations; when the flails of the matched threshers begin to thump wearily on the neighboring barn floors, and the wain comes creaking home with its freight of corn; when the first fires begin to be kindled on the social hearth, and throw their dancing light over happy old age in its easy chair, ruddy maidenhood in its life and levity, and childhood that groans in the bondage of coats restored and brogans resumed, how the heart warms to the touch of some of the sweetest associations of life, and we thank God for those changes which, each in its turn, compensates for all the severities of its predecessor, and affords a balance of characteristic joy for which it may be loved, and by which it may be remembered!

It may be a humiliating fact (and that is doubtless the reason why it has not found more prominent statement), but it is none the less an established one, that in temperate latitudes, the stronger passions of humanity become feeble, and hardly manifest themselves during summer, except in that spasmodic manner which is the most reliable symptom of debility. Thus ambition seems to dissipate in perspiration, the fires of anger subside under copious draughts of cold water, and love itself forgets its ardor beneath a burning sun. Even the most devoted attachments seem to be relaxed by the season, and are only restored to their original tone and tension by the return of the mercury to medial alti tudes and modest figures.

It was partly owing to this fact that the love which Holyoke felt for Mary Pynchon was in a measure laid aside on his arrival at the Bay, and that neither of the lovers found the attachment any obstacle in the pursuit of objects of immediate interest. They had parted with mutual faith, and with certain objects to be compassed before they should meet again—Holyoke to make his affairs ready for the contemplated removal to Agawam, and Mary to prepare for the establishment of a new home, and the assumption of new responsibilities.

The summer passed rapidly away, and with but little impatience on either side; but when the Autumn began to creep on and the crickets began to sing, and the mullein stood patiently drying its rack of seed-cups in the sun, and the corn silk grew brown, and the frost wrought its wonders, there was not a sight but brought sweet suggestions to the expectant lovers, or a sound that did not tell them of a great joy towards which they were tending.

In the plantation, generally, matters had gone on with a remarkable degree of quietness. The carpenter, Jehu Burr, with such help as he could occasionally secure, had succeeded in building a habitable house for Holyoke, to be in readiness for occupation when that individual should arrive. Its simple furniture, built at the Bay, came by water carriage, and was arranged by Mary's own hands.

The feud between Mr. Moxon and Woodcock slept, although no cordiality existed between them. Many thought that a great change had occurred in the latter, and some, in genuine friendliness, endeavored to approach him with the design of encouraging any good resolutions that he might be entertaining, but their advances were coolly met, and persistently repulsed. He was not living for himself; he was not acting himself. He was engaged in providing for his daughter, and carried under powerful restraint as independent a spirit as ever. The daughter still lived with Mary Pynchon, and week by week and month by month improved in her demeanor, until fear began to be felt by many in the neighborhood who had young daughters, that Mary Pynchon would "spoil that child, and make her forget who she was and where she came from"—baleful influences which they sought benevolently to correct at every convenient opportunity.

Peter Trimble was kept out of mischief by hard work. He was whipped but three or four times during the summer, for such offences as knocking off the hats of other boys on the way home from meeting, agreeing to give boot in a jack-knife trade, and making the payment somewhat too energetically with a leather article of that name, and other playful indiscretions of a similar character.

Mr. Moxon preached with singular earnestness, and devoted himself to the discharge of his duties with an assiduity which, receiving its primary impulse in unwonted spiritual fears and fancies, was naturally and almost necessarily convulsive and severe.

The approaching marriage of Mary Pynchon was the theme of much gossip in the plantation, and particularly so as no one out of the family knew exactly when the event was to take place. Among the first days of November, however, at an unusually full meeting on lecture day, the intentions of marriage between her and Holyoke were published, *viva voce*, in accordance with the colonial law.

Mary was present, and in the whisper and flutter and stare which followed the announcement, sat in indignant though silent rebellion, against what she regarded as a sacrilegious notoriety, as disgusting to every healthful sensibility as it was grateful to prurient and prying curiosity.

The fourteen days of "publishment" at last expired. Holyoke and a number of friends from the Bay arrived, and the evening was appointed for the performance of the marriage ceremony. Every individual upon the plantation had been invited to the wedding—an occasion fraught with more of pleasant anticipation than any in the experience of the settlement. The preparations for that wedding—the furbishing of old dresses, the polishing of rough shoes, the labor night and day to finish a home-spun garment—the contriving, the dreaming, the gossiping—the impatience for the advent of the looked-for day, and the flutter of delight as it dawned, need no description.

A cool, frosty evening among the closing days of November, produced the long expected hour. The stars were shining brightly, and the fallen leaves were lying in silent heaps upon the ground, as the neighborhood began to collect at the house of the magistrate. The candle-wood blazed cheerfully upon the hearth, and welcomed, in its own way, with flashes and sputterings, and jets of smoke, and dancing out-gushings of flame, each guest as he opened the door. There were long quiet whisperings, and half suppressed jests, and criticisms of dress; and when, at last, all had collected, expectation began to verge upon impatience; and every opening door was the signal for a renewed silence.

There was one man present who, without companionship, was more profoundly exercised by his emotions than any other. This man was John Woodcock. He had for several days been meditating a step which, to his own mind, was charged with the deepest interest and greatest importance; and he sat revolving it while those around him gave themselves up to levity and the natural excitements of the occasion. He sat at the back side of the room, and as occasionally his daughter, neatly dressed, entered the room on some errand from her mistress, his eye followed her in every movement, with an interest as apparent to those around him, as it was all absorbing to himself.

There was also something in the occasion itself that affected him deeply. Unconsciously he had become a worshipper of Mary Pynchon, as an impersonation of feminine beauty, grace, and goodness. The idea of loving her had never entered his heart. His sentiment was one which left love, with its earthly attachments and associations, its thoughts of equality and possession, entirely unconceived. He would have spurned all imputation of passion as unworthy of himself and her. He would not—he could not—have profaned her presence with any sentiment less selfish than that which lies at the basis of worship—a reverent admiration that carried with it an entire submission of will and devotion of life.

It was a strange heart—that encased in those rough habiliments. It had once loved, and might perhaps have loved again, but for a woman who had inspired him with a sentiment higher than, or inconsistent with love. He would have cursed himself, as he would any of the common men around him, for any thought of love towards her, and yet she had wrought so powerfully upon his mind, that all other feminine natures, to which he was not bound by a natural tie, became insipid and valueless. The fact that he could not love her precluded the possibility of his loving any one else. Still, unselfish as were his feelings towards the friend of his child, and earnestly as he wished for her happiness, he could not contemplate her marriage with Holyoke without a pang. It was to him (for what reason he knew not) the dethronement of a goddess—the degeneration to humanity of an angel. It was not jealousy that moved him; it was no ill will towards Holyoke, and yet, what was it?

At length, during a deepening hum of conversation, the door leading from the adjoining apartment was opened, and the participators in the ceremony made their appearance. First came Mr. and Mrs. Moxon, and they were followed by Mr. and Mrs. Pynchon, succeeded by Henry Smith and his wife. All these stood until Holyoke appeared, with Mary leaning upon his arm, and took his position before them.

Well might that little assembly be smitten with silence by that vision of noble manhood and radiant beauty—a silence that was sweet and holy—a silence pervaded with all pure and happy thoughts, and unsealing the fountains of unconscious tears. The stillness was interrupted by the voice of the minister, in the words, "Let us pray." The prayer uttered was one of genuine feeling, and in its mention of Mary was so fervent and touching that even Woodcock opened his heart to its influences, and joined in the aspiration.

At the close of the prayer, the marriage ceremony was performed by Mr. Pynchon, who, as the only magistrate present, was alone empowered to officiate upon the occasion. Parental pride and tenderness were too much for official dignity, and the simple words were said in a broken voice, and with manifest emotion. When they were concluded, the only persons who went forward to salute the bride were Ann Smith and her father.

There seemed to be a strange restraint upon the assembly. Women who had known Mary for years sat silently in their places, apparently in much embarrassment. Every out-reaching of friendly sympathy seemed to be held in painful check, and every one appeared afraid of doing something that somebody would deem wrong. The spell was at last broken by a little fellow who, unknown to his parents, had brought a present to the bride. He left his seat, and, plunging his hand into his pocket, pulled and tugged at its contents till, when he had arrived at Mary's side, his round face was as red as a beet. The lad still worked manfully, and at length conquered an intractable bag of chestnuts, which he drew forth, and presented to the bride, amidst a hearty laugh commenced by Holyoke and joined in by Mary, who seized and kissed the little boy as he commenced to retreat, with his heart full of indignation, and his pocket inverted.

This little incident broke the spell so far as the children were concerned, and they pressed forward to make their trifling gifts, and win the smile and kiss which they coveted as their reward. As soon as the children had paid their respects to the bride, the old constraint returned, and for a few minutes held the company in its painful thrall.

John Woodcock was the first to break the silence. Rising from his seat, and making his way out of the crowd around him, he crossed the room to where his daughter was standing absorbed in, and half bewildered by the scene, and, whispering a few words in her ear, took her by the hand, and led her before the married pair. Mary extended her hand to him instantly and cordially, and exclaimed, "I knew that you would come to me and congratulate me."

"That wan't my arrant any way," said Woodcock bluntly, "and I shouldn't begin with you if it was."

"Why, John! I am astonished!" exclaimed the bride. "I thought you was one of the best friends I had in the world."

"Well, you needn't change your mind till you hear agin, but the fact is, when two fellers swap guns, 'taint the feller that gets the poorest gun that feels proud, or stands treat, or gets flattered for his bargain."

Holyoke had heard much of Woodcock and his quaint humors, and, extending his hand to him good-naturedly, said, "I am the man who feels proud, and am all ready to be flattered for my bargain."

"When a basket's full of corn, shook down, what's the use of pilin' on more?" said Woodcock.

Holyoke laughed heartily at the sally, but Mary, inclined to be vexed, said, "I am sorry you do not like my husband."

"I never told anybody I didn't like him. He likes you, and you like him, and that's two things that ought to be a recommend to him anywhere. It would 'a been jest the same if the king was your husband. 'Taint in my line to say flatterin' things to anybody, but women are better'n men, and always get the little end of the trade, when they get married."

"It is a comfort to know that you have been cheated on general principles," said Holyoke to Mary, in a merry tone.

But Mary was somehow affected with Woodcock's seriousness, and, with no reply to Holyoke, beyond a smile, she asked Woodcock's reasons for the statement he had made.

"I didn't come up here to talk about this, and p'raps it aint the right time to do it, but there's no use backin' down when you begin. I've got a consait that men and women ain't built out of the same kind of timber. Look at my hand—a great pile o' bones covered with brown luther, with the hair on,—and then look at yourn. White oak aint bass, is it? Every man's hand aint so black as mine, and every woman's aint so white as yourn, but there's always difference enough to show, and there's jest as much odds in their doin's and dispositions as there is in their hands. I know what women be. I've wintered and summered with 'em, and, take 'em by and large, they're better'n men. Now and then a feller gets hitched to a hedgehog, but most of 'em get a woman that's too good for 'em. They're gentle and kind, and runnin' over with good feelin's, and will stick to a feller a mighty sight longer'n he'll stick to himself. My woman's dead and gone, but if there wan't any women in the world, and I owned it, I'd sell out for three shillin's, and throw in stars enough to make it an object for somebody to take it off my hands."

During Woodcock's delivery of this little speech, several of the company had risen from their seats, and pressing towards the central group, formed a circle around it, so that when he had arrived at the conclusion, so characteristic of himself, there was a general laugh. Woodcock looked around upon the company, but no smile came upon his features. He had been diverted from the purpose for which he had risen, and was annoyed by the intrusion of so many heads into business that he by no means considered public.

Looking around upon the expectant group, he added, "As I was sayin', they'll stick to a man longer'n he'll stick to himself, but they ain't apt to stick where they ain't wanted, and are first rate at mindin' their own business."

This direct hit was understood, and while a few turned and went smiling to their seats, all fell back and left him to himself and his errand.

"Some time ago," resumed Woodcock, "I heerd the little ones and some of the old ones tellin' what they was goin' to give Mary Pynchon when she got married; and it set me to thinkin' what I could give her, for I knew if anybody ought to give her anything, it was me. But I hadn't any money, and I couldn't send to the Bay for anything, and I shouldn't 'a known what to get if I could. I might have shot a buck, but I couldn't 'a brought it to the weddin', and it didn't seem exactly ship-shape to give her anything she could eat up and forget. So I thought I'd give her a keepsake my wife left me when she died. It's all I've got of any vally to me, and it's somethin' that'll grow better every day it is kep, if you'll take care of it. I don't know what'll 'come of me, and I want to leave it in good hands."

The bride began to grow curious, and despite their late repulse, the group began to collect again.

"It's a queer thing for a present, perhaps (and Woodcock's lip began to quiver and his eye to moisten), but I hope it 'll do you some sarvice. 'Taint anything 't you can wear in your hair, or throw over your shoulders. It's—it's—"

"It's what?" inquired Mary, with an encouraging smile.

Woodcock took hold of the hand of his child, and placing it in that of the questioner, burst out with, "God knows that's the handle to it," and retreated to the window, where he spent several minutes looking out into the night, and endeavorir g to repress the spasms of a choking throat. Neither Mary Holyoke nor her husband could disguise their emotions as they saw before them the living testimonial of Woodcock's gratitude and trust. Mary stooped and kissed the gift-child, who clung to her as if, contrary to her father's statement, she was an article of wearing apparel.

The interview of Woodcock with the bride had been somewhat extended, and during its continuance an observant eye would have seen that Mr. Moxon was growing momently more nervous, until he seemed to have arrived at absolute distress. The moment that the newly married pair were disengaged, he advanced to them with his wife, and, complaining of indisposition, expressed his regret that he should be obliged to retire, and bid them a good evening. Holyoke was very emphatic in his expressions of sorrow at the necessity of this step on the part of the minister, but Mary was simply polite, for her quick heart had divined a secret connected with his presence which deeply concerned her own heart, and made it impossible for her to regret his withdrawal.

The company all rose as the minister retired, and not one sat down as the door was closed. In an incredibly brief space of time the whole appearance of the assembly was changed. Silence broke into confused chattering, and the bride, instead of standing alone in awkward embarrassment, was surrounded by a band of loving hearts, which gave themselves up to the natural impulses and emotions of the occasion. But a few minutes had passed after the departure of the minister before Mary's hand had been pressed by every guest—even the most awkward and bashful finding some kind word for utterance to an ear they had rarely if ever addressed.

The hum of unrestrained conversation was at length broken in upon by Mr. Pynchon, who informed the company that the newly united pair were to be installed in their housekeeping that very night, and that they would be happy to be accompanied to their new home by their friends. Accordingly, all made themselves ready for the walk, and a happier party, as they laughed and sang along the leaf-strewn street, never found themselves together.

Arriving at the new house, they found it lighted, a cheerful fire blazing upon the hearth, and a bountiful and substantial repast in waiting upon the table, to which full justice was immediately done by strong and healthful appetites. The frolic that followed among the younger members of the company received no check from the older and graver portion, and when, at last, the hour for separation arrived, all retired, feeling that they had been refreshed, refined, and made better. Mr. Pynchon was the last who left the door, and closed the parting scene by a kiss, as vigorous as it was rare, and a special injunction to "see that the fire was raked up safe."

To one who has drunk deeply of life's experience, a newly married pair is always an object of strong and tender interest. Love is beautiful in itself. Its hearty and unquestioning devotion, its perfect trust, and its soft and gentle sympathies, are very beautiful; and no less beautiful are the happy souls in which these graces of the passion are realized. But the interest one feels in those commencing life together, in marriage, is based on no abstractions like these. It has its birth in our own experience. Childhood is very beautiful in itself, but we love it mostly because of its association with the simple years of happiness that form the romance of our own past life. We may smile at the frivolous pleasures of childhood, and despise its objects, and, even while we heave a sigh in view of the deep disappointments which await it, in the great discipline of life, drop hot tears that its freshness may never again be ours. Thus it is with love's childhood, and all its associations. We know that years of trial and patient suffering endured in companionship, and mutual participation in such imperfect joys as the world affords, will produce a love so sweetly sympathetic, so perfect and profound, that the bliss of the honeymoon shall mimic it only as a shallow pool mimics the ocean; and yet, as we kiss the bride, and grasp the hand of her possessor, we involuntarily do homage to the bliss of ignorance, and sigh for days that we value only as memories.

CHAPTER XVI.

THE first puff of smoke that issued from the chimney of Holyoke's house, on the morning following the wedding, was noticed by a dozen watchful and waiting eyes, and immediately reported to an indefinite number of waiting ears. The smoke produced at the original discovery of fire could hardly have been a subject of greater interest. Meanwhile, the happy little household, which had thus unconsciously telegraphed its wakefulness all over the village, was busy in its preparations for breakfast. Holyoke, after his part of the household duties was performed, in making the fire and bringing in the water, found great enjoyment in watching his wife and her brisk waiting-maid, as they bustled about the house in the discharge of their portion of the morning's labor.

At length the bountiful breakfast was smoking upon the table, and the three occupants of the house, in a charmingly merry mood, took their places at the board. In an instant, however, Mary was silent, and awaiting reverently the pronunciation of a petition to which she had been, from childhood, a listener at every meal. Holyoke did not notice the movement at once, and rattled blithely away at his chain of small talk, but when he became conscious of his position, his face reddened painfully. Mary detected his embarrassment, and, divining its cause, proceeded with the finest tact to relieve him by entering upon the courtesies of the table.

The meal was eaten in a different spirit from that with which it was approached. Buoyancy and mirth disappeared, and, while both husband and wife attempted to appear cheerful, each was aware of the shadow of a cloud, that must feel the touch of a breeze more or less powerful before it would restore the vision of a bright sun and a clear sky.

As soon as the breakfast was cleared away, Holyoke beckoned his wife to a seat at his side. Looking her calmly and solemnly in the face, he said, "Mary, did you expect me to ask a blessing at the table this morning?"

"You probably saw that I expected it," replied Mary.

"Why did you expect it?" inquired Holyoke, preserving his solemn tone and manner.

"I do not know that I have any reason better than the fact that I have always been accustomed to the ceremony, both at home and away, and saw no reason why any Christian should decline its performance."

"I shall pain you, perhaps, my dear wife," said Holyoke, grasping her hand earnestly, "but I have been so much shocked and disgusted by the manner in which this service is performed, that it seems to me to have become the popular way of dishonoring God rather than of honoring Him."

"You do not conclude," replied Mary, "that because the service is improperly performed, it is improper in itself."

"Not that, because there is nothing like intrinsic impropriety in it; but I do not deny that I believe that the habit has, very generally, a bad tendency."

"A *bad* tendency?" inquired Mary, with an exclamatory accent.

"I see that you are pained and surprised, and it is what I expected," replied Holyoke, "but it is best for us to be frank. You wonder how a service so intimately associated, in your mind, with the daily duties of a Christian life, *can* have an evil tendency. I think it has two evil tendencies. The first is, by a frequent rush into the divine presence from the distractions of the world, and as frequent and violent a leap out, into its distractions again, or into the grosser animal delights, to break down and destroy all decent reverence for God. I have heard, hundreds of times, a blessing pronounced that, in its relations, in the points of time and place, was the sequel to a very laughable story, or the connecting link between the laugh that followed it and the sharpening of knives and the clatter of trenchers. The second evil tendency is in begetting in children and in the irreligious a disregard of religious services of every kind, and a scepticism touching religious character and experience. They are the most relentless critics of inconsistency in religious matters in the world, and a Christian can no more come into God's presence with thoughtless abruptness, while they sit near, without hardening them, than he can without benumbing his own soul."

Mary did not know what to reply to this, for, while she was not convinced of the entire correctness of his conclusions, she saw that they were based upon truths which she could not deny.

Holyoke saw her hesitation, and resumed. "I have no doubt," said he, "that there are some men, perhaps many, so saintly in their walk and holy in their frame that they would be able to address the Deity many times in a day, with no violent transition of emotion or revulsion of thought; but these men are comparatively rare. I will not deny that we all ought to be such, but I do not believe that the habitual repetition of a prayer at the table, uttered without feeling, and often mumbled into entire indistinctness, is a legitimate means of grace for the production of that end. I count it a great thing for man to approach his Maker in worship and petition. It seems to me that no one should do this without a spirit stricken through with reverence, and profoundly impressed with the sublime presence in which he stands; and to go through with this form simply as a Christian duty, or tc fulfil the expectations of Christian friends, or for the sake of the example, or for any cause less than a sincere desire for communion with God, springing freshly with every occasion, and clothed in a reverence which is its becoming garb, is not only wounding religion in the house of its friends, but is keeping the wound open and bleeding."

Mary saw by Holyoke's earnest words and emphatic manner that, however much she might differ with him, it was not becoming in her to dispute his positions directly, and therefore attacked them indirectly by stating that she did not see why his facts and his reasoning did not apply in a degree, at least, to the observance of daily prayers in the family.

Holyoke's face burned with sudden color, and his heart throbbed painfully as this new subject was introduced, for, upon this, his convictions were inharmonious with his inclinations. In this subject he had a fearfully practical interest. It was one which had occupied many of his thoughts, and one which had smitten his heart with sudden misgiving every time he had come beneath its shadow.

"I do not think the cases are parallel," said he, quietly, and with evident disinclination to continue the discussion.

"Please tell me why," gently insisted Mary.

"In one case," replied Holyoke, "we approach God without preparation, and ask him, three times in a day, to bless our food, as if that were the great, and, in fact, the only gift of his providence that deserves a recognition; in the other, we come with offerings as well as prayers, and with such preparation as the contemplation of divine truth is well calculated to bestow upon those who peruse it. We come to God in the latter case with worship, with confession, with penitence, with thanksgiving, with fervent aspirations for a stronger faith, a higher life, and a broader Christian experience; we come in the fresh hours of the morning and in the hush of evening, before care has put on its fetters, and after it has laid them aside; and all these exercises and conditions of heart form the basis, if they do not the very essence of a communion with God, as honorable to him as it is full of nourishment and strength to the soul."

While Holyoke was speaking he had grown earnest and eloquent, but the instant he concluded he involuntarily put his hand to his heart, while his lips grew pale and thin with a trembling compression, for there came up again the practical question that had given him so many anxious thoughts. His embarrassment was not relieved as Mary took down the family Bible—a fresh present from her father—and bidding Mary Woodcock to be seated, commenced reading a chapter from the New Testament. Alas! his preparation for prayer that morning, so far as it was drawn from a consideration of Bible truth, was very small, for he sat as if in a dream while the reading was in progress, his mind confused and his heart in a strange tumult of emotion.

At length, the dreaded conclusion of the chapter came. The voice of the reader was hushed, the holy book was closed and replaced upon the shelf; but Holyoke still sat in silence, his features rigidly contracted, and his heart beating so heavily that it jarred his frame. Silence soon became more painful than speech, and he burst out with, "Mary, I can't pray this morning."

"*Can't* pray?" and the words came forth from Mary's lips so slowly, so charged with astonishment, and so full of a kind of solemn wonder, that Holyoke involuntarily lifted his eyes to her's, and saw them springing with tears.

He took her hand, and bowing his face upon it murmured, "My God forgive me!"

Still unmarried! Wedded, but unwed! Loving, but not made perfect in love! United, and yet separate! Thus it is with multitudes of hearts, and those not the worst in this world. The heart that has communed with God most intimately in secret often shrinks most sensitively from giving utterance to the words of prayer where other ears than God's can hear. Nay, it is not unfrequently the case that those who have the most intimate relationship in life exercise towards each other a most rigid reserve upon all matters which touch their relations to God and religion, while each preserves a spirit of devotion, and leads, so far as an individual may without coming within the circle of social influence, a religious life. There is in every soul possessing nice sensibilities an indisposition to place before other eyes a revelation of its wants, its wishes, and its aspirations; but until a husband and a wife can kneel together and realize the sweetness of communing like children, lovingly and without restraint, with their common Father, marriage, though it may be to them a band around a golden sheaf of happiness, has the weakness of the straw, and is neither perfect nor secure.

Holyoke's eyes were hidden for a minute, and then looking up convulsively, he exclaimed—

"Must I try?"

"You will never have a better time," replied Mary.

"It does not seem possible."

"What do you fear?" inquired his wife.

"I fear myself—I fear you—I fear God—and (bending his face down to her ear) I fear that child. I cannot help it. I fear my own pride—that my speech will be awkward to your ears, and thus mortify me, or elegant and make me vain. I fear that I shall think more of my language than the spirit from which it should spring. I fear the sound of my own voice in this room."

Mary sympathized very deeply with her husband in this trial, but she knew that the time for the struggle and the triumph was then. So she gave him sweet words of counsel an l encouragement, and taking his hand rose upon her feet.

At that day, in all the Puritan churches and families, the standing posture was always assumed in prayer. Kneeling, to them, was what the beautiful symbol of the cross is to many of their descendants—something that belonged to and was characteristic of Popery—something which had been tainted and had the power to taint again.

As Holyoke saw his wife rise, his determination was made, and, rising, and folding his arms upon his breast, he uttered tremblingly and with deliberate distinctness, the words, "Our Father which art in Heaven." The spell was broken, and with all the simplicity and earnestness of a child he went on, and poured out his heart,—its penitence, its love, its trust, and its many wants, and when he uttered his fervent "Amen," his eyes, as well as those of his wife, were wet with tears. And when those eyes met, they shone with a new beauty, and beamed with a more perfect trust. Both felt that their hearts had been attuned to a new and more exquisite harmony.

With hearts full, they turned to the window, hand in hand, that even a child might not be the witness of a joy that brimmed their cup with grateful fulness, and trembled to run over in appropriate expression. Holyoke felt a strength and buoyancy of spirit which he had never experienced before. There was, then, perfection of communion between him and the being he loved best; and he felt how holy and beautiful a thing was marriage when it united those whose steps lead heavenwards, and whose highest love was already there.

CHAPTER XVII.

While these last scenes were in progress at the house of Holyoke, those of a very different character were in process of enactment at the house of his father-in-law. Mr. Moxon had called upon Mr. Pynchon on private business, and had chosen the early morning hour as best suited to his purpose. The magistrate was pained to find upon the minister's face the same wild look of anxiety that he had witnessed upon a previous occasion, and dreaded another exhibition of a weakness that was suggestive, at least, of insanity.

"I came to ask you a question," said the minister, walking backwards and forwards across the room. "It is an abstract question, which I beg you to consider without any relation to its practical bearings, even if the case which prompts it should occur to you. It is one which, so far as it goes, interests me very deeply."

"I am waiting for your question," said Mr. Pynchon, after watching the minister for a minute, as he paced to and fro, and smiling at his own conceit that the gentleman was treading out the question, as if he thought it was a flooring of wheat.

"Do you suppose"—and Mr. Moxon paused for a better phrase—"does not it seem possible to you—that a man who would give away his child would sell himself?"

"And this is what you wish me to consider as an abstract question?" said Mr. Pynchon, smiling in spite of himself.

"You consider the question a foolish one," said the minister, pausing and biting his lip with vexation.

"I do," replied Mr. Pynchon, calmly.

"Mr. Pynchon, you offend me," said the minister, sharply, for he was mortified, especially as he had been exercised by a secret conviction all the time that he was doing a very silly thing.

"Well, sir," responded the magistrate, with another smile, "I am happy to believe that it is the truth I tell you which is offensive rather than the man who tells it."

"That remark, sir, is not less offensive than the other," replied the minister, with increased bitterness; "and if these are the kind of words you feel disposed to give me, I shall take the liberty to bid you a good morning." Saying which the gentleman moved towards the door.

"They are the only words which seem proper for the occasion," said Mr. Pynchon, very decidedly, "and so long as you are engaged in the insane pursuit which occupies you this morning, they are the only kind you will have from me. I did not ask you to come to me with these vagaries, and I trust you will not trouble me with them again."

So long as Mr. Moxon believed that Mr. Pynchon had no insight into his motives, he felt strong and indignant, but his pointed allusion to an insane pursuit, and his stigmatizing as vagaries the thoughts which moved him so deeply, disarmed him, and, dropping the latch he had lifted, he walked back to where Mr. Pynchon was sitting, and settled hesitatingly and unbidden into a chair.

"Excuse my heat this morning, I beg you, Mr. Pynchon, for I am not well," said the minister. "I hardly know what I have said, but you spoke of vagaries. Will you be kind enough to tell me what you meant?"

"If you will hear me calmly and patiently, I will tell you with perfect frankness, and certainly with perfect kindness," replied the magistrate.

Mr. Moxon turned his eyes solemnly upwards, and exclaimed, "Divine grace helping me, I will hear you in a Christian temper."

"From certain mysterious statements which you made to me last summer, on my return from the Bay, and from the question which you have propounded this morning," said Mr. Pynchon, "I have come to the opinion that the Devil is tempting you with suspicions that he has an agent in the settlement who is operating to your damage. You know that Woodcock bears you no good will, and he is very naturally the individual whom your imagination would clothe with the malign instrumentality. In other words, you believe in witchcraft, and are strongly suspicious that its influences are upon you and your house. I have been plain with you this morning, and, as you have chosen to think, severe, because I thought it my duty to you, to the plantation, and to the interests of religion, to be so. Were these things generally known, the naturally superstitious spirit of the people would take fire at once, and hell itself would hardly be less tolerable than our new town of Springfield."

"Do you not believe in witchcraft?" inquired Mr. Moxon, as Mr. Pynchon closed.

"I do not perceive that your question has the slightest relevancy to the matter in hand," replied Mr. Pynchon. "I do not believe that witchcraft exists here, and, least of all, do I believe that Woodcock, whom neither you nor I can buy, would sell himself to the Devil. There are half-a-dozen of your particular friends, and mine, too, I may say, in all candor, whom I would suspect of such a disposal of themselves before I would him."

"I know you have always had a partiality for him," replied the minister, without any attempt to deny the genuineness of Mr. Pynchon's interpretation of his language and actions, "and that is one reason why I have never been frank with you in relation to the subject."

"Then I am right?"

"You are not far from right."

"Let me tell you then, my dear sir," said Mr. Pynchon solemnly, "that, in giving utterance, or even secret harbor, to these suspicions, you are assuming a terrible responsibility. If you can assume it on any but the most reliable grounds, you are either a very brave or a very heedless man."

"I admit what you say," said the minister, "and if you could but see what I have seen, and hear what I have heard, you would confess that I have reliable grounds for my suspicions."

"Very well; give me a share in your experience," replied the magistrate. "Nothing would gratify me more than an opportunity to prove to you the fallacy of your conclusions."

"Well, you see," said the minister, hesitatingly, and with a slight blush, "it's Martha."

"I thought so," replied the magistrate, with a smile.

"And why should you think so?"

"Because I know the child. But this makes no difference. I wish to see her and ascertain whether she has deceived you."

"Deceive me! Martha deceive me!" exclaimed Mr. Moxon convulsively; "my little child? my little simple-hearted one? Do not pain me, Mr. Pynchon, by suspecting her of such wickedness, or me of such weakness!"

"I have no disposition to pain you, my dear sir; but it is possible that a little pain now will save a great deal in the future. But tell me something of what has taken place."

"I could not tell you a tithe of what has taken place. Besides, I can see how many things which have made a profound impression on me should only excite your ridicule, when simply narrated to you. Martha is a child who would be very easily bewitched, and is by her constitution peculiarly open to influences from the unseen world. Until recently, her impressions and revelations have been general, but they have been very strange. She has never accused any one, but she shudders when Woodcock walks by her, and was once thrown into a spasm at hearing his name pronounced.. I have questioned her considerably, but without arriving at any very satisfactory results. I only know this: that a strange and unearthly influence is upon her, and that Woodcock appears to be more or less connected with it."

"I think I can get at the matter," said Mr. Pynchon. "If you will bring your child here after dinner to-day, I hope I can show you—I think I can prove to you—that you are in this whole matter very much mistaken."

"I should be unjust to you and my child, at least," replied the minister, "were I to refuse the trial, and I consent to your wish very cheerfully;" saying which, Mr. Moxon, intent on the new aspect of affairs, walked out of the house, forgetful of all courtesies.

After the minister's departure, Mr. Pynchon sat for a long hour engaged in reflection. He was sickened with the prospect which Mr. Moxon's hallucinations had opened to him, and he was sickened with the man himself. He was not a thorough sceptic in regard to the wonders of witchcraft, and few who lived in his day could boast of entire freedom from that great figment of superstition, but he did not believe in Martha Moxon's witchcraft at all, and was vexed that her father, with the great affairs of the Gospel ministry upon his hands, could tolerate such idle whims for a moment, and not only tolerate but, as he had reason to fear, actually implant and foster them.

Having determined upon his plan of procedure, he walked out, and taking Holyoke's house upon his way in a brief call, directed his steps to the cabin of John Woodcock

He found that individual within, singing merrily away at an old stave while engaged in cobbling an extremely dilapidated shoe. Mr. Pynchon informed him that he wished to see him at his house in the early part of the afternoon, at such a time as he should signal him from a window, and told him not to be surprised if he found the business a strange one. Woodcock promised compliance, and when the magistrate departed fell into a brown study, or more properly a highly variegated reverie, not unworthy of the brain of his eccentric daughter.

The first surmise of the old man was that news had been received from England of the death of some unknown relative, who had left him his estate. It was very natural, therefore, that Mr. Pynchon should invite him to his house, and treat him with the respect due to his altered fortunes. If this should prove to be the fact what a lady he would make of Mary! He would give her such a fortune that Holyoke would be proud to adopt her as a daughter! He would build a house that should outshine any and every house in the settlement, and that should be Mary's! And then he thought of the minister, and ran into a long calculation of the number of revenges which an unlimited amount of money would enable him to execute upon that gentleman. He concluded at last, that if he were to offer to build a meeting-house for the plantation at a cost of five thousand pounds, on condition that they would dismiss Mr. Moxon from further duty, they would accept the offer and jump at the chance. This he should do without fail. Then, just as the minister was about to leave the village on his way back to the Bay, he would go up to him and say, " Here, Moxon" —yes, he would call him Moxon or George, he did not know which—" Here, Moxon, take your six pound thirteen and four; I guess I've had that out of you one way and another. When you come this way ag'in call, and if I can help you ag'in by a little slander, I shall be at your sarvice."

That would be a good cut, and then he would take off his hat and bow to him a hundred times as he retired.

This florid dream was a long time in running through Woodcock's mind, and he felt so contented in himself, and was so enchanted with his possession, that he had forgotten himself and the world of stern facts around him. When he awoke he threw his hammer to the other end of his cabin, where it fairly buried its face in the wall, and exclaimed, " You miserable old fool !"—After this, he burst into a fit of boisterous laughing, and then, picking up his hammer, resumed his work.

After working a while longer, his dreams took another complexion, and there arose in his mind the possibility that the visit had something to do with Mary. Perhaps the child had stolen something, or there was a suspicion that she had, and Mr. Pynchon wished to get him at his house to make an inquiry into the matter. Perhaps there was a conspiracy against the child, with Mr. Moxon at the head of it. If such should prove to be the case, he should take that gentleman by the throat, and exclaiming, "ah! ha ! old wolf! I've caught you killing the lambs, have I ?" he would shake him till his face was blue, and kick him out of the house; and Woodcock almost leaped upon his feet with the excitement of the imaginary encounter.

But suppose there was merely a suspicion that she had stolen something. and the circumstances were very much against her. She would stand in the middle of the room, crying as if her heart would break, and protesting that she knew nothing of the matter. The question was just about to be decided against the girl. He had begun to be convinced of the guilt of his own child. At this moment, Mary Pynchon—for he could not think of her as Mary Holyoke yet—would rush into the room, her face radiant with joy, and bearing in her hand the missing article. This she would hold up triumphantly, and placing it on her father's knee, clasp the child affectionately in her arms.

When this grand finale was reached, Woodcock was about to insert the bristle of a waxed-end into the puncture prepared for it, but, in the excitement of the moment, and partly in consequence of an uncomfortable mist that gathered about his eyes, he shot a long inch wide of the mark. This fact re-awakened him to the consciousness that he had been dreaming, and kicking, his kit into confusion and the corner, he bestowed upon himself a variety of contemptuous epithets, terminating respectively with the words "coot," "fool," and "pewter-head," and then walked out into the open air in search of a more healthy mental atmosphere.

But the morning passed very slowly away. He could not relieve his mind of the apprehension that an event very important to him was about to occur. His mind ran into nearly every possible channel but the right one, and as the hour approached, he had settled down into a belief that a great evil was impending over him and his child. His dreams began in brightness and ended in darkness, and when at last the expected signal appeared, he started for the house of the magistrate in a state of profound dejection.

Mr. Moxon and his daughter had been at the house of Mr. Pynchon for half an hour when Woodcock arrived. They were closeted with him in a small private room, and when Woodcock entered the house he was shown directly to that room. The moment that he entered, Martha Moxon uttered a piercing scream and fell to the floor in a fit, where she lay for several minutes foaming at the mouth. Mr. Pynchon was puzzled. He looked first at the child, then at Woodcock, and then at Mr. Moxon, who was praying with blanched lips for God's mercy on himself and child.

Woodcock was dumb and motionless with astonishment, it seemed so unlike a common fit, was induced so manifestly by his appearance at the door, and was regarded so singularly by the child's father, and by Mr. Pynchon. Seeing that they took no measures to relieve the child, he exclaimed in a tone well charged with reproof, "Why don't you cut the chick's riggin', and do somethin' for her?"

These words were better than a thousand arguments for the reassurance of Mr. Pynchon. The exhibition had shaken him, but Woodcock's rough reproof testified to his own thorough honesty, and the child's delusion, or intentional deception. In the meantime, the child remained upon the floor, with her eyes rolled wildly up at the ceiling, the froth issuing from her mouth, and presenting a spectacle equally terrible and disgusting. Woodcock watched the group a moment longer, and then burst forth with "What in the Devil's name!—"

He had proceeded thus far, when the child uttered another scream, and subsided into violent convulsions.

"Mr. Pynchon," exclaimed the minister, "do not permit these hellish incantations to proceed." Then turning to Woodcock he said, "Man, beware! Remember the terrible price you pay for this, and repent in time! Why will you persist in afflicting this innocent child?"

"*Me* 'flictin' *her?* Have I teched your young one?"

"Yes, it's him, father," exclaimed the child, becoming conscious in a moment, and pointing her finger at Woodcock. "It's him: don't you see the blue cat on his shoulder, whispering in his ear? Kitty, kitty, kitty, come, kitty!" and the little girl smiled wildly, and held out her hand with an enticing motion to the invisible animal.

"What do you mean, you little slobber-chops?" said Woodcock, with a glance at each shoulder, and one hand on his head to see if that were in its place. Then, looking at her a moment longer he said, "She's makin' it, Square, as sure as guns. I ain't a 'pothecary, but if spankin' ain't good for that kind, then I wouldn't try it, that's all."

Mr. Pynchon could not restrain a smile, and a pleasantly inquisitive glance at the minister. That gentleman stood looking at his child with a stern and solemn expression of countenance, but deigned no reply to Woodcock's accusation.

"Woodcock, will you leave the room for a few minutes?" said Mr. Pynchon; and, as soon as he had retired, he addressed the same request to the minister. Mr. Moxon paused, as if he would ask a question, but Mr. Pynchon checked him with a motion of the hand, and he hesitatingly complied. When both had gone, and the door was closed, he lifted the little girl, who had gradually recovered from her strange fit, to his knee, and asked her what made her act as she had done.

"*He* made me," replied the girl, pointing at the door, and meaning Woodcock.

"How did he make you?" inquired Mr. Pynchon.

"He did it with the blue cat," replied the child.

"The blue cat? He has no blue cat, and you have not seen any."

"Well, I've seen one at my brick house, and it had red rings round its eyes, and it had—oh! ever so many little red kittens, every one of them made out of bricks—"

"Stop!" said Mr. Pynchon, authoritatively. "Let me hear no more of that nonsense."

The child looked tremblingly into his eyes, and was silent. "Now," said he, "Martha, I am going to call John Woodcock into the room again, and your father is not coming. Do you see that riding stick up there? Now remember that if you fall down in a fit again, or scream, or talk about blue cats, I will whip your shoulders so that you shall have something to scream about." He then called Woodcock, who came in expecting another fit; but, on approaching the child, and finding that she was perfectly calm, he sat down opposite to her, and asked her to come and sit with him.

"Go!" said Mr. Pynchon, placing her upon the floor.

She walked immediately to Woodcock, and he lifted her to his lap. Mr. Moxon had overheard the movements that were in progress, and entered the room unbidden, at the moment when Martha, at Mr. Pynchon's command, was engaged in kissing Woodcock's rough cheek. It would be hard to tell whether it were the flush of anger, or shame, or fear, that burned upon Mr. Moxon's face, as he saw his child in what seemed to him a foul and unnatural act. Mr. Pynchon pointed to the child in triumph, and exclaimed, "Your daughter is no more bewitched than I am."

"Martha! get down and come to me," exclaimed the minister shudderingly.

In any other mood, Woodcock would have given the minister bitter language, but Mr. Pynchon had used a word which had opened to him the secret of the strange scene. Slowly he comprehended the accusation which had been made against him, and it smote him dumb. Meanwhile Mr. Moxon had folded Martha to his breast, and was bending tenderly over her, and Mr. Pynchon was turning from one to the other of his companions, uncertain what course to pursue with them. He was relieved, at last, by the minister, who, with a look full of angry reproof, said, "How do you decide so readily that the child is not bewitched? Perhaps you can tell what enchantments were used to get this trembling child into that man's arms."

Mr. Pynchon heaved a sigh that was half pity and half disgust, and evidently restrained himself from using such language to the infatuated father, in the presence of Woodcock, as he was powerfully moved to use. As the minister bent over his child she raised her head and whispered in his ear. She evidently made a request to return home, as he rose with her in his arms, and very emphatically saying "then you shall go home," passed out of the house, and left Mr. Pynchon and Woodcock looking silently into one another's faces.

The magistrate and his surprised companion preserved their position and their silence for a long minute after Mr. Moxon's withdrawal, as if they had made a private agreement not to speak until he was beyond a hearing distance. Woodcock was in distress. His mind, in a brief time, had ranged through the field of consequences that would naturally be opened by the singular suspicion which the minister had fastened upon him, and he could not avoid the conclusion that that field was springing thickly with trials and sorrows.

"Where do you 'xpect this thing is goin' to fetch up?" said Woodcock, at last, folding his arms upon his knees, and looking with renewed earnestness into Mr. Pynchon's face.

"It seems to me," replied the magistrate, thoughtfully, "that he must necessarily abandon suspicions that are proved to be so groundless."

"Well, Square," said Woodcock, "I don't pretend to be any smarter than other folks, but I know Mr. Moxon better'n that. Guessin' is a great deal stronger'n knowin' with him. Argyments don't stand no more chance with his notions than a hen's egg does with a weasel. He'd suck the yelks right out on 'em, and hide the shells in his coat tails, and swear he hadn't seen 'em. No, sir,—there's goin' to be a fuss, and I've got to catch it. He's bewitched the young one, and she's bewitched him—all the bewitchin' there is—and they think it's me. He's been peaceable a good deal longer'n I s'posed he would, but he's on the track, and he'll foller it, and yelp till all the hounds in the settlement jine him."

"It is too small an affair for Mr. Moxon to pursue, I am sure," said Mr. Pynchon, shaking his head as if he were not entirely sure, after all.

"What did he start it for, then?" said Woodcock. "It was a good deal smaller then than 'tis now. I don't know jest what you think of his preachin', Square, but I've heerd him talk half a day on littler things'n that, and I b'lieve he likes such things better'n anything else. I think a good deal of religion, if you can only get hold of the right sort, but his'n ain't that sort by a long chalk. I never see a minister stickin' to little things, such as didn't come to any given sum, any way, but what he had an onreasonable religion, and I never see one that had an onreasonable religion that didn't make a jackass of himself—so! there!" And Woodcock slapped his knee spitefully, rose to his feet, and walked across the room as if he had said something which he expected to be reproved for.

Mr. Pynchon knew that Woodcock had been sufficiently provoked, and so made no comment on his remarks about the minister, but asked him what course he supposed that individual would pursue.

"I think he'll shoot low, and save his waddin', till you go to the Bay ag'in, and then he'll let me have it jest back o' the fore-shoulder, as he did t'other time. You're a little too much for him, Square, but you've got him mad, and I've got to stand the blowin' for both on us. Not that I care any great shakes about it on my own account, 'cause I'm used to't."

"Woodcock," said Mr. Pynchon cordially, "you gratify me very much by commanding your temper so well this morning."

"Now, Square, stop that, or you'll get me mad," said Woodcock sharply, and reddening in an instant. "'Taint no compliment to tell me my pluck's gone, and if you want to raise the devil in me right straight off, all you've got to do is to stroke my back and call me a good feller."

"I may think what I choose about you, I suppose," said Mr. Pynchon smiling, "provided I say nothing about it."

"It'll be better for the minister if you keep mum, for if I r'ally thought you s'posed I was layin' low 'cause I was gettin' good, I'd make pumice of him 'fore he was an hour older."

"What serious objection have you to being called good?" inquired Mr. Pynchon curiously.

"I ain't good," replied Woodcock decidedly. "I'm bad, and gettin' worse, and I don't want to have you think I'm gettin' any better. I sh'd be ashamed to grow good on sech fodder as I've had in this plantation. It's mighty poor stock that'll do it, and I don't belong to the breed."

"We all notice that you are changed in your temper," said Mr. Pynchon, "and I see no way for you to do but to let us call it for better or worse, as it pleases us."

"Do you r'ally s'pose the folks round here think I'm gettin' good?" inquired Woodcock, with an air not unlike that of injured innocence.

"With the exception of Mr. Moxon, I presume they do."

"Then they're a sweet set of fools—that's all. Now I'll tell you, Square, jest how 'tis, and what it all started from. When I was layin' by, after that overhaulin' the minister give me, last Spring, I was walkin' in the woods, thinkin' about that matters and things, worryin' about that gal of mine, and wonderin' how I was goin' to fetch round, when out shot a hen patridge with one wing lopped clean down to the ground; and she kept hoppin' and limpin' ahead on me, and lettin' me almost get up to her till I'd chased her a good long stretch, when all at once, jest as I was hittin' her a rap, she up and off as sound as a nut and straight as a string. Then I mistrusted the critter, and turned round and went back to where she started out. I've got a tol'able good eye, and pretty quick I saw a little young patridge, jest hid under a leaf, and standin' as still as a mouse. Well, Squire, I sot right down on a stone, and went to thinkin' to see if I couldn't learn somethin' from the old bird. Says I,

'Woodcock, you ain't 'xactly a hen patridge, but you're kind o' wild, and you have got a wild young one. Now when the Square gets back, you try to get into the plantation ag'in, and if you do, get your young one under a leaf, and then limp and let your wing lop down, and make 'em think you're as good as bagged, till they forget all about the young one.' Well, you know I got the young one under just the leaf I wanted to, and I've kept my wing down, and it's done the work, too, till now; but, Lord! I ain't any more a tame patridge than I be a spavined salmon."

At this characteristic conclusion of Woodcock's exposition of his policy and motives, Mr. Pynchon laughed heartily, and, rising to his feet, said, "Well, John, you placed the young one still further under the leaf last night, and I am glad to see that you keep the wing down still."

"What do you s'pose Holyoke'll do with that gal of mine?" inquired Woodcock, with an affected carelessness of manner.

"I imagine that he has come to no conclusion yet—he has hardly had time," replied the magistrate.

"Well, I reckon he'll do pretty much as his wife says, and I know she likes her. Don't you think she's a goin' to 'arn her livin'?"

"She appears to be bright and industrious."

"Now, don't you s'pose if she didn't see the old one round she'd get tame, and folks would forget where she was hatched?" and Woodcock put on a very transparent look of unconcern, and snapped his finger with an ease that was very uneasy.

"Do you mean to ask whether for the sake of your daughter you had better leave the plantation?"

"That's jest it, Square," replied Woodcock. "You see I don't care anything about this witchcraft business myself, only, if I hadn't a young one to look after, it wouldn't be safe for a man to p'int his finger to me and say, 'broom sticks' more'n a dozen times. He'd lay down kind o' careless, and I should stomp on him. But the gal makes the trouble. You see, I don't want to be a drawback on her, and I've been thinkin' that p'r'aps I'd better say, that if you should find me gone some time, and I shouldn't come back, and you didn't know where I'd gone to, I want to have what little land I've planted here to go to Mary when she gets old enough, and help support her till she does."

Mr. Pynchon read in Woodcock's tone and manner the nature of the conclusion to which he had arrived. He saw that he believed that Mr. Moxon would pursue his persecutions further, and that it was only his consideration for his child that kept him from visiting the minister with savage vengeance; and, while he disliked to part with the man, it seemed evident that it was for the peace of the plantation and the good of all concerned, for him to quietly withdraw.

He saw that the difference between him and Mr. Moxon had become utterly irreconcilable, and that the introduction of a new element of discord, which from its nature would be likely to involve the welfare of the settlement, would serve to extend a feud which was yet within limits. So he told Woodcock that he would bear his request in mind, and see to its execution whenever the supposed emergency should occur, but expressed the hope that he would take no hasty action.

Woodcock took his leave of the magistrate, and walked slowly away, with his head bent down reflectively, and his hands grasping each other behind his back. He was thinking of a project he had formed months before—a project based on the supposition of such a juncture in his affairs as he had already reached. He had for several months thought it probable that, considering Mr. Moxon's hatred of him, a time would come when, to save the reputation of his child, or to keep her free from unpleasant or unpopular associations, it would be necessary for him to retire from the settlement, and he had laid all his plans for that event. He had not a doubt that if he should remain, the fact that he had been accused of being a wizard would, in some manner, become known, while, if he should retire, Mr. Moxon would have parental affection sufficient to induce him to keep his secret. He had arrived opposite to the house of Holyoke, when, upon raising his eyes, he saw his daughter smiling at the window. He could not resist the temptation to enter the house, where he was greeted very cordially by Holyoke and his wife, both of whom detected the cloud upon his features, and made sympathetic allusion to it.

"Well, I BE troubled," said Woodcock emphatically, "but I don't make a p'int of goin' round to tell on't; leastways, I wouldn't fetch my troubles here."

"I do not know of a better place," said Mary Holyoke smilingly, "and you certainly ought to carry them somewhere."

"I never do," replied Woodcock.

"And what do you do with them?"

"Let 'em mull."

"And here you have given me your companion, your comfort, your own child!" exclaimed the lady, the tears springing to her eyes.

"If you want to do me any good, look after her. I'll take care o' myself. My troubles are nothin' to anybody, and, if she comes out right, they aint anything to me."

"I will certainly do the best I can with her," said Mary, "and she seems well disposed to do everything she can for me."

"Can she pay her way?" inquired Woodcock earnestly, and as if the question contained the very meat of the matter.

The reply to this question was interrupted at the commencement by a rap at the door, and the entrance of Mr. George Moxon.

CHAPTER XVIII.

When Mr. Moxon left the house of Mr. Pynchon, he proceeded homewards, carrying his child in his arms the whole distance. Arriving at his house, he laid her upon the bed, and, bending over her, asked her how she felt. She made him no reply for several minutes, when she startled him by a sudden cry of pain, and the exclamation —"Oh! stop him! stop him! He's sticking pins into me!"

"Where, child! where?" inquired the distressed father.

"In my foot—in my back—all over me," replied the child.

She was immediately undressed, and from the delicate skin the blood was starting at several points upon her body and limbs. After being carefully covered she lay still for several minutes, when she began to complain of sickness at the stomach, and soon vomited forth upon the floor an offensive mass, in which were distinctly seen a number of crooked pins—a fact from which the minister concluded that the pricking had been done from within outwards. Poor Mrs. Moxon stood at a distance in great distress, looking pitifully fearful, wan, and woe-begone. Broken-spirited and feeble in body, the strange calamity in whose presence she stood had paralysed her, and she could only impotently wring her hands, and weep, and utter feeble ejaculations of prayer to God for help.

When the vomiting had ceased, Martha turned back upon the bed, as if entirely exhausted, and, after lying upon her back a few minutes, with her eyes closed, she opened them wildly, and rolling them upwards, fixed them stiffly, in an unwinking gaze, upon the rough ceiling. "I see them! I see them!" she exclaimed softly, into her father's ear, as he bent over her; "Oh! what beautiful little kittens! and the old blue cat has got one of them in her mouth! Oh! my neck! my neck! She's biting the kitten! There! the kitten has got away! Good! Good!" and the little girl clapped her hands merrily, while her face retained its strained and rigid expression. "Oh! papa!" continued the child, "do you see those six white, beautiful fingers sticking down out of the boards? Arn't they pretty! oh! they're just as pretty as they can be! and there is the old cat sucking one of them, and there go the kittens! Every one of them is sucking a finger, and there they hang, swinging at the fingers all the time—oh! wouldn't it be funny to catch hold of their tails and pull them off? * * * * There they go!" exclaimed the child, "the fingers have pulled them right up through the boards."

As she uttered the last words, her features relaxed, and returned to their natural expression, and she turned her face pleasantly towards her father, and exclaimed, "I'm so glad he's gone! He was too bad to hurt me so."

"Who do you mean, Martha?" inquired the minister tenderly.

"John Woodcock," replied the child, and then added, "wasn't he cruel to squeeze my ankle?"

The father had ceased to be astonished at any of the child's revelations, and immediately turned off the bedclothes to see what new wonders the invisible John Woodcock had wrought. He was not at all surprised to find around the child's ankle the marks of a firmly grasped hand, even to the sharp indentations of the finger nails.

"When did he do this?" inquired the father.

"Just now, when the blue cat and her kittens were

here," replied the child. "Didn't you see him! He was on the foot of the bed all the time."

"Why didn't you cry out, and tell me he was here?" inquired the father earnestly.

"Because he told me not to say a word about him, for, if I did, he would throw me out of the window."

"Did he go out of the window?"

"No; he went out of the hole where the latch-string comes through."

There was one witness to these exhibitions and revelations to whom little attention had ever been paid. This was the second child of the minister, Rebekah. She had looked on, sometimes in terrified silence, but never without an absorbing interest. Every word uttered had been indelibly stamped upon her memory, and the whole subject and all its associations had become invested with the most intense fascination. She said nothing, but she saw every motion, heard every word, revolved them in her childish meditations, and dreamed of them in her sleep.

During the scene which has just been described, she had climbed upon a chair, and gazed with wondering eyes upon her sister's contortions, and drunk in greedily her strange utterances. Just as Martha had designated the point of Woodcock's exit, her father accidentally turned to Rebekah, and saw her staring with a strangely rigid expression at the latch. He spoke to her, but she did not stir, but gazed steadily at the object upon which she had fixed her eye. He turned and took her hand, but it was rigid and cold, and, grasping her in his arms in a hurried alarm, he found her insensible, and in a trance.

This new affliction was too much for both father and mother. The child was laid upon the bed with her sister, while the parents, giving themselves up to wild ejaculations and groans and cries, alternately bent over the new victim of Satan, and walked back and forth across the room.

Martha was, however, possessed with perfect calmness. She lay quietly by the side of her little sister, embraced her with childish caresses, asked her to awake, and, finally, commenced singing to her. This brought the parents to silence, and the mother, naturally returning to her old habits, dropped upon her knees at the bedside, and buried her face in the coverlet. In any other mood, and at any other time, her husband would have reproved her for as suming so heretical a posture, but his superstitious fears had been so far wrought upon, that he had begun to mistrust that, perhaps, God was visiting him with terrible judgments for non-conformity—that he had strayed away from the true fold.

He watched his wife for a moment, looked out of the window to see if any one was near, stepped to the door and made it fast, and then knelt by her side, and gave utterance to a prayer which was momently interrupted, from its commencement to its close, by convulsive sobs and choking throes of mental pain.

Both remained kneeling for some minutes after the close of the prayer, and when, at length, they lifted their eyes, they saw their younger daughter looking silently and pleasantly into the face of the older one, who sat regarding her with a gratified and affectionate smile.

This sudden change in the aspect of affairs would have brought an unmixed joy to the heart of the minister, had it not so immediately followed a prayer uttered upon his knees. But doubts rose out of his joy like an armed host, to beat him back into the realm of misery he had so long inhabited.

Turning from his children, he paced forwards and backwards across the apartment, wondering if this were not the way God had chosen to bring him back to the true church, and to condemn his present convictions and connexions. Oh, that God would rend the heavens and come down! that he would stand and converse with him, and tell him in language that he could not misunderstand, what he should do to avert His judgments!

Then, as he reviewed the circumstances and events of the occasion, another swarm of doubts came against him, from another direction. If this were the Devil, operating directly or indirectly upon his children; if the children had been in his power, was not their release from his influence evidence that he had been conciliated by the very prayer which had just been regarded as the procurer of God's favor? Had not the Adversary been pleased by seeing him and his wife upon their knees once more? Was it not a promise from the great enemy of souls to abstain from hurting the children, on condition that the parents would return to the bosom of the church from which they had gone out? These two orders of questions could only result in confusion, and it was in the utter hopelessness of their resolution that he took his hat, and, re-assuring himself of the recovery of his children, passed out of his house into the open air.

The atmosphere was raw and chilly, portending a storm. Rustling leaves were driving across the street, sometimes in parti-colored flocks and sometimes singly, clinging here and there to a stump or a stone, and pausing tremblingly in their leaps; sometimes rushing into heaps in the hollows and smothering themselves, and here and there holding themselves by a splinter, and fluttering like a smitten bird. The clouds were dull and cold, and as the minister looked up, the very heavens seemed barred against him, while all the elements were in conspiracy around him to shut him up within the circle of his miseries. The house of Mr. Pynchon had always been his place of resort when his own home had, for any reason, become intolerable, but he had sufficient reasons for not bending his steps in that direction. He felt that he had been offended—almost insulted there, and the wound was too fresh for sudden closure.

There never had been another house in the settlement which

had any real charms for him, and, as he drew his coat around him, and buttoned it closely against the chilling wind, he walked aimlessly along the street, until Holyoke's new dwelling came in sight. He felt that he had no special errand there, at a date so closely succeeding the wedding, but he determined to enter, and inquire after the health of the family, if nothing more. At his entrance he disturbed, as has already been recorded, a conversation in progress between Mary Holyoke and Woodcock, and it may well be imagined, in view of his recent experiences, that the latter individual was the one, of all in the settlement, whom he least wished to encounter. The sight of Woodcock threw him entirely off his balance, and made him forgetful of all forms of politeness.

"How long has he been here?" exclaimed the minister, in a harsh and authoritative tone, to Mary Holyoke.

"Not long—I cannot tell you how long, sir," replied Mary, wonderingly.

"Long enough to find out that there's a lady here, and that she's got a husband," said Woodcock, answering for himself, and rising from his chair.

Mr. Moxon turned upon the old man a look of mingled anger, scorn, and fear, but without deigning to address him, said, "Mary, how *can* you harbor such a man? How can you have him near you?"

"He has never harmed me, sir," said Mary, "and I am sure he never will."

"Do you not know that he is sold, body and soul, to Satan, and that his hands are still hot from his infernal work?" half shouted the minister. "Do you not know that the strange power by which he commends his boorish manners and uncouth speech to your good will is borrowed from the Adversary? Do you not know that one of the Devil's foulest minions is here in your house, undermining your peace, and planting thorns for your feet?"

Mary looked imploringly at Holyoke, and he came forward, motioning to her to retire. Walking coolly up to the minister, and looking him steadily in the eye, he said, "You are either insane or impertinent; now tell me which."

The minister stared at him fiercely for a moment, but quailed before his unbending eyes, and apologetically said that he had doubtless acted in a manner which was widely open to misconstruction, but that when the facts should be known, Holyoke would not only understand the nature of his feelings, but would forgive any seeming extravagances into which they might have led him.

"I accept your apology, and trust that you and our friend Woodcock will adjust your differences, and have no further trouble."

"I make no compromises with Satan, or peace with the sons of Belial," said the minister, glowering fiercely upon Woodcock.

That individual, who had stood with some impatience watching the progress of affairs, could restrain his tongue no further, and burst into the conversation with, "I ain't Satan, nor I ain't a son of Belial; my father's name was John and so was his afore 'im, for that matter, but if I was, and there was any prospect of you're ever comin' to live with me, I should send you my respects, and ask you to stick to your mind, till after my door was shet."

"Imp of Satan!" growled the minister, "how dare you profane this Christian house by such godless words?"

During the conversation, Mary Woodcock, who, when it commenced, was in another part of the house, came in, and became immediately interested in its progress. She watched the minister closely, and as she faintly comprehended the terrible epithets he was heaping upon her father, her eyes flashed, the old bright spark began to burn on either cheek, and she only wanted action to be the highest impersonation of a fury; and this condition did not remain long unsupplied. The last bitter address of the minister was no sooner uttered, than she crossed the room like a cat, grasped his hand, and, drawing it to her mouth, fastened her teeth into it before he could guess what she was doing. Her jaws came spitefully together, her teeth almost meeting between the bones.

"Hell-cat!" groaned the minister in an agony of pain, and snatched his hand from her teeth with a suddenness and power that almost lifted her from her feet.

"Oh! my God! Mary," exclaimed Woodcock, in a tone of extreme distress, "it's all over with me now!"

The child had no sooner given expression to her intense anger than she ran to Mary Holyoke, who was sitting upon the other side of the room, and, burying her face in her lap, gave herself up to her old hysterical sobs and cries.

Woodcock was greatly troubled. That sudden movement of his child was like a flash of lightning, revealing upon the wall of the dark future the record of her fate. His sole aim had long been to keep her dissociated from himself, and to associate her as much as possible with those against whom no one should dare to breathe a word; but she had incurred the anger of the very man, who, for her sake, he most feared. It ruined in a moment all his hopes, destroyed his plans, and impressed him with the belief that his daughter was designed for a fate not unlike his own.

Holyoke was deeply mortified that the event should have occurred in his house, but, as the father of the child was present, he simply expressed his sorrow for the occurrence, and referred to Woodcock as the individual from whom apology and reparation were due.

"I'm sorry the thing is done, the Lord knows," said Woodcock, "for the gal's sake, and the sake of the house she belongs to, but I ain't goin to back out, and leave her in a scrape she got into on my account. She felt jest as her dad did, but she didn't know so much. She couldn't stan' it to hear me called hard names, and while I'm round she shan't be abused for it."

"Miserable hypocrite!" exclaimed the minister, scowling and holding his wounded hand in its fellow—"pretending sorrow for the savage offence of your child, and yet acting as her boastful justifier and champion!"

"Look a' here," said Woodcock, shaking his fist in the minister's face, "the school's out and the ma'am's drownded, and now, you old carri'n, I aint goin to stan' any more of your sass. You jest call me imp and hypocrite and son of Belial and father of a hell-cat once more, and I'll pound you till you're as full of batters as an old brass kittle. It don't do me any good, nor my young one, nor you neither, to treat you decent. There aint anything that'll bring you to your milk half so quick as a good double-and-twisted thrashin', and hang me if I don't give you one in less'n five minutes if you don't shet your head."

"As the head of this house," said Mr. Moxon, turning to Holyoke, while a sudden pallor overspread his face, "I claim your protection from the threats and hands of this ruffian."

Woodcock drew back his hand to strike him as he uttered the last epithet, but it was caught by Holyoke, who in a firm tone said to him, "Strike no man in my house."

"I beg your pardon," said Woodcock, "but he tempted me too strong."

At this instant Mary Holyoke came up and laid her hand upon his arm, and undertook in a soothing tone to address him and dissuade him from violence. He understood her motive at once, and deprecatingly held out his hand to her, and begged her to desist. As she still persisted in her attempt to speak, he put his hands to his ears to shut out the sound, still begging her not to interfere, for he feared her influence over him, and knew it would be exerted on the side of peace.

During this brief diversion, Mr. Moxon had retreated, stepped out of the door, and was rapidly passing away from the house. The moment that Woodcock became aware of his retreat, he wheeled, and, in a dozen bounds, which were executed as strongly and as nimbly as if the very essence of youth were dancing in his veins, he had stopped the minister, and confronted him. The latter was alarmed, but not entirely intimidated, and, seeing Holyoke at the door of his house, and one or two others starting out of their cabins and walking rapidly towards him, he endeavored to pass on; and as Woodcock interfered, exclaimed in deep vexation and anger, "Villain! Stand aside!"

The words had hardly passed his lips when Woodcock struck him a staggering blow with his flat hand across his mouth. The minister shouted "Murder!" and "Help!" and it was strange how those words—cries of simple alarm and distress as they were—infuriated Woodcock. He had patiently withstood injuries and insults, but the outcry of this large and powerful man seemed so cowardly to him—so mean and unmanly—that, having once broken over the restraint under which he had held himself, he became suddenly maddened into fury, and, striking him a second blow, the minister fell heavily upon the ground, the blood spurting from his nose and covering his face. Woodcock was instantly kneeling upon him, and putting his face down to his ear, he hoarsely whispered, "Are you goin' to tech that gal of mine?"

"Help! let me up!" gurgled forth the minister.

"Are you goin' to tech that gal of mine?" shouted Woodcock. "Say yes or no, or I'll break your head."

"Spare me," feebly whispered the minister, "and I'll promise as you wish."

"Now you remember," said Woodcock, shaking his fist menacingly before his eyes, "that if you make any fuss about her bitin' you, or let anybody else, or bring harm on her any way, you'll catch that thing between your eyes and under your ear agin, and when it comes you won't think it's a puff-ball or a piece of cold pudd'n'."

This scene had occupied a very brief space of time, and at first somewhat paralysed those who were its witnesses, but as Woodcock concluded his threat, he felt himself seized by two pairs of powerful hands. Their owners, however, had made a very poor estimate of the kind of individual with whom they had to deal, for in an instant he was on his feet, and had thrown off the double grasp as if it were the playful imposition of a child.

As he looked around him, he saw the villagers running towards him from every quarter. As they came up and gathered in a crowd, Henry Smith approached the minister, and taking him by the arm, led him away towards his house. As he was retiring Woodcock shouted, "Now remember what you've said, for I shall be round," and then turned and walked, unmolested but followed by the crowd, to Holyoke's house. He seemed to understand that there was not a man of them who dared to lay his hand upon him, and he walked through them as calmly as if he thought them so many stumps of trees. Taking Holyoke and his wife by the hand, he bade them farewell. On their inquiry in regard to what he meant, and where he was going, he shook his head, and simply replied that they wouldn't see him again.

"I've got to leave the gal with you," he continued, shifting immediately from considerations touching himself to the subject which burdened his mind, "and I want to have you do as well as you can by her. I've *got* to go now, *any way*, but I shall know how she gets along, and p'raps shall help her some."

Holyoke and his wife said but little to him. Both felt unpleasantly in consequence of being associated with the scene of violence which had just occurred, at the sudden cloud it had drawn over their happiness, and at the rupture of the peace, and the wound to the reputation of the settlement.

At last, Woodcock turned to the child, and taking a seat, lifted her to his knee. He put her head back, and looking in her face a moment, bent like a reed over her, and hiding his rough face upon her neck, gave himself up to a passion of grief and tenderness, which could only find expression in long and convulsive suspirations. The villagers, one after another, looked into the door and window, and there was no smile upon their faces as they gave their places to others.

"Don't forget me, Mary," said Woodcock, as he raised his head; "don't forget me, and don't b'lieve any on 'em when they tell you I was a disgrace to you. Good bye!" And straining her to his heart, he set her upon his own chair, and looked fiercely out upon the gathering crowd. Looking beyond the crowd, he saw the constable, John Searles, approaching the house rapidly, and he knew that he must act immediately. Passing by little more than a single leap out at the back door, he ran for the river, and as his exit was witnessed by several persons, a wild outcry was raised, and this seemed to break the spell that rested on the crowd.

They rushed after him with a wild halloo, and succeeded in reaching the river's bank in time to see him push rapidly out upon the current in his canoe. The constable and half-a-dozen others went out in pursuit, but soon returned, well knowing his superiority at the oar, and the danger there would be in attempting his capture upon the water. Woodcock's little craft, under the long sweeping strokes of his one oar, slipped through the water with wonderful velocity, and soon looked so small that, with its apparent life, it seemed more like a deer swimming the stream than the transport of a man. The speck gradually curved in to the eastern shore, ran in among the bushes, and disappeared. The crowd then turned and went chattering excitedly back to the village.

This attack upon the minister produced an excitement which was long in subsiding. The fact became known that Mary Woodcock had bitten the minister's hand, and all wondered why some corrective measures were not instituted against her. Then, little by little, in some unaccountable way, the story of the witchcraft practised upon Mr. Moxon's children became known, till at last it was notorious in every particular, and was the theme of a world of idle gossip.

But Woodcock did not return, and the affairs of the plantation soon assumed their accustomed phase. Mr. Moxon (after a month's confinement) preached on in his usual way; Mr. Pynchon bought beaver and distributed justice with his characteristic fairness and urbanity; the planters planted and builded; the women cooked, mended, and gossiped; the children grew, and seed-time and harvest came and went in the revolving circle of the years, as they have done since the birth of the rainbow.

CHAPTER XIX.

Ten years! A segment of the great circle of eternity! How much of the long past abides in so brief a period! Rivulets of influence which started, perhaps, with the subsidence of the flood, and have been joined by other rivulets flowing from rifts in the stratified centuries, or have been turned aside into sluggish circuits through long ages, have, in ten years, deposited their store of blessings or curses, and, at the same moment, sunk in the sands. Ten years! They are the high road of destiny, crowded with shouting multitudes—multitudes in chariots—multitudes in armor—multitudes chasing golden phantoms—eager-eyed and sleepless multitudes—multitudes in rags and wretchedness—multitudes trodden upon and forgotten in death. Ten years! Ten hours of joy—ten ages of sorrow! Seed-time of a harvest which shall not be fully reaped and garnered till the stars, now throbbing and flashing in the strength and beauty of their youth, shall flicker and fall. Ten sweeps of the wing of that great angel who, earthward bound, bears the proclamation that time shall be no more! Ten years! They transform helpless infants into bounding children, confer manhood on boyhood, make matrons of maidens, stamp wrinkles upon the brow of beauty, bring declining years to senile idiocy, draw millions into life, bear millions to their death, stud a heaven of hope with stars and blot them all out, and, yet, only ten years!

Ten busy years swept over the settlement of Agawam, and wrought their changes and left their traces—wiping away old memories with new experiences; raising up one, and bowing down another; bearing cups of joy to some, and clothing others in the weeds of mourning; involving old identities in new associations and circumstances, and preparing the field for a fresh and more interesting survey. In ten years, the Bay Path had been changed from a simple bridle path to a worn and frequented highway. Packed horses went and came upon it through all the summer and autumn; land hunters, in merry parties, cantered along its shady aisles; emigrants coming from and returning to the Bay, with strange freights of children and household stuffs, and droves of cows and goats, crept along the solitudes which it divided, and lighted nightly their lonely fires; Mr. Pynchon, with a pleasant retinue of companions, which not unfrequently numbered some of the women of the plantation, went twice a year to attend the General Court, and the artery connecting the distant settlement with the body of the colony throbbed more freely with the life and influence of the growing heart.

In ten years, Mr. Pynchon had greatly changed. Those years had brought him seriousness with increasing care, and determination with strengthening convictions of duty. The increase in the population of the settlement by immigration, brought in new materials, the strongest portion of which were those with which he found himself inharmonious. His heart rebelled against influences which he felt were beginning to control the minds around him. The old creed, which he hoped to see liberalized and simplified, was growing still more strait. The community which he had been endeavoring to mould into the semblance of his beautiful Ideal had become warped, so that he hardly recognised it. Driven in upon himself, forced in his declining years to see others outstripping him in enterprise, and conscious of the advance of errors which he had from motives of policy sought to neutralize in their effect, rather than oppose in themselves, he busied himself with his Bible, his thoughts, and his pen.

He began to write—uncertainly at first, reading and carefully revising as he wrote, from day to day; and then, as he became more interested in his work, he devoted himself with entire ardor to the fulfilment of the mission he had assigned himself. For weeks and months the work progressed. During the day he wrote, and during the night he studied the Scriptures and prayed; and when at last the huge mass of manuscript lay before him, he found that he had written a book on theology. Little did he dream, as he turned over its leaves, interlining a sentence here, and correcting a word there, that his own fate and that of the plantation were involved in its pages!

The changes that began in Mr. Moxon, when he first became unsettled in his religious belief, went on during ten years with great rapidity. Even his occasional fits of strength and independence became, at first, widely intermittent, and then ceased altogether, until at last he had degenerated into a weak-minded, melancholy, fearful, and humble man. He moved about the streets quietly, looking hurriedly around at the slightest noise, as if he anticipated the appearance of some danger. His little ones had become ten years older, but they were puny and stunted children, and still the sources of severe trials. They still had their strange fits; and their pitiable case had been commended to God, at the public request of their father, by all the members of the church. They were talked about, and at every new attack from which they suffered, the probabilities touching the authorship of their torments were thoroughly canvassed, until half the people in the plantation had been mentioned as objects of suspicion.

Mr. Moxon's mind, shut up within a rigid creed, which, in many points, chafed and benumbed his reason, shrank from the walls of the inclosure, and became dry and dead. He had fed on no liberal ideas. He had had no enlargement, and there, hemmed in on every side, and afraid to burst out, he had clutched at effete superstitions, and eaten them in silence and fear. His ministrations upon the Sabbath had become uninstructive and uninteresting, and had come to be regarded with lamentable indifference by his people.

Ten years came down on Holyoke's rough house, and the walls became blackened by the sun and rain; but the ground looked so pleasantly around, and so many delightful associations were connected with it, that it had a cheerful look to all. On Holyoke, ten years had wrought a great work. Satisfied in his affections, blest in his home, happy in his Christian experience, and in fellowship with a mind that fostered every good motive, nourished every good resolve, and rewarded with the sweetest and only praise he sought every difficult achievement and noble deed, he could not choose but outgrow even his own expectations of growth, and become, in his own modest consciousness, more noble and manly than he had once supposed a man in active contact with the world could be. Everyone looked upon him as one of the coming men—one who, in the future, would fill an important place in the plantation, if not in the colony. Time had fed him; experience had given him strength. The love that burned warmly at his heart, and the angel that fed the flame, kept all the chords of his being in harmony; and while, from this fact, he was able to give his whole soul and undivided energies to whatever work he undertook, his mental and spiritual growth was, from the same fact, symmetrical, and strong as a natural consequence of its symmetry.

Mary Holyoke hardly looked older by a day than when she was married, yet she had known many cares and anxieties, for three beautiful children played around the hearthstone. Yet Mary Holyoke had changed even more than her husband. With advancing years, she had grown more and more silent and diffident. She saw the growth of her husband, and in the gratification which it gave her, and the sweet cares imposed upon her by her children, she became greatly self-forgetful. The more intimately she communed with the masculine mind with which she was associated, the more she saw its depth, its power, and its beauty; and the greater became her admiration of it. She did not measure herself by it, but she was content to add herself to it and blend herself with it. She experienced no sense of humiliation at his side, but, on the contrary, emotions of noble and ennobling pride. His love was the sweetest blessing the earth had for her; his admiration the sweetest praise. When she dressed, it was for him; when she labored, it was for him; when he was absent, all time that was not devoted to him and those he loved, was a burden; when she left him, it was to fly back, at the first opportunity, to him and the home in which he had made her so happy and himself so essential to her happiness. She asserted no prominent place in the neighborhood where she might have had commanding influence, because she was content to feed the springs of love and power of one who could fill that office as she could not. In this beautiful devotion, her heart had known no cankering envy, no bitter self-revilings, no vain regrets. Passion had left no trace upon her cheeks, jealousy and pride and selfish discontent had ploughed no furrows across her brow; and even the fresh blush of maidenhood had only given place to a maturer grace—a deeper, broader, and softer glory—which happy maternity may alone bestow. She had been content to be a woman, and to follow the promptings of her own loving heart; and in devoting herself to her husband and children, had found the highest happiness she had ever known.

The difference in the character of the changes that respectively passed over Mary Holyoke and her sister, Ann Smith, was as great as that of the respective motives by which they were actuated. Ann was married to a man with whom a sense of duty was the highest motive of action. He had a strong will, and she readily took the coloring he gave her. She performed the duties of a wife. She kept the house, and clothed the children, and cooked the food, and mended her husband's garments, because as the wife of Henry Smith it came within the line of her duty, and because she knew that Henry Smith would regard the service in that light, and not as any direct manifestation of love to him. Thus labor became a burden, and sacrifice a sorrow. Thus toil lost its dignity and its dignifying influence. Thus discontent became a tenant of her heart by a perpetual lease, signed and sealed by her husband. Thus upon her face the bloom of girlhood was never replaced by any grace that atoned for its loss. Thus her features assumed permanently the hard lines which were the appropriate expression of her prevalent thoughts and emotions. Thus the corrugation of care which slept behind the fair disguise of health, or became exhausted before they reached the soft plump outlines of the surface, displayed themselves in permanent wrinkles so soon as youth and health began to wane. Thus she became old before her time.

The character of Henry Smith had grown without being enlarged—that is, the qualities of mind and heart that were his when the reader first made his acquaintance, were by the experience of ten years simply intensified or strengthened. There was no change in the outlines of his character. The identities of his being had all been preserved. He had adopted a system of opinions on almost every subject that interested him in youth, and as manhood came on he shut off the influx of light and knowledge, having got enough for his purposes. All his opinions and sentiments were clearly arranged in his own mind, and as he could and would talk of nothing beyond his range, he had the reputation of being clear-headed and strong-minded. He had tracked over every channel of his soul till he knew it as he did the paths around the plantation. He knew just what arguments and illustrations he had on hand, as well as he knew what trees grew hickory nuts and chestnuts upon his farm. In his own consciousness mind was cut up in patches like his home-lot, each patch being productive of some useful fruit, and while the whole might be made more fruitful even as the home-lot might, its area, like that, could never be increased by any intrinsic principle of growth. He was a kind of cast-iron man—a perfectly reliable man—a man whom one always knew where to find, and with humble ostentation he gloried in the character.

What did ten years do for Peter Trimble? The first of the ten found him a small lad. He had not growth enough for his years; and while he remained small, his roguery seemed to be so concentrated that a successful attempt to check the appropriate expression might have been fatal. But, at the close of the year, his master, whose attention was called to the subject, found the bottoms of the legs of Peter's trowsers in the immediate vicinity of his knees. He saw that the boy had begun to grow in earnest, and then recognised the fact that as the length of his limbs had increased his roguishness had diminished.

Year after year this process went on until he arrived at manhood with a stoop in his shoulders, bashfulness in his manners, a tuft of white beard upon his chin which was invisible at a short distance, and a populous settlement of the most inflammable and intractable pimples upon his face. Peter's legs seemed to have a great influence in his conversion to good behavior. The utter disparity between his legs and his favorite pursuits first became apparent to him on the occasion of his tripping up a small boy as the boy did not happen to be so long as his legs; and after that, he half unconsciously adopted his legs as a moral standard, and they certainly answered an excellent purpose. While his legs thus became the means of his reformation, his pimples did good service in confirming him in principles of sobriety. They made him modest and retiring, for he was as conscious of each particular pimple as if it were a burning mountain. Each florid protuberance seemed to possess an independent power of blushing, and would redden as it felt itself the subject of observation until his face appeared like a chart, representing all the stages of active inflammation.

If he had an errand at any house in the settlement, the last thing he did before knocking at the door was to draw his hands down over his face, and, as the surface was smooth or rough, he was bold or embarrassed in his interview with the individuals with whom his business lay. Sometimes, when his face felt extremely rough and uneven, he was obliged to look down upon his legs for reassurance of his manhood, and thus those organs became more than a simple moral standard—became, in fact, a motive force, by which the spurs were put to resolution. In short, Peter was so thoroughly changed that one who had not seen him in ten years, would not have recognised him at all. He was a new creation. He was as if he had been literally what he had been often denominated figuratively—"a hard little nut"—which had fallen to the ground, burst open, and given birth to a tall chestnut sapling, either absorbing the nut or entirely covering it from sight.

Mary Woodcock had become a woman, and her sharp black eye had grown large, and, softened by new sympathies, very beautiful. It was a most legible index to an uneasily balanced, passionate nature. It seemed sympathetic and inviting, and yet repulsive, with a kind of reckless disdain. To many susceptible temperaments, it was charged with the most intense fascination. Her eye was apparently all that any one saw who came into her presence. A stranger would have remembered nothing but her eye. Her size, form, face—all would have been forgotten in the recollection of that wonderful revelation of character, that subtle detecter of sympathy, that inquisitor of motive, that inspheration of soul. One watched it involuntarily, and without being conscious that that was the only object observed, as one watches a whole face for the perusal of the emotions which express themselves in its changes. It had its sunshine, its clouds, its depths of thoughtful coolness, its flashes of passion, its dances of delight, its phases of humid softness, its half-repulsive glarings of wild merriment, and all those appreciable but indescribable intermediate shadings and interminglings of emotion, passion, sentiment, and thought, which found birth and being within her soul.

Yet she had few sympathies with her own sex. Her development never lost the bias towards masculineness given to it in its initiative stages. Not that she was coarse, or offensively and improperly bold; but her individuality had the faculty and characteristic of standing alone. She leaned on no one, and had no wish to lean. She had no confidant but her benefactress—no intimate associate of her own age—and she had no desire for one. If she had any desire touching man or woman, it was that she might receive his or her confidence and trust, and to stand in the relation of a protector or supporter. In such a relation, she could dare or do anything.

Everybody felt that Mary Woodcock was attractive, and yet everybody naturally and specially subject to her attractions, was afraid of her. There was a scar upon the minister's hand which every one in the plantation had seen. All knew or believed, that there was incorporated in her nature a terrible temper.

Mr. Moxon's children were still subject to their strange fits, and there was, necessarily, in the minds of the credulous—and nearly all were such—some medium or agency by which the Satanic influence was communicated. After everybody in the plantation against whom a suspicion could by possibility be indulged, had been taken up by the reckless fingers of gossip, turned over, and dropped, the ill-starred orphan was fixed upon as the one who most probably was in the blame. The scar upon Mr. Moxon's hand was evidence of her spite against him, and the banishment and disgrace of her father, in consequence, indirectly at least, of his reputed agency in tormenting the children, were deemed motives sufficient to induce her to perpetuate the work he had commenced.

These things were not talked about openly, yet everybody knew of them, and had not the girl been under the protection of Holyoke and his wife, she would have been subjected to great annoyances, if not to unrestrained persecution. As it was, she became aware of the suspicions held, and influences operative against her, and the consciousness—as her mood might be—wearied, sickened, soured, or maddened her.

There were also shadowy reports in regard to certain interviews that Mary had been known to have with men, or forms, who came and went in the night; and a very singular looking communication had been found addressed to her. This had been passed from hand to hand, and finally came into the possession of Mr. Moxon, who put it under lock and key, with the impression that it might possibly be of use to him. These facts formed the basis of all kinds of stories, which did not require ten years for such growth and modification as to place them beyond the recognition of their first acquaintances.

At the house of Mr. Pynchon, a new spirit had taken possession. Mary had long been absent. The old lady grew more and more quiet, from year to year, and, busying herself in the small economies of the establishment, left the labor to the devoted servants of the household; while John, the boy pupil of Mary, came early into man's estate, and assumed naturally and boldly its responsibilities.

During all these years, what changes had come over John Woodcock? None in the plantation could tell. He had not once been heard of in the settlements eastward or at the south; but, though none had seen him, there were very few who did not believe that he was alive. There was one who knew him to be alive, or, rather, who had no doubt of the fact. This was his daughter. She had received, at the hand of Commuk, the Indian, a score of communications, rudely traced upon strips of birch bark, consisting of warnings, bits of information in regard to her position in the neighborhood, scraps of advice, &c. These were nearly always accompanied by presents, larger or smaller, in silver money or wampum; and though the communications had no signature, and the gifts no nominal donor, she had no doubts touching their common origin. The Indian messenger answered no questions, and made no explanations.

Within the first year after Woodcock's withdrawal from the plantation, the discharge of a gun was occasionally heard in the forest, when all belonging to the plantation were at home. An Indian was seen, on one occasion, with a musket in his hand, but he suddenly fled from sight, and as, in one way and another, the Indians generally became possessed of fire-arms, the matter was forgotten.

The reader has been made acquainted with the changes which ten years had wrought upon his acquaintances in the plantation of Agawam. As he recognises, one after another, through their faded lineaments or modified characteristics, those in whom he has acquired an interest, he is ready to join their hands in sympathy, and pass forward with them to the resolution of the problem of their lives, and, perhaps, make a few new acquaintances with them on the way.

CHAPTER XX.

It was a bright autumn day of the year to which the reader was advanced by the last chapter, when the Agawam training band, under the command of Captain Holyoke, paraded upon the village green. The band was composed of all the men in the plantation capable of bearing arms, including even boys of sixteen years, and old men with the first infirmities of age upon them. The members were not dressed with any great degree of uniformity, nor were their arms of equal length and calibre, but they formed a resolute and hardy looking corps—well fitted to act in such warfare as they were liable to be engaged in.

One would naturally suppose that the members of a body so indifferently appointed as this would have little place for personal vanity or military pride, but, when it is remembered that this company and its performances were the only embodiment and expression of the military spirit possible at the time, it can be imagined that many a young man studied personal effect, and thought of bright eyes at favorite windows, with no little interest.

During the half day devoted to training, a compliment was usually paid to the house of the captain by such officer as might be temporarily in command, and even Holyoke happened occasionally to put his little army through their evolutions in front of his own house. On the day alluded to, the company were marching steadily along the street, to the time of the old drum used to call the people to Sabbath worship, when one of the members began to betray a remarkable degree of agitation.

As they approached the house of Holyoke, he frequently looked down upon his legs, and, at the conclusion of each survey, lifted his hand to his face and brought it, spread broadly, down to his chin, at which point the fingers came in and reported what they had found to the thumb. One might go the world over, and not find so uneasy a specimen of a soldier as he. As he came nearer, and still nearer, to the house, he began to lift sudden stolen glances to the window, to ascertain whether the subject of his thoughts was there; and, as he caught sight of a pair of black eyes, flashing among a set of smiling and spirited features, the pimples upon his face became enraged, one after another, and his feet were confounded in such a manner that he was half afraid that he could never get by the house without being ordered from the ranks. He had not a doubt that Mary Woodcock saw every motion. He could actually feel her looking at him. The influence of her eyes was such that he had nervous twitches in his ankles, that brought his feet to the ground in uneven steps. He felt it up and down the muscles of his limbs; it heated his face, and confused his head. Yet he could not keep his eyes from the window; and, as the company came to a halt, and displayed their skill in exercise, his eyes and mind seemed to be about equally divided between the window and the commanding officer.

Peter Trimble was not in love with Mary Woodcock. That was a passion he was not equal to. He could love (in his small way) any woman at sight, provided the probabilities were in favor of his securing her hand. A compliment, real or fictitious, from a girl, was enough to change the current of his affections without a ruffle on the surface. He knew Mary Woodcock's origin, the nature of the prejudices that popularly prevailed against her, and her own consciousness that the majority of the young men shunned her; and the remnants of his old cunning had turned his mind towards her, as one whom, perhaps, he might obtain for a wife.

He was, therefore, not a little annoyed to find, as he came nearer to the house, that her attention was perfectly absorbed by some other member of the corps, and that she only turned to him once, and then with a smile that greatly resembled derision. When the company was dismissed, Peter had become quite unhappy—not from unrequited affection, but in consequence of a vague consciousness that he had made a miscalculation. He was unable fully to satisfy himself, even after having walked by the house a dozen times while the inmates were asleep that night.

The man who had the fortune to attract the attention of Mary Woodcock, and who became the unconscious cause of Peter's uneasiness, was one who had never been a favorite with the women of the settlement. The fact was not due, however, to any vice of his nature or habit, to any low associations, or to any ugliness of person. He was unpopular because he was not manlike in his constitution. He was a short, slenderly built man, with a feminine face, a mild blue eye, full of amiable sweetness, a soft and pleasant voice, and a manner that was all meekness and modesty. He was, in strict terms and in no unworthy or offensive sense, an effeminate man, and to his nature Mary had felt herself more and more attracted, as the years had brought her to maturity. From the stronger masculine natures she had felt herself repulsed by a force that she had neither the wish nor the power to resist.

She had grown up self-reliant, courageous, more or less conversant with hardship and danger, lonely in her thoughts, and passionate under restraint; and the idea of becoming the wife of a man to whom she would be obliged, or would feel it a pleasure, to bend her will, was one which it was not possible for her to entertain. She wished to choose, and it was natural for her—the masculine woman—to choose the feminine man. And as she saw him marching by with the training band, and watched him as he went through the exercises of the occasion, every step and motion seemed to her charged with unutterable grace.

"Dear little fellow!" exclaimed Mary, with a sigh, as she at last turned away from the window; and she thought of him tenderly all the day, and dreamed of him at night, and wondered the next morning whether circumstances would ever favor her with the means to convey to his mind the knowledge that she admired him, and could easily love him.

But days and weeks passed away before the opportunity for an interview with the object of her interest could, without a sacrifice of the proprieties of her sex and position, be obtained.

For a week after training day, Peter was in despair. At the end of that time he accidentally met Mary in the street, and, as she gave him an unusually kind smile and bow, he hastened home immediately, and, going to his little room, tried, with the aid of a small mirror, to get a side look at his legs. He walked forth and back across his apartment, but, with his facilities, he could observe only a small surface at a time, and relinquished his mirror for an unreflected survey of his nether proportions—a feat which he accomplished by stretching his head out from his stooping shoulder, giving an earnest squint inwards, and arching his eyebrows, and all the wrinkles above them, in a most preposterous manner. He saw nothing unusual, unless, perhaps, a slight increase of size in his locomotive organs. That, of course, was favorable. Then he looked at his face. It was certainly not a very handsome face, and it was not by any means smooth in its details; but, take it at a distance—say about as far as Mary stood from him when she met him—and the expression could be called good. He tried his looking-glass across the room, but, as it would only take in part of his face at that distance, he had to come back with it to close quarters.

This little circumstance fed Peter for several days with a satisfaction that began to grow into pride. Everybody said that Mary was a smart girl, and under other circumstances, and with a little less spirit, etc., would make any man a good wife. *He* was enough for her. As for her temper, *he* would let her know she couldn't play off any of her tantrums on him; and when the young men in the plantation really saw what a splendid-looking wife he possessed, and how pleasant and respectful she was to him, and, more than all, when old Woodcock's land should come into his hands, then they would say, "Hang that Peter Trimble!—what a lucky dog he is!"

After he had made considerable progress in Mary's affections in this manner, without her knowledge or consent, he met her in his frequent walks again. Her demeanor on this occasion was exceedingly gracious, and Peter was more delighted than ever, and wondered how large a slice of Woodcock's land, which was every year increasing in value, it would take to purchase a watch as valuable as Mr. Pynchon's. If he had a watch he should be a gentleman, and his wife would be Mrs. Trimble; and he could sit in his own house, and drawing his time-piece slowly from the fob say, "Isn't it about time we were having supper, Mrs. Trimble?" or, "Isn't it about time for the lecture to commence, Mrs. Trimble?" or, "I'd no idea it was so late;" or, calling at a neighbor's house in the evening, he would take the watch modestly out and say, in an off-hand, free-and-easy way, "Come, Mrs. Trimble, it's time honest folks was at home and a-bed." Yes—he was not fully certain, but—he rather thought he should have the watch.

Very few individuals get in love (or think they do, which is the same thing to them for the time), and are really very much pleased with the object of their interest, who have not a strong desire to give their confidence to some one who will take it good-naturedly—some one who will patiently hear of their successes, and listen to the praises of the being beloved. Peter felt this want very much. In his own mind he had made such advances in Mary's affections that, as he did not dare to call upon her for re-assurance, he found it necessary to brace himself against the assent and encouragement of some one else. He cast about among his acquaintances for the proper recipient of his precious secrets. He found himself afraid to speak of the matter to any acquaintances of his own age, ashamed to speak of it to any who were younger, and disinclined to allude to the subject with those who were his seniors.

There was but one face that came up to his imagination with a kind and sympathetic aspect, and that belonged to a young man with whom he had no intimacy. He resolved, however, to make his acquaintance, and see what he could do with him, and circumstances soon threw him conveniently in his way. Before the two parted Peter had invited his new friend to his room, informing him that there were certain things he wished to say to him, that he had profound secrets to impart, and important advice as well as aid to solicit.

On the following evening, accordingly, the confidant elect made his appearance at the house where Peter had his home, and walking into the kitchen found that individual bent nearly double upon a low bench before the fire, eating samp and milk.

Peter had about exhausted his supply at the moment of the arrival, and as he had not been accustomed to receive calls in the presence of the family, he began to blush with excessive embarrassment. His first movement was, almost unconsciously, to throw the remnant of his supper into the fire. Then rising and uncoiling himself, he set his porringer upon a side-table, and doubling up his pewter spoon under the impression that he was closing the blade of his jack-knife, put it into his pocket. The new comer smiled amiably upon all, told Peter that he had come according to promise, and, sitting down, extended his hand and a look of interest to a little child who stood timidly at a distance. The little one did not wait for a second invitation, but went directly to the stranger and was lifted to his knee. The child's instinct discovered a sympathetic nature, and not only trusted it at once, but conceived an affection for it at the same moment. Soon the other and older children gathered around him as an attractive centre, and without any apparent effort on his part he became in a few minutes the monopolist of domestic influence and interest.

At length, Peter had gained the extravagant concession of a tallow candle from the mistress of the house, and, lighting it at a coal, with the assistance of a very uncertain pair of lips, he told his friend, with a nervous wink, that he was "ready to cut his hair."

"Ready to cut my hair!" exclaimed the man.

"Yes! Walk right along up stairs," said Peter, pushing out of sight as soon as possible.

The visitor looked around upon the family with a curious smile, and in a quiet way saying, "I'm sure I don't know what he means," followed with such speed as half-a-dozen children clinging to his legs would permit. When both had landed in Peter's room, Peter sat down on one end of his chest, and placing his candle on the other, put his face between his hands, and his hands between his knees, and went suddenly off into a violent snicker which commenced with a snort and ended in a cough. As soon as he could speak, he bade his visitor be seated on a bench, and asked him "why he didn't take."

"Take? take what?" inquired the man, slightly nettled at the idea of being expected to play a game of deception.

"Why, you see," said Peter, "I'm great on cutting hair.

I don't s'pose when you come right down to the real thing, there's anybody in the settlement can shingle like me. I do it for pretty much all of 'em. I reckon you might stuff a bed with the hair I've cut off in the last five years."

"I hope you get well paid for it," remarked his companion, not knowing at the moment what else to say.

"Land ahead!" said Peter, using a favorite exclamatory phrase, "you don't s'pose I charge 'em anything, do you? I do it 'cause I like it. Between you and I, it ain't everybody that can do it. You see, a great many that cut hair pull like time, and I've come across several,—now very likely you won't believe it, but it's a fact—I wouldn't lie to you, for I think too much of my word, 'pon my honor I do, —several who had slits in their ears, made by these botches —I don't think it's any too bad to call 'em botches, that's a fact. Well, when a man gets his hair pulled every time the shears comes down—it's done by slipping by, you know—cutting off some, and taking along the rest—and gets a slit or two in his ears, he looks out, and doesn't get catched in the trap again. But I suit 'em, you see. Land ahead! I guess I do suit 'em; I don't s'pose if I should live here till I was as old as the hills, but what I should have all the hair to cut. Do you know how to shingle?"

"I hav'n't the slightest idea how it is done," replied the man, with a smile playing about the corners of his eyes, that showed that he was beginning to enjoy the interview.

"Well, it's a good deal of a knack, ain't it? The fact is there ain't but a few that's got it in 'em. Just look at my hair."

The concluding direction was accompanied with an exhibition of his head, in every aspect possible with a head still fastened to a pair of shoulders.

"That," continued Peter, "is what I do in the night. I come up here, and nobody to say anything to, and so I sit down on the old chest, and cut my hair in the dark. I keep it jest about so all the time. Do you see how smooth 'tis behind? Don't you call that pretty even trimming? Don't it look as if it was shaved, now, r'ally?"

After securing a general assent to his separate questions, Peter took his candle, and set it upon the floor. Then, lifting the lid of his chest, he took out from the till his shears and comb, and, holding them up to the amused visitor, exclaimed, "There's the tools! and if they ain't the tools, land ahead! there never was any tools.. I s'pose, if the truth was known, there's better stuff in them shears" (giving them a click) "than there is in any razor this side of the Bay. I call 'em a little too hard—jest a leetle grain—but that's a good fault in shears."

The visitor had begun to tire of the subject, interesting as Peter had the power to make it; and, shifting uneasily on his seat, he interrupted that enthusiastic amateur barber in his attempt to explain the trick of the shingling process, by saying, "I believe there were some things you wished to say to me."

"Land ahead!" exclaimed Peter, dropping his shears upon the floor, "I come pretty near forgetting that. What if I had forgot that, now? By the way, don't you want your hair cut? I don't know how I'm going to get along, unless you do have it jest shingled a little?"

The visitor could see no direct connexion between his hair and Peter's secrets, and declined the operation.

"You see," said Peter, "the folks down stairs will wonder what in time made you come here; and if I don't cut your hair, or make believe cut it, perhaps you won't believe it, but the way they'll pump me will be awful. I guess I can fix it," pursued the ingenious fellow, "by coming a small rig. I'll keep the shears a-going while we get along with the business, and they'll hear 'em down stairs, and think it's all right."

Thus deciding, and thus delivering himself, Peter lifted

the shears from the floor, and, performing half-a-dozen clips upon an imaginary head before him, reached forward, and grasping the hand of his companion, said, "You sit there, and I sit here. You are Hugh Parsons, and I am Peter Trimble. We understand ourselves, and what we say is between us."

"Just as you say," responded Hugh, with a slight struggle to drown in a smile a little irritation which sought the surface; for the study of Peter, while it had been an amusing one, showed him that there was not an element in his character with which his own could harmonize.

Peter gave a long tune upon the shears, in order to hold the people in the kitchen to the delusion to which, in imagination, he had committed them; then executed a subdued whistle, and, crossing his hands, and leaning forward with his elbows on his knees, he said to Hugh, in the slyest possible manner, "Between you and I, I think of taking a pullet."

"Robbing a henroost, in other words?" said Hugh interrogatively, with a quizzical expression on his handsome face.

"Land ahead!" exclaimed Peter, "don't you know what taking a pullet is?"

"I can guess, perhaps."

"Well, I thought you knew, and now I want to ask you —it's all between us, you know"—furious clips at the phantom head of hair, "what you think a pullet looks at most, when she's picking out a man?"

"His corns?"

"Come now! honest!" exclaimed Peter, beginning to see that Hugh was making fun of him.

"Well, if pullets are girls," said Hugh, quietly, "I presume they look at the man they like the best."

"That isn't what I mean," said Peter, "and it wouldn't be true if it was. I've seen it tried. I remember one training day,—but"—and Peter suddenly recollected himself, "but it was a good many years ago—before you come here, I guess. What I want to find out is whether I'm right on a man's p'ints."

"What do *you* think they are?" said Hugh, becoming the questioner.

"Well," responded Peter, squinting at the rafters, and slashing his shears high into the air, "if you was walking out some day, and there should come along a darn pretty, black-eyed girl, and should look you square in the face, and smile jest as sweet as she could, and say 'how do you do?' and she never had done this before, and you should go home and think it all over, and couldn't find anything about you to make her change her mind, but a fair pair of legs and a face that wasn't very bad (and Peter drew his hand gently over his own), wouldn't you say that legs and face was the word?"

"I should think they might be," replied Hugh, with utter good-nature.

"Think? Don't you know it?" cried Peter, becoming vehement so suddenly as to surprise himself; and then, with the idea that his violence might compromise his interests, he apologetically added, "but perhaps you never thought of these things so much as I have. I've thought of 'em any quantity. I don't s'pose you'd believe me, if I should begin to tell you half of the time I spend in thinking of them—I don't, that's a fact, now." And Peter closed with an expression of entire placability, which said plainer than words could say, that he should not blame Hugh in the least were he to be incredulous, in case the real facts should be divulged.

"We'll call it so, at least," said Hugh, very positively. "Now go on."

"Let's see—where was I?" said Peter, slowly and thoughtfully snapping his shears. "Oh, yes! I remember now. Well, s'pose a little while after that you should meet the same girl again, and as quick as you see her coming you should straighten up, and brush up your hair, and go by her something like this" (and Peter strode across his apartment with a dashing swing and a complacent smirk), "and she should look sweeter than ever, and kind o' look at you all over, as if she felt tickled and wanted to say something and darsn't, and you knew, jest as well as you wanted to know, that your legs and face was the best part of you, what should you think then?" And Peter snapped his shears triumphantly, and reiterated his question—"Say! what should you think then?"

"Well, what did *you* think?" inquired Hugh, smiling.

"I didn't say it was me, did I?" said Peter, with a flattered and half fatuous look of cunning.

"No, but it was you, wasn't it, Peter?"

"Now what made you think so?" inquired Peter, very much pleased; "what made you think it was me? What did you guess by? Perhaps, if you'll tell me, I'll tell you whether you was right."

"Oh! I knew; I'm not going to flatter you; you're proud enough now."

"Hugh Parsons, give us your hand," exclaimed Peter, grasping the man's slender and shrinking palm, and shaking it violently. "You're the best feller I ever see in my life. It's true now—you needn't say you ain't. I know all the rest of 'em. They ain't anything. Land ahead! they think they are, but I've shingled their hair this five years, and I never found it out, and perhaps you don't think so, but if *I* hav'n't found it out, there ain't many fellers that would."

"Now tell me who the girl was," said Hugh, as soon as his aching hand was released, and carefully wiped upon his handkerchief.

"Between you and I," replied Peter, "it's the pullet that I think of taking."

"Have you said anything to her about it?" inquired Hugh.

"Land ahead! I hav'n't got to that yet; and between you and I that's what I want to see you for. Now you see you've got a smooth tongue, and nobody is afraid of you; and you can do what I want better than anybody else—now you needn't say you can't, for I know you can—and the iron being hot on both sides, all you've got to do is to strike."

"But perhaps I don't know the girl," said Hugh.

"Yes, you do. I guess she kind o' likes you, as a friend, you know. I don't s'pose you're jest sech a feller as she'd want for a husband; not that there's any good reason for it, but she's a large girl, and women have queer ideas about such things, you know," said Peter, patronizingly.

Hugh's eye flashed with a sudden contempt, but he was one who never quarrelled, and so, letting the insult pass, he said, somewhat impatiently, "Come! give us her name."

"Well, don't be in a hurry," responded Peter. "You're the greatest feller to go off half cocked that ever I see in all my life."

"But it's almost bed-time," said Hugh.

"Land ahead! so 'tis," said Peter. "We must be getting along—that's a fact. Now, Hugh, you're first rate at guessing, and before I tell you, I want you should tell me what M. W. stands for?"

"Mehitabel Warriner?" said Hugh, interrogatively, and with a smile of amusement that he did not try to restrain.

"Didn't hit!" said Peter, looking up at the rafters. "Guess again."

"My wife?"

"That's it! by the jumping Moses!" exclaimed Peter, bursting into voiceless convulsions of laughter, and becoming so far mirthfully excited that he seized Hugh by the shoulders, and shook him till he laughed in self-defence.

"How come you to think of that? My wife!" And he stretched up towards the ridge-pole, and swung his shears three times around his head. "Land ahead!" pursued Peter, still unable to work off his admiration of Hugh's inventive powers, and his delight with the pleasantly ominous coincidence, "I'd no idea you was up to that sort of thing."

"My wife—Mary Woodcock," said Hugh, interrupting him.

"No—guess again," said Peter, looking up at the rafters with one eye, and at Hugh out of the corner of the other.

"Mary Woodcock," reiterated Hugh.

Peter plunged into a snicker, and came up with, "Hugh Parsons, you're the greatest feller I ever see in my life. Now about the business."

"What do you want?"

"Well, I want you to go to a certain girl," said Peter, slowly, and with an extremely sly look of intelligence, "and tell her that you know of a young man—you can say what you're a mind to about him—you know me and you know my p'ints—who has seen her several times, and every time he sees her he thinks that he has got a friend that would think everything of her, if she would be kind enough to take a notion to him, provided she hasn't done it before this. Tell her she's seen him, and likes his looks, and that if it wasn't because he was bashful, he would have been to see her some time ago, and finished up the business. When she asks you who the young man is that has got the friend that thinks so much of her, you can tell her it's me—Peter Trimble."

"What if she asks who your friend is?" inquired Hugh.

"Well, you must go then by what you see. If she acts as if she was disappointed, or says she won't have anything to do with him, you can be pretty sure, you see, that there ain't anybody in the plantation that she likes besides me, 'cause if there was, she wouldn't know but it was jest the one I was making believe I was after for her, and she'd be careful not to tread on her own shoestrings. But if she acts tickled, which I don't believe she will between you and I,—I don't now 'pon my word—then it's all day with me, but you see she won't know then that I'm hit, and no won't anybody else."

When Peter closed, Hugh was looking at him in blank astonishment, for as he talked, his eye grew bright with an intense cunning, his face seemed to contract to a small, sharp mass of features, his form was bent earnestly forward, and his whole expression was so widely different from anything that he had previously exhibited, that Hugh sat for a minute wondering and unresponsive, while Peter, without moving, looked steadily in his eye. The moment that Peter began to consult his own safety from ridicule and raillery, a vein of his original nature was struck, and the old cunning bubbled up as pure and fresh as ever.

"Don't you see?" continued Peter, breaking the silence. "If you tell her it's me to start with, perhaps she wouldn't let you know that she liked me, if she did ever so much. May be she wouldn't like anybody to know it; and then again, if she didn't happen to like me, she would go and tell on't, and the boys would raise thunder with me."

"Then you want to get your head in, and keep your neck out," said Hugh, regaining his voice.

"That's it! By George! you've hit it. Now you talk," said Peter, with enthusiasm.

"Do you really wish to have me go through with all this manœuvring for you?" inquired Hugh, seriously.

"Land ahead!" exclaimed Peter, with a disappointed air, "I thought you'd like it."

"I'm not one of that kind," replied Hugh.

"You ain't going to back out now?" said Peter, with an anxious interrogation.

"I must, positively."

Peter looked at Hugh, and his lip began to tremble. He undertook to say something, but he broke down, and putting his head between his knees, he began to sob like a baby.

"Peter," said Hugh, in a kind and relenting mood, "I didn't suppose you cared so much about it as this. I'll try to do what I can for you."

"Will you, though?" said Peter, jumping up and grasping his hand, the scant tears in his grey eyes changing from those of disappointment to those of sudden joy. "I was mighty 'fraid you wan't going to. Between you and I, I was beginning to feel about as cheap as turnips, 'pon my word I was. Any feller that had seen me a minute ago, and should come in now, would think I'd had a rich uncle die, wouldn't he, Hugh?" and Peter pitched head first into a snicker, and taking Hugh by the shoulders he shook him till he cried, "Oh, stop, Peter, for pity's sake."

"There's great times ahead for us," continued Peter, and then remembering that for at least fifteen minutes his shears had remained idle, he slashed the air forth and back furiously for awhile, and then subsided into a steady clip, as if he were shearing a sheep.

"By the way," continued Peter, changing the subject, "I want to show you a hone I've got. It come from the Bay last week, and it's a hone, now, I tell you. Look at it" (and Peter lifted the lid of his chest, and drew out the article). "You've no idea of the difference there is in hones. Some cut away the steel fast, and leave a hair edge, and some kind o' gum down."

"What are you going to do with that?" inquired Hugh.

"Perhaps *you* wont believe it," said Peter, "but in a year from this time I shall hone every razor in the plantation. It ain't everybody that can hone a razor. You see, they don't carry it even from heel to p'int, and then there ain't half of 'em that knows when it's done. They hone it clear by. If you'll bring your razor here some rainy day, I'll show you all about it, and perhaps your hair will want cutting by that time, and between you and I, though it's none of my business, I don't think a little shingling would have done it any hurt to-night. Who in time cut your hair last?"

Before Hugh could answer this question in any way, Peter gave another furious lunge into a snicker, as if a sudden thought had visited him with a blow upon the back of his head, and, pointing to four long poles or rods, bound with regularly recurring strips of old felt, said, "Did you ever hear anything about my quilting frames?"

Hugh assured him that he never did.

"Well, you see," said Peter, "everybody has to do more or less quilting, but nobody has quilting frames. They have to send round for 'em, and I r'ally s'pose, if the truth was known, that there ain't in this settlement such a set as mine; I don't, now, 'pon my word, if 'twas the last thing I had to say. Well, everybody comes for mine, and other people's quilting frames ain't anywhere. I s'pose if the truth was known there's been quilts enough put together on them sticks to reach acrost the river."

"How do you make it pay?" inquired Hugh.

"Land ahead! It's pay enough to have 'em come after 'em, and go right by a house where they keep 'em, for the sake of getting mine. Four little staddles with the bark off ain't quilting frames, and the women know it. Besides, between you and I, they always invite me to the quilting, and I've been home with three girls since I've had them things, that, 'pon my word, I believe would have gone home with other fellers if they hadn't wanted to borrow."

How much longer Peter would have continued in this strain had he not been disturbed, it is impossible to tell, but just as he finished the quilting frames, the chamber door opened, and two boys whom he kept from quarrelling every night, by sleeping between them, came growling up stairs.

"You'd better put your hat on," said Peter to Hugh aloud, "you may catch cold after losing such a fleece," and then added in an under tone, "the old folks are going to bed down stairs, but you keep your hat on, and go right through the room. They'll think it's all right."

Hugh felt, as the interview closed, extremely irritated in the position into which his good-nature had led him. He had been amused with Peter's oddities, but disgusted with his low cunning and shallowness, and he was vexed with himself for having agreed to serve him in an enterprise every way preposterous and hopeless. Peter saw the cloud upon his brow, but it was too late to attempt its removal (although he had his hand upon an eight-bladed knife, which he had intended to exhibit, as it was furnished with a corkscrew, which several of the neighbors had used with entire success), and following his visitor down stairs told him as he passed through the kitchen to be careful about taking cold. Poor Hugh, as he walked home, felt worse and worse, and wondered more and more why he had not had the strength to stand up like a man, and tell the silly coxcomb the truth in regard to himself and his plans. And then to think that he was the tool of such a fellow—that he had agreed to intercede for him as a friend with one who, he could not help but feel, would despise the mediator for his office even more than his employer for his impudence, was too much for his equanimity, and he went home and tossed nervously upon his bed all night.

CHAPTER XXI.

After the house of Mr. Moxon was built a room was finished in one corner for a study. This looked out upon the street, and being furnished with a snug fire-place afforded the occupant a pleasant view, whether he confined his attention within the room or dissipated it in looking abroad. In this room the minister spent the most of his time. The late passenger at night often saw his shadow on the wall or curtain, as he paced up and down his little apartment, or observed him at the window looking out into the night or gazing abstractedly at the stars. After occupying himself at his sermons during the day he often gave himself up to reveries, which possessed him until his fire had expired in its own ashes, and he was reminded of his bed by a feverish head and a cold and benumbed frame.

It was here that he brooded over the trials and disappointments of his life. It was here that he wept over the afflictions of his children, and speculated upon the cause of the calamity with which they had been visited. It was here that in weakness and blindness he wrestled with the angel of God in prayer. It was here that dim suspicions entered his mind, coming in like shadows and growing into form and fulness under his searching vision, until the door at which they entered became too small for their egress, and they remained in throngs.

It was during a crisp and cool evening in the latter part of autumn that Mr. Moxon, having concluded the labors of the day, drew his chair before the fire and subsided into one of his frequent reveries. He went back in memory to the time when Woodcock was a resident of the plantation, and as he called up the scene near Holyoke's house where that individual visited him with personal indignity, and thought of the girl who in a moment of blind passion inflicted a wound whose scar seemed to be always thrusting itself into his sight, the old flush of shame and humiliation mantled his face and thrilled through every sensitive fibre of his frame. This was the sorest spot in all his experience, and one which he could never touch without the keenest pain.

As the pang struck him and diffused its subtle frenzy he rose from his chair with a hurried sigh, and after pacing up and down his apartment for a few minutes, stopped before the window and looked out. He had stood but a moment when a singular figure crossed his vision. It was that of a man clothed like an Indian, but clumsy and moving with a different gait. The man had evidently been standing at a short distance from the window, and was induced to move by the impression that the minister saw him. He was, however, soon out of sight, and Mr. Moxon forgot the circumstance as he resumed his seat at the fire.

Soon the old subject recurred, and, this time, his thoughts stopped with Mary Woodcock. From the time she had bitten him until then, her act had never been alluded to by him. She had grown up to womanhood, and with such a determined character that he did not choose to violate his promise to her father not to molest her. But he could not give up the desire to detect the agent in the affliction of his children, nor the suspicion that she was the guilty party.

At that time, sorcery and witchcraft were prevalent in England, and had been, for the previous fifty years. He had written for and received books, giving the details of numerous cases, and had sought for light upon the subject in all possible directions. While, upon this occasion, he was wondering what means could be resorted to for the detection of Mary Woodcock, he recalled the singular communication which has already been mentioned as having fallen into his hands. Immediately rising, he went to his desk, and, opening a drawer, withdrew a small package. Taking off the wrapper, he selected the communication alluded to, and replaced the package in the drawer.

As he was turning to leave the desk, he knocked from a shelf an apple—one of the first fruits of the new orchards of the plantation, which had been presented to him—but, instead of returning it to its place, he took it with him to the fire, and set it upon the hearth to roast. He sat down, and opened the communication. It was evidently written with a pencil of common lead, upon a strip of birch bark:

"*Mary:—Be gentle and good, and please your master, and you shall be helped by one you cannot see.*"

These words, clumsily traced and sadly misspelled, comprised the entire text of the wonderful manuscript. The minister inserted his knife under a layer of the bark, and, separating it, threw it upon the coals. The flash from it was as instantaneous as if it had been gunpowder—so sharp and powerful that he started with affright, and retreated to his desk with the communication, in order that it might be beyond the reach of the flame.

He had hardly reseated himself, when he heard a rap at the door, and, on opening it, greeted and admitted a resident of the plantation with whom the reader has not yet made an acquaintance. This man was Deacon Samuel Chapin, a tall, austere-looking individual, whom the minister saluted with much warmth, and who, on advancing into the little study, looked around, with a not unpleasant expression in his keen grey eyes, and said, "It seems pleasant, now and then, to visit the place where you prepare the food for the flock of Christ. I warrant I have disturbed you in meditations which belong to the whole of your little Israel."

"No, sir, sit down," said Mr. Moxon pleasantly, "I have been thinking of something more strictly selfish and personal."

Deacon Chapin's eyes looked pleased, while his face still maintained its austere expression, as he accepted the minister's invitation, and, slowly rubbing his hands before the fire, said, "I esteem your society a great privilege, Mr. Moxon, and shall be very happy to enjoy it, if I can do so without disturbing you, and being the means of sending leanness into the bones of the other members of your flock."

The reader will at once perceive that Deacon Chapin was a good man, and thoroughly understood the road to his minister's heart. He did not become a settler at Agawam until several years after the first planters, but his severe manners, pliable tongue, and shrewd personal policy, had carried him along rapidly in the path of advancement. On being made a deacon of the church, he had moved for the erection of a meeting-house, and it had risen, with its six blank looking windows, and its two turrets—a belfry and a watch-tower—and had become the place for holding meetings upon the Sabbath, and all the public assemblies of the plantation. He had been the means, too, of bringing several members of the church under wholesome discipline. In short, he had been an active man, in everything pertaining to the spiritual well-being of the community, a strict adherent to orthodox doctrine, and one who, in coming from the Bay, brought the spirit of the Bay with him.

It was noticed that after the meetings of the plantation were removed from the house of Mr. Pynchon to the new meeting-house, the influence of the latter gentleman in the minor affairs of the settlement had declined, but no one supposed that Deacon Chapin had an eye to this result in obtaining the erection of the house. Everybody knew him for a thrifty man—a man who slid into prosperity and preferment with a kind of facility that betrayed a pushing will and a track made smooth by a never-tiring urbanity. The young men and young women were afraid of him. The boys took off their hats to him by instinct, as they had been taught to take them off in obeisance to the minister, the magistrate, and Mr. Holyoke.

Deacon Chapin sat and rubbed his hands with pleasant dignity before Mr. Moxon's fire, after his considerate expression of care for the church, and waited for the minister to begin the conversation.

"I have long desired," said the latter, hesitatingly, "to say something to you upon a subject which interests me deeply, but have been prevented by the wish not to burden others with trials sent upon me."

Dea. Chapin made a bow, said nothing, and kept slowly rubbing his hands before the fire.

"You have probably heard of occurrences which took place previous to your settlement in Agawam."

Dea. Chapin bowed again, as if he perfectly understood the allusion, and would spare the minister the pain of referring to them more definitely.

"You doubtless know something of the trials I have experienced in my family since your residence here."

Dea. Chapin bowed again, and, shifting in his seat, leaned his ear towards the minister, in a way quite expressive of a desire to learn something more.

"The children are different," said Mr. Moxon, instantly seeming to catch the deacon's meaning, as the deacon had caught his own. "Martha is extremely wild at times, and is open and free in her accusations of the one who afflicts her. I have told no one but you of this, but the people, I understand, have fastened their suspicions upon the same individual."

Dea. Chapin bowed again, and turned his face directly towards the minister, as if he expected that gentleman to unbosom himself entirely.

"Rebekah, on the contrary, is gentle, and seems to be in some mysterious manner connected with her sister. It has been so from the first. They seem to suffer together, though in different kind and degree. I have read extensively in regard to witchcraft, and the open manifestations of the Adversary among men, and I have been convinced, for ten years, that Satan is afflicting me through my children, and them through the wicked agency of individuals in this plantation."

"It will hardly be necessary for me," said the deacon blandly, "to remind my minister that whom the Lord loveth he chasteneth, and scourgeth every son whom he receiveth."

Mr. Moxon drew a painful sigh, as he replied, "It is long since I have been in the habit of appropriating to myself the promises of God. It seems as if His threatenings were intended for me, and they hang above my soul always, as if ready to fall upon and crush me."

"But you must remember," said the deacon, "that if you were not a true branch of Christ, you would be taken away. The branches that bear fruit are those which are purged, that they may bring forth more fruit."

Now the deacon was not consciously insincere in his address to the minister. He was in the habit of saying comforting things, and pleasant things, to those who held position and influence. It was the habit of his life. It did him good, and it did them good; and his policy in this matter had wrought, in deed and in truth, a very good work in the plantation. Many a man went about his business from an interview with Dea. Chapin with a self-respect that was a rarity in his experience, and played a better and more dignified part in life, until the influence of the interview had departed. Some flattering or encouraging word, some expression of respect, or some marked attention, always made impressively grateful by the dignified politeness of its style of exhibition, had a marvellous effect upon all with whom he came in contact.

It is true that it all made the deacon's path more pleasant and easy, and gave him consideration and power with all, but few ever dreamed that he had an eye to his own interests in the premises. The minister knew him, and was glad to see him. The deacon knew the minister, and, while he really had a desire to cheer him, and had brought honestly before him the comforts of religion, he had also a desire to learn certain things which the minister knew, and with that object definitely in view had thus far pursued his course and conversation.

"You spoke," said the deacon, "of one individual whom you suspected of being the agent of Satan in your affliction;" and he paused, as if that were a direct and definite question.

"*His* daughter," replied the minister.

The deacon threw up his chin decisively, as if it were a confirmation of his own suspicions.

"Just before you entered," said Mr. Moxon, "I was examining a little communication which you probably heard of at the time it was discovered. Perhaps you would like to look at it again," and he rose and handed to him the mysterious note.

The deacon read it through, held it against the light, and then inquired of the minister whether he knew the hand-writing.

"I do not," replied the minister. "It is not that of any man in this plantation. What do you think of it? Who is he whom she cannot see? What is he going to help her to do? Who is her master? What does he mean by being gentle and good?"

These questions were pronounced at little intervals, the deacon bowing at each, as if he were swallowing it for digestion. When they were concluded, he simply said, "It's all very strange, is it not?"—and reaching down to the minister's apple, where it was sputtering and becoming brown before the fire, he turned it round by the stem in order to expose the other side.

"I suppose, of course," said the deacon, as he resumed his position, "that you have talked this all over with your friend Mr. Pynchon. He is somewhat advanced in years, and grey hairs should bring wisdom."

"I formerly communicated with him upon the subject," replied the minister, "but he gave me neither comfort nor instruction."

"Perhaps we expect too much of him," suggested the deacon. "He has a great many cares, and I understand that he spends a great deal of time in study. Do you know anything of the book he has recently written?"

"Yes—I have seen something of it," replied Mr. Moxon.

"Something which will edify the church—something sound and well adapted to these Zions in the wilderness, I presume," continued the deacon, affirmatively and suggestively together.

"Doctrinal, mostly," said the minister.

"Orthodox, I'll warrant. Ah! that's a very fine old man!" and the deacon rubbed his hands and pushed his chair back from the hearth, as if, with such a generous glow of friendship in his bosom, the fire was a little too much for him.

Mr. Moxon moved uneasily in his seat, for the deacon, when he resolutely set about boring for a secret, never released him till the fountain was reached, and had relinquished its treasure. He understood him on this tack in the progress of conversation, as well as on those which had preceded it, but he hesitated to speak fully of matters concerning which he knew it became him to preserve silence; so he simply assented to the latter clause of the deacon's exclama tion without any allusion to the former.

"Man's inability?" suggested the deacon, with an inquiring turn of the head.

"No. Oh! no."

"Depravity?"

"Not if I remember correctly."

"Atonement?" and the deacon turned directly around, and looked the minister in the face.

"No—that is—not exactly. The subject is connected with the atonement, somewhat intimately, to be sure, but—" and the minister hesitated whether to put a stop to the conversation where it was, or to go on, and reveal what he knew.

"That is a favorite subject with the old man," interrupted the deacon. "What view did he take?"

"Well, sir," proceeded the minister, reluctantly, "on the subject of the nature of Christ's sufferings, he has not advanced and defended the views which prevail in the Bay churches. I differ with him, and perhaps it is my duty to make his views a matter of inquiry in the church,—perhaps I have been remiss."

"It cannot be anything very heretical, I know," remarked the attentive deacon. "It would not be like him to conceive it, nor like you to conceal it. What are his peculiar views?"

"Well, if I understood him, he does not believe that Christ suffered the essential torments of hell for the salvation of men, and contends that God did not impute the sins of men to him."

"I think you must have misunderstood him," said the deacon positively, and with every manifestation of charitable confidence in the magistrate.

"That could hardly have been," replied the minister, "for I argued the matter with him at length."

"What did he say? What *could* he say?"

"Well, he said it was an absurdity to accuse a God of justice, while vindicating his justice, of imputing sin to an innocent being; and that hell torment, being directly connected with a consciousness of personal guilt, could never be experienced by Jesus Christ, from the fact that personally he was never guilty. I found it a difficult matter to overthrow his subtle reasonings, and left him, praying that he might fall into no fatal errors."

The deacon looked for a long minute into the fire, and then, with a sigh, remarked that it was strange how the best minds in the world would sometimes be left to the entertainment of dangerous heresies. He thought it was a lesson to the ministry, on the importance of keeping before the people constantly the great doctrines of the Gospel in all their simplicity and purity. He had been running back in recollection to see if Mr. Moxon had preached a sermon against this peculiar form of heresy, and ended by informing that gentleman that he had doubtless preached upon the subject on some Sabbath when he (the deacon) was detained at home by sickness. Mr. Moxon colored slightly at the reproof, and confessed that he never had felt called upon to preach directly to Mr. Pynchon, as, if he could not convince him of his error in a personal argument, it would hardly avail him more to engage in a pulpit demonstration against his private opinions.

"That would depend something upon what the book was written for," replied the deacon. "If it was written for private gratification, to be shown only to friends, it would doubtless save scandal in the church to refrain from its exposure. I presume that Mr. Pynchon would hardly think of publishing his book."

"On the contrary," replied the minister, desperately, for he saw that it must come, "the book has long been in the hands of the printers in London, and may be expected at the Bay within a short time."

Deacon Chapin shook his head slowly as he sat gazing into the fire, and said, "I'm sorry—very sorry," and then, as he had sifted this matter sufficiently, he suddenly remembered that he had drawn the minister away from the subject upon which he had commenced, and turning to him, he observed that gentleman engaged in snuffing suspiciously at the piece of birch bark which he had not yet returned to the desk.

"Excuse me, sir," said the deacon gravely, but with a smile in his eyes, "are you on the scent?"

The minister, without noticing the attempt at raillery, handed the deacon the bark manuscript, with a nod which meant "Smell of it yourself."

The deacon did so, and exclaimed "Musk!"

"He's around to-night," remarked the minister nervously. "I feel him myself, and so do my children, I presume. You will find this scent all over the house. You will find it, I have no doubt, in the very centre of that apple, which has been roasting before the fire ever since you have been here."

The deacon stooped to lift the apple, and drawing out his knife, cut it in two. The stench reached his nostrils before the apple itself was half way there, and impulsively he dashed the whole upon the hearth, where it lay, crushed and steaming, and filling the room with its odor to a greatly offensive degree. The man was evidently astonished. It was such a demonstration as he had not dreamed of witnessing, and one which he regretted to have witnessed. But his equanimity did not forsake him, and he coolly asked the minister whom he alluded to.

"Martha, and those generally who are bewitched, call him the Black Man," replied the minister. "I have no doubt that he is one of the emissaries of the Adversary, and that he has been drawn here by our conversation about this piece of birch bark," and rising, the minister returned it to the desk.

He had hardly reseated himself when his oldest daughter, in a loose night robe of white, and with her long black hair dangling upon her shoulders, threw the door hurriedly open, and, gliding into the study, went directly to the fire, seated herself close up to the ashes upon a stick of wood, and gazed with a vacant stare into the flames.

The movement was accomplished so quickly and so silently, that both of the witnesses were entirely absorbed in the vision, and remained quietly in their seats. Mr. Moxon looked at his daughter a moment, and then, covering his eyes with his hand, gave his mind to silent prayer.

It was a strange, wild sight. The girl was pale, and her countenance seemed almost deathlike in the contrast with her black hair and eyes; and as the flame flashed high in the chimney, and fluttered about the jambs, and painted dim and uneasy shadows upon the walls and ceiling of the room, and irradiated her impassive features with its trembling and fitful glories, the imagination of the deacon became inflamed with fears which he could not repress. He felt almost as if he were within the power of the Adversary himself. Every hair upon his head prickled with a preternatural apprehension, and he felt himself shivering and the cold perspiration starting from his forehead. Before the power of speech came to him, and while, half fascinated, he sat absorbed in the weird vision, the girl whispered faintly, "Where is my supper?" Then, as if her question had been answered to her mind, she turned around upon her seat, with an expression of delight upon her tongue, but with no corresponding expression upon her face, and dropping her hand suddenly to the hearth, took up the crushed and still steaming and offensive apple, and devoured it with a greediness that was sickening. When she had swallowed the apple, she turned again to the fire, and gazed unblinkingly into the blaze.

"Martha!" said Mr. Moxon tenderly, as he uncovered his eyes.

The girl lifted her eyes to him, but made no reply.

"Martha, what did you come in here for to-night? What made you come here?"

"I came after my supper," said the girl. "She told me to come."

"She means the one we were talking about," remarked the minister, in a side explanation to the deacon.

The deacon nodded and drew a long breath which must have filled the furthest recess of his lungs, and it was well that he received, at the moment, its fortifying influence, for, in the high tension of his nervous sensibilities, he detected a slight sound at the door, and on turning his eyes in that direction, the younger sister made her appearance, walking slowly, with her eyes fixed on some object before her. The attention of both the deacon and the father of the child became absorbed in observing the movements of Rebekah, who, with perfect serenity upon her features, advanced towards the desk, and taking up the bark manuscript, held it to her forehead, and stood motionless with it there, for several minutes.

In the meantime, Martha had risen from her seat, and, advancing towards her sister, gently removed the manuscript from her hand, replaced it upon the desk, and led her to the fire, where the two stood in a sisterly embrace, and in apparent unconsciousness of the presence of the deacon. The latter individual had seen much more than he anticipated, and was really anxious to leave the house. His superstitious fears had never been so much excited, and had never been excited on so rational a stimulant.

"Perhaps," said the deacon kindly, addressing the minister, and rising and rubbing his trembling hands, "you would prefer to be left alone with your poor children. I think I had better bid you a good evening."

The minister rose, as Deacon Chapin addressed him, and the latter observed that he was under a new and strange influence. He was deadly pale, and was trembling violently. On turning again to the children, they were observed to be similarly affected. The father drew them to him, and sank into his chair with them in his embrace, and there the three shuddered and shook together. The deacon's equanimity was fairly upset, and he began to draw his breath spasmodically, and to tremble with fear and sympathy.

Looking up, with a determination to break from a scene whose horrors were every moment increasing, his eye detected a black, grizzly face at the window, looking fixedly in upon the group. He wiped his eyes to assure himself that it was not a phantom of his excited imagination, but there it stood; and, as the fire danced in the chimney, and played upon the walls, and sent out its flashes into the darkness, it painted that face alternately with scowls and sneers, or lighted its eyes with a fiendish glare, or shaped its lips to a horrible grin. He stepped across the room to assure himself that it was not an illusion wrought by the imperfect glass, but the face remained. He would then have left the house, but he did not wish to encounter the owner of that face in the darkness.

"Do you know that there is a very singular-looking face at the window?" said the deacon softly, bending down to the minister's ear.

"I know that the tormentor is very near," replied the minister with a renewed shiver. "I feel his presence, and these poor children feel it even more than myself. We can do nothing but submit, and give ourselves to prayer."

The deacon turned his attention to the window again, and there still hung the face, paling and flushing, and scowling and grinning fantastically in the fire-light, but the eyes were evidently looking at an object on the desk, near the window, and did not observe, for a moment, their observer. In an instant, a pane of glass was burst through, and a rough arm, reaching to the desk, snatched the dark manuscript, and withdrawing it, disappeared with the face in the darkness. The children uttered a wild scream as the glass flew out and came tinkling across the floor, which was echoed by the retreating visitant with a peal of derisive laughter; and that, in turn, seemed to be echoed by intermingled screams and laughter that were repeated from the walls of houses, or came more faintly back from distant hill sides.

When the last hollow murmur had died away, the children rubbed their eyes, looked up in surprise upon the face of the deacon, then down upon their night dresses, and were beginning to cry, when their father hurriedly led them from the room.* The visitor could not leave, of course, until the return of the minister, and so stood, hat in hand, in the middle of the little study, until that gentleman came feebly back, and closed the door behind him. They stood face to face for a moment, when the deacon, having been thoroughly melted into sympathy, the two impulsively laid their hands on each other's shoulders, and bowed before a common emotion. The embrace was not long, but it did the minister good, for he thought there was one heart at least thoroughly won to an apprehension and appreciation of his trials.

The deacon did not linger, but, with a few kind words of counsel and sympathy, took his leave, and, with a sense of relief, drew a long breath again in the open air. The coolness of the night restored tone to his trembling nerves, and as he bent his steps homewards, he found himself calmly revolving and analysing what he had seen. There was something in it very mysterious—that was certain. There

* It can hardly be necessary, at this day, to suggest animal magnetism as the explanation of the strange phenomena connected with this family. That this mysterious agency or influence has always had an intimate connexion with witchcraft, associated in a greater or less degree with deception and delusion, will not, it is presumed, be denied.

was such a thing as witchcraft—everybody admitted that—and this was a genuine case. What was the true policy in regard to its treatment? Was it best for him—Deacon Chapin—and for the settlement generally, to engage in a vigorous crusade against the foul sin, and be the means of expurgating the community of it, or to keep in the background, and wait for the indication of occasions? He would think of it after he had slept.

When the deacon arrived at his home he found a neighbor waiting to transact some business, and met him with a dignity of manner and austerity of countenance that characterized him in his usual intercourse,—with not a trace of the emotions by which, within the previous hour, he had been agitated. The shrewd and pleasant eyes moved calmly in their sockets, the little word that should make that man's heart feel warm all the way home—warm towards the world in general, and Deacon Chapin in particular—was said, the bargain was closed, and the neighbor was on his homeward way, smiling and talking pleasantly to himself.

When the deacon calmly closed his eyes in sleep that night, the minister rose from his chair, replenished his fire, and until after midnight his sturdy shadow mingled upon the wall with those that play hide-and-seek with the freakish flashes of the fire-light.

CHAPTER XXII.

Two or three days after the interview between Peter Trimble and Hugh Parsons, those individuals accidentally met. The former was ready for the meeting, but the latter was not. Peter had arranged his inquiries for every possible contingency, and (there being several individuals present) he asked Hugh if he had "been to Spain." On receiving the reply that he had not, he asked him if he had "seen the queen." Having obtained the same reply, he inquired if it were not about time he was taking the voyage. Hugh obligingly told him that perhaps it was, and Peter, as he parted from him, remarked that he should think so.

The next day the two met again, when Peter asked whether Hugh had succeeded in "treeing the squirrel" which he understood he was after, and propounded various other inquiries based on that peculiarly happy figure of speech. Hugh saw that he was to have no peace until something had been done towards fulfilling the mission he had so foolishly assumed, and desperately determined to call on Mary Woodcock, and make known his unpleasant business.

On a convenient evening, therefore, Hugh made his toilet with such taste as his means would allow, walked to the house of Mr. Holyoke, and hurriedly knocking at the door, as if apprehensive that his courage would fail him should he delay, he stood with a pale face and a throbbing heart awaiting the answer to his summons. The door was opened by Mary herself, and Hugh could not choose but notice the delight that flashed in her dark eye, and illuminated—as the lightning a cloud—her strong and expressive features, when she took his hand, and invited him into the house.

Fortune had favored Hugh with the choice of an evening when Holyoke and his wife were absent, and in Mary's smile there was a satisfaction and delight that were based upon an instant comprehension of the circumstances of the visit. Mary retained Hugh's passive hand within her own as he crossed the threshold, and then she led him to a seat with a gallantry and tenderness of manner which were the appropriate expression of the sentiments which possessed her. When she had placed Hugh's hat upon the table she returned to the fire, and taking a seat where she could look him fairly in the face, regarded him with an affectionate admiration which she took no pains to conceal. Hugh timidly lifted his eyes to her face, and for the first time in his life thought her the most beautiful woman he had ever seen. Instead of being abashed as he had expected to be in her presence, he suddenly felt his heart going out to her in confidence and trust, and self-possession came with the assurance that his spirit was in harmony with her own.

Mary inquired for his health and that of his father's family, wondered he had never called upon her before, frankly declared her delight with the opportunity of an interview, and then referred to the day on which she saw him in the training band, when (she told him without reserve) she was "looking at him all the time."

There was nothing in Hugh's nature that revolted at this forwardness. On the contrary, he felt that he had never previously met a woman so agreeable. There was something in her frankness, her self-confidence, her strength and fearlessness, that impressed him with admiration, and as he sat and gazed upon her, and listened to her impulsive utterances, all the women he had ever known sank to mere nothings in his estimation.

Just as a faint idea of the real character of the impression she was making upon him crept into his consciousness, the object of his visit obtruded itself, and in dissipating a beautiful dream which had begun to overshadow him quite upset his equanimity.

"I came," said Hugh, determined to keep his promise at all hazards, and blushing to his temples, "on a queer errand, and I hope you will not blame me for it, for I really could not get along very well without promising to come."

"Did you wish to see Mr. Holyoke?" inquired Mary—adding, "if you do, he is not at home, and his wife is absent also."

"No, I came to see you, and I hope you will not be offended with me for coming on such an errand."

"Just think of my being offended with *you!*" exclaimed Mary, bursting into a hearty ringing laugh which disturbed the sleeping children in the next room. Then, as her merriment subsided, she bade Hugh get rid of his errand as quickly as possible and fear nothing.

"Why, you see," said Hugh, "I was down to see Peter Trimble the other night—he wanted me to come—and he wanted to have me go to see you, and tell you that he had a friend that thought a good deal of you—"

Hugh paused. A pair of glowing eyes were flashing full upon him, and the sense of the utter meanness of his position and the subterfuge of which he had become the mouthpiece, with a consciousness that Mary saw and detested both, overcame him with shame, and with a burning face he dropped his eyes, while his tongue refused the performance of its office.

Mary rose to her feet, and, giving vent to her exuberant contempt by a vigorous onset with the tongs upon the back log of the fire, she turned around with the tongs still in her hand, and exclaimed, "Peter Trimble is a fool! A spindle-shanked, squash-headed fool! And if you are so good at doing errands, I wish you would have the kindness to tell him just what I have said; and, while you are about it, tell him that if he sends any more of his impudent messages to me, I'll slap his ugly face for him."

Having said this with an angrily impulsive utterance, Mary gave the back log another punch, set the tongs in the corner, and looked at Hugh in silence.

That individual was dumbfoundered, and his admiration of the woman before him was fast dying out, when her countenance relaxed from its harsh expression, and, breaking into a low, musical laugh, she said, "Hugh Parsons, how could you let that poor puppy impose upon you so?" Then she laughed again, and bent down and looked into Hugh's eyes—conscious of having offended his sensibilities, but determined to win a smile of forgiveness before another step was taken. "Did I scare you?" said she, resuming her chair, and laying her hand upon his arm. "Well, you can't imagine how much I despise that Peter, and you do not know what reason I have to hate him. He has no memory, and he imagines I have none. It made me mad to think he should suppose it possible for me to show him anything more than common politeness, and madder still to see that he made you a pack-horse of his impudence, as well as his lies."

"I was afraid it would offend you," said Hugh, "but he seemed to feel so badly about it that I couldn't refuse him."

"Hush! hush! hush!" exclaimed Mary, tapping her finger upon Hugh's lip. "Don't tell me any more, or you'll make me mad again!"

"You really don't wish me to carry the message to him which you just now gave me," said Hugh, deprecatingly.

"Oh, no!" replied the girl; "I'll tell you what to say to him. Say that I have given my heart to another, and that he must forget me," and Mary laughed outright at the idea of her sending such a message to such a man. "If he asks you who it is," added Mary, "tell him you do not know, but that what I say is true."

As the girl closed, Hugh rose to his feet, his errand being finished, and, as he met the direct gaze of her marvellous eyes—bright with an unwonted excitement, searching for sympathy down into the very depths of his soul, and pouring out upon him (as he felt) an influence which, though strange to him, found just as strange a response within him, he trembled in every fibre of his frame—trembled under a power all-pervading in its effect, prostrating for the moment his will, and shaking the very foundations of his being.

A strange feeling crept into his heart, as he stood there, looking Mary in the face—a feeling that he was in the shadow of a nature stronger than his own—that that shadow was his home—that he was not in will and purpose, in thought and feeling, in strength and determination, a man. These emotions were quickly experienced, and those more indefinite and confused succeeded, so that Mary's hearty grasp at parting, and his promise to call again, and tell her how Peter received her message, were matters that were remembered rather than realized.

Hugh found himself in the open air, in a state of mind bordering upon insanity. Her eyes were still looking into his, her laugh still rang in his ears, her storm of contemptuous passion swept wildly through his memory, and every artery was throbbing with a passion as new as it was delicious. His heart, with a truthfulness which he could not doubt, had told him the secret of her own, and oh! how precious was that secret. He longed to get home—to get into his room—to lock his door, and think it all over—to surround himself with it as a cloud in which he might bathe—to drink it in as if it were nectar—and tremblingly to open the door that stood between him and the future, and look upon the charmed land.

Perfectly absorbed in his new thoughts, he had proceeded but a short distance on his way homewards when Peter stepped forth from a road-side cover, and silently joined his startled messenger.

"You see," said Peter, in a subdued voice, "I go down there pretty much every night, and walk by the house, and, once in a while, I get a squint into the windows, and see her washing dishes and cutting round in the kitchen; but, land ahead! I'd no more idea of seeing you there to-night —a talking with her—I didn't s'pose you'd dare to—I didn't, 'pon my word. Says I, as I stood out there a peeking in, Hugh Parsons is the greatest feller I ever see in my life—I did now—that's jest what I said, word for word."

Hugh lifted his eyes to his voluble companion, to ascertain from his countenance, if possible, in the dim light, whether he had in any measure made himself acquainted with the result of his visit. He was interrupted in his scrutiny, and relieved in his apprehensions, by Peter himself.

"I didn't wait," continued that individual, "to hear what she had to say, for I wasn't ready; but I jest come right out under the cover here, and got myself all fixed for whatever she might say. It's a great contrivance now, I tell you, and you'll say so jest as quick as you come to see it. Where shall we go?"

"We will go to my room," said Hugh.

"Have you got a board there, or anything for me to make a few chalk marks on?" inquired Peter, and then added, "never mind about the chalk, for I always carry that in my pocket. Everybody is wanting chalk, and nobody has it. You never catch me without chalk."

"It wouldn't hurt the floor, would it?" inquired Hugh.

"Hurting the floor depends upon what woman makes up the bed. It wouldn't do to chalk the floor where I live. I've tried that, and I've always kept a loose board there ever since. Land ahead! what a row that was!" and

Peter shrugged his shoulders as the memory of the stirring occasion to which he alluded swept over him.

Hugh replied that he imagined that some method could be devised for Peter's accommodation when the room should be reached, and they walked on in silence until they arrived at the house.

A minute sufficed for the lighting of a candle, and the two proceeded up the rough stairway to Hugh's room. As Peter followed Hugh up the steps, he became possessed with a feeling of importance that he had never before experienced. His throat swelled, he held his breath with an inflated chest, he looked down upon his remarkable legs with utter complacency, and said to and within himself, "These are great doings! This pays if it doesn't amount to anything. It takes me to put these little chaps round, and get the work out of 'em." Peter terminated his interesting soliloquy by a grand flourish of his fists at Hugh's back, as he entered his chamber, and a kick into the darkness he had left behind him, both of which demonstrations were intended as an expression of his momentary exaltation above all the humanity in his immediate vicinity.

Arriving in the room, both of the young men sat down, and Peter drew forth his carefully preserved chalk. "Now," said he, "I s'pose you want to see how I'm going to fix it. Well, I'll tell you first how I come at it. She's made you one of two answers. It's either all right, or all wrong. If it's all right, there's one thing for me to do; if it's all wrong, there's another thing. You see that, don't you?"

Hugh assented.

"Well, now you see I'm standing right in the crotch of the roads, don't you?" (and Peter made chalk marks on the floor representing a road branching off into two roads, the whole being a rude representation of a hay fork.) "Up this way," continued Peter, designating the left hand path, "is where I live. Beyond there is Deacon Chapin's house, and his lot that he offers to let me plant next year to halves, and the lot that I shall clear on the commons. There's women on the road, but you can't see 'em now, and there's a pretty little house that isn't built that I own. Enough said. Now, on the right hand road, where I've been wanting to go, there's Holyoke's house, and Mary Woodcock inside of it, and all Woodcock's land, and a cabin on it, and everything all right. Now you see I'm at the crotch of the roads, don't you?"

Hugh assented again.

"Now I'm bound not to make a fuss, any way, and you see if Mary turns up her nose to me, I shall take the left hand road, turn my back upon the right, and make believe I never see it in my life; and then I shall take the deacon's lot to halves, build a house on the commons, take a wife out of them pretty women you can't see now, and have a great time. If Mary is all right, I shall take the right hand road, walk into Holyoke's house, take Mary and walk out, fix up the cabin on old Woodcock's land, and invite in my friends. Now, what do you say?" (inquired Peter, rising and taking his position upon the point he legitimately occupied upon his diagram), "shall I take the right hand or the left?"

Hugh, who, though still under the excitement induced by his interview with Mary, could not avoid being excessively amused with the measures Peter had instituted for the preservation of his equanimity, replied to Peter's inquiry with a freedom he had not anticipated—"The left."

"Forward, march!" exclaimed Peter, stepping off in the direction indicated, until he reached the wall, where he measured time upon a squeaking pair of shoes for at least a minute, with a neck and back as stiffly set as if they were made of cast iron. Then he turned briskly round, and, walking back to where Hugh was sitting, said, in a tone of curiosity rather than of apprehension, "Is it r'ally so, Hugh?"

Hugh asserted that the left was the only direction he could give him.

"Well, how did you get at it, Hugh, any way? What did she say? Tell a feller all about it. By George! you must have had a great time!"

"She said," replied Hugh, with a strange thrill in his brain, "that she had given her heart to another, and that you must forget her."

"Did she say that, though? I don't know what you think of that, Hugh, but it seems to me as if it was darn pretty. How was it? You jest say that again."

"That she had given her heart to another, and that you must forget her."

"It seems to me," continued Peter, his lip quivering, and his eyes becoming suffused, "as if that was jest about the prettiest thing I ever heard in my life. Don't you think so, now, r'ally? By George!" exclaimed the enthusiastic young man, in a burst of admiration that was accompanied by a slap upon Hugh's back, "I hope she'll do well—I do, 'pon my word."

"Yes—I hope so," responded Hugh.

"Anything said—'bout—p'ints?" inquired Peter, turning his eyes upwards, with an occasional side glance at Hugh, and drawing his fingers slowly down over his face.

"Nothing that I shall tell *you*," replied Hugh with a smile.

"She didn't though, did she, Hugh?" said Peter, bursting into a snicker. "Well, I hope she'll do well—I do, 'pon my word, if it was the last thing I had to say. I hope she'll do first-rate. Hugh, you get off that word she sent to me again. I can't seem to hold on to it."

"That she had given her heart to another, and that you must forget her."

"I don't know how you feel about it, Hugh," said Peter, "but that pays *me.* I tell you, it's something to get such a word as that from a girl. It's about as good as marrying her. Jest think how it sounds! By George! I've no reason to complain—now that's a fact. I r'ally hope she'll do well."

Hugh was about expressing his gratification that Peter had borne his disappointment so well, when the latter rose to take his leave.

"If you'll jest whip them chalk marks," said Peter, looking considerately down upon the diagram of his life, "they'll come out, but if you rub 'em, you'll only rub 'em in. When you've used chalk as much as I have you'll know without being told."

Peter looked round the room, and finding no more to say, turned and walked down stairs, Hugh following him, and seeing him safely landed in the street.

On arriving in the open air, he pulled his coat collar up about his ears, and burying his face in it as far as possible, whispered and chuckled, and shook his fists all the way home.

Hugh was alone at last, and, hastily undressing, he committed himself to his bed. In an instant, the face and form of Mary Woodcock were before him. He transported himself in imagination back to the room in which he had had his interview with her, recalled every word she uttered and every look she gave him, and feasted his memory upon what he had suddenly discovered to be her wonderful beauty. She filled his heart and head full. He felt that he had given himself to her, and that only in her possession could he thenceforth be happy. His head grew feverish with excitement, and he tossed upon his bed for hours without sleep, dwelling upon and recalling constantly the same images, the same words, and the same wonderful emotions.

In his first dream, Mary's eyes were looking with their

wonted fascination into his own—her hand was upon his arm—warm, electrical, subduing. A deep sense of harmony and happiness played about his heart—and yet, he felt his whole nature yearning for something unpossessed—something without him, yet supremely necessary to him.

And Hugh was not alone in his restlessness and dreams that night. Mary was exultant. She had hardly a doubt after Hugh retired that she should conquer him, and win him to herself; and this she determined to do in spite of any opposition that might interpose. She would walk barefoot to the Bay—nay, she would walk the world over—through danger and darkness and despair, before she would relinquish her design to make him her own. Her heart brimmed with the most perfect tenderness towards him—it overflowed in gushing words, softly whispered to her pillow—words of endearment—words that were caresses—words of gentlest idolatry.

CHAPTER XXIII.

Morning came to both, and it was morning in a new world. They had been translated in their relations, and everything had a new value and a new significance. With Mary, life had resolved itself into an invincible purpose. She knew that she should have opposition from her best friends to the accomplishment of her wishes, but she determined to burst through it all. She knew that she should be met with jeers on every hand from her acquaintances, for choosing so insignificant a husband. She knew also that Hugh would be pitied as if he were a boy in the claws of a tigress; and yet these facts were no more than straws beneath the feet of her determination.

Hugh was possessed by a very different spirit—a spirit of helplessness—of fear of Mary's power over him—of sorrow that so many thought and spoke evil of her—and yet a spirit smitten through by a fascination that exalted its author to the pinnacle of feminine power, grace, and glory.

All day long, Hugh walked about his business as if in a dream, and when night came on, he found himself moving in the direction of Holyoke's house. The longing to see her face, to listen to her voice, and to feel the influence of her magnetic eyes was irresistible. As he approached the house, he saw a dark object, closely wrapped, leaning upon the garden gate; and when he had arrived sufficiently near, a low, firm voice said, "I knew you would come—I knew you would come." These words were uttered in such a tone of conscious power, that Hugh felt that self control was not possible in her presence.

"You will take a short walk with me to-night, will you not?" said Mary, in the same confident tone.

"Certainly," responded Hugh.

"Oh! I knew you would," said Mary, as she passed out of the gate.

Hugh did not offer her his arm—he did not even think he had an arm to offer, but she moved to his side, and took it within both her own, and drawing it to her, carried her face so near his that he could feel her breath, and exclaimed, "You cannot tell how glad I am to see you this evening." But Hugh could say nothing. He walked along as if he were a culprit, oppressed with a sense of his worthlessness, his awkwardness, and ignorance, wondering what Mary could find in him to admire; and, for the moment, feeling that he had neither part nor lot in the strange intimacy she had assumed.

"Hugh," said Mary, and the word thrilled him as if it were a breath of music, "Hugh, I have long had something to tell you, and you must let me tell it to you to-night. We will walk out to the old cabin, and there we can be out of the way, and say what we choose."

Hugh understood what was meant by the old cabin. It was the building formerly owned by John Woodcock, which had occasionally been repaired and temporarily occupied by immigrants, while providing themselves with a shelter upon their own lots. The mention of it filled him with fear, for there were stories told concerning that lonely old shelter—of lights having been seen in it at midnight—of ashes upon the hearth left by fires which no one had kindled, and of confused voices heard by distant watchers—and the association of Mary, in her tainted reputation, with the building was such as, for a moment, almost to impel him to break from her side and flee. But he could not have done it if he would, and the impulse soon subsided.

They passed several houses in silence, and at last approached the cabin. The door of the old structure was closed, and knowing that it was quite as cold and cheerless within as it was outside, they took a seat upon a rough bench at the door. Mary hardly knew how to broach the subject of her thoughts, and the object of the interview. At last, summoning her resolution, she said, "Hugh—I want to ask you a question, and you must answer it. I want to know whether, if you loved such a girl as I am, you would dare to go independently to her and tell her of it."

Hugh shook his head, but uttered not a word.

"I thought so," responded Mary, "and now if you should love such a girl as I am, and such a girl as I am should love you, how would the two find it out unless the girl should tell you?"

Hugh felt that his proper answer to both these questions involved his shame, and so, still speechless, he shook his head again.

"I know that the people would not think it right for a girl like me to tell a man like you that she loved him, but I don't care anything about that, and I've come out here to-night with you, Hugh, to tell you that I love you better than anybody and everybody else in all the world. Nobody living can love you as I do—I know it—I know it just as well as I know that I live."

Mary paused in her passionate utterance, and, slowly passing her arm around Hugh, continued: "It seems to me that if you were mine, and I could live with you always, I should be perfectly—perfectly happy. I don't care what people say—I don't care what they do. If I could live here, away from them, in this cabin, where we could be all by ourselves, and where I could work out-doors and in-doors, I shouldn't care whether you worked or not—I should rather you wouldn't work, for you ain't made for this rough country. I could take care of you—I could nurse you when you are sick, and do everything for you when you are well, and I should rather work for you than for myself any time and all the time. Oh, Hugh!" (and Mary's voice sank to a low, tender tone) "how happy—happy—happy I should be! How happy I should be!"

As she closed her impassioned declaration, she drew Hugh to her heart, and there, his sensitive frame wrought into the most painful nervous frenzy, he shook and shivered as if a subtle poison were creeping through his veins, or a miasmatic blast had smitten him with a fever. He could say nothing. He could only sigh convulsively. He knew that Mary's eyes were upon him, and he felt that, if he should lift his own to them, he should fall to weak and womanish tears, or be guilty of some drivelling silliness that would disgrace him in her eyes for ever.

"Can you not love me?" said Mary, tenderly kissing his forehead as it lay upon her shoulder. "Can you not love me? Can you not be mine—all mine—always mine?"

Hugh pressed her hand, and there, in the cold night air, for a good half hour, the lovers sat, wrapped in a feverish sense of happiness, so wild, and vague, and nebulous, that one proper word uttered in the midst of it might have crystallized the whole into something definitely and permanently good, while an improper one might have broken it into eddies that would have drowned heart and brain in forgetfulness and madness. But no word was spoken, and the spell was broken at last by a slight noise within the cabin, followed by a half whispered exclamation, which, in the ears of both the lovers, shaped itself to the words "O God!"

Hugh was nearly overcome with fright, while Mary, for the first time in her brief love history, was stricken with a sense of guilt. She could pour out her soul to Hugh, she could woo him and win him, without the sense of shame. In his presence, alone, she felt that she was sacrificing none of the proprieties of her sex by telling him her love and suing for his hand, but the thought that other ears had heard her seemed to inform her action with new qualities; and, as both started hurriedly away from the spot, she drew her arms under her shawl, and hung her head in silence. Half the distance of return had been accomplished, when Mary burst forth with, "I don't care anything about it. It is no one's business but yours and mine, Hugh. Do not walk so fast."

The remainder of the walk home was occupied in a low and busy conversation on the subject of the future. Mary told Hugh of the land left to her by her father, of the money she had received from the same source (though she did not tell him by what agency the latter came), of the difficulty she should have of carrying out her plan to marry him, and explained to him the origin of the stories which he had heard about her. And Hugh, as he became convinced that she had been wronged, and that she was really honest-hearted and guiltless, felt himself attached to her by a new and nobler sympathy, that did much to fix his determination, assure his judgment, and give body, form, and spirit to his affection. When they parted, each was calm, and each felt assured of the strength of the mutual tie.

Only a few weeks passed away before it was known that Hugh and Mary were betrothed to each other, and such a commotion as it produced in the settlement had never previously been experienced. The first declaration made by each man and woman, as the news was told, was that "Mary did all the courting." It was singular that so just a suspicion should have been so universal, but none were found to dispute it. It was a natural deduction from their relative constitutions and characters. Everybody felt it to be a bad match.

Mary had anticipated all the opposition to her plans which she actually experienced, and all the abuse of which she was the subject. Against all this she had steeled herself, and carried a calm, brave, and determined face wherever she went, or in whatsoever company she found herself. Only in Mary Holyoke's kind presence had she melted, and confessed the means she had taken to gain Hugh's affection and his promise of marriage. But there she received no reproaches. She heard fears expressed—fears springing from genuine Christian love—and she drank in gentle counsels that were dictated by a heart that realized the full preciousness of human affection; and she found one who looked upon the match more than charitably—pleasantly—even hopefully.

On the day when the intentions of marriage between the two were published, Peter Trimble took occasion, as the audience was dismissed, to tell Hugh that he had done a neat thing. "I tell you," said Peter, "it was just exactly as I should have done if I'd been in your place. Yes, sir—if you'd sent me, as I did you, I should 'a nabbed her as true as guns, and you might have whistled. Yes, sir, you did that well."

CHAPTER XXIV.

HITHERTO the office of the Bay Path had been one of peace. It had been worn by weary but hopeful feet in the service of commerce and friendship, and by the migrations incident to a new territory; but the hour was approaching when new and more stirring influences should pass over its track, fraught with great changes to the plantation which it connected with the Bay.

While Mr. Pynchon was in attendance at the October term of the General Court, in 1649, the book with which the reader has become imperfectly acquainted, through Deacon Chapin's interview with Mr. Moxon, arrived in a vessel from London, and the author, with many misgivings concerning the result, but with a determination conscientiously to risk it, and bravely to abide by it, committed it to the public.

Saying nothing to any one of his proceeding, and leaving his book to its fate, and to its influence upon his own, he preserved, day by day, his quiet dignity in his seat among the magistrates, and performed his duties. A few days passed away before he was made aware in any manner that his book had arrested the public eye, but the cool greetings and the altered manners of those about him, and those whom he met in the streets, soon betrayed the depth of the unfavorable impression which it had made. At the meeting-house, upon the Sabbath, he was reminded of the errors which he had promulgated, in the minister's prayer; and half unconsciously looking around, he saw several worshipful and worshipping gentlemen gazing over their noses at him. At length, the state of public feeling became so intense that the bounds of politeness were fairly broken over, and one or two of his old friends visited him personally with severe reproaches. As no direct action had been instituted against him by church or state, and as he found his position comfortless, he thought that the best policy for him would be to relieve the town of his presence, and return home—thus giving to all time to consider his work more calmly, and allowing opportunity for the subsiding of the storm. Accordingly, he asked for leave of absence from the Court—a request which was readily granted—and, with two or three friends, commenced his journey homewards.

In the meantime, half-a-dozen members of the plantation had been in Boston, and thus became acquainted with the position of affairs relative to their magistrate. They had seen him, and had returned home with his assurance that he should soon follow them. Wherever they had made their appearance among the Bay settlements, the subject of the heretical book was brought up, and they found the man whom they had for years loved and revered notorious to an offensive degree. They returned to the plantation much excited, and full of indignation towards those who were thus insulting the person and maligning the reputation of their friend and counsellor, and but a few hours were necessary to diffuse their news and their excitement throughout the plantation.

In Mr. Pynchon's family, there was much distress; for what the men had related on their return, was fully confirmed in a letter from Mr. Pynchon himself. John felt every indignity offered to his father as a personal offence, and could hardly be dissuaded from starting immediately for the Bay, to take his place by his side, and resent all the insults offered him. Mary Holyoke was very deeply affected. The love which she had always borne her father, her confidence in his thorough Christian principle, her knowledge of his deep conscientiousness, and her insight into his delicate pride and sensitiveness of character, all tended to swell the sympathy with which she regarded him, and which not only filled all her waking thoughts, but destroyed her sleep through many feverish nights.

Poor Mrs. Pynchon, in her plodding old age, and in the profundity of respect which she entertained for her husband, would not at first believe a word of what was told her. She could not imagine it possible for William Pynchon to be treated anywhere or by anybody with disrespect. His letter was read to her, but she "could not see into it," and shook her head so long and so determinedly that all attempts to impress upon her the nature and extent of the difficulty were abandoned.

At the close of the lecture on Wednesday succeeding the announcement of Mr. Pynchon's difficulties to the settlement, all the men remained within the meeting-house, while their wives and families mostly followed their example. These difficulties were, of course, the topic of discussion, and each of the news-bringers was surrounded by his little knot of auditors, replying to a multitude of questions, and retailing the particulars he had gathered to very attentive ears.

Conversation had progressed but a few minutes, when three or four horsemen cantered up to the door of the meeting-house, and, dropping their bridles, leaped from their saddles, and entered. Twenty individuals caught sight of the first intruder, who was no other than Mr. Pynchon himself, in his rusty travelling gear. A cordial smile illuminated his face as he contemplated the assembly, which remained silent and motionless for a moment, and then, by a common impulse, turned to greet him. "Three cheers for Mr. Pynchon!" shouted one, leaping to a seat; and they were given with a will. "Three more!" shouted

Peter Trimble from another part of the house, swinging his hat high in the air; but as he became immediately convinced that he had gone too far, he settled into a profound snicker that carried him nearly to the floor, and excluded all attempt on his part to answer to the call.

Mr. Pynchon was at first greatly surprised to meet with such a demonstration in the house of worship, but he was surrounded immediately by his family and more intimate friends, who explained the cause of the convocation, and of the explosion of enthusiasm which he had witnessed. The old man's lip trembled, and his eye moistened with emotion as he asked for silence, and thanked the assembly for their confidence and sympathy. As they passed out of the house, on that mild autumn afternoon, and took their way homewards, in a glow of happy excitement, Mr. Pynchon regarded them all with an affection he had never before experienced, and his heart swelled with gratitude that he was once more among hearts that loved him.

As the people divided into little parties on their way homewards, there was one group besides that immediately around Mr. Pynchon, which excited considerable attention and comment. It was composed of Hugh Parsons, Mary Woodcock, and no less an individual than Peter Trimble. The face of the latter had taken on the aspect of an aggravated case of the small-pox, while his legs, judging from the manner in which they managed themselves, labored each under intense personal embarrassment. He had happened to be near to Hugh and Mary as they left the meeting-house, and, being hailed by the former, joined them in their walk.

"You are jest the man I wanted to see," said Peter. "When you get ready" (and Peter looked at Mary), "I should like to see you alone about three minutes."

"What secret have you got for Hugh, now?" inquired Mary good-humoredly.

"We've had considerable between us, first and last, hav'n't we, Hugh?" said Peter.

Hugh replied that he rather thought they had.

"I guess," continued Peter, "some folks don't know how some folks happened to get hold of some folks;" and then he burst into a snicker that he found it impossible to terminate without reaching across the walk, behind Mary, and giving Hugh a sly kick.

Mary understood the allusion, for she had long previously heard the whole story, and she joined Hugh in a laugh so merry as to attract attention from a considerable distance.

"Peter," said Mary, "why didn't you make a speech to-day?"

"By George!" exclaimed Peter, excitedly, "that's jest what I wanted to do; and, between you and I, that's what I want to see Hugh about. Mr. Pynchon wouldn't hear anything to me, but perhaps he would to Hugh; and I want to put him on the track of something that'll stick them Bay fellows where they wont hear from their friends over and above often. Land ahead! If I was in his place, I could fix 'em all in less than twenty-four hours. It's so, now; you needn't laugh."

"But can you not inform both of us?" inquired Mary, assuming a sober face.

Peter shook his head. That was not the way in which he was accustomed to deal. It was too public—there was nothing sly about it.

At last, the singularly composed trio arrived at the house of Holyoke, and Mary released her lover to Peter, who led him behind a huge tree, a short distance off, and there unveiled his plan for the relief of Mr. Pynchon.

"You see," said Peter, "I've got a plan. I didn't want to tell it to the other fellers, for they're always laughing at me; but you can tell Mr. Pynchon, or somebody else that will tell him. Did you ever hear of a wind-gun?"

Hugh thought he had heard such an article of warfare mentioned.

"It goes by wind, you see," continued Peter; "and it'll plug a bullet right into a man, and never make a bit of noise. A feller's alive one second and dead the next, and nobody knows what hurts him. Well, if I was in Mr. Pynchon's place, I'd get a short wind-gun, and have it fastened under my arm, and just cover up the whole concern with a cloak; and then I'd have a string run down my coat sleeve from the thing that pulls it off, and when one of these fellers comes up and says, 'Mr. Pynchon—that's a miserable book of your'n—you ought to be taken in hand for writing it,' I should jest look him in the eye, and pull the string, and slap goes the man right down in the middle of the road, all curled up as if he was full of choke cherries. When the next feller comes along with his sass, pull the string again, down he goes, and so on. By the time I'd laid out about half-a-dozen that way, they'd begin to think that apoplexy was catching, and that it wasn't exactly safe to be minding other people's business. Land ahead! I should jest like to be William Pynchon for about three days. I'd be dangerous now—you'd better believe I would, if I was to be strung up for it."

Hugh was not at all certain of the soundness of this scheme, as a matter of policy, to say nothing of its morality; while his faith in wind-guns was not such as to make the enterprise look practicable; but he nodded as Peter said, "You think of this"—and parted with that modest and ingenious young man, to forget his injunction and think about Mary.

The return of Mr. Pynchon was an event which had, for several weeks, been associated in his mind, and in that of Mary Woodcock, with their marriage; and that was the subject of their first thought as the magistrate made his appearance at the meeting-house door. Hugh, therefore, only went home to return to the house of Holyoke in the evening, where the intentions and prospects of the lovers were made the subject of family conversation during his call. Mr. Holyoke and his wife kindly lent their counsel to the lovers, and promised to lend them their interest and aid.

It was concluded that the marriage should be celebrated so soon as the cabin could be put in complete order for the winter, and sufficient stores of wood and corn procured, or rendered certain of procurement. Mary Holyoke promised to speak of the matter to her father, and obtain his approval of the match and the arrangements for the consummation of the marriage.

The feeling towards the lovers among the young men of the plantation had become softened by the passage of a few weeks, and, through Mary Holyoke, John Pynchon had become much interested in them. After a consultation with Holyoke, he proposed to the young men of his own age to do something in the way of assisting Hugh and Mary in the commencement of their housekeeping.

Accordingly, upon a morning appointed, Woodcock's old cabin was invaded by a busy host, who in the course of the day changed the humble structure from a mere shell to a tenantable dwelling. They were on the roof and under the roof—at the door and at the windows—topping out the chimney and closing up the walls—and a very merry and noisy set they were. At last, they built a huge fire within, and collected for consultation. John proposed that they should appoint a day to draw to the door a winter's stock of fuel. Peter Trimble insisted that it should be done some moonlight night, so as to take Hugh and Mary by surprise. He even went further, and expressed his opinion that if they could so dispose of the wood as to fence in the cabin, it would be one of the finest jokes ever perpetrated. But Peter was overruled by the majority, and the wood made its appearance at the time and in the mode appointed.

Mary found the stores of money and wampum which she had received from her father greatly convenient in her arrangements, and, between those and the generous presents of Holyoke and his wife, she was able to supply herself with very respectable housekeeping articles and furniture, and a trousseau quite up to, if not a little beyond, the Puritan standard. She managed everything, attended to everything, did everything. Night after night Hugh went to see her, and ask her about her progress. It did not seem to him that it was an affair with which he had, actively, anything to do. The house had been put in order for him, his wood lay at the door ready for his axe, and, living within the charmed and charming circle of his all-absorbing passion, he seemed to feel as if miracles were to be wrought for his benefit, and that there was absolutely nothing for him to do but to receive them.

All this—strangely as it may seem—pleased Mary well. She loved him for his helplessness—his amiable placidity, and above all for his implicit faith in, and entire reliance upon, her. She had never been so happy in her life as when, all day long and half the night, she labored ceaselessly and tirelessly to prepare for an event which seemed to her to be so fraught with bliss that whole years of misery would purchase it cheaply. The vision of the retired cabin with its blazing fire, its inviolable secresy, its independence, and the amiable treasure which she was soon to make her own and to instal there, was constantly before her.

The day appointed for the wedding at last arrived, and in the morning Hugh and Mary walked down to the cabin, to see to some of the closing preparations. The stock of provisions which Hugh had been able to procure had already been deposited there, and everything was nearly ready for immediate occupation. They kindled a fire in the huge fireplace, and sat down, Mary talking all the time, and telling what changes she should make, so soon as she should become settled in housekeeping, and giving expression to her delight with the arrangements around her, and the prospect before her.

The pair were sitting thus when the door was opened, and a tall Indian walked in, unbidden, carrying upon his back a basket filled with corn. He was followed by another and another, until the room was filled with Indians, each of whom relieved himself of a burden, and stood in silence, as if awaiting the orders of a chief.

When all had arrived and deposited their freight, a somewhat clumsy and singularly painted old man waved his hand, and the company turned and retired in silence as they came. Mary and Hugh were dumb with surprise and astonishment. The former looked at the superior of the squad with an eye burning with strange curiosity and apprehension, and an impulse moved her to seize him by the arm. She did so, almost with fierceness, but relinquished her hold as he turned mildly upon her, and regarded her with an eye so full of tenderness that she bowed her head in sudden emotion, and burst into a paroxysm of tears.

The man turned to leave the room, but, perceiving his intention, she stepped between him and the door, and, planting herself against it, still continued weeping. The visitor was overcome, and, making no attempt to pass her, stepped back towards the fire.

"Do you know who I be?" inquired he at last, with a trembling voice.

Mary compressed her lips firmly, raised her eyes to his, and bowed her affirmation.

"Does *he?*" with a nod and look at Hugh. Mary shook her head.

"I never expected to speak to you agi'n, and I shouldn't now, if you hadn't made me, but I'm glad you did, 'cause I may do you a good turn, though I haven't anything good to say to you."

During all this scene Hugh had stood as if in a dream—his mind filled with strange fears and fancies. The abundant stores that had been deposited in the cabin did not surprise him, until he saw that Mary was surprised, and that she was exercised by very strong emotions. Then, as he saw a mutual recognition of acquaintance between the two, all the stories he had ever heard of Mary filled his mind, and he trembled with excitement. The man did not look or talk like an Indian. He was disguised. Perhaps those who had retired were disguised. Perhaps they were but servants, after all, of one whom many firmly believed to be Mary's master. The gifts they had left, immediately upon these considerations assumed a new and alarming significance, and he began to feel that, in very truth, he might be within the toils of the adversary. If so, he knew that he was hopelessly there, for his heart told him that his destiny was linked with Mary irrevocably.

"Mary," continued the stranger, "I know all what you're goin' to do. You're goin' to marry this boy, and it's a bad bargain for both on you. It won't be your fault nor his'n, but your enemies ain't dead yet, any more'n mine. You're leavin' a good place, and it's been a safe one so fur, and you're comin' here, away from Mary Holyoke and her husband, and I'm afraid it'll get you into trouble; and this little body that you've got here can't do anything to help you."

Mary's eyes flashed with an angry gleam as she exclaimed, "I can help myself. I should like to see the man who would dare to lay his hand on him, or on me. Hugh and I shall mind our own business, and if other people do not mind theirs I shall tell them to." And Mary walked forth and back across the cabin, her face flushed with excitement.

"Well, I hope it'll come out right," said the man, "but I haven't got any faith. I like your spunk, but it don't count in a fight with crazy folks and fools. It'll only tell ag'in you when the thing comes to a pinch, and be laid to the devil that's in you. But, Mary, I didn't come here to trouble you this morning. I come here to do you good, and I didn't expect to find you here. There's lots of corn and dried venison and salmon on the floor, and you're welcome to it all. God knows I want to see you happy, and all I can do to make you happy I shall keep a-doin'. You won't tell anybody who you've seen, and you won't let anybody else—you know too much for that—and now I reckon I'd better go back to where I come from."

He went towards the door, but hesitated and hung his head. Raising it at length, he approached Mary, and took her hand. "Mary," said he, "I've been leadin' a rough life, but I don't forget anything. I know how good it is to be like folks, and be with 'em, and I miss a thousand things that there wouldn't anybody give me credit for. I look rough, and I be rough, but there's one thing I want to do before I die, and that I know'll warm my heart till it stops beatin', and give me somethin' to think of that'll keep me human, and kind o' jine me on, if it is a good ways off, to somethin' that's good. Mary, the last woman's face that I ever kissed was a cold one, and none but the worms kissed it after me; and now, if you'll let me kiss your'n before I go, I'll never kiss another in this world, and I'll remember it always."

Mary, thoroughly melted, and thoroughly charmed by the same strange eloquence that had haunted her memory for many years, threw her arms impulsively about the old man's neck, and kissed him again and again. It was enough. Drawing a purse from his belt filled with coins and wampum, he pressed it into her hand, and hurried from her sight.

Mary stood looking through the vacant doorway long after he had vanished, but at last turned, with a cloud of deep disturbance upon her face, and regarding her astonished lover with a strange expression in her wonderful eyes, she said, pointing to the articles upon the floor, "These are to be packed away out of sight, and you are to say nothing of what you have seen this morning. Some time I will tell you all about it; and remember, till then, that I have done nothing wrong in kissing that old man. You will love me better for it when you know why I did it."

Hugh was contented with the explanation, and putting his arm fondly around her, begged her to be pleasant and happy, as her looks chilled him, and made him miserable.

"Hugh," said Mary, looking him in the face with an expression of the deepest tenderness, "we don't know what's before us. There are people in the plantation who think I'm bad, and you see what this man thinks, and he knows better than anybody else. He thinks that as soon as I get out of Mr. Holyoke's house these people will be after me, and give me trouble."

"Let's not get married then," said Hugh, deprecatingly. "We can live as we have lived, until things change. I should die if they were to take you away from me, or if my marrying you should get you into difficulty."

"Not get married?" said Mary, with fierce determination mantling her face. "Do you suppose that I would put it off an hour for fear? I would see Mr. Moxon (and her voice sank to a low whisper) and the miserable fools who believe in him and his crazy children, sunk to the bottom of the river before I would change a plan of my life the breadth of a hair. They are more cruel than bears. What have I done to them? How have I hurt them? Why can't they let me alone?—always talking about me—always worrying me, and trying to make me miserable."

"Don't look so—don't talk so!" exclaimed Hugh, with tender importunity.

Mary kissed him passionately, and resumed: "Ah, Hugh!

They've tried to get you away from me, but they shall never do it. We shall be married to-night. They cannot cheat me, and I shall give them no chance. No, Hugh, we'll be married—we'll be married—if we never see another happy day. Let them do their worst."

Hugh had nothing to say, and in his silence yielded assent to her determination, as one from which there was no appeal. After disposing of the provisions which the Indians had brought in accordance with her previous decision, the two replenished the fire, and took their way back to Mary's home.

The wedding was solemnized in the meeting-house just at night-fall, Mr. Pynchon performing the ceremony, as was his office on all such occasions in the settlement. It is not necessary to speak of the whispers that echoed around the chilly house as the strangely matched pair made their appearance; of the shrugs of shoulders in the audience; of the poorly disguised spite of nearly every woman in the congregation; of the cold greetings that were bestowed upon the pair as they passed out of the house; of the evil prophecies, the poor jokes, the sly calumnies that were uttered on every hand.

Only the family of Mr. Pynchon and the young friends of the bridegroom treated the married pair with cordiality. For them, Mary had a tear of love and gratitude, but, for the remainder, only cool defiance. She looked at them, from side to side, until each eye that met her own quailed as if under an irresistible influence.

A social gathering in honor of the occasion was held at the house of Holyoke, but it was not a happy one, and was broken up at an early hour. Mary wore an air of deep abstraction during the evening, and responded but feebly and incoherently to such good-natured raillery as was addressed to her; and was evidently rejoiced when the party separated, and when, with a choice company of friends, she took her departure for her own home. There she was left, at last, with many kind expressions of interest and sympathy—her schemes all accomplished, and the prize she had so fiercely coveted, and boldly striven for, secured.

CHAPTER XXV.

The first month of Mary Woodcock's married life passed pleasantly away. The cloud which overshadowed her as she entered it, was temporarily lifted, and a calm and sweet content succeeded to the apprehensions and disquietudes that had gathered so closely about her. Slander having done its worst to thwart her plans and ruin her hopes, withdrew for a time its cruel offices, and waited for renewed strength and fresh opportunities. She saw but little company, and hardly ventured beyond the inclosures of her dwelling. Hugh was rarely out of her sight, and, so long as he was near, she cared for nothing beyond. She lavished upon him all the deep fondness of her powerful nature, and, in her own happiness and his, demonstrated the perfect legitimacy of the union between them—a union popularly deemed faulty, not because it was unnatural, but because it was unusual, in its relations.

Little by little, however, the slanderous murmur was renewed. Hugh, whenever he stirred abroad, came home with a troubled brow and a heavy heart. Poisoned words were flung in his ears from brawling tongues, and calumnies were breathed in sly insinuations. Much as he endeavored to cover their effect upon his mind from her sight, he could never succeed in doing it. She read his face on every return as if it were the most legible of tablets, and he could never refuse her demand to tell her everything. The effect of these things on Hugh's mind made them doubly oppressive to her.

For herself, she could defy and despise those who sought

her injury, but the thought that they were endeavoring day by day to undermine her husband's confidence in her, and had fully succeeded in filling him with perplexity and anxiety, cut her to the quick, and often fairly disrobed her of her strength.

At times, when she was alone with Hugh, talking upon the ever prevalent subject, she gave way to wild bursts of impatience and passion that fairly frightened him; and then she would weep upon his neck like a child, telling him that he was all the comfort she had in the world, and begging him never to forsake her, and never to distrust her.

Mary found, whenever she ventured abroad, that she was regarded with a kind of impudent curiosity by every one she met, and that nearly all with whom she conversed seemed to lie in wait for her words and to ask her strange and irrelevant questions. Sometimes, in her contempt for the efforts made to entrap her in her expressions, she gave derisive replies, humoring her questioners in their conceits touching herself, and confirming their suspicions by her own confessions, uttered with an irony of tone that none but those wilfully perverse, or wholly stultified, could fail to understand.

During these conversations, few though they were, she unfortunately, and perhaps unwisely, let drop many expressions that were tortured into slander, and perverted into confessions of guilt. These expressions were bandied about from mouth to mouth, till once more she had become thoroughly and offensively notorious.

Matters had gone on badly in this way, until, one evening in the depth of winter, as Hugh and Mary were sitting by their glowing fire, a rap resounded upon the door of the cabin, and the same was slightly opened, though not sufficiently to reveal the visitor. Hugh went to the door and undertook to open it wider, but it was held where he found it, and, through the crack, Hugh heard the words: "Can't you come out here a minute, Hugh?"

Hugh was slightly frightened, and did not detect the voice as quickly as Mary, who, rising suddenly from her chair, advanced to the door, and, seizing it strongly, pulled Peter Trimble plump into the room. Peter was very evidently taken by surprise, and had not a single pimple ready for exhibition.

Drawing his hand suddenly down over his face, and taking a hurried survey of his trousers, which were somewhat seriously patched, he took the chair offered him, and held out his blue and horny hands to the fire, warmed first one ear and then the other, slid from a violent shiver into a snicker, and turning and slapping Hugh on the shoulder exclaimed, "By George! Hugh, you've got the stoutest wife there is in this place. Now, you needn't say you haven't, for I know you have. There ain't another woman in the plantation could have pulled me in as she did. I couldn't hold the door—upon my word I couldn't—any more'n if an elephant was hold of it."

Mary and Hugh both greeted Peter's highly appreciative compliment with a merry peal of laughter, which Peter impulsively united in at first, but a sudden thought struck him into soberness, as if it had smitten him across the mouth. Mary and Hugh both noticed it, and the former spoke of it, and rallied him upon it.

"The fact is," said Peter, "I didn't come hear to laugh, and I didn't mean to come in at all; but there's something I ought to tell you, and something that you ought to know, and I sort o' mistrusted that I could help you out of it."

"*You?* Who are you talking to—Hugh, or me?" inquired Mary with sudden energy.

"Well, I meant you, but I was talking to Hugh, because I didn't expect to say anything to you."

"What is the matter?"

"It's nothing that I've had anything to do with," replied Peter, "but I heard something that was going to be done, and I thought perhaps I could tell Hugh how you could dodge it."

"Peter," said Mary, rising and grasping him by the arm, "tell me what you mean."

Peter began to blubber, but managed to keep the mastery of his emotion and his tongue sufficiently to say, "Mary, they're agoing to take you up to-morrow, for saying something bad about widow Marshfield;" and as he saw her looking blankly into his face, endeavoring, as she was, to comprehend the disgrace before her, he continued—"and I thought perhaps I could tell you how to dodge the whole thing."

"Something bad about widow Marshfield? Take me up?" said Mary slowly and wonderingly.

"I don't say you said something bad about her," replied Peter, "but they're r'ally going to do something. Now don't feel so, for I think it can be dodged by coming a small rig. If it was me that was going to be took up" (continued Peter, with an encouraging expression of countenance, and a lively tone of voice), "I shouldn't lose any sleep, and I tell you how I should work it. I'd have rheumatism enough to kill three men, and get the case put off. Or I'd break my leg or something of that kind. Land ahead! there aint any surgeon here—they wouldn't know—and all you've got to do is to holler like bloody murder if they touch you." Peter saw that his revelations were rather enlivening the countenance of his auditors, and went on. "Or I'd make believe I was crazy, and spit all over my clo'es, and take off my boot and wipe my nose on it, and flip beans all day at a mark, and walk around among the trees, and make believe they are men, and say, 'How are you, Mr. Beech? How do you do, Mr. Pine? Hullo! Mr. Apple! how do you do, and how's your orchard?' Land ahead!

that ain't a beginning. I could do any quantity of things. The fact is, there ain't any end to the things I could do, if I r'ally set out for it."

All this would have been amusing enough under less serious circumstances, but Mary could only give it a tolerating smile, and ask Peter if he knew what charges were to be brought against her. Peter did not know, but he rather thought there would be enough of them, and that perhaps it would be safe to assume the double affliction of rheumatism and insanity.

All three sat in silence for some minutes, when Peter rose with lively energy in his feet, with the inquiry, "Have you got any money?"

"Yes—why?" replied and inquired Mary.

"Because, if you should happen to break down on the rig, you might want some. If it goes agi'n you, we all know mighty well what it will be. We ain't rich enough to have a jail yet, and it's nothing but money or whipping."

At the last word Mary sprang to her feet, and uttered a groan so full of acute pain that Hugh and Peter both turned pale with fright. Then, while her eyes flashed, and the old bright spots burned upon her cheeks, she paced up and down the apartment, her lips tightly compressed, and her arms folded closely across her breast. If she had been stung in the bosom by a viper, she could not have been more terribly agitated.

The possibility that she should be subjected to such a disgrace as a public whipping was maddening. The consciousness that she was generally suspected and hated, the uncertainty in regard to the nature of the charges to be made against her, her anxiety for Hugh, and her desire not to be disgraced in his eyes—all this conspired to induce a state of mind bordering on distraction.

Peter was greatly agitated by the effect he had produced, but not being particularly sensitive himself, he could hardly appreciate the real cause of her suffering. "If it really comes to that," said he, soothingly, "I've got a piece of buckskin that you can put under your clo'es, where the constable can't see it, and he can't hurt much through that, now I tell you."

When he had concluded, Mary came up to him, and said, "Peter, be kind enough to leave us now. You mean us well, and I thank you for having told us what you have, but you cannot do us any good, and we want to be alone."

"Well, I'll go," replied Peter, and buttoning up his shabby coat to the chin, and drawing his cap down over his ears, he bade the sad pair "good night," and picked his way along the poorly made snow-path homewards.

The first thing which Mary attended to after his departure was the counting of her money. It was a handsome little sum, and one which seemed competent to cover any fine that might be imposed upon her for any offence that malignity might charge her with or perjury convict her of.

The pair sat and talked late into the night, and retired at last to a sleepless bed, where they tossed in feverish wretchedness until the morning. Breakfast was prepared, and each tried to sustain the other by an appearance of appetite, but it was a hard task, and was soon relinquished. After the table was cleared, both sat down to wait impatiently, and with anxious uncertainty, the development of events.

There were frequent visits to the window looking out upon the village, and questions asked and answered in an under-tone, until, at last, Mary started suddenly back from one of her visits to the window, and took her seat in silence at the fire. Hugh understood the movement, and arose to look for himself. He saw what he looked for, and returned and tremblingly took his seat, and gazed with painful sympathy upon his wife. She was looking into the fire, whispering to herself, and nervously shaking her head, as if she were holding an imaginary altercation. Hugh dared not address her, and hardly ventured to draw a long breath. At length, the feet of a briskly walking man were heard approaching, and, as he came into the yard, Mary rose to her feet, walked to the door, and throwing it open, exclaimed, "Thomas Merrick, do your devil's work, and have it over with."

The constable stopped as if he had been thunderstruck. He had never seen such an impersonation of desperation, and had anticipated quite a different scene. He could only stand speechless for a minute, and look into her face; and he did not stir until Mary imperatively demanded of him his errand.

"I came," said the constable, recovering himself, and advancing into the cabin, "to arrest you on a charge of slander."

"And whom have I slandered?"

"Widow Marshfield."

"What am I accused of saying about the precious widow Marshfield?" inquired Mary with a bitter sneer.

"You will learn that soon enough, I dare say," replied the constable.

"Goodman Merrick," said Mary, walking closely up to him, and looking him fiercely in the eye, "what can they do to me, if lies enough are told about me to prove what I am charged with?"

"The magistrate can fine you, or order you to be whipped, or both together. He could do more and worse than this, but those are the common punishments here."

"You do the whipping, do you?"

"The constable always does it."

"And would you whip me?"

"I have sworn faithfully to perform the constable's duties."

"Well, now, mark you, Thomas Merrick (and Mary kept

her fierce eyes fixed upon him), I am as innocent of the charge that you have arrested me on as an unborn child—as *my* unborn child—(and her voice sank to a trembling whisper) and if you abuse me, or bring peril on my burden, I will pray God to curse you with the last breath I draw. You are a husband and a parent. Act like one. The people of this town are determined to make hell of my home; don't you be guilty of making a devil of me."

The constable was overcome. He knew that Mary despised his office and disliked him, but there was something in her fiercely courageous earnestness that commanded his respect, and something in her appeal which softened him wonderfully. "All I can do consistently with my oath to make your sentence light shall be done," said he. "What can I say more?"

"Nothing. I am content. Shall I go now?"

"Now, if you please."

Mary whispered a few words to Hugh, who, in accordance with her instructions, went to the closet where she kept her money, and drawing forth the purse deposited it in his pocket. She then put on such extra clothing as the cold weather demanded, and, drawing her hood closely down over her face, declared her readiness to accompany the constable. Hugh had, in the meantime, prepared himself to go with them, and all issued from the door together. The morning was biting cold, but the air was still and peaceful, and the smoke went up from all the chimneys of the settlement like incense. Children were shouting in the distance, the teamster was merrily cracking his whip, tidy housewives were brushing off their door steps with their heavy birch brooms, and all seemed careless, lively, and happy. But in Mary's heart, as she passed one house after another, where she knew that her name had met with foul treatment, there was rebellion and wretchedness. All were happy but herself, and the one dearest to her.

13*

Her appearance with the constable was the subject of lively gossip along the street, and many a gratified stare was directed to her from the windows. These she did not see, but, as she passed the house of Holyoke—the home of the happiest portion of her childhood—she could not forbear raising her eyes to see if her truest friend were the witness of her disgrace. Mary Holyoke stood at the window, pale with recent illness, and smiled so sweetly as she bowed to her, and wafted to her a kiss so affectionately, that, softened into tears, she bowed her head, and sobbed during the remainder of the distance to the house of the magistrate.

Leaving them in the room in which the trial was to be held, the constable retired to summon the witnesses, or, rather, to announce to them the readiness of the court. The passage of the constable with his prisoner through the street, was a sufficient advertisement of the affair in progress, and one after another dropped in to witness the trial. Peter was the first, having secured his release from labor for the day during the previous evening. He was a good deal affected by the appearance of the pair. They seemed to have grown haggard and old since, but a few hours before, he had unintentionally greeted them at their hearthstone. Mr. Moxon, Mr. Holyoke, Deacon Chapin, and nearly a dozen women, were also among the crowded audience. Mary wondered who the witnesses against her might be, but she paid little attention to the throng about her, for she was conscious of being the subject of their conversation.

At last, Mr. Pynchon made his appearance, and took his seat at his desk. Looking over it, he gazed long and anxiously at the prisoner, who turned with a look of honest innocence and trust, and met his inquiring eyes. Mr. Pynchon had seen the girl much, as she had grown up under the care of his daughter, and had always entertained a peculiar regard for her as the child of a strange man whom he had never ceased to love and respect. Her present position was one which gave him severe pain, but, from the industrious representations made to him by many persons in the plantation, and in consequence of definite though frivolous charges, he had, at last, concluded to issue a warrant for her arrest.

As he met her look—so pleading and trustful—he repented of the step he had taken, and wished the business off his hands. As he sat there, looking half vacantly at the spirited woman whose mute appeal he had felt, he could not help recalling a scene that occurred on the same spot many years before—when her father was on trial for the same offence, nominally, with which she was charged, and when she was an ill-trained and wayward child.

Then his eye passed over to Mr. Moxon, in whose hatred and hallucinations the troubles of both father and child had originated, and he felt how poorly justice was meted out in this world, and especially how impossible it was for him to render equity in judgment to the people of his charge. The laws were defective, as their human authors were, and, even when operating for the general good, sometimes discriminated in favor of the doers of evil against the holders of the right.

"Mary Parsons," said the magistrate, at length, in a mild voice, "you will stand, and listen to the charge upon which you have been arrested."

Mary rose, and, turning boldly around, looked her judge in the face with an eye so bright and strong that it almost overthrew his equanimity, and he hesitated before proceeding.

"You are charged," continued he, "with defaming the good name of the widow Marshfield, in reporting her to have been suspected for a witch. The bringing of such a suspicion as this—a suspicion of having familiar dealings with the Adversary—against a respectable and innocent woman, is a very grave offence. Are you guilty or not guilty?"

"Not guilty!" exclaimed Mary, with a sudden shake of her head, and a voice almost spiteful in its decisiveness.

The interested individuals in the audience exchanged significant glances, and Mr. Moxon shifted uneasily in his seat, as if he were in some way connecting her answer with the previous remark of the magistrate. Goody Marshfield, the spirited looking widow who had made the complaint, sat but a short distance from the prisoner, and, tossing her head saucily, nodded at two or three friends with a smile which, being interpreted, said, "Did any one ever see such impudence!"

It was evident from the expression upon the faces of all the men present that the widow was a woman equally courted and feared—one who assumed the place of a popular favorite, and maintained it at the point of her wit and the edge of her sarcasm. In fact, it was owing to her cutting speeches in regard to Mary that the latter had been led into remarks from which the present charge was trumped up.

"Goody Marshfield," said the magistrate, "who are your witnesses?"

Now the term "Goody" did not sound pleasantly to the spirited widow, and a flush of anger passed over her features as she replied, "John Matthews and *Goody* Matthews."

"The witnesses named by Goody Marshfield will arise and receive the oath," said the magistrate.

The man and his wife did as they were bidden, but, as they arose and advanced to the stand, they shunned the burning eye which Mary Parsons fixed upon them, and looked far more like culprits than she.

"John Matthews," said the magistrate, after administering the oath to the pair, "have you ever heard Mary

Parsons say that Goody Marshfield had been suspected for a witch?"

"Yes, sir, I have," replied the man, while his heart bumped so heavily against the walls of his chest as to jar his voice.

"Will you tell me when and where, and give all the circumstances connected with the matter?"

"Well, Goody Parsons come to my house one time when my wife and I was both to home, and we got to talking about one thing and another, when my wife, says she, 'Mary—Widow Marshfield says you'v'e took a child to bring up, but he's so small he'll never make much Hugh-and-cry." (A titter all about the room, and a nod from the widow which meant, "Pretty good—wasn't it.") "Well, this made Mary mad, and says she to my wife—Widow Marshfield has been grudging every child that's been born in the plantation, because her girl didn't have any; and as soon as she had one, it died, and her cow died at the same time, and died a' bellering, 'cause she thought the child was her'n." ("Sharp shooting," whispered Deacon Chapin to Mr. Moxon, the widow meanwhile assuming an air of charming imperturbation, and the magistrate drawing his hand slowly down over his mouth, as if he rather enjoyed it.) "And then she went on, Mary did, and said that widow Marshfield was suspected for a witch when she lived in Windsor, and, for all she knew, the child and the cow were bewitched when they died, and that was what ailed them. I told her she ought to be ashamed of herself to talk so about a respectable woman, and that I didn't believe a word of it; but she stuck to what she said, and when I asked her what she knew about it, she said it was known all over Windsor that the Devil had a private room in her house, where he met all the witches once a week, to have a grand feast and lay out his work; and she didn't see any reason why she shouldn't have dealings with him in Springfield as well as Windsor. That is pretty much all I heard, but she and my wife were keeping up the talk when I come away."

"Was Goody Parsons talking in earnest, or was she only trying to see what she could say, as an offset to Goody Marshfield's sharp words?"

"I never see a woman more earnest in my life," said the witness, forgetful of tense and truth together.

"And you really believe she meant all she said?"

"Yes, sir."

"You may sit down, and Goody Matthews will take your place."

The new witness was a woman greatly given to gossip, carried a glib and ready tongue, and presented a thin form and face whose sharp outlines accorded well with her character. In all her allusions to her husband, she ignored everything else masculine in the universe, by speaking of him as *he*—that pronoun, in its several cases, being assumed as descriptive of and applicable to, that individual alone whom she had sworn to love, honor, and obey, and whom she had repeatedly made to swear, by declining to do anything of the kind.

"Goody Matthews, what do you know about this case?" inquired the magistrate.

"I know just the same as him, only he left before we got through talking, and didn't hear it all."

"Then your husband's testimony is correct, so far as it goes, is it?" inquired the magistrate.

"He ain't in the habit of swearing to lies;" and the offended wife pursed up her mouth, and assumed an air of offended sensibility that drew a smile upon Mr. Pynchon's face in spite of himself.

"Very well—what did you hear more?"

"Well, I was telling her about something that happened the day before, when I was getting ready to get dinner.

I'd put about half a pound of veal into the pot—*he* don't care much about meat, and veal ain't very good warmed over——"

"Was this operation performed when Mary was in the house?"

"No," replied the witness; "this was what I was telling her. I was saying to her that I'd put about half a pound of veal into the pot—it wasn't much, but he never did like veal—and I'd put the water in, and put on the cover, and when the time come to hang it over the fire, I hung it right on, without thinking of looking in, because I knew I put the veal in, and poured in the water, and put on the cover—I remember it, because I did it just after I'd washed out the pot, and I know I thought to myself *that's* clean enough for anybody; and right after that I put in the veal. Well, after it had been over the fire, I should think pretty near half an hour, I took off the cover to see if the water wasn't pretty near biled away, and there wasn't a particle of veal in the pot, and it didn't look as if there had been, and I haven't seen hide nor hair of the piece ever since."

"What has this to do with the case?" inquired the magistrate.

"I was just going to say, that as soon as I had told Mary of this, I said I wondered what *had* become of that veal; and says she, 'don't you think it was witched away?' and says I, Mary, what is it makes you all the time talking about witches? You don't believe there's any witches in the town, do you? Says she, yes—I know there is; and she come into my house, when I was carding wool, and as long as she was there, I couldn't make the wool into rolls. Says I, who is it? Says she, it's *her*."

"Who do you mean?" inquired Mr. Pynchon.

"I mean widow Marshfield, that we'd just been talking about; and then says she, Mr. Stebbins told me all about it, and told me how she was always set down for a witch in

Windsor, and how, ever since she'd been in Springfield, we'd had the strangest lights in the meadows over the river—blue ones, and green ones, and red ones—and—I don't know—there was a great many things she said, but I can't remember them."

"What was it about the grudging of other people's children?"

"It is just as he said," replied the woman, "about the grudging, and the child and the cow dying at the same time."

"And you have no doubt that she told you these things expecting and intending that you should believe them?"

"Not any."

"And you have reported all about the neighborhood, I suppose, that Mary Parsons told you these things, and done all you could to make the widow Marshfield suspected for a witch."

"I have told you all I know about it," said the witness, sharply.

"Very well—you can sit down," said Mr. Pynchon. Then, addressing Mary, he said, "What have you to say to this testimony?"

"I say that it is a downright lie," replied Mary, stamping her foot decidedly.

"Do you say that you have said none of these things that they have testified to as your statements?"

"I said what I said," replied Mary, her eyes flashing angrily, "to a couple of fools about a woman who hated me, and who had made them believe that I was a witch myself. I said it not because I cared anything about the woman or her slanders, nor because I supposed they were going to believe me in earnest in what I said. I said it laughing all the time—just to show them how easy it was to lie about people, if one had the mind, and that I could say 'witch' as easy as anybody else could. They have said many things that are absolutely false, and what they have repeated from me was said with no intention of injuring anybody."

"Then it is not *all* a downright lie."

"It is, as they have given it."

"I notice," said Mr. Pynchon, looking around the room, "that we have a greater number present than is usual at trials of this kind, and if Mr. Moxon or any officers of the church present wish to make any remarks in reference to this case, they can have the liberty."

Mr. Moxon rose partly from his seat, and then the thought of what he had promised Woodcock many years previously, struck him, and he sat down, and bowed to Deacon Chapin.

The deacon was conscientiously opposed to the practice of slander as it existed in many of the Puritan communities, and it was his policy to crush it with an iron heel. So he rose with a good deal of alacrity to say that it seemed to him that a clear case, and a very aggravated case, of slander, had been made out; and, for one, he hoped that at least exemplary punishment would be administered to the offender, who, it seemed to him, carried a very haughty and froward spirit. Such matters were treated at the Bay with great severity, as the only true policy. He wished that the magistrate, whose moderation all knew and admired, would yet see it in the line of his duty to deal more severely and effectively with these little sins, than it had previously appeared proper for him to deal. He thought, too, that a woman of the widow Marshfield's respectability, situated somewhat defenselessly, as she was, personally, had peculiar claims upon the protection of the law.

The magistrate then asked Mr. Holyoke if he had any remarks to offer.

"Not at present," replied that gentleman. "I have no wish to interfere with the strict operation of the law in this case, or in any other; or to influence the magistrate's decision in the slightest degree. He is bound by his oath to administer the law, and the case—a very frivolous one it appears to me—is before him. If, when the decision is rendered, there are any who would like to hear what I have to say, I shall have no objection to speaking very plainly upon the subject."

As Mr. Holyoke resumed his seat, the magistrate turned to the prisoner, and bade her rise and receive her sentence. Mary now grew pale and trembling for the first time during the trial, and pressed against her heart with both hands, while poor Hugh hung his head, and wrung his hands in the profoundest distress. "Mary Parsons," said Mr. Pynchon, "I find you guilty of defaming the good name of the widow Marshfield, and I sentence you to be well whipped on the morning after lecture, with twenty lashes by the constable—"

Mary stood and heard him thus far, and then uttered a scream so shrill and terrible, so charged with intense agony —that it brought nearly all the individuals in the room upon their feet, and thrilled them with a terrible shudder. But there stood Mary still, her eyes strained wildly open, but horribly vacant and meaningless.

Hugh burst into a flood of tears, and cried like a child—cried as if his warm and womanish heart had been swept by the fiercest breath of desolation, and his nicely strung sensibilities thrown into irredeemable discord. The sentence was a crown of thorns to the phantom of her fears, and as it was pressed down, her heart gave way, and she fell for the moment into a wild, hysterical insanity.

"Except you pay," continued the magistrate, in concluding his sentence, after the momentary interruption and excitement were past, "to the widow Marshfield the sum of three pounds, in satisfaction of the damages inflicted by you upon her reputation."

As he concluded, Mary still stood, looking vacantly at him. Immediately Mr. Holyoke arose, and, advancing to the desk, commenced to count out the amount of her fine. This she seemed to comprehend, for she turned and said, "Hugh, if there's money to pay, pay it."

"Have you money to pay the fine, Hugh?" inquired the magistrate.

"I have," replied the poor fellow, going forward and placing his heavy purse upon the desk.

As the sum of the fine was counted out, there was a shrug of the shoulders among the audience, a general whisper and a stare of wonder. Holyoke's movement, too, combined with the altogether unlooked for exhibition of sensibility on the part of the prisoner and her husband, had turned the current of sympathy for the moment into a new channel. The spirited widow saw only averted or vacant eyes around her, and felt greatly uneasy with the cheaply gotten gold.

As soon as the fine had been counted out from Hugh's purse, and the remainder handed back to him, he took Mary by the arm, and endeavored to lead her away. As the magistrate saw that she hesitated, he told her that she was at liberty, and with some hesitation, as if she but dimly comprehended the fact of her release, she suffered Hugh to lead her from the apartment.*

* At the risk of the loss of credit for originality, the report of this trial, as it appears in the Pynchon Record Book, is subjoined, for the purpose of showing that no exaggerations have been made, and that the picture is a true one. It is *verbatim*, with the exception of two illegible words, indicated by asterisks:

"The Widdow Marshfield complained against Mary, the wife of Hugh Parsons, of Springfield, for reporting her to be suspected for a witch, and she produced Jo. Matthews and his wife for her witnesses, who were examined upon oath.

"Jo. Matthews said that Mary Parsons tould him how she was taught to try a witch by a widdow woman that now lived in Springfield, and that she had lived in Windsor, and that she had 3 children and that one of them was married, &, at last, she said it was the wid-

As the door closed upon the distressed pair, Holyoke, who had not resumed his seat, pointed at their retreating figures, and said slowly and solemnly, "You have had an exhibition of law. Do you call it justice? Here is a poor girl who had the misfortune to have a father made lawless by law, and who has been for years a most offenceless object of suspicion in this plantation. She was complained of by a woman who I very well know has slandered her; and testified against by individuals who richly deserve the punishment she has received, for reporting and garbling her idle words. She is brought here by law, shocked into insanity by law, has paid a fine according to law, and has been wounded irrecoverably in her feelings by law. If this is in accordance with the spirit of the Bay, I pray God the Bay Path may be obliterated, that no more of the spirit

dow Marshfield. Jo. Matthews answered her that he believed no such thing of her; but, whereuppon said he, Mary Parsons replied—you need not speak so much for Goody Marshfield, for I am sure (said she) she hath envied every woman's child in ye **** till her own daughter had a child, and then, said she, ye child died and ye cow died, and I am persuaded, said she, they were bewitched; and she said moreover it was remarked to her by one in town that she was suspected to be a witch when she lived in Windsor, and that it was publickly known that the Devill followed her house in Windsor, and for aught I know, says she, follows her here.

"Goodwife Matthews saith upon oath that when Goody Parsons came to her house she said to her—I wonder what is become of the half pound of Veall—Goody Parsons said that she could not tell, except the witch had witcht it away. I wonder, said I, that you talk so much of a witch. Doo you think there is any witch in towne? Yes, said she, and she came into my house when the wooll was a cardinge. Who is it? said I. She said that Mr. Stebbinge had told her in Mr. Smith's chamber, that she was suspected to be a witch in Windsor, and that there were divers strange lights seen of late in the meddow that were never seen before the widdow Marshfield came to town, and that she did grudge at other women that had children, for her daughter had none, and about that time (namely of her grudging,) ye child died and ye cow died.

"Goody Parsons did stiffly deny the truth of these testimonys: but as the said witnesses had delivered their testimony upon oath, and finding that she had defamed ye good name of the widdow Marshfield, I sentenced her to be well whipped on the morrow after lecture with 20 lashes by the constable, unless she could procure the payment of £3 to ye widow Marshfield, for and *** the reputation of her good name."

reach us. I believe this whole system of brutal punishments for inferior crimes, and all these nicely drawn laws against the venial sins of imperfect communities, are infernal—unworthy of a Christian people, and demoralizing to every one living under, or in association with them. I do not speak reproachfully of the magistrate, or condemnatory of his decision. He has acted in accordance with his oath, and as you all cannot help but know, against his inclinations."

During this brief and impassioned speech, each word of which seemed to burn into every one's ears with a strange, irresistible power, and to sweep away from every eye the mists of prejudice and error, Mr. Pynchon sat with his head leaning upon his hand. At its close, one after another rose and left the house, until, at last, Holyoke and his father-in-law were left together. "Elizur," said the old man, raising his head and extending his hand, "you are nobly right, and if you could only know how wholly sick I am of this poor business of dealing out justice according to law you would pity me."

Holyoke had said what he had to say, and, with a sad and indignant heart, walked homewards, to tell his wife of the disgrace and suffering of her protegée, and to think of, and labor and pray for, a reformation in public sentiment, and its liberal expression in the colonial statutes.

Poor Hugh and Mary, in their deep distress, walked home regardless of the observation they elicited on the way, and entered their dwelling—once the brightest spot to them in all the world—now dark, spiritless, and gloomy. Mary had hardly taken a seat before a terrible chill assailed her, and in a few hours Hugh was sitting at her bedside, wetting her parched lips and bathing her throbbing temples, and heaving sighs and dropping tears of distress, as he listened to her incoherent ravings.

As Hugh sat like a patient girl, watching by the bedside

of his wife, day after day, and saw her spirit broken down by shame and sickness, and witnessed the wasting of her noble form, and the falling of the rose leaves from her cheeks; and as he nursed her in impatience and petulance, during the protracted period of her convalescence, Mr. Moxon, instead of visiting her, rose from his table a dozen times in a day, and asked the question: "*Where did she get that money?*"

CHAPTER XXVI.

If Mr. Pynchon really supposed that time and a more extended examination of his book would palliate the harsh judgments that had been rendered upon it by the leading men of the Bay, he was doomed to a grievous disappointment: for the winter, spring, and summer passed by, and the clamor concerning it only subsided to give place to a settled determination that the book should be condemned by the highest tribunal in the colony, and the author disgraced in every practicable manner.

This was not unanticipated by the people of the settlement, who, in order to give him such aid as he might desire in the General Court, consulted him in regard to their selection of a deputy to attend that body. He frankly indicated his preference for Mr. Holyoke of Lynn, the father of his son-in-law, and that gentleman was returned by the unanimous votes of the freemen.

When Mr. Pynchon set out for the Bay, he was accompanied by his son John, and by several of the leading men of the town, who went down to make interest for one who was bound to them by so many relations and associations, but all departed with sad forebodings. The trees that hung over the Bay Path, blushing with the surprises of the first frost, never canopied a more silent company of travellers. Here and there, some shrub or vine had shed down its shower of foliage in radiant flakes, until it lay fetlock deep upon the ground; but the hoofs of the horses, brushing it and crushing it, scarcely broke the thread of league-long reveries. The squirrel chattered upon the bough; the blue jay chided the dull-eared silence that lay dreaming among crickets, under the forest arches; coveys of partridges, like well delivered files of musketry, discharged by single birds their platoons of sound, and rolled off among the trees; the startled deer leaped from his roadside cover, with tangling vines upon his antlers, and with them wildly streaming over his back bounded away as if he were a pet tricked out for a holiday; and the wild turkey called to his mates, or some answering stranger, far out among the hills. But all these sights and sounds were unheeded by the men who felt the importance of the stake involved in the events that awaited them at the termination of their journey.

On the arrival of Mr. Pynchon and his friends at Boston, they became immediately aware that their worst fears were about to be realized. The magistrate was treated wherever he appeared with entire neglect, and not unfrequently with marked discourtesy. Everybody seemed to regard him as one whose fate was sealed, and as one with whose fortunes no one could be identified without detriment of personal character and business or political prospects.

He entered the chamber occupied by the magistrates, and took his seat, only to hear an order, just sent up from the deputies, read and passed, that a protest against the doctrines of his book should be drawn up to satisfy all men that the Court not only did not approve them, but that it disliked and detested them; that one of the ministers of the colony should be appointed to refute the errors of the book; that the author should be summoned before the next General Court to answer for the promulgation of his heresies; and that the book itself should be burned by the executioner in the market-place at Boston, on the following day, at the conclusion of the lecture.

This order was the consummation of his worst fears, and deeply offended, and still more deeply wounded at heart, he rose in his place, and exclaimed: "May God forgive the malice of the author of this order, and the cruel blindness of those who have passed it! I pronounce it an outrage upon the rights of human reason, a denial of the liberty wherewith Christ maketh his disciples free, an offence against conscience, and a sin against God."

As Mr. Pynchon slowly measured his language, quick, angry glances crossed the room, among his associates, and, save for the assumption of the floor by a cool and imperturbable member, he would have been assailed by harsh and bitter language: but the speaker who rose in response begged the magistrates to make all due allowance to one who had momentarily given way to a very natural excitement, and then suggested to Mr. Pynchon the propriety of his withdrawal from the room, as further action upon his case would doubtless follow, and he might possibly be led into imprudences that he would regret.

Mr. Pynchon proudly looked the man in the face until he sat down, and then calmly surveying the room, said,—"I have been an adviser in this body since the establishment of the colony, touching the affairs of the colony and the administration of justice, but neither this body, nor any one of its members, has been constituted my adviser. Under God, I am my own keeper, and though this Court may deal grievously with me in my person, station, and estate, I have the privilege, as I shall take the liberty, of watching the sword that is thrust at me, both in this and the second house, that no unfair advantage be taken of my unwariness. Save the Governor and his honorable deputy, I am to-day the peer of any man in this chamber, and I challenge the respect due in everything to myself as an honorable gentleman, and an assistant in the government of this colony. I have neither been displaced nor disgraced. Neither impeachment nor proscription has been visited upon me. Happily, injustice is not dishonor; and truth—blessed be God!—does not depend for its authenticity, vitality, and power, on the breath of the General Court of the Massachusetts!"

Thus outspoke the man at last. The book which he had written committed him before the world to his own opinions, and when he felt the consequences of the clash with the straitened creed that cramped the minds around him, the chains that had been upon him for long years fell off, and he stood in his own Christian manhood, and felt himself to be stronger than ever in his life before. The fear of man had passed away. The fear for the interest of truth had vanished before the conviction that truth was able to stand of itself. He stood upon a height from which the bigotry around him seemed so contemptible that, while he proudly claimed the honors due to his position, he regarded with pity those who associated with him. He felt that, in however false a position he might be placed before the Christians of the Englands, Old and New, he was a freer man, a larger Christian, and a better magistrate, for having given a thorough expression of himself—for asserting his own reason—for vindicating his own independence.

Previous to the scene which has been thus briefly described, quite as exciting and interesting a one had transpired in the House of Deputies. The order which had been sent up for the concurrence of the magistrates covered really the whole ground of proceedings which it was proposed to institute against the heretical bookmaker; and it was upon this order that a struggle most unusual was made.

The general knowledge that the case would come on filled the hall with spectators, among whom were many of the reverend elders of the colony, who came in to watch the operations of the deputies—partly from curiosity, partly from a wish to encourage the timid to stand boldy by their duty, and partly, doubtless, to impress them with a due sense of the importance of a faithful performance of the same.

Among them, conspicuously, were Mr. John Cotton of

Boston, and Mr. John Norton of Ipswich, the latter one of the most learned men and able controvertists in the colony. All of them had a scent for heresy so subtle and acute that they could discover it lying *perdu* beneath a word, or smell it in a puff of air awakened by a flourishing figure of speech. They were great, gaunt, keen-eyed, learned, self-devoted, powerful men of God, with more religion of intellect than thorough spirituality, and more zeal for doctrine than care for the nourishment of the Christian affections. This occasion was one which called them out from their studies, and gave them exciting food for thought and discussion; and if their care for the interests of orthodoxy was sometimes merged in the seductive delights of controversy, it would prove only that nature and grace made men and Christians then as they very frequently do at the present day.

The deputy who offered the order, made a speech containing no small amount of personal abuse. He felt that he could do this with perfect safety, as he knew that the sympathy of four-fifths of the members was with him, and that of the whole of the audience. He spoke of the impudence of a man like Mr. Pynchon—a learned fur-dealer, as he was pleased to call him—in assuming to interpret the oracles of God, and especially in controverting the doctrines held by the New England churches, and expounded by such learned and orthodox divines as he had the pleasure of seeing in the house on that occasion. He spoke of the damage that must inevitably result to the cause of true religion, from the attack upon it of one who had been mistakenly honored by a seat among the magistrates. He challenged the friends of Mr. Pynchon, if any such there might be among the deputies, to undertake his defence—to have the hardihood to do it—to place themselves on record as having done it—to disgrace themselves before the Christian world by doing it.

All this was said, and much more of the same import, with very slight allusions to the real merits of the book which the order, in effect, condemned. The heretical character of the book seemed to be taken for granted. The ministers had preached upon it, and condemned it from their pulpits. It had been discussed in private circles, and condemned there. There was no voice raised in its behalf. When the member took his seat, he looked around with a triumphant air, as if he supposed no one would answer him; but he was disappointed, in a manner which showed that Mr. Pynchon was not mistaken in his estimate of the man he had selected to guard his interests and character in that house.

Mr. Holyoke rose amid whispers, and sneers, and poorly disguised laughter, to reply, and, addressing the speaker, said: "About twenty years ago, a worthy gentleman of education, living comparatively at his ease in England, became one of the patentees of the colony of Massachusetts Bay; and in England, and New England, has been a magistrate, and assistant in the government of the colony ever since. He has been connected with all its affairs, has had, at times, the charge of its treasury, and has labored amid great discouragements and discomforts for its welfare. On arriving in this country, he founded a settlement of importance, which to-day has its representative in this house; and when that settlement had passed through the dangerous period of its infancy, he took with him a chosen band of companions, and sought a new home in the wilderness. The fields that he planted lie along the banks of the Connecticut, and there are the houses which he builded. He has been there these many years—the leader, father, magistrate of his people—loyal to this jurisdiction, though almost joined to the people of the South; and between his duties there and at the Bay, has spent his time and strength among the fatigues and dangers of long passages through the forest. In every relation which this man has sustained—public and private, legislative and judicial—he has done honor to himself and the colony. As a member of the church of Christ, his life has been blameless. As a man bearing heavy responsibilities, he has never failed in his duty. He has never abused a public or private trust. A wise legislator, a just judge, a consistent Christian, a ready counsellor, a true friend, a lover and supporter of order, and an honest, noble man, he has lived without suspicion or reproach. And this is the man—good, noble, venerable as he is—the abuse of whom has been so grossly indulged in, and so heartily enjoyed in this house to-day! I envy not the hand that dispenses, nor the maw that accepts, such miserable slanders and such unchristian calumnies as human food."

The concluding words were uttered in a tone of contemptuous indignation, and produced a most decided sensation among spectators as well as members. The speaker paused for a minute, amid profound silence, and then continued:

"What is it proposed to do with this man? It is proposed to disgrace him—to ruin him, for what is, at worst and most, an error of judgment. To his thorough Christian disposition, his life testifies; and this life of his, so pure, and devoted, and noble, has confirmed to him, or should confirm to him, in the eyes of the Christian world, the right to form opinions upon Christian doctrine and the privilege to propound them. The Christianity which makes a man a true Christian—which controls his life, and sanctifies his affections, and builds him up into a saintly estate, growing more holy with more years, and more meek with more honors, is a Christianity good enough for me, good enough for the world, and good enough to teach. And when new opinions come from good sources, it is rather the dictate of Christian modesty to examine them with prayerful attention, than boldly to condemn them and their author, because they run counter to the common judgment. Has it not always been the few who have held the right? Has not the common judgment been wrong, in all this world's history? Shall we sit in judgment on one of Christ's disciples? Have we more wisdom than he? Have we more grace? Have we lived better lives? Has God committed judgment into our hands? Are we infallible? Do we, as a political body, assume the interpretation of the Scriptures by any power received of men or of God? I tell this House of Deputies that they are doing, or trying to do, a very fearful thing. I tell them not to lay their hands on this man, lest they touch one of God's anointed. I tell them to refrain from this man, and let him alone, for if this counsel or this work be of men it will come to naught; but if it be of God, they cannot overthrow it; lest haply they be found even to fight against God.

"We have come to this country, nominally for the enjoyment of the liberty of conscience, the liberty of speech, and the liberty of action; but what liberty is that which is led bound at the wheels of state, or stands captive at the pillars of the pulpit? The liberty which is most in exercise here to-day, is the liberty to oppress conscience. There is no such thing as liberty of conscience, aside from perfect individual liberty; and the restraint of this, is oppression no different in kind, no less outrageous, than that exercised at home, or even in the den of The Beast himself, at Rome. I tell you that if this man be condemned for the utterance of his religious opinions by this body, which has legitimately no more to do with them than a council of savages, the world—aye—the devil himself, may have us in derision, and pointing, say, 'behold how these Christians love one another!'

"I see present here, to-day, several ministers of the Gospel of Jesus Christ. It cannot be that they have been brought here from any desire to see an independant thinker and writer sacrifised; and I only wish that it were consonant with the rules of this body for them to rise here, and testify to the paramount importance of a Christian life, and the essential necessity to vital Christianity of entire liberty of conscience. I wish that they might rise here, and, in their own eloquent words, point forward to that trial and tribunal to which we all tend, where the question will not be in regard to what church a man belongs, what creed he subscribes, what dogmas he adopts, what opinions he holds, but will be concerning the improvement of the one talent, or the ten talents, with which he has been intrusted. I pray that we may stand blameless of any violence upon his rights, or wounds upon his reputation."

Mr. Holyoke sat down, and, at the moment, his audience had forgotten where and what they were. A principle which they had never recognised, or had long forgotten, had sprung into life before them, and they were struck with its marvellous power and beauty. The idea that a man could possibly be good, and yet fail to be orthodox after their pattern—that life was something higher than light—that character was something more essential than opinion—and its correlative, that, with all their orthodoxy, they might possibly be destitute of true Christianity, received for the moment the homage of their reason, and threw the materials of the world in which they moved into new positions and new relations. The revelation was, however, but momentary. The spell passed away before the cool breath of spite, and the hot words of zeal which responded; and when the vote was taken, only five of the whole number of deputies were enrolled with Mr. Holyoke among the dissentients. But the effect of his words could not wholly die. Such seed is never sown in vain.

As soon as the order was passed, the declaration, or protest, for which it provided, was introduced and read, and the deputies and reverend elders bent their heads to hear its language:

* "The General Court now sitting in Boston in New England, this sixteenth of October, 1650. There was brought to our hands a book, written, as therein subscribed, by William Pynchon, Gent., in New England, entitled *The Meritorious Price of our Redemption, Justification, &c., clearing it from some common errors, &c.,* which book, containing many errors and heresies generally condemned by all orthodox writers that we have met with, we have judged it meet and necessary for vindication of the truth, so far as in us lies, as also to keep and preserve the people here committed to our care and trust, in the true knowledge and faith of our Lord Jesus Christ, and of our own redemption by him, as also for the clearing of ourselves to our Christian brethren and others in England, (where this book was printed, and is dispersed,) hereby to protest our innocency, as being neither parties nor privy to the writing, composing, printing, nor divulging thereof; but that, on the contrary, we detest and abhor many of the opinions and assertions therein, as false, erroneous, and heretical; yea, and whatsoever is contained in the said book which are contrary to the Scriptures of the Old and New Testament, and the general received doctrine of the orthodox churches extant since the time of the last and best reformation; and for proof and evidence of our sincere and plain meaning therein, we do condemn the said book to be burned in the market-place, at Boston, by the common executioner, and do purpose with all convenient speed to convent the said William Pynchon before authority, to find out whether the said William Pynchon will own the said book to be his or not; which, if he doth, we purpose (God willing) to proceed with him according to his demerits, unless he retract the same, and give full satisfaction, both here and by some second writing, to be printed and dispersed in England; all which we thought needful for the reason above alleged, to make known by this short protestation and declaration. Also, we further purpose, with what convenient speed we may, to appoint some fit person to

* Copied from the Colonial Records, Vol. iii., p. 215. The orthography is modernized.

make a particular answer to all material and controversial passages in the said book, and to publish the same in print, that so the errors and falsities therein may be fully discovered, the truth cleared, and the minds of those that love and seek after truth confirmed therein."

After the adoption of this declaration, and the passage of an order to have it printed and distributed in England, it was agreed upon by the whole court that Mr. Norton, one of the reverend elders of Ipswich, should be entreated to answer Mr. Pynchon's book with all convenient speed. The court then decided that Mr. Pynchon should be summoned before the next General Court of Election, on the first day of the session, to answer for the publication of his heretical book, and not to depart without leave from the court.

Notwithstanding the action that had been taken against Mr. Pynchon, he went out of the court with a better case than he carried in. In the magistrates, he had reclaimed the respect which he had momentarily lost; and in the deputies, a secret sympathy in his behalf had been awakened, which did not find its legitimate expression in their vote. It had appeared that he was not a man to be trampled upon without care, and that his case was one which did dishonor neither to his intellect nor his heart—whatever disgrace the court might, in the exercise of its prerogatives and power, see fit to visit upon him.

To the ministers who heard Mr. Holyoke, Mr. Pynchon became immediately an interesting subject of labor and discipline. They longed to get hold of him, and talk his errors out of him—to show him the loops in his logic, the weakness of his argument, and the fallacy of his conclusions; and they resolved, before leaving the hall, that they would, for the honor of Christ and the salvation of Mr. Pynchon, procure from him a retraction of his errors, and achieve for him a restoration to the confidence of the court and the colony. The resolution was a bold one, when it is considered with whom they had to deal, but the result, as will hereafter appear, was complimentary to their perseverance and power.

As the session broke up, the deputies divided into excited parties, and engaged warmly in the discussion of Mr. Holyoke's speech. The more they talked, the more clearly they apprehended the fact that something very unusual—something revolutionary, in fact—had been said. They wondered they had sat so quietly, and heard such sentiments and opinions boldly put forth. They wondered that they had not risen, at the close of his remarks, at least, and denounced him as a traitor to the country, and a betrayer of true religion. They wondered that they had not seen the tendency of the doctrines proclaimed, and that they could have been so weak as to sit silently, and listen to sentiments so entirely subversive of the existing order of things.

Mr. Pynchon and Mr. Holyoke walked to their lodgings together, and were the least excited and the happiest men of the number. A report of the independent bearing of the former before the magistrates, and of the noble speech of the latter, had preceded their appearance in the street, and, by the common people, they were regarded as heroes—as men who must have possessed a courage almost superhuman.

Towards evening, as Mr. Pynchon was sitting in his room busily engaged in writing, his landlady appeared, and informed him that a couple of reverend elders were at the door, and desired to speak with him. He bade her invite them in, and, on passing to the door himself, met Mr. Cotton and Mr. Norton, the two divines who have been mentioned as in attendance at the Deputies when Holyoke's speech was made. Mr. Pynchon received them with more than his usual dignity, and it was with much circumlocution, and with no assistance from him, that they approached the object of their visit.

"We have come," said Mr. Cotton, at last, "to speak with you in relation to your book."

Mr. Pynchon bowed.

"We have felt it to be our duty, as ministers of the gospel, to approach you privately, to explain to you the effect which your work has produced, to endeavor—praying for God's blessing upon our effort—to point out the more grievous errors into which we believe you have fallen, and to labor, as God hath given us ability, for your restoration to the favor of the General Court and the colony churches."

"God give you such speed in your work as may bring honor to truth and glory to Him!" exclaimed Mr. Pynchon, while an excited flush passed over his face.

"Amen!" ejaculated the ministers in concert.

"Mr. Pynchon," said Mr. Cotton, "you are doubtless aware that the doctrines you have advanced in regard to the character of the price paid for man's redemption are very unlike those entertained by the colony churches."

"I am, sir. Had I supposed there was no point of difference, I should not have written the book."

"Well, we will not discuss that matter now, for there is not time. We come now to you as a Christian man—as one who has the cause of true religion at heart, to show you that, however honestly you may have written, that cause is receiving damage at your hands."

"I should be very sorry to believe so sad a thing," replied Mr. Pynchon, touched by the earnest tone in which the minister spoke.

"And yet you cannot believe otherwise, if you will open your eyes to see, and your ears to hear, the commotion which you have aroused in the mind of the churches of this colony, and even among those of the Plymouth. A rock may be turned over where it lies, upon the level ground, and no man hear the report or feel the shock, but starting from the top of the mountain, it leaves a scar upon the mountain's side, and fills the plain with smoke and ruin."

"But a scar is the indication of a healthy action, and smoke and ruins are not necessarily companions," replied the magistrate.

"I cannot accuse you of jesting," rejoined the divine, "but surely you must have seen enough in the General Court to-day, to show you that much bitterness of feeling has been aroused, and that charity and brotherly love have been very sadly compromised."

"For all of which, I presume, you propose to hold me responsible. You might as well hold me responsible for your own unreasonableness in such an imputation, as for what you have seen to-day."

Mr. Pynchon uttered this rebuke with an excited flash of the eye and flush of the cheek, but Mr. Cotton received it meekly and returned to the charge.

"Mr. Pynchon, man is, at his best estate, fallible. You have written a book upon one of the greatest and most important subjects that can engage the mind of a mortal, and there is a possibility, you will admit, that you have made a mistake, and even many mistakes. I have no doubt that you will admit this. If so, then it becomes you, as a Christian, to open your mind to those who attend continually upon this very thing, and try your opinions in the light of their learning. At any rate, the consciousness that you may be in error, and be the cause of stumbling to many a weaker brother, and, perhaps, may lead many souls to the gates of death, should make you very careful before men, and prayerful before God."

"I thank you for your plainness of speech," said Mr. Pynchon, rising, "and shall be glad to see you and Mr. Norton at some other time, but you must excuse me now, as I have pressing business on hand."

The two divines rose from their chairs, and Mr. Norton, who had remained silent from the fact that he only wished to engage the magistrate in a discussion of doctrine, asked that gentleman if, on some future occasion, he would have any objection to take the text of the controverted book as the basis of conversation. Mr. Pynchon assured him that he should be ready to engage in such a conversation at any convenient opportunity, and then politely bowed the gentlemen out of the house.

As soon as his door was closed, he turned to his desk to pursue his writing, but, to his surprise, he found that a new and most troublesome discontent had been implanted in his heart. He had supposed that he was firmly fixed in his opinions, but he could not but admit that he might possibly be wrong, and he could not fail to see that the foundation of the beautiful edifice he had reared partook—however strong it might be—of his own frailty.

Then came up to his imagination the ordeal through which he had agreed to pass. He had agreed to pit himself against the most learned divines and the subtlest dialecticians of the day in a discussion of some of the fundamental doctrines of Christianity. This thought was full of excitement, and his mind ran off into the field of thought and argument with which it had become so familiar, as if anxious to see whether the old fortifications were still standing, and the pieces upon which he had always relied still looked out from their embrasures. Then his mind glanced off upon another course, as Mr. Cotton's suggestion recurred touching the effect of his book upon the Christian cause. This gave him more trouble than all the rest. The possibility that he had wounded the cause of Christ—that he had endangered the soul of believer or unbeliever—that he had failed to do full honor to Him who had his affections, or had detracted from the dignity of His mission—sat gloomily at the door of his heart, and breathed into it the most painful disquietude.

A few minutes' indulgence in thoughts like these unfitted him for business, and he found himself unable to pursue his writing. As he rose, and walked the floor of his apartment, the change that had passed over his spirit within a short time, occurred to him. He had entered the room calm and almost exultant—his mind firm, contented, and elastic. He was then free from the fetters he had worn through many weary years, but, somehow, his visitors had slipped them upon him again, and, full of doubts and fears, he felt once more half stripped of his manhood.

Mr. Pynchon had many interviews with the divines before he returned home. His mind became, little by little, obscured by the fear that he might be wrong—a cloud no larger than a man's hand at first, but growing until it darkened his whole mental vision—and he found himself unable to cope with the cool heads and ready speech of his antagonists.

At last, their interviews had become little more than solemn farces, in which the divines threw down his positions, and then setting them up, threw them down again. After they supposed that the foe had been thoroughly reduced, they proposed to Mr. Pynchon that he should recant his errors. This he refused to do, until he had had opportunity coolly to consider the whole matter after his arrival in Springfield. He felt that he was not himself among them, or under their influence, and that he should be faithless to God's honor as well as his own to yield well conceived and thoroughly considered opinions to such an unnatural pressure.

As the party which accompanied Mr. Pynchon to the Bay set out upon their return, they were even sadder than when they left their home; and the dead leaves that strewed the Bay Path in one continuous line of desolated beauty, well represented the fallen hopes that, like these very leaves, were fluttering in suspense and tinged with blight when their bearers passed eastward not many weeks before.

CHAPTER XXVII.

During the tedious period of Mary's sickness—its long days of watching and longer nights—Hugh heard of many strange things; and, although he knew that Mary was deranged, her words seemed informed with a peculiar significance, as if they were warnings or prophecies of some awful event in the future. There was one object—invisible to Hugh—of which she was always endeavoring to obtain a view, and her trials all grew out of the presence of other objects which obstructed her vision. Sometimes Hugh stood between her and the object she sought, and when, at her command, he stepped aside, Mr. Moxon appeared; and if Mr. Moxon at last retired, some one, or some thing, almost always took his place, and still left her wandering imagination unsatisfied and distressed.

It was strange to see how a peculiar mood of mental being and action had leaped over a barrier of sane and hearty life, to join itself to a similar mood far back in the past. As Mary lay upon her bed, tossing in feverish restlessness, the familiar vision of her mother's eyes came back to her. She recalled a long conversation with her father when he asked her if she could not see them; and their sweet and loving expression arose upon her memory, and soon dawned upon her distempered fancy, with the old semblance of reality. She sought for them through clouds and darkness, and when, at times, she felt their influence upon her aching head, and no intervention prevented their soft and soothing light from falling deep down into her heart, a smile so beautiful and heavenly irradiated her pallid face that Hugh's fainting heart throbbed with a new hope, and gushed with a long unwonted delight. But each smile was brief. Some phantom face or form—some grim enemy—some distant cloud or clinging mist—came between her and those blessed eyes, and often she struggled with these obstructions through whole nights, and waked in the morning only for a brief hour, to enter again into the unsatisfying and tormenting quest.

Nor did these fancies leave her as she slowly recovered a portion of her strength. Those eyes were always above her, in her dreams, and, as life freshened its pulses, she sometimes slept in their light through whole nights—as still, and white, and placidly beautiful as the earth beneath the moon in early spring-time.

At other times, great ghostly clouds swept over her, and tangling shapes of darkness twined their dim forms above her, through the rifts of which those eyes, at long intervals, looked in upon her spirit with a spell of peace, as the moon sometimes looks from the clouds through openings towards which it has waded in their deceitful depths for hours.

Through all these long weeks of weakness and confinement, Hugh and Mary could hardly have been better cared for had a special miracle been wrought for their benefit every day. Morning after morning Hugh found at the door some choice bird, or fish, or piece of venison, which left him at perfect liberty to devote all his time to the care and comfort of his wife. Further than that these timely gifts came from the same generous hand that supplied their earlier stores, Hugh knew nothing; but he became so much accustomed to find at the door just what he wanted, that he was disappointed whenever the resource failed him.

Occasionally, neighbors called to see how Mary was getting along, or from some motive of curiosity, and, as they frequently came in at meal times, and saw what excellent fare Hugh enjoyed, and was able to spread before Mary, they asked many awkward questions in regard to the mode of its procurement. It became known and notorious, at last, that though Hugh did not step his foot out of doors to obtain any kind of food, he was always supplied with the best game in the forest, the best fish in the river, and the best meal from the mill. Every effort made by the gossips of the place to ascertain who supplied him, was without avail. The matter was discussed at quilting parties, in family circles, and even among the grave and important men of the plantation.

As a natural consequence, the general belief ran in the old channel, and infernal agency received the credit of more Christian charity than existed in the whole settlement; or perhaps, more properly, of fulfilling the terms of a bargain to which Mary, or Hugh, or both, were parties. Mr. Moxon always formed one link in the chain of gossip that reached around the neighborhood, and was the receiver and careful treasurer of every idle story concerning the ill-fated pair; for his children were still afflicted, and with all his circumspection he was unable to discover any one, except Mary, who could safely be charged with being their tormentor.

Every circumstance in the unfortunate woman's life seemed fated to feed his suspicions concerning her. If she exhibited anger, she was under the influence of the devil. If she won a friend, it was through Satanic wiles. If she was fed in her helplessness, it was by the power of sorcery. Even the insanity of her sickness was regarded as demoniacal possession; and her sickness itself as nothing less than the prostration of her bodily powers before a supernatural occupation.

At long intervals, Mary's old mistress, who also suffered from ill health, went to visit her. The meeting was always a sad one, for each saw in the other the cruel havoc made by disease and care. There was not one in all Mr. Pynchon's family who felt the wounds inflicted on that gentleman's reputation so keenly as Mary Holyoke, and, as his trials came upon him when she was weak with indisposition, the intelligence wrought upon her with a terrible power. Her mental organization was so fine, and her physical powers so exquisitely adjusted, that, irritated by the harsh influences of a new settlement, oppressed with maternal cares and hardships, destitute of medical advice or aid, and shocked by the treatment dealt out to her father, whom she still loved and honored with more than the devotion of childhood, she could not retrieve her failing strength, or shake off the sorrow that lay heavily upon her heart. Yet her lips dropped only kindness, and, however irritable and petulant Mary Parsons might be, as she entered the cabin, the serene carriage of her friend, the sweet words of comfort which she spoke, the manifestation of true friendship which she never failed to make, soothed the poor girl's wounded spirit, and filled her with gladness and gratitude that gave life almost its only sweetness through many after days.

It was a joyous day for Hugh when his wife sat in her chair once more, with a favorite dress upon her, and her hair neatly parted and tied up in the way she used to wear it when he learned to love her. He was as playful as a child, and quite as happy; and as he drew the table to her side, and pressed her with the viands he had prepared, and heated the rough plank for her feet, and kissed her pale cheek, and lavished upon her the thousand little attentions and caresses that naturally sprang from his gratitude for her recovery, and his wish to make her as happy as himself, it seemed a pity that Mr. Moxon could not be a spectator of the scene—that so he might receive an impression of the artlessness and innocence of the unfortunate pair.

As Mary slowly recovered her strength, a new care, which during her insanity had been forgotten, asserted the leading place in her mind. She was, within a few months, to become a mother. The thought thrilled her with a strange, sweet pride, that quite subdued her natural fears and apprehensions; and the first work to which she turned her long unused hands was bestowed upon the preparations for the advent of the promised comer.

One evening, three or four weeks after she had commenced this work, and sat pleasantly talking with Hugh in regard to it, she brought out for exhibition the store of clothing she had rapidly prepared—the little shirts, the little dresses, the little caps and socks, and the hundred-and-one little things that make up humanity's first wardrobe. One after another these were held up, and then laid down upon the table, until that article of furniture supported such a spread as it never had before, and presented quite the appearance of a museum of curiosities. In the very midst of this display, the cabin door opened without the slightest warning, and gave ingress to Peter Trimble.

"I knew you must be alone here to-night, and I heard Mary had got well, and so I thought I'd come down, and walk straight in, jest to see if it wouldn't scare you a little," said Peter, carefully closing the door, and advancing to the fire. "I didn't 'spose it would scare you much," continued he, "because I didn't know as that would do; but I thought it would make you open your eyes sudden, and wake you up. How do you do here—eh?" and Peter gave one hand to Mary, and the other to Hugh, in a manner so different from that which he usually bore that they opened their eyes with a very genuine surprise.

"Take away these things," said Mary to Hugh, very hurriedly, and in an under tone. Then turning to Peter she endeavored to engage him in conversation, and commenced by asking how he had been for so many weeks.

"Oh! I've been fust rate," said Peter, sitting down in the best chair, and stretching his feet towards the fire; "but

I'd no idea you'd got so well. By George! Mary, you look as red as fire! It's true, now, isn't it, Hugh? I never see your cheeks so full of blood; did you, Hugh?"

All this, of course, did not tend in the slightest degree to restore Mary's equanimity, especially as Hugh stopped exactly in the midst of his work, in order to verify Peter's statement.

"If you're taking them traps away because I've come, you may as well let them be, for, between you and I, I am getting used to them." And then Peter put his head down between his knees, at the infinite peril of roasting his brains, and abandoned himself to such a powerful snicker that Hugh and Mary were obliged to laugh outright, from very sympathy. While he was thus engaged, however, Mary managed to get the remainder of the "traps" out of sight, and, with a feeling of relief, sat down and asked him what he meant.

"Oh! I see these things pretty much every night, and they don't scare me; and if they don't scare me, they hadn't ought to scare anybody, and you'd say so, if you knew what I do." The knowledge to which he alluded quite overcame him, and he could only check the snicker into which it threw him, by turning around, slapping Hugh on the back, and exclaiming—"It's the old hen, now, Hugh!"

"The old hen?" inquired Hugh, with an expression of wonder on his face.

"Don't you remember about the pullet?" inquired Peter, with the slightest possible sidewise nod towards Mary.

Hugh believed that he did, and smiled at the recurrence of the term, and the scene with which it was associated.

"The pullet was took by a fox, I expect," said Peter, giving Hugh a sly nudge. "By George!" continued he, his old admiration of the feat recurring, "you did that well, Hugh! You did jest as I'd 'a done, exactly. Yes, *sir!* that was a clean thing."

"So you're after another, now," suggested Hugh.

"Yes, I'm after another, but it ain't a pullet," responded Peter, and then he continued: "I might as well tell you, for between you and I, that's jest what I come here for to-night. You know where Deacon Chapin sets, pretty regular, in the meeting-house, don't you?"

"Yes," replied Mary and Hugh together.

"Can't you think of a hen and six chickens that always set three seats back of him?"

"A hen setting in the meeting-house?" inquired Hugh, with well feigned astonishment.

Peter rose, and, seizing Hugh by the shoulders, shook him till he could hardly breathe,—meantime saying: "Hugh Parsons, you're the greatest feller to be tripping up a chap's heels I ever see. That's jest the way you served me before. You're always putting me out and breaking me down in the wrong place! Land ahead! there wouldn't anybody think, to look at you, that you was up to that sort of thing."

"Do you mean the widow Tomson?" inquired Mary, with marked curiosity.

"No," replied Peter, very positively.

"Well, who do you mean?"

"I mean," replied Peter, charmed with his own ingenuity, "a woman that looks so much like her you can't tell them apart."

"Do you mean to say that you are going to marry widow Tomson?" said Mary.

"I can if I'm a-mind to,—I know that," responded Peter, rising to his feet proudly, and looking down upon his legs.

Mary saw that there was really something serious in the matter, and that Peter thought he was about to secure a prize. She therefore refrained from any remark that would injure his feelings, and asked him to tell her how the affair was brought about.

" Well, you know Tomson left her in rather a tight place, don't you ?—six children and a cabin to keep them in, but nobody to do the work for them, and stay in the house nights. One morning, as I was going by, she called to me, and said she, " Peter, I was almost scat to death last night. I know, jest as well as I want to know, that an Indian tried to get into the house, and I haven't got a bit good flint in my gun.' Well, I knew what that meant. She knew I always carried flints—everybody is always losing a flint, you know, and nobody has one, and so I went to the house, and put the best flint into the lock I had in my pocket, and jest drew the old charge, and snapped it two or three times, to let the children see the fire roll. Byme-by I looked up, and there stood the widow, crying. Says I, ' What's the matter ?' Says she, ' I was thinking how Tomson used to snap that same gun, with the children all standing around him.' Says, I, ' Goody Tomson, there is no use in crying for spilt milk.' Says she, ' I know it, but what'll become of the children ?' Says I, ' Can't you put them out to live ?' Says she, ' I don't know how I should get places for them, for I can't leave them a minute.' Says I, ' Perhaps you'd like to have me try for you.' Says she, ' Peter, that is jest what I've been wanting to ask you to do for me a long time.' Says I, ' I'll do it.' Well, I made a good beginning, and got rid of one child the first evening ; you'd better believe I told a pretty good story. The next morning I got rid of another, and then the widow said I could jest as well have their bed as not, and she should feel so much better with a man in the house.

" So I've been there to sleep ever since ; but it took me nigh about a week to get off the third child. You see they grow smaller as you get along down, and people are scary about taking them because they can't pay their way. Now there's one more that'll do to be sent off—don't you want a little tot, Hugh, to be skiving round the cabin here, and making a fuss, and learning to do things, and full of fun? By George! Hugh, she's as lively as a little squirrel, and *I* think she's the prettiest one of the lot. Land ahead! I hadn't thought of you before."

Hugh and Mary were both disposed to decline any portion of the widow Tomson's dividends, and Peter, having satisfied himself on that point, proceeded.

"One night, after I'd come in, and we was both feeling pretty well, to think how nicely we'd got along with the children, says Goody Tomson to me, 'What do you s'pose folks think, because you're here so much, and have done so much in getting my children put out?' Says I, 'I don't know, nor I don't care. Whose business is't?' says I; says she, 'You men don't feel such things as we women do. We don't have anybody to take care on us, and stand up for us—we that have been left alone—' and then she put her handkerchief up to her eyes, and I should think she cried for half an hour."

As the memory of this afflictive scene came back to Peter, he rose from his chair and walked across the room, and then returned and dropped himself into his seat.

"I ain't a'going to tell you the rest of it. You both of you look just as full of Cain as you can hold," said Peter, as he caught the expression upon their faces, on resuming his chair.

"Oh! go on! go on!" exclaimed both, Mary adding with peculiar significance, "we were not laughing at you."

"I shan't do it," replied Peter, with a dim suspicion that he had been humbugged, and a slight feeling of shame at revealing the tender passages in his acquaintance with the widow. "I shan't do it. You know how them things are got along with. Anyhow, we came to an understanding, and I tell *you* she's a good *deal* more of a woman than she has the credit of being, and she ain't but thirty years old either. Now you wouldn't have thought that, would you?"

"So you are really going to marry the widow Tomson, are you, Peter?" said Mary, affirmatively and interrogatively together.

"I shan't say that I *am*, and I shan't say that I *ain't*," replied Peter, "but I *do* say," continued he, with an extremely intelligent look, "that such traps as you had on the table when I came in don't scare me. Land ahead! I'll bet I've dressed and ondressed that baby of Goody Tomson's—Esther she wants me to call her—more than twenty times."

This statement was too much for the gravity of his auditors, and Hugh, exclaiming, "Ah, Peter, you are in for it," burst into a hearty laugh, in which Mary joined him. Peter began, at last, to think there was something extremely funny in the matter, and laughed louder than either of them, until he wished to stop, and managed to effect his object by seizing Hugh by the shoulders, and exclaiming, "Say! what are you laughing at? I only did it for fun."

Peter's friends finally found breath to congratulate him on his success, as well in getting rid of the children of the bereaved Esther, as in securing her and the balance of her family; and Peter closed the interview by informing them of the exact value of the widow's cabin, the number of acres in her possession that had been planted with corn, and the general desirableness of the match, in a worldly point of view. Assuring them, with a feeling of complacent exultation that almost choked his utterance, that he began to feel as if he was "one of them," he retired to the widow Tomson's cabin, to lend the protection of his presence to its inmates, and to dream of the time when, with all its contents and environments, it should become his own.

Long conversations, between Mary and Hugh, upon the all-absorbing subject, were of frequent occurrence during the months which followed, but, meanwhile, new anxieties descended upon both.

Mary, instead of recovering her accustomed health, as time passed, relapsed into a strange and very miserable state, and, during much of the time, betrayed the most positive and painful symptoms of mental alienation. These were frequently accompanied by a very decided aversion to the presence of her husband, and the acceptance of any offices of kindness and affection at his hands—a condition which filled him with the deepest perplexity and distress.

As the spring advanced, there arose another disturbing cause, which, though harmless in itself, became, in her imagination, charged with terrible evils. Mr. Moxon had received advice concerning his children from an eminent medical gentleman at the Bay, which required him to see that they were thoroughly exercised for an hour every morning in the open air; and as the best walk passed by Mary's cabin, the passage of the minister, with a daughter at each hand, became a matter of daily recurrence. They never passed by the cabin, however, without instituting the closest scrutiny of everything around it, and if the door or window happened to be open, of everything within it.

This daily inquisition became, at last, so intolerable, that every symptom of Mary's disease was aggravated by it, and it frequently gave rise to whole days of excessive nervous irritation and mental distress.

Thus passed away the spring and the summer; and a sad, weary time was it for poor Hugh. Through many a warm summer night he sat sleepless at Mary's bedside, endeavoring to soothe her heated fancies. Hour after hour she lay upon her bed, gazing upwards with her large, lustrous eyes, and brushing away with her white and spectral hands the long succession of filmy shapes and shadows that interposed between her own and those eyes whose loving and gentle gaze was all for which her soul seemed to long and labor. Sometimes she asked him for assistance, and was vexed at his awkwardness. Sometimes he was the obstruction, and fled before a wild burst of her impatient temper. Then, after laboring ineffectually for hours, she would renounce the essay, and sink into a long fit of hysterical weeping and sobbing.

One morning in the early part of autumn, only a day or two after Mr. Pynchon's departure for the Bay as recorded in the preceding chapter, Mr. Moxon and his children were taking their accustomed walk by the cabin, gazing intently at it during their slow progress, when a feeble wail fell upon their ears, but of a character so peculiar—coming as it did very faintly through the closed door and windows—that they paused in blank stillness and astonishment. The wail was again and again repeated; and Mr. Moxon, on looking down upon his children, saw that it was producing upon them a very marked effect. Martha listened with a pleased and most interested smile upon her face, and, at last, reaching out her hand, exclaimed "Poor pussy! poor pussy!" Then she stooped to the ground, as if she saw the object she had named approaching her, and was ready to fold it in her arms.

Mr. Moxon saw that a fit was actually upon her, and that Rebekah was rapidly approaching her usual sympathetic condition, and, fairly tearing Martha away from the spot, in spite of tears and entreaties, he hurried with both of his children homewards. Arriving there, the minister, who had begun to feel hopeful in regard to his children, was again plunged into despair by their continuance in the paroxysm which had come upon them. All day long Martha had the blue cat, of the years long gone, with and about her. She folded her in her arms with childish fondness, and was offended that neither her father nor mother could hear her purr, or feel her as she rubbed against their garments.

During the day, Mr. Moxon was informed by a neighbor of the birth of Mary Parsons's child; and heard the announcement with a sigh so deep as to startle his informant.

He regarded the event as the accession of another baleful influence to the number of those which had for years been operative against him and his family, and as he turned to the contemplation of his children he exclaimed, from the depths of a heart bursting with distress, "How long, O Lord, how long!"

Little did Mary and Hugh imagine, while they were laughing over Peter Trimble's story of his somewhat remarkable courtship, that they should be indebted to the good-natured widow Tompson for some of the kindest and most important offices of friendship.

Mary, for weeks and months after the birth of her child, saw not one sane day or hour. Hugh, in the midst of his perplexity, called upon his friend Peter to help him; and Peter, with his uniform policy, was ready to lend the services of anything he had in the world—even to those of the self-devoted Esther. And Esther came with her hearty baby at her breast—the youngest of the Tompsons—and after doing what she could in the cabin, and ascertaining that Mary's child would have to be kept away from her, took the puny little creature to her own home, and cared for it, and nursed it as tenderly as if it had been her own.

Many a long fight of words did she have over the strange baby; for two days had not passed, after its birth, before the story of the peculiarity of its tone in crying and its effect upon the Moxon girls, had become notorious throughout the plantation. All the gossips of the town visited the widow's cabin for the purpose of seeing the baby that cried like a cat. Little girls came to the window, and looked in, and then ran away to tell the story to their mates.

It would be difficult to account fully for the peculiar gloom that settled upon the town during the winter that followed Mr. Pynchon's misfortunes at the Bay, and the birth of Hugh's unwelcome child. Mr. Pynchon shut himself closely in his room and hardly appeared at all, except at the public religious exercises in the meeting-house. There was a general air of thoughtfulness throughout his household, and among his connexions. There were no merry-makings in the neighborhood during the winter—no huskings—no weddings. It seemed as if a great crisis in the affairs of the plantation were approaching, and as if every one's heart were blindly prophesying.

No man appreciated the general state of feeling and the change that had occurred in the tone and temper of the people more thoroughly than Mr. Pynchon, and it all tended not only to increase his unhappiness, but to fill him with the most distressing anxieties and the deepest self-questionings. In his lonely contemplations, the thought had occurred to him that perhaps all these calamities had come upon his people in consequence of his own unfaithfulness to duty and to truth.

To a sensitively conscientious mind, a thought like this would be the most painful it could possibly entertain. Was he, after all his efforts to build up the plantation, and to order its affairs in a Christian manner, only a curse to it? Had he been presumptuous in setting aside the learning of his teachers, and in assuming their robes and responsibilities? Was he but a Jonah upon the vessel, who must be thrown overboard before the waves could be quieted? These questions fell, one after another, upon his mind, and fairly crushed it to the earth, and prepared the way for one of the most painful and humiliating passages in his whole life.

As soon as the Bay Path became passable, and the streams that crossed it fordable, in the following spring, Mr. Pynchon set out, with a heavy heart, for the Bay. Henry Smith accompanied him as a deputy from the town to the General Court, and as they turned the steps of their horses eastward, followed by prayerful adieus, they left a very sad community behind them. All believed and felt that a great and good man was about to be sacrificed. Even Deacon Chapin, who, with a number of the best and most reliable men in the plantation, did not sympathize with Mr. Pynchon's views of doctrine, and disapproved his general policy, was touched by his personal distresses, and gave him, at parting, the hand of genuine commiseration.

At the end of his journey, he found his old friends, the ministers, ready to receive him, and ready again to labor, in any way that offered, for his restoration to orthodoxy. During his absence, they had gone over the whole ground together, and had arranged their forces for a battle in which they felt certain of becoming the victors. Mr. Norton's reply, written in accordance with the request of the General Court, had been completed and fully discussed among the self-constituted board of reverend censors; and it was, as a matter of course, the strongest document in that behalf possible to be produced in the colony. The divines found Mr. Pynchon debilitated by a winter's confinement, and greatly fatigued by his journey. His mind suffered as well as his body, and it became a task of comparative ease to worry him down, and secure the preliminary steps to a recantation of his alleged errors.

At this juncture, an event occurred which brought a sudden alarm upon Mr. Pynchon, and a burden of terrible pain—an event which thrilled with horror the members of the General Court, and spread a sudden excitement throughout the Bay settlements. This event will take the reader back to Springfield, and to that town—for the time—the scene is transferred.

CHAPTER XXVIII.

Mr. Pynchon had been absent from the settlement but a few days when symptoms of amendment appeared in the sad case of Mary Parsons. For months she had not spoken of her child, but, at last, her memory and reason seemed to return together, and as the fact that she was the mother of a child that had once slept upon her bosom had been fixed upon her mind during some lucid moment, she turned to look upon the long alienated baby, as if she had just awaked from the sleep of an hour. She gave Hugh a pleasant smile as he bent over her, and asked him for the object for which she sought; and he—unwittingly and with much agitation—told her where the child was, and how long and for what cause it had been away from her. The facts were too much for her weak brain, and, under their pressure, she relapsed again into an insane mood, in which her child divided her wandering and wayward fancies with her mother's eyes, and in which, in some way, the two became united by a thousand conflicting or harmonious associations.

Hardly a minute passed that did not hear her calling for her child; and, as darkness closed down upon her memory, and the path between it and Goody Tomson's cabin was blotted out, the child was elevated by her imagination to direct companionship with the beautiful eyes from which had descended upon her the only calm and comfort she had enjoyed during her long illness. Then came between her eyes and the double vision the old tormenting shapes with which her long struggle had been held, and her efforts to reach her baby and reclaim it to her arms became so pitiful, that Hugh could only look upon her and weep.

At last, he sent for Mary Holyoke, and asked for her advice in regard to restoring her child to her. The pleadings of the poor insane mother touched Mary Holyoke's heart at once, and she begged Hugh to go to Goody Tomson, and bid her bring the child. The kind-hearted nurse was soon on the way, in obedience to the summons, and Hugh walked back in her company, with a vague hope in his breast that the child would carry to its stricken mother a soothing if not a healing power. As the pair softly entered the cabin, they found Mary Holyoke sitting at the side of the poor patient, who, as if conscious of the presence of her old friend and mistress, had fallen into a quiet sleep. The child, too, was sleeping in its nurse's arms, and both the women—mothers as they were—by an impulse that sprang in each alike from simple nature, moved to lay the little one by its mother's side. The clothes were softly turned down, and the baby's head—once more at its home—pressed its mother's arm; and the little one smiled with a sweetness that thrilled the trembling Hugh to the very depths of his heart, as it composed itself, from a momentary disturbance, to a sounder sleep.

It was a moment of profound excitement. The cabin was as still as if there were not a breathing inhabitant within it, and every waking eye was upon the sleeping mother and child. Half an hour—an hour—passed thus, when Mary, who had enjoyed the best sleep that had visited her for several days, opened her eyes, and again called for her child.

"Hush!" said Mary Holyoke, softly, "the baby is sleeping on your arm. Do not wake it!"

The mother turned her large eyes, full of wonder and strange curiosity, upon the child, and, without speaking a word, gazed at it until the big tears brimmed her eyes, and ran down upon her pillow, drop by drop, as if an accumulated flood had found vent, and were pouring forth its waters, alike unbidden and uncontrollable. Then she carefully put her face down to the little head that lay pillowed upon her arm, and pressed her lips upon it with a gentle power, and, from the recesses of her ardent nature, poured out upon it, in a fervent and silent effluence, the first healthy outgoings of a mother's love. The room was silent still, save as Hugh gave expression to his feelings in occasional sobs. Goody Tomson had, as noiselessly as possible, gone out of the cabin, and seating herself upon a rough bench at the door, given herself up to a hearty fit of crying.

The sleep of the unconscious cause of all this emotion began gradually to release its bands, and the child opened its eyes for the first time upon its mother's face. It looked but a moment, when its face became suffused with fright, and, closing its eyes again, it burst into a fit of crying as vigorous as it was pitiful.

Mary Holyoke watched with intense interest the effect of this development upon the mother, and was pained to witness a strange wild change coming upon her countenance, and breaking in a more powerful expression from her eye. The mother looked at her weeping child for a minute, then pushed it from her violently, and exclaimed, "That is not my child—take it away; and don't let Goody Tomson bring any more of her brats here to cheat me with!"

"My dear!" said Mary Holyoke, "this is your own sweet child. It has grown so much that you do not know it."

The only reply made to this address was a stare of mingled incredulity and resentment, from which the poor patient's benefactress shrank with a sigh of distress. Goody Tomson no sooner saw her little protegé pushed rudely aside than she seized the treasure, and, hugging it to her bosom, retired to a distant part of the room, whither its mother's eyes followed her with an expression of mingled intelligence and fatuity that crushed the newly springing hopes in Hugh's bosom, and showed how thoroughly her mind had been committed to its shadowy keepers.

Goody Tomson was soon joined by Mary Holyoke and Hugh, and a consultation was held in regard to the proper course of procedure. Mary Holyoke could not give up the idea that, in some way, the presence of the child would do the mother good; how, it did not appear, but so it seemed to her. The nurse was not so sure, from the fact that her sympathies attached rather to the child than the mother. Hugh was willing to do what the others thought for the best, and, as they could not agree, it was finally decided that Goody Tomson should return to her cabin with the child, and, if Mary should again call for it, in such a manner as in any way to show that she wished to see it—the little one she had disowned—it should be sent for.

As the nurse wrapped her little charge in a blanket, to guard it from the chill of the evening which was approaching, and undertook to pass out of the door, she was arrested by Mary with the words, "Where are you going with that child?"

"Home," replied the nurse.

"I thought Mistress Holyoke said it was my child," said the mother.

"But you said it wasn't," replied Goody Tomson, very bluntly.

"I don't know," responded Mary, while a shadow of doubt passed over her face, "but she never told me a lie before. Bring the baby here again."

The babe, at Mary Holyoke's request, was brought back, and exhibited to the mother, who made no effort to take it in her arms, and was content to look at it in the nurse's possession.

"Don't let her take it away!" exclaimed the mother to

Mary Holyoke, with a beseeching expression that seemed the very opposite of that which she had previously exhibited.

"She shall not go!" replied the lady, with an affectionate and decided impulse.

It was then arranged that Mary Holyoke should return home, and send word to Goody Tomson's cabin—still in the keeping of Peter Trimble—that that young man would be obliged for the night to dispense with the presence of the mistress of the house, and discharge the duties of a nurse as well as protector to her little family of children. After giving Hugh and the nurse some general directions touching the management of affairs, Mary Holyoke bent her steps homeward to attend to the duties of her own household.

After her departure, the patient lay in deep silence, as if absorbed in thought, and Hugh and the nurse kept at a distance, hoping that she might fall asleep. But not a motion was made that she did not see. The babe which the nurse had succeeded in keeping unusually quiet during her presence in the house, occasionally nestled uneasily in her arms, and gave utterance to a low cry; and at such times the mother raised herself upon her elbows in the bed, and gazed upon it with a painful intensity.

At last, Hugh brought to Mary her supper, but not a mouthful passed her lips. She shook her head at every offer of food, and kept her eyes fastened upon her child as the nurse fed it at her own breast, or walked across the cabin with it closely folded in her arms, or hummed a drowsy tune in its ears, or whispered to it in sweet and soothing words.

Hugh and the nurse ate their supper in silence, and soon afterwards the baby fell asleep. As the two were sitting at a small fire that had been kindled upon the hearth, alternately looking at the flickering flame and the patient at the opposite side of the room, the wind began to moan dismally, and the rain to patter upon the cabin roof, while, at brief intervals, a drop fell intact through the short chimney, and died with an angry pang upon the coals, as if it had been stung. Then the rising wind wailed more and more dreadfully among the trees, and roared in and around the chimney—sometimes sweeping the gradually increasing rain against the window panes, persistently and with spasmodic reinforcements of power, and then retiring, and roaring away among the woods; sometimes pouncing upon the cabin like an army of shadowy beasts, shaking the door as if human hands had hold of it, rattling the window, tossing the rain down the chimney in showers, scrambling over the loose sticks upon the wood pile, and, at last, tired and baffled, scampering off over the leaves to make way for its successors; sometimes making a feint, and, wheeling around the corner, spending its strength at an unexpected point—at last falling lifeless in a lull through which the rain came down steadily, as if it had been waiting the result of the wind's manœuvres. In a brief hour, a still, sombre day had descended into a wet, wild night.

Hugh sat for a while and listened to the dreary music of the storm, and then barred his door, and made fast the windows, so that they should not rattle, and stuffed old garments under the door to keep out the driving rain, and set a pail to catch the water that began to fall, drop by drop, from a leak in the roof. After these preparations for a stormy night had been made, he resumed his seat at the fire, and, oppressed with weariness and long watching, began to doze.

The dropping into the pail quickened its measured fall, until each drop struck the surface with a metallic, musical clink, that might, in that weird and dreary room, have been mistaken for an elfin bell, calling the sprites of the woods to a revel upon the midnight hearth.

Hugh opened and closed his eyes wearily, and the nurse nodded over the baby in her low chair; but upon the bed, which, in their weariness and drowsiness, they had momentarily forgotten, lay a brain teeming with fancies born equally of the storm without and the storm within.

As the watchers became still, Mary waited for a noisy blast of the storm, and then raised herself upon her elbows in the bed, and sought for a glimpse of the child. Then, in another blast, she settled upon the bed again. This movement was several times repeated. At last, she subsided into silence.

The blast rose and fell upon her ears, the rain poured ceaselessly upon the roof, and the water drops clinked faster and faster in the pail, as if the fairy bell had been changed to a set of silver chimes, sending forth their liquid music from towers that swayed with the sound. The flickering fire, the roaring wind, the sweeping rain, the lively chimes, the strange child, and the twilight of the room, formed a combination of circumstances and influences which harmonized marvellously with her mood of mind, and filled her with a strange, delicious joy, that she had not experienced for many months. She seemed to breathe the native atmosphere of delirium, and to find her mind, for the first time since her sickness, adapted to, and in accordance with the circumstances that formed the externals of her life. In this mood, she turned her gaze upwards, and never had such a sweet vision of her mother's eyes smiled upon her. No cloud obstructed, no shape intervened. Calm and sweet—full of love and tender sadness—those orbs which had watched over her infancy, which had beamed in upon the darkness and sorrows of her childhood's dreams—those eyes met hers, and, beneath them, as if folded to a shadowy bosom, was her baby—*her* baby—a little cherub, wrapped in rosy sleep.

As she gazed and gazed again, and drank in the beauty

and the blessedness of this dear vision, the wind seemed to lull in the forest around, and the clinking water changed to a low, sweet measure, like bells heard in the desert, or the dreamy tinkle of flocks grazing on the sunny slopes of summer hills.

As she lay thus in beatific possession, through what seemed to her almost an age of bliss, the wind began to rise again, and, roaring in the chimney, driving the rain upon the roof and walls of the cabin, and screaming among the forest branches, brought clouds before her mental sight, and shut out the vision that had so long held her in sweet enthralment. The first and only shape that interposed was that of the strange child. She changed the position of her head, but the stranger came between. She tried to sweep it away with her hand, but she could not reach it. Then, slowly raising herself upon her elbows again, she looked at the nurse, still nodding over her little charge in the corner, and, settling back to her place, she very softly pronounced Hugh's name.

Hugh, long accustomed to watching and sleeping lightly, was at her bedside in an instant.

"Tell Goody Tomson," said Mary, in a low, composed voice, "to lay the child on my bed, over upon the other side, and to lie down herself upon the bunk, and get some rest."

"Do you think you had better have the child on your bed?" inquired Hugh, doubtingly, and with an effort in the faint light to get the expression of her eye.

"Why—isn't it my child?" said Mary.

"Oh! certainly it is, Mary," replied Hugh, with all the tenderness and persuasiveness he could throw into his voice; "certainly it is, Mary—it is your child and mine."

"Well—can't I have my own child?" inquired Mary.

There was something in the tone of her voice—something in her manner—that filled him with misgivings and fears, but he could not tell what it was; so he went to Goody Tomson and knelt down by her side, and whispered in her ear the substance of Mary's wishes and directions.

As he knelt there, the rain came down freshly upon the roof, and the clinking drops struck the pail with a rapid and irregular fall—a wild and hurried tone—as if the bells of a city were ringing the alarm of a pressing danger. They almost spoke—and bounded up from the surface upon which they fell, and broke into strange articulations, and sharply modulated shouts and cries that had their echoes. No ear heard or noticed them but Mary's. To her, they spoke a plain language; and she wondered that Hugh and Goody Tomson did not hear it; and, as they whispered together—cautiously, so that they might not waken the babe—she watched them closely, to see whether they had not taken the alarm.

Goody Tomson, oppressed with sleep and not doubting that Hugh would look well after the child, seemed glad to accede to Mary's wishes; and, taking the little one to the bed, gently released it from her own arms, and deposited it upon a pillow on the side opposite to its mother. The sleepy nurse did not see the glaring eyes that scanned her every movement, and Hugh was engaged in watching the child which, though his own, he had hitherto hardly known.

When the child was covered, the pair went on tiptoe back to the hearth, and Hugh, pointing to the bunk at the side of the room, sent the nurse to her rest. Then, adding two or three sticks to the fire, he stretched himself in his chair to sleep. Ten minutes had hardly elapsed when both Hugh and the nurse were soundly snoring. But the storm still continued without, roaring and sweeping around the cabin, and masking if not entirely drowning the minor sounds within.

Within a few minutes, the cabin had grown solemn to its only wakeful tenant. The roof had swollen with rain until the leak was so small that the drops came in at long and measured intervals upon a body of water whose increased depth gave forth a sad strange resonance, like the tolling of a lonely bell.

Mary lay in death-like stillness listening to the knell, and revolving in her confused mind a purpose which had crept into it and fastened itself there. Once more she looked upwards—long, patiently, and earnestly—but she could see nothing but the strange child. Then slowly, she turned her head upon the pillow, until her eyes were glued to the little sleeper. She watched the babe for a few minutes—all the time keeping distinctly in her sharpened apprehensions the rhythmic respirations of its nurse and father, and alive to every movement they might make—and then, as a serpent creeps toward the victim it has charmed, she passed her emaciated hand towards the child.

With the first movement, the wind seemed to die away, and the rain to withhold its fall upon the roof. She paused, and the drops fell into the pail still more slowly, and with a sadder intonation, as if they were grief-burdened, or growing faint with despair. Between each drop, inch after inch, the white hand slid along the sheet, coming nearer and still nearer the unconscious babe, whose nurse seemed to snore more loudly as the danger to her charge increased. At length its little hand was reached, and Mary accidentally touched it. It was soft and warm, and irritated by the slight disturbance, the child raised it and slowly dropped it upon that of its mother. In the utter tension of her sensibilities, she could feel the pulsations of its heart at the very tips of its fingers, and there was something so delicate and sweet in its touch, something so unconscious and innocent in its sleep, that she paused for another look in its face. She could not be mistaken. It was the same face—the same child—that had come between her and her own child—it was the little impostor.

The wind came up again with a wail from the woods—and her brain caught the impulse and the influence. Again her hand was in motion, and onward it moved, inch by inch, towards the babe's head—the slowly dropping water meanwhile uttering low, tearful, pleading notes of deprecation.

Again she paused, looked towards the distant sleepers, then towards the pail, and half rose with a sudden impulse to move it from its place, that so its admonitions might be silenced. Her cautiousness checked her in the act, and again she turned to the child.

At this moment, her eye was burning with excitement, but her hand and arm were as steady as if the nerves that strung them were of iron. Slowly that hand passed over the little sleeper's throat, and there, as still and rigid as the hand of death, it paused. The conscious palm, with the strained tendons underneath the bloodless skin, felt the warmth of the little chin and neck and breast, like a palpable emanation or atmosphere, as it hung above them at scarcely a hair's escape from contact; but still it paused. Then, from the far northeast, Mary heard a blast stirring among the trees. On it came, roaring and wailing and screaming through the night, until it reached the cabin, where, bellowing in the chimney and sweeping over the roof, it drowned all other noise without and within.

At the height of the confusion, that pale hand, with the grip of a vice, was fastened upon the little sleeper's throat. Not a breath did it draw—not an utterance did it make—afterwards. Its hands instinctively tugged at Mary's wrist, in the vain effort to tear it away, and its chest heaved in quick throes, and its legs were drawn up in struggling convulsions. These grew fainter and fainter until the victim's eyes—strained wildly open—slowly deadened into a senseless glaze, and its soft, sweet face became turgid and purple. At last, all was still—the babe was stone dead. The wind died away, and the last brand had ceased to crackle in the fire-place, and the clinking drops had forgotten to ring their changes in the water pail. The silence grew awful, for death, violence, madness, and sleep were gathered in one room.

The murderess clung to the little neck that had grown long and lank within her grasp, until she began to feel the chill that was creeping into her victim's frame, and then she slowly and cautiously withdrew her hand and covered the body as the nurse had left it covered. In an instant a wild thrill of exultation passed through her brain—a strange, mad joy—whose manifestation in some manner she had no power to repress, and she shivered the silence with a laugh so loud, and meaningless, and long continued, that it seemed to the suddenly awakened sleepers more like the laugh of a demon than of a human being. Hugh leaped to the bedside, and found her sitting up at the end of the bed, madly laughing still. He no sooner appeared than Mary pointed to the dead child, and went into renewed convulsions of her terrible merriment.

"O Mary! O God! Oh! what shall I do! what shall I do!" exclaimed Hugh, bursting into a wild cry of anguish, as he dimly saw the child, and placed his hurried and trembling hand upon its cold little face.

At this time the drowsy nurse stumbled blindly towards the bed, wondering what had occurred, and more than half forgetful that she was not in her own cabin. She put her hand upon the child, dropped to her knees to look at it in the dull twilight of the room, felt its neck, and then looked at the mother, whose laughter had been arrested by Hugh's exclamations of terror and distress. The terrible fact stole into her apprehension by degrees, and, sinking upon the floor, the simple and devoted creature clung to Hugh's knees, and gave utterance to such exclamations of distress as burst naturally from her heart—bemoaning the hour and day she ever brought the little innocent back, and insisting that God would never forgive her, and that she could never forgive herself for the act. She might have known a crazy mother would kill the child, she said.

Hugh disengaged himself from her, and passing around the bed to Mary, put his arm around her, and looking in her wild eyes a moment, hid his face upon her wasted bosom, and crying convulsively said, "Oh, Mary, Mary, Mary, Mary! you don't know what you've done!"

"Yes, I do, too; I've killed that woman's ugly brat, and if she don't leave the cabin and stop troubling you and me in this way, I'll kill her."

"Why, Mary! it was not her child—it was yours! Oh, dear! what will become of us now!" and Hugh—poor, worn, weary, and despairing fellow—cried as if his heart were wholly broken.

Goody Tomson was not long in making her determination. Throwing her shawl over her head, as the most expeditious way of covering herself, she unbarred the door, and, before Hugh became conscious of what she was doing, was on her way to give the alarm—her own heart so full of alarm that she flew rather than ran along the muddy path. The storm lay spent upon the ground, the old moon with inverted horn hung over the woods, the wolf's long howl from the eastern hill came drearily down into the valley, as the woman ran screaming "Murder! murder!" from house to house.

Not until she had run nearly the length of the village could she be stopped, so as to direct the steps of the attendance she sought. As soon as the first fact of the case was learned, nearly all the men of the settlement, who had risen and hastily dressed themselves, were on their way to Hugh's cabin. Few of them could disguise their fears, as they turned out upon this errand. The old stories that clung around Mary all recurred, and, aside from them, the first murder in the settlement was something well calculated to shock and sicken.

While Hugh was engaged in the endeavor to restore composure and some degree of rational consciousness to his wife, he heard the tramp of approaching feet, and the confusion of excited voices. On they came, along the road; they entered the yard, threw open the door of the cabin, and, in a few minutes, the room was crowded. All were there—friends and foes. Conspicuously among the figures moving around the room was that of the minister, who, instead of endeavoring to quell the excitement, was engaged with the constable in opening drawers, prying into nooks and crannies, lifting loose planks upon the floor, and making inquiries of this one and that, in a low voice, and acting in a manner that showed that he regarded the murder as the key to his own deliverance. Heaven, in his belief, had descended in judgment, and Satan had completed the ruin of his deluded devotee.

During all the first of the disturbance, Mary sat still upon the bed, leaning upon Hugh's shoulder, and looking wildly around upon the excited assemblage which soon filled the room to suffocation.

Peering through the doorway into the morning twilight, she could see others coming in the distance—men, women, and children—some running at the top of their speed, some walking, some shouting, some pointing towards the cabin, and all pressing forward with a fearful earnestness towards her.

Then rude men gathered round her, and asked her harsh questions, and told her that she would be hung; while half-dressed women, with their hair upon their shoulders, came rushing excitedly in, and, pressing to the bed-side, burst into wild lamentations over the little body which, in life, they had accused of looking like a cat; or gave vent to their excitement in upbraidings of the poor mother. What was passing in her shattered spirit, what meaning she attached to the confusion around her, what forebodings darkled through her mental gloom, what fancies she built up from the new materials around her—the pale faces, the straggling hair, the confused voices, the gaze of menace, curiosity, and fear, the fierce reproaches—cannot be pictured, but, in her fright—in her trouble—there was one face which she sought, and which was long in coming.

At last, by the operation of the powerful influences around her, the cloud of her delirium was borne slowly away from her spirit—or repelled, perhaps, by her spirit, under the action of the new and terrible stimulus—and consciousness swept over her with a shudder as cold as that of death. The longed for face appeared at length, and the poor infanticide burst with an appealing cry of distress from the arms of her husband, and hid her face upon Mary Holyoke's bosom, who, too weak with excitement to stand, fell back into a chair, and received her old ward upon her knees.

Mr. Holyoke, touched by this scene, ordered the room to be cleared, and the door to be shut. Goody Tomson had returned, and was weeping over her cold little nursling, and Mr. Moxon, Deacon Chapin, the constable, and two or three of the principal women of the place remained, while the others gathered into knots outside, or took their way silently and solemnly homewards. Then Hugh and Goody Tomson—in tears and terror—told the story faithfully and truly—Hugh simply insisting on Mary's insanity, and Mary hearing every word, as the awful fact grew slowly into her convictions.

Then the minister and the other men present drew themselves apart, and soon became excited, so that none of their conversation escaped the ears of the others. "I tell you," said Mr. Moxon, "the day of retribution has come. The tormentor of my children has been pointed out to you and to me, by this shocking and most unnatural murder. The witchcraft is the primary crime, it is the crime which procured this crime, and she should be arrested for witchcraft as well as murder."

"I do not see very well how her arrest for murder can be hindered, in the state of feeling which exists here now, in the absence of the magistrate," said Mr. Holyoke, "but I do object to loading her down with the odium of witchcraft when she is brought before her judges for the only crime she has been guilty of."

"How do you know it is the only crime she has been guilty of?" inquired the minister, sharply.

"By the same means by which I know you to be a monomaniac," replied Mr. Holyoke firmly, "and, in this matter, I beg you will not be so unreasonable as to provoke me to give your insanity less consideration than I do hers."

The minister's mind rebounded from this rock into the region of doubt and uncertainty again, and he fell to his usual resort of walking to and fro across the cabin. At length, he withdrew a package from his pocket, and, calling Deacon Chapin's attention to it, opened it in Mr. Holyoke's presence, and asked the former if he had ever seen anything like its contents before.

The Deacon reluctantly replied that he had, and then Mr. Holyoke took from it a piece of birch bark, with a sentence written upon it, in the handwriting of that so rudely withdrawn from Mr. Moxon's study window, on an occasion well remembered by Deacon Chapin and the reader.

"I knew," pursued Mr. Moxon, eyeing Mr. Holyoke closely, as he perused the manuscript, "that if ever I could have an opportunity, I could find in this house evidence that Mary Parsons has had dealings with the Evil One; and if Deacon Chapin will tell what he has seen, he will identify that, and all the manuscripts I have in my hand, as the product of Satan, or his emissary. But perhaps" (added the minister in a tone of irony) Deacon Chapin is a monomaniac."

"This is too solemn a place for jesting," said Mr. Holyoke, bitterly, "but if the devil writes as bad a hand as this, and can afford no better paper, he is too ignorant and too poor to do much damage among people possessing common sense, and decent stationery."

Saying this, he was about to turn away, when Deacon Chapin interposed, and said that he considered it no more than proper, as he had been alluded to, to say that while he had seen some things connected with a similar manuscript which were wholly unaccountable, and while, at that time, he had supposed it in some manner connected with witchcraft, he had been inclined to reconsider his conclusion. So far as Mary Parsons was concerned, he saw no way to get along with her but to send her to the Bay, if she could be carried there. It was a sad case—a terrible judgment.

Holyoke listened impatiently, as the minister and the deacon approached the bed. "There," said he, as he laid his hand upon the cold forehead of the dead child, and turned to his two companions, "there is another victim of law without justice. Its mother's insanity dates from her trial for slander, and the full measure of horrible evils, of which this is but one, has been, and is to be, turned out by such clumsy machinery as men make when they take the work out of the hands of Christianity, and endeavor to regulate altogether minor and subordinate social evils."

Mr. Moxon was too blind to see the full force of this cutting and unanswerable rebuke, but Deacon Chapin saw it, and felt it, and never forgot it.

During this brief side scene, Mary Holyoke and Hugh and his poor wife were weeping together, in one touching group. The infanticide had rarely seemed more natural and rational than at that moment, and new strength had taken possession of her. She sat up in her chair, and, as her old mistress, kindly and with many tears, and with such words of comfort and counsel as she could command, told her of her probable fate—of the trial which awaited her, and its uncertain issue—the old, strong spirit swelled within her, and, grappling, as it were, with her destiny, she exclaimed, rising firmly to her feet, "Let them kill me! I am ready! It will be no comfort to me to live, and I am nothing but a curse to the only man I love on earth!"

Hugh begged her not to talk so, but she told him to be silent, and, turning to the constable, asked him when he would be ready to start, stating that she should never be as well prepared as during that very hour.

Why pause to tell of the events that quickly followed, like shadows passing the vision in a dream;—of the hurried inquest, the burial, the throngs of curious eyes that peered into and around the cabin during the day, the hasty preparations for the journey, the farewells, the prayers, the final departure, the winding of the cavalcade up the hill along the Bay Path—the saddest and yet the most excited cavalcade that had ever trodden it.

It was a terrible journey for an invalid like Mary to undertake. She was seated upon a horse, behind her husband, and supported herself by leaning upon and clasping him. As she turned to take a farewell view of the valley and village, she knew that she should never see them again, and only hoped that she should die before she reached the Bay.

The party was made up of the constable, Mr. Moxon, Mr. Holyoke, three or four other men who adopted the occasion and company for errands of their own, and Goody Tomson, who, with Hugh, were the important witnesses. Mr. Moxon went down determined to have her tried for witchcraft, but, in Holyoke's company, preserved silence in regard to his designs. The party were more than a week upon the way. The prisoner grew weaker from day to day. Several times she fainted upon her horse, and once fell to the ground, dragging Hugh with her. At last, more dead than alive, she arrived at Boston, and was taken directly to the lodgings of the magistrate.

The distress into which the case threw him may well be imagined. His first thought related to the sentence which he had administered to her, in which had originated her sickness and her sin. He never had thought of its first effect without a pang, he had never heard of her sickness without sad regrets, and the last blow stunned him. It was this event which burst in upon his own personal trials, which thrilled with horror the General Court, and spread a sudden excitement throughout the Bay Settlements. It was this event which afterwards gave a new coloring to his own case, and helped to involve him in his deepest humiliation. The grand crisis in his affairs had arrived.

CHAPTER XXIX.

The trial of a witch and a murderess was an event well calculated to excite the General Court and the people of the Bay settlements; and not a few of the more superstitious freely expressed their convictions that both the witchcraft and the murder were consequences of Mr. Pynchon's defection, either as a direct, legitimate result, or a special judgment from Heaven. In this manner, the cases of the venerable heretic and witch-murderess became associated in the public mind; and, as no man, possessing common human susceptibilities, can live by the side of a great superstition without coming more or less into its shadow, so Mr. Pynchon became touched with the prevalent sentiment, and was unable entirely to separate himself from the responsibility of events with which he had no direct connexion.

Mary Parsons was taken to the jail, for safe keeping and for rest. She was so feeble as to be entirely unable to appear before the General Court, and plead to the charges against her. During the days that intervened, Mr. Moxon had very little difficulty in so arranging matters as to bring the trial for witchcraft into the order of precedence, and, before Mary was sufficiently removed from death to be tried for her life, considerable impatience began to be felt in various quarters for her appearance.

During this period, Hugh, though rarely allowed to see his wife, was not without sympathetic companionship; for, upon the second day after his arrival at Boston, his old, unknown, and still disguised benefactor, arrived, severely worn by the journey, and giving evidence of recent illness, which explained to Hugh a neglect which he had noticed for several weeks previous to the murder.

The old man was more thoroughly disguised than on the occasion of his first and only interview with Hugh, and passed for an Indian wherever he appeared. Matters had arrived at such a condition that he had no hesitation in informing Hugh of the nature of his connexion with Mary, and the pair became united by a tender and touching sympathy. Day after day they lingered around the door of the jail, and, whenever Hugh was admitted, the old man waited without until he re-appeared, and then listened, with painful interest, to the report which he brought, and the messages she sent.

To Mary, the decay of vitality brought the full return of reason. The terrible journey over which she had passed, while it seemed to destroy the very foundations of her physical strength, restored, through some mysterious process of nature, the balance of her mind. The past was with her in all its brightness and all its darkness. The terrible present was something which she fully realized. The future —dark, uncertain, and strewn thick with dangers—lay before her. But the ties which bound her to the world had nearly all been severed. There was but one left, and that was her husband. Even this was losing its power, under the conviction that she was destroying his position and his happiness, and, perhaps, dragging him into infamy. And when the possibilities of the future impressed themselves upon her mind—when she saw that she might, and very probably should, lose her reason again, and perhaps be left to the performance of still further deeds of violence, the prospect of death became more and more tolerable, till it was entertained with pleasure.

There was one thought which, more than all others, reconciled her to the fate which seemed inevitable. She believed that she had her husband's confidence—that no power could deprive her of it. She believed that, when she should die, he would mourn her sincerely—that he would think of her tenderly, and cherish her memory, even should it be trodden under feet by malice, prejudice, and superstition. There were so many things with her that were worse than death, and so little in her life that was desirable, that the thought of dying sometimes filled her heart with an unutterable peace.

The time at last arrived for her to be brought forth. The fact that she was to appear for trial had been noised abroad, and a large crowd had collected about the jail, in order to catch a glimpse of one who had been represented to be a monster of sin. Hugh and his disguised companion were at the door, and, as she made her appearance, feebly walking between two officers, and saw the sea of upturned and excited faces, and comprehended the fact that she was the object of curiosity, her cheek, which was deadly pale at first, grew bright as if it were burning, and her dark eye flashed defiance. After the first glance, she looked around as if to seek familiar faces, and, as she met that of Hugh and his trembling companion, a sweet smile overspread her face, and she bowed to them with a cordiality and composure that, for the moment, won upon the sympathies of the crowd, and betrayed it into a murmur of admiration.

A preliminary examination under the forms of law peculiar to the period, resulted in the finding of two indictments against her—one for witchcraft and one for murder; and when she was brought into the General Court and arraigned on the first, she pleaded "not guilty" with a vehemence of tone that startled the ears of all.

The tale of her trial for this offence would be a disgusting record—weary to write, and sickening to read. Mr. Moxon was the principal witness, and as he brought forward his flimsy and ridiculous testimony, and exhibited his bits of epistolary birch bark, and laid out the whole ground of his evidence, he saw for himself that the case was hopeless for him, for he met on every hand only smiles of derision, or blank stares of incredulity. The facts upon which he had relied for proof, began, even in his own mind, to assume a shadowy and unsatisfactory aspect, so that when he was allowed to resume his seat, it was with a sensation of relief, and a somewhat indistinctly formed conviction that he had ruined his own reputation, and saved that of the prisoner.

The trial occurred at a date more than forty years previous to the great delusion of New England on the subject of witchcraft, and found the court sufficiently calm to be able to judge between valid and worthless evidence, so that Mr. Moxon's impression in regard to the effect of his testimony was almost literally correct. The other evidence offered amounted to nothing against the prisoner, and she was immediately acquitted. The fact seemed rather to detract from than increase her strength, and she almost swooned upon her seat.

As soon as she was sufficiently recovered to stand, the second indictment was read to her. This accused her of murdering her child, and to this she as unhesitatingly pleaded guilty as she had denied the charge in the first indictment. Of the proceedings in this case, preliminary to her sentence, there is neither record nor hint. It could not be that one whose infirmities were so well known as those of the prisoner, and one who had such friends near her as Mr. Pynchon and Mr. Holyoke, as well as a townsman in the General Court who was disposed to regard her charitably, should have been left to the fate which naturally hung upon her confession, and that no effort whatever was made to save her. The fact was doubtless proved, that although she had had the reputation of being insane, she had been to all appearance rational from the hour of the murder; or from the time when the people crowded into the cabin upon Goody Tomson's alarm. Whatever the efforts in her behalf may have been, or whatever aspect the evidence may have assumed, she was condemned to death, and received her sentence with entire calmness and fortitude.

The prisoner was carried from the court room in the arms of the officers, being entirely unable to walk; and the open air failed to revive her when it was reached. A carriage was called, and amid a throng of curious faces, and a tumult of insulting cries, the poor convict was conveyed to her prison to await the time of her execution.*

As Mary Parsons retired from the court, a large number of spectators bore her company, and among them, Elizur Holyoke, who was accompanied by the deputy from Springfield, his brother-in-law, Henry Smith. The cause of the retirement of the two last soon became apparent, for silence had no sooner been secured than it was announced that Mr. Pynchon had made a retraction of his errors, in a formal note in the hands of the clerk, and it was accordingly received by the court, and read. The steps which led to this recantation have been sufficiently apparent in the progress of the narrative. An over sensitive conscientiousness, which, when acted upon by popular denunciation, learned casuistry, and a superstitious interpretation of providential occurrences, had beclouded his reason and benumbed his will, was the active agent in bringing him to an unwilling

* "Mary Parsons of Springfeild, having two bills of inditement framed agaynst her, the one for havinge familyarity with the devill, as a witch, to which she pleaded not guilty & not suffycyent euidence appearing to proue the same, she was acquited of witchcraft.

"The second inditement was for wilfully & most wickedly murderinge her owne child, to which she pleaded guilty, confest the fact, & accordinge to her deserts, was condemned to dy. per Curiam."

Colony Records, vol. III. page 229.

relinquishment of opinions which he had formed in his strong and healthy years.*

The effect of this retraction on the General Court was just what it ought to have been under the circumstances. They could not help but see that, insomuch as Mr. Pynchon had been convinced of the errors of his book, he had been convinced against his will, and in fact against his convictions. Their action in the matter, while it greatly disappointed and terribly mortified him, was exactly what was necessary to restore him thoroughly to himself, and re-invest him with the native dignity of his character.

As the retraction was read there were nods and winks among the members, which meant much to Mr. Pynchon's disadvantage. He had humiliated himself, and the instant effect of his action was to diminish a certain degree of respect which the court had not ceased to entertain for him since Mr. Holyoke's manly defence of him at the previous session. There seemed to arise in the minds of nearly all the members a disposition to humiliate him still further.

* The halting, unwilling, unconvicted spirit in which this retraction was conceived and written, is sufficiently apparent in the document itself, which is copied from page 229 of vol. iii. Colonial Records, where it immediately follows the record of the case of Mary Parsons:

"Accordinge to the Courts advice, I have conferred with the Reverend Mr. Cotton, Mr Norrice & Mr. Norton about some poynts of the greatest consequence in my booke, & I hope I have so explayned my meaning to them as to take off the worst construction; & it hath pleased God to let me see that I have not spoken in my booke so fully of the price and merit of Christs suffrings as I should have done, for in my booke I call them but trialls of his obedience, yet intendinge, thereby, to amplyfy & exalt the mediatoriall obedyence of Christ, as the only meritorious price of mans redemption; but now, at present, *I am much inclined to thinke* that his sufferinges were appoynted by God for a further end, namely, as the due punishment of our sins by way of satisfaction to divine justice for mans redemption.

"Your humble servant in all dutyfull respects,

"WILLIAM PYNCHON."

As he had allowed himself to be cajoled and threatened and argued into a virtual surrender of his position, they were determined that the surrender should be complete and in terms. So they voted that as through the blessing of God on the efforts of the reverend elders, Mr. Pynchon appeared to be "in a hopeful way to give good satisfaction," they would give him, in accordance with a request which it appears he had made, leave to return home in the following week, taking with him Mr. Norton's reply to his book—in order that at the next session of the court, to be held in the following October, he might appear, having had full time to consider the matter, and then "give all due satisfac tion." They considered that he had only half accomplished the work of recantation, and judged that it would be comparatively easy, and perfectly proper, for him to conplete the task.

Mr. Pynchon was not present during this action, but when it was conveyed to him by Henry Smith, he was stung to the quick. In an instant the whole secret of the affair flashed upon him, and, with one struggle of will, he had cut loose from crafty advisers, zealous counsellors, private misgivings, and the whole train of agents and influences that had enslaved him, and was once more, what he ever afterwards remained, a man.

The court was not unaware of the sympathy felt for Mr. Pynchon at home, and, while doing what lay in its power to humiliate him, felt it necessary to do something to conciliate his friends in the distant settlement. As Henry Smith was a son-in-law of Mr. Pynchon, and had received the confidence of the settlement in his election as deputy, he was appointed in Mr. Pynchon's place to be the magistrate of Springfield. How much there may have been of political craft in this appointment—how far it was intended to stop the mouth of the deputy, and retain the good will of the family, it may be hard to determine.

Without making any remarks, Mr. Smith rose in his place, and, stating that it was very necessary for him to return home, requested permission to do so. Permission of absence for the session was immediately granted, and when he sought Mr. Pynchon, he announced to him, not only the action of the court upon his case, but also his own appointment as magistrate, and his intention to return home with his father-in-law in the following week. He also asked for his advice in regard to accepting the appointment which had been conferred upon him. Mr. Pynchon adjured him by all means to obtain his commission and retain it, until it should seem best to relinquish it, that so the court should not appoint some one in his place whose incompetency or unpopularity would make the place unpleasant, and subject the family to unnecessary mortifications.

Once more to the mind of the venerable controvertist, returned the elasticity and confidence, the firm poise and free action, which had been its experience when he boldly asserted himself among the magistrates. Men who met him were surprised to find him in excellent spirits—almost careless of the opinions of those around him, unconcerned in regard to his position in the colony, and hopeful and confident in regard to the future. He had at last and for ever learned that self-respect is a better possession than the good opinion of others, that nothing is too costly and nothing too precious to be sacrificed to perfect liberty of thought and action, and that his declaration, made once before the magistrates, and half unmade by his confession, "that truth does not depend for its authenticity, vitality, and power on the breath of the General Court of Massachusetts," was one to be maintained and acted upon in all his future dealings with that body.

CHAPTER XXX.

The arrangements were all made, at last, for the return of the Springfield party, and, on the evening previous to the day appointed for setting forth, the majority of them were assembled at Mr. Pynchon's room, when an officer from the jail arrived with a message from Mary Parsons, requesting the attendance of Mr. Pynchon and Mr. Holyoke at her bedside. Upon inquiry, the officer stated that Mary was very low, and would not probably survive the night; and her old friends lost no time in complying with her request, and following him to her cell. They found her lying upon a low cot, and very evidently breathing out her last hour. She turned towards them her black and fearfully hollow eye, and a faint smile of recognition and gratitude illuminated her features, as she opened her hand to Holyoke to receive his silent pressure. The two gentlemen hardly noticed Hugh, as he sobbed at the opposite side of the cot, and were entirely unmindful of the old Indian who sat with compressed lips leaning against the wall of the cell.

Mary looked into Holyoke's eyes, and moved her lips, as if she would speak to him. He put down his ear, and caught in whispers, "Tell Mistress Holyoke that I thought of her while I was dying, and hoped that she would never forget me. Tell her to be a friend to poor Hugh, and to believe that wilfully I never did anybody wrong; and oh! ask her to thank God for me—for I am weak and troubled—that He has taken me from the terrible death I was sentenced to."

Holyoke could not restrain his tears, and, as there was

16*

something in her closing words, as well as in the occasion, which very naturally suggested prayer, he asked her if she would like to have Mr. Pynchon pray with her. She signified her assent, and the old man, forgetting custom, prejudices, and self, knelt down upon the cold stone, and taking the dying woman's hand in his own, gave utterance to a prayer so tender, so fervent, so full of the genuine spirit of charity, that, borne on the wings of its language, her own spirit went calmly upwards in resignation, trust, and hope. He committed her soul to God. He prayed for her husband, and then, as if he could forget nothing that might come into the dying woman's mind, he prayed that wherever in the broad earth the feet of her father should wander, they might, at last, be found walking heavenward in the straight and narrow path, and that both father and child might be re-united in a land where sorrow and sighing should never come.

There was not a dry eye in the room, and when he concluded, or, rather, while his closing words were sounding, the old Indian left his seat, and falling upon his knees by Mr. Pynchon's side, buried his dusky face in the bed, and gave himself up to most distressing groans.

Mr. Pynchon and Mr. Holyoke were both astonished, and were still more surprised when the old man took the hand which Mr. Pynchon had relinquished, and pressed it to his lips and covered it with tears. Such emotion commanded respect, and the two visitors stood back, and regarded with deep feeling the afflicted group before them. Hugh was receiving the last whispered words of tenderness from his wife. She told him with her dying expirations how much she loved him—how much more than everything else she was leaving in the world, and how gladly, to save him from sorrow and trouble, she should die.

The minutes passed away until an hour had expired, and it became evident that her time was short. Mr. Pynchon and Mr. Holyoke pressed her hand, and bade her an affectionate farewell. A long passage of laborious breathing terminated all intelligible conversation with her, and her thin, white hands became chill with the retiring tide of life; yet, while all were looking to see her breathe her last a beautiful smile spread over her countenance, her eyes turned upwards, and, raising both hands, she brought them together and crossed them over her breast, at the same time uttering the whispered exclamation, "My mother and my child!"

There, above her, looking down through the prison roofs and celled floors, smiled, at last, with an undimmed and unobstructed radiance, her mother's heavenly eyes; and folded to the shadowy bosom beneath them, wrapped in ineffable repose, lay her child. Death and the presence in which she lay—all earthly loves and regrets—were forgotten in the blissful vision, and her spirit left the body at last without one struggle, as if it had been lifted out of its tenement by the serene attraction to which she had surrendered her being.

"She is gone," said Mr. Pynchon, solemnly, as he advanced and tenderly closed her transparent eyelids.

Hugh abandoned himself to grief's wildest convulsions, but the old Indian rose calmly to his feet, and, turning to Mr. Pynchon, said in a deep voice, "Gone where?"

"I cannot tell," replied Mr. Pynchon, startled equally by the question and the manner in which it was propounded. "I hope she has gone to heaven."

"Well, Square," pursued the old man, "here we be, and the wheel has come round. There lies my gal, and I wouldn't wake her up if I could do it with a feather; for I've been thinkin' on't all over, and I've made up *my* mind that God will deal square with her, and I'd rather have her in his hands than anybody else's. If I didn't think the Lord would see jest how she's been abused and knocked round, and would allow for the way she was brung up, and would strike out all he's got ag'in her exceptin' that that didn't come from bein' meddled with, and insulted, and plagued, I should want to have her and me and everybody else I care anything about blown into a thousand flinders, body and soul, and all the pieces lost."

"Woodcock!" exclaimed Mr. Pynchon, as soon as he became convinced of the identity of the speaker, and overcame his astonishment so as to be able to speak.

"Square Pynchon, God bless you!" exclaimed Woodcock, and the two old friends grasped one another's hands with a mutual cordiality that betrayed the honesty of their long friendship.

"Square," resumed Woodcock, "when I heard that you had sentenced my gal to be whipped—which was worse than the whippin' a great sight—for jest givin' widow Marshfield as good as she sent, I felt wicked towards you, and I never should 'a felt right ag'in if I hadn't heard you prayin' with her. I stood it as long as I could, but when you begun to pray for me, that fetched me." And the tears ran down upon the old man's painted face as freely as if he were but a child.

"I am glad," said Mr. Pynchon, "that you are able to sustain your afflictions with calmness and resignation; and it seems to me that if your state of mind is based simply on a belief in God's justice, you might have positive joy in thinking of and trusting in His mercy."

"I've been thinkin' of these things pretty busy for a few years," responded Woodcock, "and I don't look at 'em jest as you do. I believe there's a God, and that he's jest as good as he can be. If he wasn't, he'd be a devil. Now, if God made us he knows all about us, and he knows how hard it is for us to toe the mark, and how little we know, and how one thing and another is always cuttin' into us, and how we get knocked round, and *I've* no notion that he's goin' to come down on all alike. Now, I don't say that Mary was very good, but I say she was pretty good considerin', and any sensible man would say so, and I b'lieve God is a good deal more sensible than any of us."

"He knoweth our frame; He remembereth that we are dust," half unconsciously repeated Holyoke, who was listening to the conversation.

"That's it exactly," pursued Woodcock, "but that's nothin' to do with mercy! If I had a small boy, and should tell him to make a first-rate ash hoe-handle out of a pine stick, and to do it with his jack-knife, I should expect he'd fall consid'able short of it any way, and not have very good courage to do the best he could; and it would only be doin' the fair thing by him to give him his board and clo'es, and tell him he'd done pretty well considerin'. There wouldn't be any mercy in it."

"Comparisons of that character can very rarely be just," said Mr. Pynchon, biting his lip to repress a smile. "The relations between man and man are very different from those existing between man and God."

"Well, I can see that—that's plain enough—but it always seemed to me as if we was apt to set ourselves too high. We ain't anything but a lot of little fellers trottin' round among the bushes, and it's sometimes mighty queer to me that the Lord takes any notice on us at all. Any way, He can't think so much of us as we do of ourselves. It always makes me laugh to hear a man tellin' how the world was made for us, and how the sun, moon, and stars was made to give us light, and all creation was got up to our order, jest as if we wan't born 'fore we knew it, and didn't die 'fore we got ready. I've got a consait that the Lord made us 'cause he wanted to, and he didn't do it for the sake of abusin' on us, and givin' on us trouble any mor'n you and I, Square, would abuse anything we had got up, when it wan't strong enough to do us any damage."

"There is a good deal of truth in your notions," replied

Mr. Pynchon, "but you have not got hold of the whole of it. I know that we are too apt to feel that everything was made for us, partly because we are proud, and partly because we enter so harmoniously into the structure of a universe, each part of which ministers to our wants, that it is a very natural mistake to suppose that it was made only for that ministry. Yet there is such a thing as thinking so meanly of ourselves as to dishonor our Maker. Nothing is insignificant that God thought worthy to make and takes care to preserve. If an insect is not to be despised, then surely man is of importance, and if he is of sufficient importance to receive the constant care and protection of God—to be the subject of His kind and never failing providence—then he is worthy, in some high sense, to be honored by himself, and accountable in some high and positive respect for his behavior."

"I presume you're right, Square, and p'raps I said more'n I meant to. All I wanted to say was that I didn't b'lieve that the Lord would expect so much of us as if it was all a straight road and no stumps."

When Woodcock closed his characteristic explanation, a sigh that was half a groan found impulsive utterance at his lips. Returning suddenly from his momentary diversion, he saw, lying cold and lifeless before him, the object of long years of care and self-denial; and, for the first time, the question arose within him. "What am I to live for now?" He could not mourn for his daughter. He was glad that she had escaped from a long and most unjust persecution. He was glad that she had died acquitted of the crime of witchcraft, of which she had long been suspected, and glad that she had evaded the execution of an ignominious sentence; yet the thought that he had no one left to labor and be anxious for was one of unmingled pain.

There came to him, also, the thought of the companionship to which he had so long submitted, and to which, if he should continue in the country, he must still submit, and life seemed sad and even disgusting to him. Outlawed, at first, by comparatively trivial offences, new enactments severely punishing those who might lead a vagabond life among the Indians had forbidden his return to civilized life, and he saw nothing before him but an insipid and valueless existence. With a sad voice and dejected air, he gave expression to his feelings to Mr. Pynchon.

"I can sympathize with you," replied that gentleman, "for all the great aims of my life, with one exception, are either frustrated or accomplished. You have heard, doubtless, how they have been dealing with me, and know that I have no longer any power in the colony, and have become the object of persecution."

"I know all about it, Square, but I never should 'a said a word, if you hadn't. It's come out jest where I s'posed 'twould fetch up, more'n ten years ago. I knew there was some of the same stuff in you that there was in me, and I knew it was a kind of stuff that always leaked out of a man 'fore he died. If you are any like me, you feel a mighty sight better with it out than in.—Now if it's a fair question, what is the thing that you hav'n't done that you're goin' to do?"

"To endeavor, by God's grace, to become fully prepared to meet death, and the scenes to which it leads," replied Mr. Pynchon, with a solemn voice; adding, as he saw a thoughtful shadow passing over Woodcock's face; "it is a great aim—worthy of the last years of your life as well as mine—more worthy probably than any object for which you have thus far lived."

"I've been thinkin' of this, too, in my way," responded Woodcock. "I was thinkin' on it when I was settin' on the floor, jest as you come in. I've made up my mind that the Lord keeps a pretty close look-out for us, if we be small,

There was my wife—she lived out all her happy days, and when the Lord saw what she was comin' to, she died. I thought it was mighty hard, but bein' left with my little gal kind o' altered me, and her livin' with your Mary was good for her, and she was happier'n I ever could make her. Well, Mary lived out all of her happy days, and now, jest afore the law is goin' to murder her, she goes to sleep like a baby, and can't be hurt by anybody. Now He's choked me off from pretty much everything I wanted, and *I* can't think of anything that he wants me for now but to get religion and 'tend up to it." The old man's voice was honest and earnest, and his lip quivered with genuine emotion, as, in his homely way, he thus recognised the operations of Providence, and adopted the lesson they were designed to inculcate.

As the two old friends closed their conversation, the officers of the jail appeared, and announced that preparations were to be made for the disposal of the body of the deceased. This recalled Woodcock to the painful features of the occasion, overwhelmed Hugh with a fresh influx of grief, and informed the visitors that it was time for them to retire. A conference was first held, and, it being determined by the officers that Mary's burial should occur early on the following morning, Mr. Pynchon promised for himself, and in behalf of his party, to be in attendance, and so, passing out with Holyoke, bade Woodcock and Hugh a good night.

The events that followed were all like the experiences of a troubled dream to the grief-stricken Hugh—the sleepless night passed with Woodcock within the jail, the homely but hearty words of comfort uttered by the latter, the gathering of friends in the early grey of the morning, the words of a prayer pronounced in deep solemnity by a minister, the nailing of the rough coffin, its transportation in a yard back of the jail to a spot where a grave had but just been completed, the hollow resonance of the coffin as the first earth fell upon it, the final closure of the opening, and the trampling down of the sward above a bosom which had loved him as none other could—all these events were dimly realized, and, before he began calmly to apprehend the scenes through which he had passed, he, with the whole Spring field party, had left the sea-coast, and once more within the Bay Path—with the fresh leaves of June above his head, and the sweet air of June around him—was plunging into the broad forest that intervened between the Bay settlements and the Connecticut. Woodcock, after a private conference with Mr. Pynchon, was left behind, to find his way westward at his own convenience.

As the party arrived at Springfield, after a tedious ride, various emotions exercised its different members. Mr. Pynchon was happy at heart—and most happy to grasp the hands of his closely clinging friends. Henry Smith was mortified with his commission, and was pained by any allusion to it. It somehow seemed to him that he had received and appropriated the price of his father's dishonor. Mr. Moxon was discontented, and excessively mortified at his failure to sustain his charge against Mary; and Hugh felt that life, which had once been so sweet and joyous to him, was a ruined and pleasureless possession.

The impression produced upon the residents of the plantation by the recital of the events that had transpired at the Bay, was painfully profound. There were open threats of leaving the jurisdiction, but Mr. Pynchon begged all to wait for the development of events, and, by his own cheerfulness and equanimity, succeeded in controlling the rising discord, and restoring patience and peace to the people.

CHAPTER XXXI.

No member of the party returning from the Bay could have been more rejoiced upon arriving within sight of the Connecticut than Goody Tomson. Her three youngest children had been left in the care of Peter Trimble, as, in fact, the only willing nurse to be found; and, when it is remembered that the youngest of the three had but recently missed some of the tenderest ministries of maternity, it may well be imagined that Peter and the mother would be oppressed, the one with onerous cares and the other with feverish anxieties.

It may also be imagined that, under all the circumstances, they would be extremely happy to see each other; and in truth they were. The woman found Peter within her cabin, engaged in the endeavor to ascertain the effect of turkey's oil in softening his heavy shoes, and, as he used his hand in the application of that article, the first necessity arising from the impulsive greeting that passed between the two friends was a basin of water and some soap, in order that Goody Tomson might so far clean her hands as to be able to "take off her things." Before any progress was made, however, she inquired for her children. Peter told her that they were well, and quieted her curiosity in regard to the place where they were all hidden by mysterious nods and winks, which were intended to convey the command to wash her hands and take care of herself, and the intimation that he would then be ready for particulars.

After the preliminaries were finished, and Peter had brought out and placed before the mistress of t e house a plate of severely broken victuals, he sat down opposite to her, and, assuming an air of great complacency, began.

"You see, pretty quick after you went away, the baby began to cry like smoke. I'll bet she cried one night as much as five hours. Land ahead! I never see a little critter tune up so in my life. Well, that set the other two a-going, and I found I couldn't stand it. So, after they'd all cried till they got tuckered out, and went to sleep, I went to thinking of it, and I made up my mind I could do better than tend babies while you was gone, and I reckoned I might do something towards working them off. Anyhow, I locked them into the cabin the next morning, and put for the neighbors. I told them I believed the children would die if they couldn't go where there was women; and I hung on till I got rid of one here, and another there, and another there, in the course of the day; and, come night, I went to bed laughing over it, and slept as sound as a nut. By George! Esther" (exclaimed Peter, smitten with a sudden spasm of affection, and rising to his feet and walking around the table to her side, to give her hand a renewed shake), "I'm glad to see you! Why don't you say something to a feller?"

Poor Esther, grievously disappointed at not meeting with her children, and her motherly sensibilities shocked at Peter's apparent heartlessness, was obliged to give over her efforts to repress her feelings, and, filling her mouth, as if to dam up the accumulating flood as long as possible, burst, at last, into a complex paroxysm of mastication and tears.

"Land ahead!" exclaimed Peter, rising and shaking his fists with excess of sympathetic irritation, "why don't you have that old tooth out? You never'll take any comfort till you do."

Esther, quite willing to see Peter misled in regard to the real cause of her grief, continued to fill her mouth and weep, but did not dare to trust herself with speech. Her unrestrained mastication, however, led Peter to mistrust that he had not judged correctly of the cause of her unhappiness, and he inquired if her back did not ache terribly after riding so far, stating that it not unfrequently affected him in that manner, and that he didn't wonder she was perfectly used up.

Goody Tomson must have been uncommonly perverse not to be soothed by this deep and appreciative ministry, and Peter was rejoiced, at last, to see her jaws work less actively and powerfully, and her tears fall less copiously, as she subsided into her usual genial placidity.

"Where did you say the baby was?" inquired Esther, looking fixedly upon her trencher.

Peter had not said, but he informed her.

"Don't you think she is too young to be put out?" continued the mother, still busy with her victuals.

"Well, I tell you what I think," replied Peter, putting his feet upon the table and leaning back in his chair. "If the people that take her don't find any fault, it stands us in hand to keep mum. Young ones are in the way unless you happen to take to them pretty strong; and they eat like mischief anyhow, and if anybody's willing to keep them, why, there's so much saved in elbow grease. That's the way I look at it."

"Yes, of course," responded the bereaved mother, with renewed sobbing.

"I kind o' reckoned," pursued Peter, "that when you got back, you'd be sick for a few days, and wouldn't want to have the children round; and that would give the people that have got them a chance to get tied to them more; and perhaps they'd want to keep them for good and all. Now, if you'll go to bed I'll go round and tell them you've got home, and are crying for your children, but that you're all tired to death, and ain't fit to take care of them, and that they'll have to keep them a little longer."

At this moment the plans of Peter were dashed to the ground by the sudden opening of the door, and the entrance of a dirty girl, who carried in her arms a dirty bundle, which she deposited in Goody Tomson's arms, with the words, "There's your worryin' little young one that I've been takin' care of till I've about broke my back. Next time you go away I hope you'll leave somebody else to home besides this lazy lummox of a Peter Trimble."

This saucy speech was greatly broken in its effect upon both Peter and Esther by the emotions which had taken pre-possession of them. Peter was distressed to witness the return of the child. He had been extremely anxious to see a very decided reduction of the stock before coming permanently into the establishment. In the widow's first distress, he saw her willing to get rid of the older children, and he could conceive no reason why she would not willingly part with all of them, provided they could be got into good places. He perceived, at last, that the baby was a fixture. He saw it, as well in the caresses which its mother was lavishing upon the child, as in the insolent language which its involuntary nurse had used.

The mother, in her joy at once more clasping the babe in a pair of arms that, by eight or nine years' practice, did not know what to do with themselves without one, hardly heard the insult offered to the man she had chosen to supply the place of the lamented Tomson. In fact, she seemed to forget his presence in the superabundance of her joy upon again gaining the possession of her treasure.

"By the way," said Peter, after the unpleasant girl had departed, and Goody Tomson had become in some measure conscious that there was a whole world outside of her baby, "how about Mary Parsons, and the rest of them?"

"Mary Parsons!" exclaimed Goody Tomson, surprised that the subject had not been thought of before, "why, she came within an inch of being hung, and she would 'a been if she hadn't 'a died."

"Mary Parsons isn't dead, is she?" exclaimed Peter, in a tone of genuine concern.

"Well, you may ask the rest of them, if you don't believe me. They'll tell you she's dead, and that she died in jail."

"Died in jail? Mary Parsons died in jail?" and Peter slapped his thigh, and walked across the room under strong emotion.

"What makes you act so?" inquired his companion.

"Won't you never tell anybody if I'll tell you something?" inquired Peter, sitting down, and drawing his chair up to the widow.

"No—never, as long as I live."

"Well," pursued Peter, "I come *very* near marrying that girl once—*very* near;" and he nodded emphatically, and looked out of the window as if some object at an immense distance were absorbing his attention.

Goody Tomson blushed scarlet, and while attempting to feed her child with the scant remains of her meal, said, "I never thought so bad of Mary as other folks did, but I *do* wonder what such a man as *you* could see in such a woman as *her*."

Peter detected the motive that lay coiled beneath the widow's somewhat emphatic language, and followed up the attack. "I believe," he pursued, "that she didn't make any fuss when her baby was took away from her, and brought here. Some people are willing to do what is best for them, and some ain't. I don't find any fault. Perhaps it isn't any of my business, but there's such a thing as having more in a family than is comfortable all round, especially" (and Peter rose and swaggered towards the window) "if a man is pretty independent, and don't care much what becomes of him."

As Peter finished this cruel speech, he saw the widow putting a huge bone into her mouth, and her eyes all afloat again. What concession she would have made at this juncture, it is impossible to state; but, at the moment, the door was again opened, and another child, who had had a kind keeper, came in, and bounded to a seat in his mother's lap, by the side of the baby.

This one had hardly been thoroughly kissed (the bone having suddenly been withdrawn from the mother's mouth for that purpose), when the third, quite old enough to pull the latch herself, being the identical child that Peter had recommended to Hugh and Mary on a previous occasion, rushed into the widow's arms, and quite overwhelmed her with caresses.

Peter looked at the group with an expression of mingled vexation and resignation, took his hat from a nail, put it on, walked out of the door, and turned his steps down the street, giving utterance to a kind of music that he had the happy faculty of producing by the change of a hiss into a whistle, without the necessity of puckering his lips. He went out to think, and to make up his mind, if possible, upon what it was best for him to do.

Those three children, it had become evident, must remain, at present, with their mother. Nobody wanted them —nobody would keep them; and if he and Goody Tomson should consummate the little arrangement that had been initiated between them, he would be obliged to work for and support the children. From this subject his mind ran off upon Mary Parsons, whose name very naturally suggested that of Hugh; and Peter quickened his pace, under a determination to seek his old crony, and ask for his advice.

Quite unexpectedly he met him on his way to the old cabin. The tears sprang into the poor fellow's eyes as he grasped Peter's hand; and the latter, with all his shallowness, could not but be touched by his grief, and the wonderfully sad change it had wrought upon him. Peter was even sufficiently considerate to allow Hugh to tell his story

—his long story of Mary's terrible sufferings, of her calm death, her early morning burial, and of all his sorrows—his sorrowful memories, and his sorrowful prospects.

When he had relieved his burdened heart, and Peter had, so far as it was possible for him to do it, given him his sympathy, the latter assumed the lead of the conversation, and revealed to Hugh the peculiar trials that were associated with his matrimonial prospects.

"If I could get rid of them children," said Peter, "the widow would stand me in at a snug little profit, but if I've got to feed them, they'll swallow the whole place, and all I can do on it. I've got to look out for number one. By the way, Hugh, I wonder if the magistrate will make me promise to support the children as well as the widow, when he comes to marry me?"

Hugh said he presumed not, and then commenced very warmly in behalf of his child's old nurse. He extolled her generosity, her genial temper, her excellent good-nature and her industry, and even went so far as to compliment her for her youthful appearance—urging Peter not to disappoint her, vindicating her parental sympathies, and pronouncing her an excellent match for any man whom she might honor with her choice. Hugh did not close his eulogium of the widow until he had discharged, so far as possible, the large debt of gratitude he owed her, and had thrown out the intimation to Peter's selfishness that the children would soon be able to help him, and would require but little of his care.

During all this address, Peter stood and stroked his face in thoughtful complacency, and looked down upon his legs with a pleasant smirk that showed his intense gratification. At the close he looked up at Hugh, and said, "Well, what did I tell you? You begin to find out that I know something about women, don't you? As you say, the children may help a little one of these days, and, on the whole, I suppose I may as well marry her, and have it over with. Between you and I, Hugh, I believe she'd die if I should quit her."

"Oh, you will marry her, I know you will," said Hugh. "You'll marry her to please me, won't you, Peter?"

"By George!" responded Peter, with a chivalric touch of self-devotion, "I'll do it if you say so, any way. I never refused you anything yet, and I ain't going to begin now. If you say marry, marry it is; and if you name the time when you'd like to eat a few of Goody Trimble's nutcakes, I'll see that the chair is set and the platter on the table."

Thus devoting himself to matrimony and his friend, Peter took leave of Hugh, and hurried back to Goody Tomson, under a vague impression that so precious a creature as the former had described her to be, must necessarily be overwhelmed with suitors as soon as it should become known that she had returned from the Bay.

It is needless to say that, notwithstanding Goody Tomson's fatigues and maternal incumbrances, she was most happy, before closing her eyes in sleep, to receive Peter's plighted troth without reservation, and to promise in return to make him a happy man after the crops should be gathered in, in the fall. In the meantime, it was arranged that he should expend his labors upon the estate of Tomson deceased, and act as the nocturnal protector of the family, as he had done for several months.

Two or three days after his return from the Bay, Mr. Pynchon invited his children to his house—at the same time giving them an intimation that important business was to be advised upon, at the interview. The party was—strange as it may appear—the most joyous one that had gathered in the old family house for many years. The children of Holyoke and Henry Smith, loosened from the strait rules of decorum which at that time curbed the natural overflow of childish hilarity, filled the house with their mirthful music, while parent and grand-parent listened, not only without remonstrance but with positive delight.

It seemed refreshing, after the wrangles, and discomforts, and trials, and distresses, to taste once more of life at its fountain—to take it to the lips as it leaped up into the sunshine from youthful spirits, and once more to forget, in innocent pleasure, the various ills that had beset the path of each. Of all this joy Mr. Pynchon was, in truth, the radiating centre. It was his buoyant spirit that released the burden from the spirits of his children, and their happiness that gave license to the limbs and the laugh of the grandchildren; and the mutual reaction from spirit to spirit that made the meeting happier than the family had known, even in the times of its power and prosperity.

When at last the older members of the party had become tired of the frolics of the younger, the latter were sent into another room; and Mr. Pynchon, with a warm smile upon the affectionate group left around him, said, "Well, children, I have something to say to you which, as it concerns my happiness, certainly should concern yours. You have been pained to see me lose my influence in this colony, for which I have suffered so much—and I will not deny that it has been to me a cause of very deep unhappiness, but the pang is past. I have never felt more buoyant-hearted than now, and life never seemed sweeter or more desirable. But I cannot, and I must not, live in bonds. After having been, during my whole lifetime, subject to bondage, and among its last years having tasted of freedom, I shall not again come under the yoke. In this plantation, my usefulness is at an end. I am not allowed to forward its affairs by my counsels, and I am too old to aid it with my hands. Therefore" (and the old man's eye moistened as he looked around upon the expectant group), "I am going back to die in England."

This was the first intimation they had had of this determination, and they looked at one another in blank astonishment. Mary Holyoke was the first to break the silence. Rising, and pushing aside the reserve that advancing years had placed between her father and herself, she was the girl Mary Pynchon once more; and, throwing herself into his arms, she kissed the old man fervently, and exclaimed, "If you go to England, I shall go with you—we will all go with you."

"No, no, my child," replied the old man, putting his arm affectionately around his old-time idol. "No, no, you must stay here. If you are going to leave for me, I shall remain. This is the place for you, and the rest of my children. You do not write books, and I am not yet done with Mr. John Norton. You do not wish me to remain, and be subject to the annoyances which the General Court are determined to visit upon me; and if I do remain, I shall certainly give them greater cause for persecution than has actuated them thus far. I have but a few more years to live, and, while it would be very pleasant to me to have my children around me in my last hours, I will never consent to receive the blessing at the expense of their usefulness and prosperity. You have all a future before you, and your children will come into a noble inheritance when you are gone."

Mrs. Pynchon, while these remarks were in progress, was evidently in distress, and they were no sooner concluded than she took the opportunity to say that she knew Mr. Pynchon had been treated shamefully, and no doubt that it would be uncomfortable for him to live here. She did not know but, if a person was prepared, it was just as well to die away from one's children as any way. It was very unpleasant to live where one wasn't respected, especially if one had not been used to such a state of things; but she *did* think that before a decision had been irrevocably made to return to England, Mr. Pynchon ought to have thought of the salt water, and to have found out what sort of a vessel he was going in. Her remarks, for some reason she did not fully appreciate, did not materially deepen the solemnity that attended their opening, and so, having been heard, she subsided to her knitting, and sailed out into her placid sea of thought, on a woollen vessel with steel spars and blue-mixed cordage.

Mary Holyoke still sat on her father's knee, but she was engaged in deep thought, and when her mother concluded, she said, very emphatically, "Some of us must go to England. Father and mother must not go alone."

The matter had appeared in this light to all, yet all were equally undecided in regard to what was individual propriety and duty in the premises. Henry Smith, who had said nothing thus far, decided the question at last. He had no doubt that it was the duty of one or more of the children to return with their parents, and, as he was bound to them by a double tie, Mrs. Pynchon being his own mother, he believed that the duty was pointed out to him. At any rate, he should so consider it with his present light.

"I had not reckoned upon the companionship of any of my children," said Mr. Pynchon, with a grateful suffusion of the eye, "but it will be very pleasant; and, while it will cost me a great struggle to leave the remainder here, and bid them good-bye, never more probably to meet them in this world, I cannot but confess that the thought of being able while I live to act freely in matters that have come to make up so much of my life, and the prospect of dying among the scenes of my youth, and of being buried among those with whom are connected some of my happiest memories, bring to me many pleasant anticipations. I could almost wish that the farewells had been said, that the winds were bearing me away from you, and that those I must leave behind had prosperously recommenced pursuits with which my presence can only interfere."

A long conversation ensued, suggested by this development in the history of the plantation—a development which all could not fail to see was to inaugurate a new era in their lives and affairs. By some association the past was called up, and the family sat for a long hour talking of the people and times gone by. Among the topics of the hour was the sad case of Mary Parsons, of which there were so many things in the house, in the history of the family, and in the plantation, to remind them.

To relieve the distressing details of her last days, Mr. Pynchon, under pledge of secresy, told his family of his discovery of John Woodcock, of his long residence near them among the Indians, of his charities to Mary and Hugh during the sickness of the former, of the authorship of Mr. Moxon's bark manuscripts, and so described him that all declared that they had seen him repeatedly, and called up a multitude of occurrences to which his presence among the Indians furnished the key.

All were very deeply interested in the narrative, and were astonished when informed by Mr. Pynchon that he had, during the comparatively brief interview that he held with Woodcock on the morning of his departure from the Bay, not only learned the particulars he had communicated to them, but had informed Woodcock of his determination to return to England, and received from Woodcock the assurance that he would gladly return with him. The family had always known the sympathy that existed between Mr. Pynchon and Woodcock—two individuals as widely diverse in their character, apparently, as could be imagined—but now that they more fully comprehended the character of both, they were less at a loss in accounting for the pleasant anticipation that lighted up the old man's eye, as he spoke of having Woodcock near him in his last years; of recalling with him, in their distant retirement, the details of the wonderful episode in their lives furnished by their residence in America; of listening to his fresh and quaint humors, and of coming into invigorating contact with his free and original spirit.

"There is one man," said Holyoke, in a very decided voice, "who I wish could be induced to leave the plantation when you do, if he will not go before, and the wider the sea which separates him from us the better. If you are going to leave, I beg you not to leave behind you Mr. Moxon. He has been the author of great calamities amongst us, and, whatever may have been his position once, he can now do us no good."

The others spoke less boldly, but with no less strength of conviction, in the same behalf. All felt, not only that the day but the capacity for usefulness with him had passed, and that, thereafter, his presence in the plantation must be an offence, if nothing worse.

Mr. Pynchon coincided with the general opinion, and, moreover, intimated the probability that Mr. Moxon would make the proposition to return with him, without a request or invitation from any quarter.

The company little imagined that, at the very moment when they were talking of him, Mr. Moxon was passing through another of those trials to which he had been so frequently subjected, and were startled by a loud rap at the door, and a general summons to come with haste to the minister's house. The messenger only knew that Martha Moxon was bewitched by somebody, and that her father was anxious that every one should see her.

Mr. Moxon was not unaware that there were open and secret murmurings in regard to his treatment of Mary Parsons, and doubts touching the soundness of his reason. He had, therefore, upon the renewal of the attack upon his children, determined that every one should have an opportunity to witness the scenes which had made such an impression upon him, and by that means to vindicate as well his opinions as his proceedings.

It was remarkable to see the air of deep sadness which pervaded the Pynchon family as this announcement was made to them. "Who, in Heaven's name, is to be the victim now?' exclaimed Holyoke impatiently.

It was an unpleasant conclusion to a most interesting family re-union, and as the gentlemen of the party left the house to obey the summons it was with many expressions of perplexity and discouragement. As they emerged upon the street they perceived that quite an excitement was on foot, and that the call to the entertainment to which they were invited had been very general. When they arrived at the minister's house they found it already full, but room was made for them; and, advancing to the bed where Martha lay, they found the minister exhibiting to the gaping crowd one of her limbs, which was covered with black and blue spots, inflicted, as he assured them, by her invisible tormentor. As he raised his head and recognised the new comers, he informed them that his daughter had just recovered from a terrible paroxysm, and had made an accusation which gave him as much pain as it could any one present.

As he was speaking, there was a slight stir among the crowd, and a small form pressed forward to get a view of the bewitched girl. He had no sooner worked his way to her bedside, his face flushed with painful excitement, than she sprang up with frantic energy, and pointing to Hugh Parsons exclaimed, "There is the man who struck me—there he is! there he is! there he is!" Saying this, she was thrown into renewed convulsions, in which she gave wild screams of torment, and declared alternately that he was pounding her and sticking pins into her.

All eyes were turned upon Hugh, who, frightened not only by the wild words and wilder screams of the girl, but by a vision of the dangers to which he had become exposed by her accusation, began to grow dizzy as he gazed;—the room swam around him, and he sank to the floor in a swoon as deep, almost, as death.

"My God!" exclaimed Holyoke, quite overcome by the spectacle; "where is all this to end?"

"It will never end until justice shall be done," replied Mr. Moxon, in an excited voice. "So long as the devil's agents go unpunished—so long as they evade or triumph over law, so long will he continue his torments. He will never cease until those who call themselves the children of God cease to assist him in his work, by accusing his innocent victims of deception, and their distressed friends of insanity."

As Hugh was removed from the room into the open air Holyoke followed without uttering a word. He was sick at heart. He saw before him another dark tragedy—in fact a brood of them, for, upon the faces of the simple planters who were assembled, he could not but detect the credulity—the conviction—necessary to sustain, by testimony, the charge against Hugh, and the groundwork of a mental epidemic as hostile to all worldly prosperity, as to intellectual growth and spiritual religion. Directing that Hugh should be carried to his own house, he returned with Mr. Pynchon for his wife and family.

Thus again, and for the most deplorable of causes, was the plantation in commotion, but the end was approaching, and was nearer than any imagined.

CHAPTER XXXII.

The summer which followed these events was a brief and hurried season. So many things had occurred to divert the planters from their labor that little time was left—for any purpose—from the toils of the forest and the field. Mr. Pynchon was busy with preparations for closing his trade or turning it entirely into the hands of his son, and arranging the preliminaries, both on this and the other side of the Atlantic, for his return to England.

Mr. Moxon employed himself, during the time he could spare from his poorly performed pastoral duties, in looking after evidence against Hugh, upon whom, as was seen in the last chapter, the mantle of witchcraft had fallen. He was determined to pursue this case to the end, and leave no means untried to secure conviction. While the people of the plantation could not help regarding Hugh as a very harmless individual, their mouths were stopped in his defence by what they had seen, and he seemed to be in danger of meeting with a fate as lamentable as that which had befallen his wife.

As a community, the people of the town were more united in their feelings than they had ever been, and Mr. Pynchon had the satisfaction, during the last months which he spent upon the plantation, of being the centre of devoted sympathy and attachment, as well to those who had once been at difference with him, as to his long-time friends. Everybody saw, through the bland judiciousness of Deacon Chapin, a decided sympathy with Mr. Pynchon. By what perverse principle in human nature a heretic shorn of temporal power becomes heroic to the imagination; how

17*

persecution makes converts where reason fails; why opposition to a principle often dies when its defender is stricken down, are questions not readily answered; and yet it was true that Deacon Chapin no sooner saw Mr. Pynchon politically powerless—yet falling with dignity back upon his manhood—than he became one of the best friends he had. Whether, if his power had been restored, and his old standing regained, this new affection would have been constant, Deacon Chapin himself probably did not know. Few appreciate, or even examine, the influences which direct or divert the currents of their lives.

As the autumn came on, the time approached for Henry Smith to depart for the Bay, to attend upon the October session of the General Court; and as he was, at that time, the only magistrate in the settlement, Peter Trimble saw that it would be impossible for him to become the husband of the widow Tomson before winter, if he did not avail himself of Mr. Smith's services previous to his departure. Having, therefore, secured his legal publishment, he called upon the new magistrate one evening to engage him to perform, for the first time in his experience, the interesting and important ceremony. Informing the gentleman that he would like to see him out of doors, he proposed, in a manner not wholly free from embarrassment, though sufficiently charged with a sense of self-importance, the buisness upon which he had called.

"So you are really going to be married, Peter," said Mr. Smith, in his grave but not unpleasant way.

"Well," responded Peter, "I might as well, I reckon, if I'm ever going to be, for you see Esther may change her mind, and I've been to work on her land all summer, and I've no notion of losing that."

"Very well," said the magistrate. "I shall be happy to marry you at any time you may appoint, before I leave for the Bay."

Peter's business was really completed, but he lingered still, and, finally, as the magistrate turned to walk into his house, he mustered sufficient resolution to ask him what the fee would be.

"Oh! anything you choose," replied Mr. Smith, stepping into the house, and closing the door behind him.

Peter did not stir from where he stood, for several minutes. An idea had entered his mind of so novel and important a character that walking could only have diverted his attention from its consideration. Having viewed it in its various aspects, he manifested his satisfaction with it by shaking his fists violently at the door beyond which the magistrate had disappeared. Judging by the expression upon Peter's face, Mr. Smith was not menaced with any fearful calamity, but simply with some choice bit of over-reaching which filled the man who had conceived it with unmixed delight. Taking his way hurriedly back to the widow's cabin, he entered, and, hanging his hat upon the accustomed nail, sat down on a low bench, and, in his old attitude, with his head between his hands and his hands between his knees, surrendered himself to those half stifled ebullitions of laughter of which he was the victim.

"What *have* you got hold of now?" inquired the admiring widow, pausing in her work.

"Got hold of my head," responded Peter, with a readiness of wit which astonished himself, and threw him into renewed convulsions.

"Well, that ain't anything very great, I'm sure," retorted the widow, entirely unconscious that she had the best of the joke.

Peter, however, was more appreciative. Struck with the peculiar force of the retort, he jumped to his feet, and, grasping the woman cordially by the hand, exclaimed, "By George! Esther, you are up to pretty much everything, ain't you? Land ahead! I've got to look out; I ain't nowhere."

The new admiration on the part of Peter, and the glow excited in the heart of the widow by the compliment she had received, had a very pleasant effect upon the confidential conversation which followed. In this conversation, Peter made a revelation of the new idea which had occurred to him, and, although it did not strike his companion with such force as he had expected, and as she felt that it ought to strike a woman of her recently achieved reputation for acuteness, she acquiesced in its practicability.

The evening for the marriage was at last fixed upon, and Peter invited a few of his choice friends to meet him at the magistrate's upon the occasion. The night upon which the wedding was to take place became generally known, and when Peter, with his betrothed hanging upon his arm, and the oldest of her resident children pulling at the opposite hand, arrived at Mr. Smith's house, he was surprised to find it literally full. The discovery abashed him; and, from the merry countenances of those he met, he became distressed with an apprehension that he was to be made the butt of ridicule. This was quickly relieved, however, by the polite attentions he received on every hand, and the efforts made by every one to place him at his ease, and restore to him his self-confidence. In fact, Mr. Smith was quite as much an object of curiosity as the bridegroom and the bride. He had been rallied for a week on his new dignity, and exhorted to have the ceremony well committed to memory; and when the moment came for him to commence the duties of his office, his face was flushed and his voice tremulous, while Peter and his simple bride were models of self-possession.

As soon as Peter and Esther had been pronounced husband and wife, they received the hearty congratulations of all present, many of whom turned, and jocosely congratu lated the new magistrate on the happy achievement of the most grateful and graceful honors of his office.

"That is your child, is it, Peter?" remarked one of his acquaintances, who was shaking his bony hand.

"Perhaps 'tis, one way, now," replied Peter, "but it won't be a great while."

"Have you found a place for it?" inquired his friend, for the efforts Peter had made to get rid of the children were notorious.

"Well, I reckon you'll find out before you go home," replied the bridegroom, with a wink. Then, turning to Esther, he remarked, "I guess now would be as good a time as any, wouldn't it."

The bride having signified her assent, and bestowed some attentions upon her child which involved the use of a handkerchief, Peter stooped, and, taking the little one in his arms, advanced to Mr. Smith—grinning and snickering all the way—and said, "I believe, Square, you told me I might give you anything I was a-mind to for marrying me, and so I fetched down this young one; and if you'll hold open your arms I'll put her into them."

At least half-a-dozen individuals heard every word of the speech of presentation, and, as Peter suited his action to his words, and placed the child so far in the magistrate's arms that he was obliged to grasp it, to keep it from falling, the laugh that was excited at his expense was irresistible.

As the story spread from mouth to mouth, the wedded pair found themselves suddenly forgotten in the general anxiety to get a sight of the magistrate's fee, and congratulate him upon its beauty and value. The fee itself, though of a not remarkably timid character, became very much alarmed at finding itself in the arms of a man whom it had been taught to regard as one of the great ones of the town; and, annoyed by the boisterous laughter that was resounding in every direction among the closely crowding company, it achieved its liberty by two or three vigorous kicks, and dodging among the intervening legs, found its way back to the side of its mother, whom it clasped in a most awkward manner, and whom it distressed by a yell so obstreperous that it would have drowned all the tumult of the room, if it had not tended most decidedly to increase it.

"I wish we'd went out jest as quick as 'twas done," remarked Peter to his wife, thoroughly vexed with the child, and apprehensive that the manœuvre was a failure.

Before the wife could reply, the magistrate approached, and assured Peter, in a spirit of merriment that was very unusual with him, that the fee was too large, and being of a character so similar to an article with which he had the good fortune to be abundantly supplied, he must positively decline its reception. That settled the matter, and Peter mentally resolved upon the spot, that he had made his last effort to reduce the size of his family. In a state of mingled joy and disappointment, he soon afterwards announced his determination to retire, but the company interfered in a good-natured way, and some plain refreshments were served in honor of the event. When at last, in compliance with the request of his wife, who was afraid the children at home might be fretting, Peter prepared to take leave of the magistrate and the party, he found his child asleep in the corner; and taking her in his arms, he departed, followed by the smiling Mrs. Trimble. Both were glad to be out of the house, and were heartily rejoiced when they found themselves quietly seated before a brisk little fire in their own cabin.

"Well, by George! Esther," said Peter, after rubbing his knees and looking into the fire for a while, "it hain't cost anything, has it?"

Peter's marriage was an event to be merry over in the plantation, but, while its events were retailed with charming exaggerations from house to house, the Pynchon family were engaged in the adjustment of the important affairs with which were associated their future prospects.

Until within a few days of the proposed departure of Henry Smith for the Bay, he, as well as the more immediate family of Mr. Pynchon, had supposed that the latter gentleman would accompany him. They all knew that the General Court had enjoined him to be present at the October session, to complete the satisfaction he had commenced in the spring, touching his alleged heresies; but he had long previously determined that the General Court had received all the satisfaction they would win from him in any form.

The announcement of his determination to his family filled them with uneasiness. They feared the result of thus tempting the relentless persecution of those who held the power to persecute, and made some attempts to dissuade him from his purpose. He only smiled at their fears, and, bidding Henry Smith tell the court—if inquiry should be made for him—that it was inconvenient for him to be present, and that he could give them no satisfaction were it otherwise, dismissed his son-in-law and the subject together.

On the arrival of the deputy at the Bay, inquiries were immediately made of him concerning Mr. Pynchon, and much surprise expressed that he had seen fit to trample upon the orders of the government. On the return of some of the members of the party who accompanied Mr. Smith, numerous letters were sent to the old man—some of them from real, but more from pretended friends, urging him—if he would save his character and save himself—to show himself to the General Court before the close of the session. Mr. Pynchon read the letters, laid them aside without exhibiting them to his family, and as he had no opportunity to reply, contented himself with the conviction that he, and not they, judged correctly in regard to what the General Court would dare to do in his case.

The failure of the venerable heretic to appear was a sub

ject of excessive annoyance to many of the leading members of the General Court. They were vexed at being treated with contempt by a man whom they had disabled; and felt that they had over-reached themselves, in not accepting Mr. Pynchon's own terms of humiliation, offered in his hour of distraction and weakness.

After the court had been in session a few days, and Mr. Smith had become conversant with the state of feeling which prevailed, he asked for leave of absence for the remainder of the session. The request was readily granted, with the secret hope that he would carry to Mr. Pynchon such a story as would convince him of the advisableness of his appearance before the General Court as quickly as possible.

They were doomed, however, to disappointment. The session was lengthened out a day or two, in the vain hope of hearing of his arrival, but they found at last that all they could do would be to enjoin him to appear before the next General Court, and to attach a penalty to a non-compliance with the requisition.*

The action of the General Court was not seen by Mr.

* "This Courte doth judge it meete & is willinge that all patience be exercised towards Mr. Wm. Pynchon, that, if it be possible, he may be reduced into the way of truth & that he may renounce the errours & hæresies published in his booke; & for the end doe give him time to the next Generall Courte in May, more thoroughly to consider of the said errours & hæresies in his said booke, & well to weigh the judicious answer of Mr. John Norton thereto; and that he may give full satisfaction for his offence, which they more desire than to proceede to so great a censure as his offence deserves, in case he should not give good satisfaction; the Court doth therefore order, that the judgment of the cause be suspended till the Generall Courte in May next, & that Mr. Wm. Pynchon be enjoyned under the penalty of one hundred pounds, to make his personal appearance at & before the next Generall Courte, to give a full answer to satisfaction (if it may be) or otherwise to stand to the judgment & censure of the Courte."—*Records of Massachusetts, vol. III. page* 257.

Pynchon until some months after it was taken and recorded. He read it with many smiles, and with a pleasant compliment to its excessive kindness and toleration. The manner in which he treated this new order may be judged from the fact that it is the very last mention of the case to be found on the records of the court.

Thus ended, so far as legal measures were concerned, the persecution which befell one of the noblest men and truest Christians in the Massachusetts colony. It is impossible to learn now what controlling cause operated in the withdrawal of legal measures against him. The General Court, before which he had been ordered to appear, may have been of a more liberal character than its predecessor, and may have dropped the case from lack of sympathy with the end sought. This however is hardly probable, unless there had been a popular reaction, of which there is no evidence. The real cause was probably the fact that he had determined upon returning to England. They doubtless neither wished him to return, nor if he should return, to make his case notorious at home.

The mind sickens on recurring once more, among the closing scenes of Mr. Pynchon's residence in the colony, to Mr. Moxon and his hallucinations. It would gladly leave him, his worn and emaciated wife, and his children—stunted in body and mind, so that, although approaching womanhood, they were but children still—all to the fate which alone could be their legitimate inheritance; but there is one individual who, through his personal innocence and dependence, and the associations of his later life, has enlisted the sympathies of the reader, and is still beneath the ban of the minister's fatal superstition. Hugh Parsons—his wife in her grave—a woman whom he felt more and more to have been originally intended by Heaven to be his good angel—his reputation tarnished by his association with her name and crime itself, the subject of the most terrible suspicions possible at the time to be entertained, was a blighted man. Never strong, either in heart or hand, his great calamities crushed him. He felt like one benumbed. He walked like one afraid. He looked like one conscious of having been forsaken alike by God and man.

Throughout the year which succeeded the death of his wife, the evidence against him went on accumulating, aided in the process by the increasing superstitiousness of the villagers. By some strange fatality, every movement that he made seemed to involve him in new difficulties. Suspicious circumstances seemed to walk with him like companions wherever he went, to stand at his side whenever he paused, to group themselves about him whenever he talked, re-echoing all his utterances.

At length, complaint was entered against him as a wizard, and he was arrested and taken to the Bay, to be tried for his life. At this time, the state of feeling in the plantation had arrived at such a pitch that many believed that Hugh had been in the practice of his hellish abominations for months before the death of his wife, and that the minister's daughters were not the only individuals who had been their subjects. He was brought before the grand jury, and indicted, and then before a trial jury, which, by an unanimous verdict, found him guilty. The verdict came before the magistrates for review, who, on examination of the evidence upon which it was based, set it aside. The case then came legally before the General Court, which sustained the view taken by the magistrates, and acquitted him.*

* "Whereas Hugh Parsons of Springfield was arrajned and trjed at a Court of Assistants, held at Boston, 12 of May, 1652, for not having the feare of God before his ejes, but being seduced by the instigation of the divill, in March, 1651, and divers tjmes before and since, at Springfield, as was conceived, had famillar and wicked converse with the divill, and hath used divers divillish practizes, of witchcrafts, to the hurt of diverse persons as by severall witnesses and circumstances appeared, was left by the grand jury for further trial for his life.

The ruin of Hugh could not have been more complete had the verdict of the jury been sustained, and the sentence of death executed upon him. He returned to the plantation broken down in health and reputation—one more victim to that strangest and most terrible of the delusions with which God has permitted man to deceive himself. But the issue of the case was followed by a healthy and much needed reaction in the sentiment of the town. The veil was lifted from the eyes of those who had been misled, and a thousand things which, in their previous mental condition, had appeared mysterious, were explained, until, heartily ashamed of themselves, and indignant that their leader in spiritual and religious affairs should have drawn them into such guilt of injustice and cruelty, they became open in their complaints against him.

Mr. Moxon was discouraged. He was thoroughly grieved, not only in consequence of the fact that Hugh had escaped from the punishment which he fully believed was his due, but because the people had turned against himself, the only individual, besides his family, whom he believed to have been injuriously and unjustly dealt with. He felt that he could no longer fight with Satan, and that he must forsake the field and flee.

In looking over his future, and thinking of the departure of Mr. Pynchon and Henry Smith—men who, from the first, had been his friends—men who had pitied his calamities and exercised charity for his frailties—he felt that none would be left behind who would trust him as they had done.

" The jury of trjalls found him guilty. The magistrates not consenting to the verdict of the jury the cawse came legally to the Generall Courte. The Generall Courte, after the prisoner was called to the barr for trjall of his life, pervsing and considering the evidences brought in against the sajd Hugh Parsons, accused for witchcraft, they judged he was not legally guilty of witchcrafte, and so not to dye by lawe."—*Records of Massachusetts, Vol. IV. part* 1, *page* 96."

There seemed to be no way left open for him but to return to England, with his old friend and patron, and fill out the measure of his life among the scenes of his youth and early manhood. His proposition to this effect was received with no surprise by Mr. Pynchon, who had for some time seen that it would be his only practicable course of procedure; while it was received by the town with a degree of relief and satisfaction which showed how their discontent with him and his ministrations had become confirmed.

The details of preparation for the return to England of these three men—Mr. Pynchon, Mr. Smith, and Mr. Moxon—do not require a recital. It was upon a midsummer morning of the year 1652—only two or three months after the issue of Hugh's trial for witchcraft—that all the members of the plantation were assembled at the house of Mr. Pynchon, the majority of them to bid him and his companions a final farewell, and the remainder to bear them company on their journey to the Bay. It was the most touching scene that the people had ever witnessed. Mr. Pynchon addressed them from the doorway of his house with kind words of counsel, with the warmest terms of paternal endearment, and with such allusions to the future as the occasion would very naturally suggest.

At the close of his brief and simple address all pressed forward to give his hand the parting grasp. Some of the simple-hearted villagers wept aloud. Besides the members of the plantation, a large number of Indians were present to bid adieu to their friend. They pressed around or stood apart in silence, struck with a tender solemnity which impressed Mr. Pynchon quite as deeply as the more boisterous demonstrations of his neighbors. He bade them farewell in some kind words to their chief, distributed to them a multitude of little gifts which he had prepared for them, and conjured them to live in peace, as they had thus far done, with their white brothers.

The entire family of Mr. Pynchon bore him company on his journey to the Bay, but they did not form one half of the party. Nearly all the horses of the plantation were put in requisition for the transportation of packs and passengers, and the cavalcade was the most imposing which had ever passed over the Bay Path. It was a beautiful sight, on that bright summer morning, as the long line started on its passage eastward; and yet it was as solemn as a funeral procession. There were the magistrate and his aged companion, Mr. Moxon and his wife and daughters, Henry Smith and his family, Holyoke and Mary, and drivers and friends in a long array.

Arriving at the summit of the hill upon the east—upon the very spot where, sixteen years before, Mr. Pynchon and his family had paused to look down into the valley which was to be their future home—upon the very spot where Mary had met her lover, at the side of her slaughtered pet—the very spot where they stood when they crowned the northern mountain tops with the names they bear to-day—all paused by a common impulse, and turned the heads of their horses westward.

This was the most affecting moment of all. A throng of the tenderest and strongest associations crowded upon every mind, warm tears sprang into nearly every eye, and all looked and lingered for whole minutes, without a thought of the journey which lay before them. It was a moment for prayer. Even the horses seemed to lose all impatience, and to nibble at the tender foliage within their reach delicately and without disturbance. Mr. Moxon's head was bowed upon his breast, in deep bitterness of spirit, and he did not seem to catch the sentiment which pervaded the others; but Mr. Pynchon, with uncovered head, his silver hair shining in the sunlight, dropped his bridle rein, and stretching both hands towards the valley, gave utterance to his emotions and his aspirations in the words of prayer and thanksgiving. He prayed for the community he was leaving—for their safety and prosperity, for the natives of the valley, in whom he had always entertained a deep interest, and for all who might be directly or indirectly affected by the change which was then in progress in the affairs of the settlement. He committed himself and his companions to God, and thanked his Father in Heaven for the discipline—severe as it had been—through which they had been led. As the "Amen" trembled upon his lips, every horse seemed to turn of his own will into the path, and silently resume the journey; while tearful eyes caught their last look of a valley which through life they recalled as the scene of a long and eventful dream.

Of the journey to the Bay—the multiplied interviews with friends at Boston and in the other settlements, the preparations for the voyage, the return of alienated friends of Mr. Pynchon to their old fidelity; of the tender partings—partings which, in some instances, were like the sunderings of the heart's quickest fibres, the embarkation, the dropping down the Bay with the tide, the spreading of the vessel's great white wings, and their vanishment in the dusky distance, the return of the silent and sorrowful planters homeward, and their arrival among their friends—the particulars do not call for a rehearsal. They brought to a close, as the devout planters fully believed, a providential dispensation, for the purpose of making way for another, which should be longer and more prosperous; and as the man upon whom they had so long relied disappeared, they felt themselves clothed with new strength and a new mission.

On the vessel, the minister and his family, with several others of the party, were confined to their cabins during the entire voyage. Mr. Pynchon was less affected than the others, and made his way upon deck as early as possible, and there, day after day, spent his time in conversation with an old man, dressed in a sailor's costume, with whom he seemed to be on the most confidential terms.

There, together on one bark fleeing homeward, were three outlaws, each one of whom, from widely varying causes, had found himself dissonant with the spirit of the colony to such an extent that he could not live in it. Independence of religious opinion, a becoming restiveness under laws unnecessarily rigid, and a practical belief in gross superstition, were all really, and most decidedly, at war with the spirit of the colony at that time. They could not live in it, and so returned to the place from whence they came out.

In his conversations with Mr. Pynchon upon the vessel, Woodcock (for the reader will have recognised him in his sailor's dress) settled the plans for his future life. He had promised his friend that he would neither make himself known to Mr. Moxon, nor take any measures to revenge the injuries he had received upon the deluded minister; and that he would remain near Mr. Pynchon, and in his employment, while they should be spared alive.

Mr. Moxon, on his arrival in England, made an endeavor to throw off the cloud which rested upon him, but he found it all in vain. He was mentally a wreck, and both he and his family were soon lost sight of, to all his old acquaintances. Previous to his disappearance, he had been silenced as a preacher, and doubtless spent the remainder of his life in inferior, if not menial employments.*

Mr. Pynchon and his family, which embraced that of Henry Smith, settled down at Wraisbury, in Buckingham-

* "There is a tradition that he" (Mr. Moxon) "was silenced after he returned to England, and died in great obscurity, and as a common servant."

Historical Sermon by Rev. Wm. B. Sprague, D.D.

"He" (Mr. Moxon) "died, very poor, out of the ministry. Sept. 15, 1687."

Bliss's Historical Address

shire, a small place on the Thames, where he spent the remainder of his days in the undisturbed enjoyment of those pursuits which had become so pleasant to him. It was there, within sight of the river which washed the shore of his garden, that he dreamed of the past, and recalled the beautiful Connecticut, with all its interesting associations. It was there that he spent many a day in conversation with Woodcock, upon the trials of the past, the duties of the present, and the interests of the future. It was there that he had the deep satisfaction of seeing the old man—deemed reprobate by his former acquaintances—becoming meek, and tractable, and penitent. It was there that he endeavored, in a book still extant in the Harvard College Library, "to clear several scriptures of the greatest note in these controversies, from Mr. Norton's corrupt exposition," and there that he regained full command of his own reason, and reiterated the opinions which, under a terrible pressure, he had mistakenly recalled. It was there, in the last years of his life, that he wrote other theological books and tracts, and sent out around him a healthy and vigorous religious influence. It was there that the infirmities of age crept silently upon him; there that at last, crowned with years and venerated by all who knew him, he sank to rest in the blessed hope of joyful resurrection; and it is there that, after the lapse of nearly two centuries, still sleeps his most honorable dust.

Mr. Pynchon's wife did not long survive him. Simple-hearted, honest in her piety, venerating her husband while he lived, and cherishing his memory as her most precious treasure after he was gone, her last days were peaceful and serene.

Woodcock survived his old friend for many years, and, in his altered spirit, became a favorite with all who knew him. Many a wise and learned man called at his cottage, to listen to the recital of his experiences in America, the quaint views of society and the leading questions of the time which he put forth, and especially to hear him talk upon religion. This subject became the leading one of his mind during the last years of his life, and it was one upon which he brought his strong and unwarped common sense to bear with remarkable power. He was contented and happy. He believed that God had done all things well, and hoped and expected to meet the wife and daughter of his youth in Heaven. He died a very old man, falling asleep in confidence and trust; and those who bore him to his burial-place, and covered the earth upon him, interred a heart which could count as many pulses true to manliness as any that had throbbed in that century.

Henry Smith and his family lived through the remainder of their days and died in England. They were a sober, godly family of the Puritan stamp, and maintained a standing of high respectability. But he and his became dust in their appointed time, and all those who parted on the shore of the ocean years before, have since met on the bank of a river that has crossed the path heavenward of all the generations of men.

CHAPTER XXXIII.

The plantation had passed through a long convulsion; the crisis had arrived and passed; a healthy calm succeeded. No rumors of witchcraft filled the neighborhood with blasting slanders and deadly suspicions.

After the General Court and the people of the colony had become thoroughly aware that Mr. Pynchon had virtually been banished from the country, they began to realize that there had been a great wrong done. They began to feel that the settlement of Springfield had good cause for dissatisfaction; and a reaction took place which delighted in an opportunity to show honor to the family of the prescribed bookmaker. John Pynchon, Elizur Holyoke, and Samuel Chapin, in the order in which their names are here recited, were appointed a board of magistracy, with a commission precisely like the one granted the previous year to Henry Smith. This commission was held by renewal for many years, and acting under it, these three men became an important and most respectable legal tribunal—the first in the western part of the colony which assumed the dignity of a court.

Its inauguration was the opening of a new volume of life and affairs to the plantation, and properly belongs to another drama. John Pynchon, its head, became the foremost man in the Connecticut valley. There is hardly a deed of land from the Indians, in the Connecticut valley, in which his name is not mentioned. He was the leader in trade as well as in public and military affairs. His excellent wife, who was the daughter of Gov. Willis of

Hartford, bore him a large family of children; and, full of years and honors, and known everywhere as the "Worshipful Major Pynchon," he lived to see the dawn of the eighteenth century, when he fell asleep. He lived to see the banks of the Connecticut settled throughout the width of the Massachusetts patent, to pass through the terrible scenes of King Philip's War, and suffer more than any other man by its reverses, and to become assured of the expansion of the colonial germs, planted here and there, into a mighty empire.

Holyoke was honored during a long life with the confidence of the town and the colonial government. He was blessed with brave and beautiful children, worthy alike of him and the noble and beautiful mother who bore them.

Deacon Samuel Chapin lived a long and useful life. He was a diligent, persevering, reliable man—a faithful public servant, and an invaluable man in the church. He was blessed with a large family of children, and they were all boys; and they had large families of children who were all boys, who, in turn, had large families of boys. The consequence was that Springfield became filled with good people bearing that name, and the name was spread all over New England, so that, at this day, there are many thousands who bear the blood and the name of Deacon Samuel Chapin.

On the departure of Mr. Moxon, the town was deprived of the ordinances of religion, but there was a general determination that no minister should be called until one could be fixed upon who would fill the place honorably for God and himself, and profitably for the people. At length, their many prayers for a man who should be after God's own heart were answered, and their long and patient efforts crowned with success. The Reverend Pelatiah Glover of Dorchester came among them, a young man, crowned with the graces of his blessed Master, and walking in the light of God's countenance. He went in and out before them, and broke to them the bread of life for thirty years, and then, in the precious words of a record that dared to speak in Christian language, the Reverend Pelatiah Glover "fell asleep in Jesus." He made his office honorable, and rescued its fame from the terrible delusions with which his superstitious predecessor had associated it.

The Bay Path became better marked, from year to year, as settlements began to string themselves upon it, as upon a thread. Every year the footsteps of those who trod it hurried more and more, until, at last, wheels began to be heard upon it—heavy carts, creaking with merchandise. Spots of the forest which it divided were cleared, and as the settlements upon the Connecticut were multiplied—as the white men gathered in plantations at Woronoco, Nonotuck, Pocomtuck, and Squakeag—they went more rapidly and more frequently to the Bay.

A century passed away, and the wilderness had retired. There was a constant roll along the Bay Path. It had grown and was still growing into a great thoroughfare. The finest of the wheat and the fattest of the flocks and herds were transported to the Bay, whose young commerce had already begun to whiten the coast, and to stretch off upon broader enterprises in competition with the staunch old bottoms of the mother land; and whose commodities came rumbling back in prosperous exchange.

The dreamy years passed by, and then came the furious stage coach, travelling night and day—splashing the mud, brushing up the dust, dashing up to inns, and curving more slowly up to post-offices. The journey was reduced to a day. And then—miracle of miracles—came the railway and the locomotive. The journey of a day is reduced to three hours. Where the traveller toiled over swamps and through thickets, and slept under the canopy of the trees, disturbed all night by the howls of savage beasts, the train flashes and thunders by, bearing a thousand happy hearts, travelling for pastime, or bound upon errands of business or friendship.

How fared Peter Trimble amid the changes of the succeeding years? In the first place, his pimples disappeared. Nobody knew where they went. It was only known that they had been, and were not. As the sun of his married life arose, they vanished and very probably exhaled. At any rate, they went away never to return; and Peter became a long, lank, feeble man, more or less given in his later years to rheumatism, which he attributed to getting up so much nights to look after the children. The Tomson children he found of vast service to him, when he came to have a family of his own, for he, like his deceased predecessor, was abundantly blessed with offspring; and he did not regret on the whole, that he had not been able to get rid of them. Labor upon the farm became at last too severe for him, and he took to coopering, doing the most of his work in the house, and thus assisting Esther in taking care of the family, occasionally drowning their noise with his adze, and always furnishing them with shavings to play with. He preserved until his dying day his superiority as a cutter of hair and a sharpener of razors, and in the latter part of his life, consented to receive a small fee for his services in those fields of effort.

And the widow Tomson made him an excellent wife, and was quite equal in every respect to his deserts. She might have been more elegant and refined, keener of intellect and more profound and thorough in culture, but she would have been but little more highly appreciated by him in consequence, and could not have changed her relations to him, in the matter of sensitiveness and intelligence, without a great loss of personal comfort, and the necessity of obtaining and losing a modicum of self-respect. That the pair were very poor need not be written; but if, after their frugal supper at night, the reader could have seen Peter making rabbits on the wall in a kind of animated fresco for the amusement of the children, or giving the youngest one an imaginary ride to Boston on his foot, cantering feebly away in the stimulus of Esther's voice, he would not have thought them unhappy. But Peter spent a good deal of his time away from home, and he enjoyed it, and made it profitable in snaring partridges, and catching beaver, and hooking various fish, and gathering sundry medicinal herbs. Esther did not complain.

Hugh Parsons carried with him a lifelong sorrow and a lifelong humiliation. Mild and inoffensive, he was beloved and treated by the majority of those who knew him with such attentions as only the unfortunate receive—some of them so kind that they started the tears in his eyes, and all of them so marked that they could not but remind him that others remembered as well as he.

But there is one character—the most lovely that has found its place in the narrative—which still remains to give the reader a parting smile, and yet she parted from the others early. The stone, if the reader have patience, shall tell her beautiful story.

On the banks of the Connecticut, close down where the bending turf hangs its ear over the rippling wavelets that kiss the beach, and murmur and whisper to it night and day, the first grave in the plantation of Agawam was made. There swelled the first mound over a white man's breast, and there, one by one, as the years rolled away, rose other mounds. The rank grass waved over them, the night-straying cow stumbled among them, and unseemly shrubs sprouted between them, and, at long intervals, were cut away. There, one after another, those whose life has informed these pages were gathered, and there the brown sandstone, roughly finished, and quaintly carved, and clumsily inscribed, was placed above their heads. Years and scores of years flew by, the heaps multiplying on every hand, from period to period, till the yard seemed full, yet it ever took in more. There they lay when the wintry blast was driving, and when the summer sun was shining; when the trees were shedding the purple of autumn, and assuming the green of spring; when the ice, a lid of crystal, lay over the waters of the river, and when those waters laughed in the breeze and the sunlight, or swayed and staggered with the weight of the stars upon their bosom. There they lay—the silent settlement of Agawam. Some fell by the red man's arm, and were borne thither in fear, and buried in the presence of faithful muskets and threats of vengeance. Some were borne there in old age—an old age that died in fear after a life of fear. Among these slept the maiden with the bloom upon her cheek and life's discipline all untried, and the sweet infant of days, and the mother parted prematurely from the children of her love, and the man just risen to manhood.

Year after year the frost came down and heaved the ground—now this way, now that—till the mounds settled down to the level around them, and the stones sank down into the mould, or leaned in indiscriminate and inharmonious angles, or fell prone along the graves, face to face with the skeletons whose name they bore. It was a rude spot—sacred, oh, very sacred—but dressed in few of the charms that the sensitive Christian mind loves to gather around the place where its silent friends lie, and where it expects to lay down its own frail tenement. So, in the later times, when the steamboat came thundering up against the bank where the sleepers reposed, and the Bay Path had been mounted with tracks of iron, and the long trains flew over it, another field was chosen—a field laid out by God's own hand as a sleeping-place for his children. A tinkling brook dragged its silver chain over the pebbles through the midst of it, and old gnarled oaks with scanty foliage spread their arms and nodded upon its hill-sides, and maples rose on every hand, so darkly and freshly green in summer, and so richly draped in gold and purple in autumn, that they betrayed the crystal springs which gushed at their roots, and laughed and played like children among the alders.

Into this new field came a swarm of living forms, and ratified by Christian rites Nature's recognised act of consecration. And then commenced the work of reformation and culture. The brook was led down from the spring where it was born, like a pet lamb, with a bell upon its neck—made to leap precipices and practise dainty antics at their feet, to steal silently along under the grass for a score of rods, and then dash into the sunshine, then to stumble down graduated steps, to find its feet at the last, and bound merrily away out of sight and hearing. From the foot of the oak was thrown out a terrace, and on the terrace rose a shaft of marble. And the springs which gushed from among the roots of the maples, and had spent their lives playing among the alder bushes, were taught a new path to the valley, and there sprang like living trees, swaying and dissolving, sighing and whispering, in the midst of their crystal basins. The rough face of the earth was smoothed, picturesque little nooks that had caught the leaves for centuries were cleaned out, the hills were rounded off, and paths were made to wind into every sinuosity of the renewed landscape.

To this beautiful spot were then borne the dead. On every hill, in every silent nook, on every jutting promontory, rose the sandstone and the marble. There was laid the pastor, among the fathers and mothers and lambs of his flock. It became the resting-place of the people—so beautiful that the living never tired of wandering through it and lingering in it, and so sweet with its music of brooks and trees and fountains, and the sight and smell of flowers, that death became more amiable in the association. In the long Sabbath afternoons of summer, many a lonely wanderer sat under the trees, and dreamed away the peaceful hours; and groups with chastened hearts and springing tears assembled around their cherished inclosures, to think and talk of the departed ones at eventide.

At last, there arose the need of another iron path to the settlement. Like the original Bay Path, that which at first connected Agawam with the Connecticut settlements was a bridle path. Then, as on the Bay Path, descended the era of enlargement and improvement. The baggage wagon, the stage coach, and all the old conveniences for travel and transportation came in their time, and, by their side, the sail boat and the steamer. But the age demanded something more, and the engineer, as he adjusted his levels, struck gravestones in his glance, and the surveyor's chain was dragged across the old inclosure where the fathers were sleeping, and where they had lain down without a dream of rising until the resurrection. The decree of commerce was issued, and it was arranged that the accumulated dead of two centuries should be removed to the new cemetery. The spade was dipped deeply down through the mould and sand at one side of the field, and every pound of earth, spadeful by spadeful, was scrutinized for such frail memorials of those who had been buried there as remained undissolved. Each bit of plank, each ghastly skull, each remnant of a bone was treasured in coffers prepared for it, and wherever a stone marked a deposit, both were removed together, and preserved from dissociation. At last, the work was completed, and the sacred old spot surrendered to the engineer.

There, on the summit of the hill, overlooking the valley and the western range of mountains, rests the fallen generation. The old stones, with inscriptions very imperfectly traceable, invite the attention of the curious passer-by, and there he will read, if he can make out the half obliterated letters, the names of many who have become familiar to him in these pages. Among the old stones, he will find one which seems to have bidden defiance to time, and to have escaped the mossy and crumbling decadence of its fellows. It has marked a precious resting-place for nearly two hundred years, and these are the words which it bears, as clearly cut and as fairly engraven as if they were traced by the chisel within a twelvemonth.

Here lyeth the body of Mari,
the wife of Elizur Holyoke,
Who died October 26, 1657.
SHEE YT LYES HERE WAS WHILE SHE STOODE
A VERY GLORY OF WOMANHOODE;
EVEN HERE WAS SOWNE MOST PRETIOUS DVST
WHICH SURELY SHALL RISE WITH THE JVST.

THE END.

www.ingramcontent.com/pod-product-compliance
Lightning Source LLC
LaVergne TN
LVHW011155110826
845150LV00006B/1225

* 9 7 8 1 4 2 5 5 4 6 0 6 9 *

Memorial Edition

POEMS OF

HENRY TIMROD

WITH

MEMOIR AND PORTRAIT

BOSTON AND NEW YORK
HOUGHTON, MIFFLIN AND COMPANY
The Riverside Press, Cambridge
1899

CONTENTS

POEMS WRITTEN IN WAR TIMES

SONNETS

POEMS NOW FIRST COLLECTED

NOTE. The frontispiece portrait of Henry Timrod was engraved from the portrait in the possession of Hon. William A. Courtenay, for the Century Company, who have kindly presented it for use in this volume.

INTRODUCTION

"A TRUE poet is one of the most precious gifts that can be bestowed on a generation." He speaks for it and he speaks to it. Reflecting and interpreting his age and its thoughts, feelings, and purposes, he speaks for it; and with a love of truth, with a keener moral insight into the universal heart of man, and with the intuition of inspiration, he speaks to it, and through it to the world. It is thus

> "The poet to the whole wide world belongs,
> Even as the Teacher is the child's."

"Nor is it to the great masters alone that our homage and thankfulness are due. Wherever a true child of song strikes his harp, we love to listen. All that we ask is that the music be native, born of impassioned impulse that will not be denied, heartfelt, like the lark when she soars up to greet the morning and pours out her song by the same quivering ecstasy that impels her flight." For though the voices be many, the oracle is one, for "God gave the poet his song."

Such was Henry Timrod, the Southern poet. A child of nature, his song is the voice of the Southland. Born in Charleston, S. C., his life cast in the seething torrent of civil war, his voice was also the voice of Carolina, and through her of the South, in all the rich glad life poured out in patriotic pride into that fatal struggle, in all the valor and endurance of that dark conflict, in all the gloom of its disaster, and in all the sacred tenderness that clings about its memories. He was the poet of the Lost Cause, the finest interpreter of the feelings and traditions of the splendid heroism of a brave people. Moreover, by his catholic spirit, his wide range, and world-wide sympathies, he is a true American poet.

The purpose of the TIMROD MEMORIAL ASSOCIATION of his native city and State, in undertaking this new edition of his poems, is to erect a suitable public memorial to the poet, and also to let his own words renew and keep his own memory in his land's literature.

The earliest edition of Timrod's poems was a small volume by Ticknor & Fields, of Boston, in 1860, just before the Civil War. This contained only the poems of the first eight or nine years previous, and was warmly welcomed North and South. The "New York Tribune" then greeted this small first volume in these words: "These poems are worthy of a wide audience, and they form a welcome offering to the common literature of our country."

In this first volume was evinced the culture, the lively fancy, the delicate and vigorous imagination, and the finished artistic power of his mind, even then rejoicing in the fullness and freshness of its creations and in the unwearied flow of its natural music. But it fell then on the great world of letters almost unheeded, shut out by the war cloud that soon broke upon the land, enveloping all in darkness.

The edition of his complete poems was not issued until the South was recovering from the ravage of war, and was entitled "The Poems of Henry Timrod, edited with a sketch of the Poet's life by Paul H. Hayne. E. J. Hale & Son, publishers, New York, 1873." And immediately, in 1874, there followed a second edition of this volume, which contained the noble series of war poems and other lyrics written since the edition of 1860. In 1884 an illustrated edition of "Katie" was published by Hale & Son, New York. All of these editions were long ago exhausted by an admiring public.

The present edition contains the poems of all the former editions, and also some earlier poems not heretofore published.

The name of Timrod has been closely identified with the history of South Carolina for over a century. Before the Revolution, Henry Timrod, of German birth, the founder of the family in America, was a prominent citizen of Charleston, and the president of that historic association, the German Friendly Society, still existing, a century and a quarter old. We find his name first on the roll of the German Fusiliers of Charleston, volunteers formed in May, 1775, for the defense of the country, immediately on hearing of the battle of Lexington. Again in the succeeding generation, in the Seminole war and in the peril of St. Augustine, the German Fusiliers were commanded by his son, Captain William Henry Timrod, who was the father of the poet, and who himself published a volume of poems in the early part of the century. He was the editor of a literary periodical published in Charleston, to which he himself largely contributed. He was of strong intellect and delicate feelings, and an ardent patriot.

Some of the more striking of the poems of the elder Timrod are the following. Washington Irving said of these lines that Tom Moore had written no finer lyric: —

TO TIME, THE OLD TRAVELER

THEY slander thee, Old Traveler,
  Who say that thy delight
Is to scatter ruin, far and wide,
  In thy wantonness of might:
For not a leaf that falleth
  Before thy restless wings,
But in thy flight, thou changest it
  To a thousand brighter things.

Thou passest o'er the battlefield
  Where the dead lie stiff and stark,
Where naught is heard save the vulture's scream,
  And the gaunt wolf's famished bark;
But thou hast caused the grain to spring
  From the blood-enrichêd clay,
And the waving corn-tops seem to dance
  To the rustic's merry lay.

Thou hast strewed the lordly palace
  In ruins on the ground,
And the dismal screech of the owl is heard
  Where the harp was wont to sound;
But the selfsame spot thou coverest
  With the dwellings of the poor,
And a thousand happy hearts enjoy
  What *one* usurped before.

'T is true thy progress layeth
  Full many a loved one low,
And for the brave and beautiful
  Thou hast caused our tears to flow;
But always near the couch of death
  Nor thou, nor we can stay;
And the breath of thy departing wings,
  Dries all our tears away!

THE MOCKING-BIRD

Nor did lack
Sweet music to the magic of the scene:
The little crimson-breasted Nonpareil
Was there, his tiny feet scarce bending down
The silken tendril that he lighted on
To pour his love notes; and in russet coat,
Most homely, like true genius bursting forth

In spite of adverse fortune, a full choir
Within himself, the merry Mock Bird sate,
Filling the air with melody; and at times,
In the rapt favor of his sweetest song,
His quivering form would spring into the sky,
In spiral circles, as if he would catch
New powers from kindred warblers in the clouds
Who would bend down to greet him!

These lines, addressed to the poet by his father, have a pathetic interest: —

TO HARRY

HARRY, my little blue-eyed boy,
  I love to have thee playing near;
There 's music in thy shouts of joy
  To a fond father's ear.

I love to see the lines of mirth
  Mantle thy cheek and forehead fair,
As if all pleasures of the earth
  Had met to revel there;

For gazing on thee, do I sigh
  That those most happy years must flee,
And thy full share of misery
  Must fall in life on thee!

There is no lasting grief below,
  My Harry! that flows not from guilt;
Thou canst not read my meaning now —
  In after times thou wilt.

Thou 'lt read it when the churchyard clay
  Shall lie upon thy father's breast,
And he, though dead, will point the way
  Thou shalt be always blest.

They 'll tell thee this terrestrial ball,
  To man for his enjoyment given,
Is but a state of sinful thrall
  To keep the soul from heaven.

My boy! the verdure-crownèd hills,
  The vales where flowers innumerous blow,
The music of ten thousand rills
  Will tell thee, 't is not so.

God is no tyrant who would spread
  Unnumbered dainties to the eyes,
Yet teach the hungering child to dread
  That touching them he dies!

No! all can do his creatures good,
  He scatters round with hand profuse —
The only precept understood,
  Enjoy, but not abuse!

The poet's mother was the daughter of Mr. Charles Prince, a citizen of Charleston, whose parents had come from England just before the Revolution. Mr. Prince had married Miss French, daughter of an officer in the Revolution, whose family were from Switzerland. It was the influence of his mother also that helped to form the poet's character, and his intense and passionate love of nature. Her beautiful face and form, her purity and goodness, her delight in all the sights and sounds of the country, her childish rapture in wood and field, her love of flowers and trees, and all the mystery and gladness of nature, are among the cherished memories of all her children, and vividly described by the poet's sister.

William Henry Timrod, father of the poet, died of disease contracted in the Florida war, and his family thereafter were in straitened circumstances. Nevertheless, the early education of his gifted son was provided for. Paul H. Hayne, the poet, was one of his earliest friends and schoolmates at Charleston's best school. They sat together, and to his brother boy-poet he first showed his earliest verses in exulting confidence. This friendship and confidence lasted through life, and Hayne has tenderly embalmed it in his sketch of the poet. We have this faithful picture of him at that time: —

"Modest and diffident, with a nervous utterance, but with melody ever in his heart and on his lip. Though always slow of speech, he was yet, like Burns, quick to learn. The chariot wheels might jar in the gate through which he tried to drive his winged steeds, but the horses were of celestial temper and the car purest gold."

His school-fellows remember him as silent and shy, full of quick impulse, and with an eager ambition, insatiable in his thirst for books, yet mingling freely in all sports, and rejoicing unspeakably in the weekly holiday and its long rambles through wood and field. "The sweet security of streets" had no charm for him. He rejoiced in Nature and her changing scenes and seasons. She was always to him comfort, refreshment, balm. She never turned her face from him, and through all his years he "leaned on her breast with loving trustfulness as a little child."

But he had other teachers. He studied all classic literature. "The Æschylean drama had no attraction for him; he reveled in the rich and elegant strains of Virgil, and of the many toned lyre of Horace and the silver lute of Catullus." From the full and inexhaustible fountain of English letters he drank unceasingly. Spenser, Shakespeare, Milton, Burns, Wordsworth, and, later, Tennyson were his immediate inspiration.

His college life at the University of Georgia was interrupted by sickness and cramped by lack of means, and his literary plans were foiled by necessity. Nevertheless, he left his Alma Mater with a mind stirred to its depths, and with a large store of learning, and had already sounded with clear note those chords which were afterwards so vocal in melody.

Dr. J. Dickson Bruns has left this graphic description of Timrod's personal appearance, and of some prominent traits of his social character: —

"In stature," he says, "Timrod was far below the medium height. He had always excelled in boyish sports, and, as he grew to manhood, his unusual breadth of shoulder still seemed to indicate a physical vigor which the slender wrists, thin, transparent hands, and habitually lax attitude but too plainly contradicted.

"The square jaw was almost stern in its strongly pronounced lines, the mouth large, the lips exquisitely sensitive, the gray eyes set deeply under massive brows, and full of a melancholy and pleading tenderness, which attracted attention to his face at once, as the face of one who had thought and suffered much.

"His walk was quick and nervous, with an energy in it that betokened decision of character, but ill sustained by the stammering speech; for in society he was the shyest and most undemonstrative of men. To a single friend whom he trusted, he would pour out his inmost heart; but let two or three be gathered together, above all, introduce a stranger, and he instantly became a quiet, unobtrusive listener, though never a moody or uncongenial one!

"Among men of letters, he was always esteemed as a most sympathetic companion; timid, reserved, unready, if taken by surprise, but highly cultivated, and still more highly endowed.

"The key to his social character was to be found in the feminine gentleness of his temperament. He shrank from noisy debate, and the wordy clash of argument, as from a blow. It stunned and bewildered him, and left him, in the mêlée, alike incapable of defense or attack. And yet, when some burly protagonist would thrust himself too rudely into the ring, and try to bear down opposition by sheer vehemence of declamation, from the corner where he sat ensconced in unregarded silence, *he would suddenly sling out some sharp, swift pebble of thought*, which he had been slowly rounding, and smite with an aim so keen and true as rarely failed to bring down the boastful Anakim!"

In Charleston, as a first effort in life, for a brief period Timrod attempted the law, but found that jealous mistress unsuited to his life work, though he had all the opportunity afforded him in the office of his friend, the Hon. J. L. Petigru, the great jurist. Leaving the bar, he thenceforward devoted himself to literature and to his art.

Charleston to Timrod was home, and he always returned with kindling spirit to the city of his love. There were all his happiest associations and the delight of purest friendships, — W. Gilmore Simms and Paul Hayne, and the rest of the literary coterie that presided over "Russell's Magazine," and Judge Bryan and Dr. Bruns (to whom Hayne dedicated his edition of Timrod's poems), and others were of this glad fellowship, and his social hours were bright in their intercourse and in the cordial appreciation of his genius and the tender love they bore him. These he never forgot, and returning after the ravage of war to his impoverished and suffering city, he writes, in the last year of his young life, "My eyes were blind to everything and everybody but a few old friends."

Suited by endowment and prepared by special study for a professorship, still all his efforts for the academic chair failed, and, finally, he was compelled to become a private teacher, an office the sacredness of which he profoundly realized. In his leisure hours he now gave himself up to deeper study of nature, literature, and man. It was in these few years of quiet retreat that he wrote the poems contained in the first edition of his works, 1859–60, which, laden with all the poet's longing to be heard, were little heeded in the first great shock of war. Indeed, in such a storm, what shelter could a poet find? An ardent Carolinian, devoted to his native State with an allegiance as to his country, he left his books and study, and threw himself into the struggle, a volunteer in the army. In the first years of the war he was in and near Charleston, and wrote those memorable poems and martial lyrics: "Carolina," "A Call to Arms," "Charleston," "Ripley," "Ethnogenesis," and "The Cotton Boll," which deeply stirred the heart of his State, and, indeed, of the whole South. His was the voice of his people. Under its spell the public response was quick, and promised largest honor and world-wide fame for the poet. The project formed by some of the most eminent men of the State, late in 1862, was to publish an illustrated and highly embellished edition of his works in London. The war correspondent of the "London Illustrated News," Vizitelly, himself an artist, promised original illustrations, and the future seemed bright for the gratification of his heart's desire, to be known and heard in the great literary centre of the English-speaking world. But disappointment again was his lot Amid the increasing stress of the conflict, every public and private energy in the South was absorbed in maintaining the ever weakening struggle; and with all art and literature and learning our poet's hopes were buried in the common grave of war; not because he was not loved and cherished, and his genius appreciated, but because a terrible need was upon his people, and desperate issues were draining their life-blood. Then he went to the front. Too weak for the field (for the fatal weakness that finally sapped his life was then upon him), he was compelled, under medical direction, to retire from the battle ranks, and made a last desperate effort to serve the cause he loved as a war correspondent. In this capacity he joined the great army of the West after the battle of Shiloh. The story of his camp life was indeed pathetic. Dr. Bruns writes of him then: "One can scarcely conceive of a situation more hopelessly wretched than that of a mere child in the world's ways suddenly flung down into the heart of that strong retreat, and tossed like a straw on the crest of those refluent waves from which he escaped as by a miracle." Home he came, baffled, dispirited, and sore hurt, to receive the succor of generous friendship, and for a brief time a safe congenial refuge, in 1864, in an editor's chair of the "South Carolinian," at the capital of his native State. Here his strong pen wrote the stirring editorials of that critical time, and there, tempted by the passing hour of comparative calm, he married Miss Kate Goodwin, "Katie, the fair Saxon" of his exquisite song. Here the war that had broken all his plans, and wrecked his health and hopes, and made literature for a time in the South a beggar's vocation, left him with wife and child, the "darling Willie" of his verse, dependent upon his already sapped and fast failing strength for support. Here he saw the capital of his native State, marked for vengeance, pitilessly destroyed by fire and sword. Here gaunt ruin stalked and want entered his own home, made desolate as all the hearthstones of his people. Here the peace that ensued was the peace of the desert! Here the army, defeated and broken, came back after the long heroic struggle to blackened chimneys, sole vestige of home, and the South, with not even bread for her famished children, still stood in solemn silence by those deeper furrows watered with blood. The suffering that he endured was the common suffering of those around him,—actual physical want and lack of the commonest comforts of life, felt most keenly by his sensitive nature and delicate constitution. In the midst of this fierce stress, his darling boy, the crown of his life, died. All his affections, it seemed, were poured out at once, as water spilled upon the ground. He was dying of consumption, and earth shadows crowded around him.

Though long in feeble health, his last illness was brief. The best physicians lovingly gave their skillful ministration, and the State's most eminent men, in their common need, tenderly cared for him and his. With death before him, he clung passionately to his art, absorbed in that alone and in the great Beyond. His latest occupation was correcting the proof-sheets of his own poems, and he passed away with them by his side, stained with his life-blood.

In the autumn of 1867 he was laid by his beloved child in Trinity churchyard, Columbia, S. C. General Hampton, Governor Thompson, and other great Carolinians bore him to the grave, — a grave that, through the sackcloth of the Reconstruction period in South Carolina, remained without a stone. But as he himself wrote of the host of the Southern dead of the war, —

"In seeds of laurel in the earth
The blossom of your fame is blown,
And somewhere waiting for its birth,
The shaft is in the stone."

In later years loving friends reared a small memorial shaft to mark his grave. It was in that dark period that Carl McKinley's genius was touched to these fine lines.

AT TIMROD'S GRAVE. 1877

HARP of the South! no more, no more
Thy silvery strings shall quiver,
The one strong hand might win thy strains
Is chilled and stilled forever.

Our one sweet singer breaks no more
  The silence sad and long,
The land is hushed from shore to shore,
  It brooks no feebler song!

No other voice can charm our ears,
  None other soothe our pain;
Better these echoes lingering yet,
  Than any ruder strain.

For singing, Fate has given sighs,
  For music we make moan;
Oh, who may touch the harp-strings since
  That whisper — "*He is gone!*"

See where he lies — his last sad home
  Of all memorial bare,
Save for a little heap of leaves
  The winds have gathered there!

One fair frail shell from some far sea
  Lies lone above his breast,
Sad emblem and sole epitaph
  To mark his place of rest.

The sweet winds murmur in its heart
  A music soft and low,
As they would bring their secrets still
  To him who sleeps below.

And lo! one tender, tearful bloom
  Wins upward through the grass,
As some sweet thought he left unsung
  Were blossoming at last.

Wild weeds grow rank about the place,
  A dark, cold spot, and drear;

The dull neglect that marked his life
  Has followed even here.

Around shine many a marble shaft
  And polished pillars fair,
And strangers stand on Timrod's grave
  To praise them, unaware!

"Hold up the glories of thy dead!"
  To thine own self be true,
Land that he loved! Come, honor now
  This grave that honors you!

The one characteristic above all others that marked the poet's life was his unfaltering trust, — the soul's unclouded sky, a quenchless radiance of blessed sunlight amid the deep darkness that encompassed him.

As in his poetry there is no false note, no doubtful sentiment, no selfish grief, even when he sings with breast against the thorn, so in his life do we find no word of bitterness or moaning or complaining. Even amid the terrible blight of war and its final utter ruin, prophet-like, he speaks in faith and hope and courage. His own heart breaking, and life ebbing, he writes of Spring as the true Reconstructionist, and pleads her message to his stricken people. It is so true and prophetic that we quote the words written in April, 1866.

"For Spring is a true Reconstructionist, — a reconstructionist in the best and most practical sense. There is not a nook in the land in which she is not at this moment exerting her influence in preparing a way for the restoration of the South. No politician may oppose her; her power defies embarrassment; but she is not altogether independent of help. She brings us balmy airs and gentle dews, golden suns and silver rains; and she says to us, 'These are the materials of the only work in which you need be at present concerned; avail yourselves of them to reclothe your naked country and feed your impoverished people, and you will find that, in the discharge of that task, you have taken the course which will most certainly and most peacefully conduct you to the position which you desire. Turn not aside to bandy epithets with your enemies; stuff your ears, like the princess in the Arabian Nights, against words of insult and wrong; pause not to muse over your condition, or to question your prospects; but toil on bravely, silently, surely.' . . .

"Such are the words of wise and kindly counsel, which, if we attend rightly, we may all hear in the winds and read in the skies of Spring. Nowhere, however, does she speak with so eloquent a voice or so pathetic an effect as in this ruined town. She covers our devastated courts with images of renovation in the shape of flowers; she hangs once more in our blasted gardens the fragrant lamps of the jessamine; in our streets she kindles the maple like a beacon; and from amidst the charred and blackened ruins of once happy homes she pours, through the mouth of her favorite musician, the mocking-bird, a song of hope and joy. What is the lesson which she designs by these means to convey? It may be summed in a single sentence, — forgetfulness of the past, effort in the present, and trust for the future."

Such was the lofty creed and last hopeful, but dying message to his brothers of the South, whose war songs he had written, and the requiem of whose martyred hosts he had chanted.

Such was the tragedy that ended in October, 1867, with the hero at the age of thirty-seven; glory, genius, anguish, tears, but unconquerable faith and heroic fortitude. His larger life scarce begun, his full power felt, but only half expressed, he realized deeply —

> "The petty done, the vast undone!"

He yearned with passionate longing and hope and conscious might to fulfill an even greater mission; but in the infinite providence of God the full fruitage of this exquisite soul was for another sphere. He was indeed "one of those who stirred us, a friend of man and a lover. In no country of this earth could he long have been an alien, and that may now be said of his spirit. In no part of this universe could it feel lonely or unbefriended; it was in harmony with all that flowers or gives perfume in life."

The story of his last days, as given by his poet-friend, Paul Hayne, at the latter's cottage among the pines, is of tender and peculiar interest, and we quote it here, as it was written in 1873 : —

. . . In the latter summer-tide of this same year (1867), I again persuaded him to visit me. Ah! how sacred now, how sad and sweet, are the memories of that rich, clear, prodigal August of '67!

We would rest on the hillsides, in the swaying golden shadows, watching together the Titanic masses of snow-white clouds which floated slowly and vaguely through the sky, suggesting by their form, whiteness, and serene motion, despite the season, flotillas of icebergs upon Arctic seas. Like Lazzaroni we basked in the quiet noons, sunk into the depths of reverie, or perhaps of yet more "charmed sleep." Or we smoked, conversing lazily between the puffs,

> "Next to some pine whose antique roots just peeped
> From out the crumbling bases of the sand."

But the evenings, with their gorgeous sunsets "rolling down like a chorus" and the "gray-eyed melancholy gloaming," were the favorite hours of the day with him. He would often apostrophize twilight in the language of Wordsworth's sonnet : —

> "Hail, twilight! sovereign of one peaceful hour!
> Not dull art thou as undiscerning night;
> But only studious to remove from sight
> Day's mutable distinctions."

"Yes," said he, "she is indeed sovereign of *one peaceful hour!* In the hardest, busiest time one feels the calm, merciful-minded queen stealing upon one in the fading light, and 'whispering,' as Ford has it (or is it Fletcher?), — '*whispering* tranquillity.'"

When in-doors and disposed to read, he took much pleasure in perusing the poems of Robert Buchanan and Miss Ingelow. The latter's "Ballads" particularly delighted him. One, written "in the old English manner," he quickly learned by heart, repeating it with a relish and fervor indescribable.

Here is the opening stanza: —

"Come out and hear the waters shoot, the owlet hoot, the owlet hoot;
Yon crescent moon, a golden boat, hangs dim behind the tree, O!
The dropping thorn makes white the grass, O! sweetest lass, and sweetest lass
Come out and smell the ricks of hay adown the croft with me, O!"

With but a slight effort of memory I can vividly recall his voice and manner in repeating these simple yet beautiful lines.

They were the last verses I ever heard from the poet's lips.

Just as the woods were assuming their first delicate autumnal tints, Timrod took his leave of us. In a conversation on the night but one previous to his departure, we had been speaking of Dr. Parr and other literary persons of unusual age, when he observed: "I have n't the slightest desire, P——, to be an octogenarian, far less a centenarian, like old Parr; but I hope that I may be spared until I am *fifty* or fifty-five."

"About Shakespeare's age," I suggested.

"Oh!" he replied, smiling, "I was not thinking of THAT; but I 'm sure that after fifty-five I would begin to wither, mind and body, and one hates the idea of a mummy, intellectual or physical. Do you remember that picture of extreme old age which Charles Reade gives us in 'Never too Late to Mend'? George Fielding, the hero, is about going away from England to try his luck in Australia. All his friends and relations are around him, expressing their sorrow at his enforced voyage; all but his grandfather, aged ninety-two, who sits stolid and mumbling in his armchair.

"'Grandfather!' shouts George into the deafened ears, 'I 'm going a long journey; mayhap shall never see you again; speak a word to me before I go!' Grandfather looks up, brightens for a moment, and cackles feebly out: 'George, fetch me some *snuff* from where you 're going. See now' (half whimpering), 'I 'm out of snuff.' A good point in the way of illustration, but not a pleasant picture."

On the 13th of September, ten days after Timrod's return to Columbia, he wrote me the following note: —

"Dear P——: I have been too sick to write before, and am still too sick to drop you more than a few lines. You will be surprised and pained to hear that I have had a severe hemorrhage of the lungs.

"I did not come home an instant too soon. I found them without money or provisions. Fortunately I brought with me a small sum. I won't tell you how small, but six dollars of it was from the editor of the 'Opinion' for my last poem.

"I left your climate to my injury. But not only for the sake of my health, I begin already to look back with longing regret to 'Copse Hill.' You have all made me feel as if I had *two* beloved homes!

"I wish that I could divide myself between them; or that I had wings, so that I might flit from one to other in a moment.

"I hope soon to write you at length. Yours," etc.

Again on the 16th I heard from him, thus: —

"Yesterday I had a still more copious hemorrhage! . . .

"I am lying supine in bed, forbidden to speak or make any exertion whatever. But I can't resist the temptation of dropping you a line, in the hope of calling forth a score or two from you in return.

"An awkward time this for me to be sick! We are destitute of funds, almost of food. But God will provide!

"I send you a Sonnet, written the other day, as an Obituary for Mr. Harris Simons. Tell me what you think of it — be sure! Love to your mother, wife, and my precious Willie [since the death of his own child he had turned with a yearning affection to my boy]. Let me hear from you soon — *very* soon! You'll do me more good than medicines!" etc.

On the 25th of the month confidence in Timrod's recovery was confirmed by a letter from Mrs. Goodwin: —

"Our brother," she writes, "is decidedly better; and if there be no recurrence of the hemorrhage will, I hope, be soon convalescent!"

A week and upwards passed on in silence. I received no more communications from Columbia. But early in October a vaguely threatening report reached my ears. On the 9th it was mournfully confirmed. Forty-eight hours before, Henry Timrod had expired!

On the 7th of October, the mortal remains of the poet, so worn and shattered, were buried in the cemetery of Trinity Church, Columbia.

There, in the ruined capital of his native State,

whence scholarship, culture, and social purity have been banished to give place to the orgies of semi-barbarians and the political trickery of adventurers and traitors; there, tranquil amid the vulgar turmoil of factions, reposes the dust of one of the truest and sweetest singers this country has given to the world.

Nature, kinder to his senseless ashes than ever Fortune had been to the living man, is prodigal around his grave — unmarked and unrecorded though it be — of her flowers and verdant grasses, of her rains that fertilize, and her purifying dews. The peace he loved, and so vainly longed for through stormy years, has crept to him at last, but only to fall upon the pallid eyelids, closed forever; upon the pulseless limbs, and the breathless, broken heart. Still it is good to know that

"After life's fitful fever, he sleeps well."

Yet, from this mere material repose, this quiet of decaying atoms, surely the most skeptical of thinkers, in contemplation of *such* a life and *such* a death, must instinctively look from earth to heaven; from the bruised and mouldering clod to the spirit infinitely exalted, and radiant in redemption.

"A calm, a beautiful, a sacred star."

The poetic creed of Timrod, expressed in his "Vision of Poesy," set the impress upon all his work. Conscious of his power, he reverently believed in the mission of the poet as prophet and teacher, —

"The mission of Genius on Earth! To uplift,
Purify, and confirm, by its own gracious gift,
The world," —

and he has consecrated his gift to its noblest uses in the discharge of that "high and holy debt."

As lover of man and nature, his sympathy was universal; no theme was too humble for his pen. "The same law that moulds a planet forms a drop of dew." "Humility is power!" "We may trace the mighty sun above even by the shadow of a slender flower." Yet he dealt not with the fleeting; that was only the passing form of the abiding. Passionately fond as he was of Nature, and nourished and refreshed by her always, he never wrote a line of mere descriptive poetry. Nature is only the symbol, the image, to interpret his spiritual meaning. He felt with Milton, in his noble words, that the abiding work is not raised in the heat of youth or the vapors of wine, or by "invocation to dame Memory and her siren daughters, but by devout prayer to that Eternal Spirit who can enrich with all utterance and knowledge, and send out his seraphim with the hallowed fire of his altars to touch and purify the lips of whom He pleases."

Under that inspiration and revelation the poet is a divine interpreter of (in his own words) —

"All lovely things, and gentle — the sweet laugh
Of children, Girlhood's kiss, and Friendship's clasp,
The boy that sporteth with the old man's staff,
The baby, and the breast its fingers grasp —
All that exalts the grounds of happiness,
All griefs that hallow, and all joys that bless,

"To me are sacred; at my holy shrine
Love breathes its latest dreams, its earliest hints;
I turn life's tasteless waters into wine,
And flush them through and through with purple tints.
Wherever Earth is fair, and Heaven looks down,
I rear my altars, and I wear my crown."

It was this mission of Poetry that filled his mind and heart and life with abiding light, which made him cling passionately to life, not because of any physical fear of death, but because in that mission Art and Nature were so inexpressibly rich and sweet to him to reveal his message to man. In the benediction of his dying words, "Love is sweeter than rest!"

The moral purity of these poems is their distinctive quality, as it was of the man. With a universal sympathy for all life, still he moved always on the highest planes of thought and feeling and purpose. He seemed always to be impressed in his art with the truth of his own lines, —

"There is no unimpressive spot on earth,
The beauty of the stars is over all."

His earnestness and deep poetic insight clothed all themes with the beauty and light that is in and over all.

Timrod's melancholy, the finest test of high poetic quality, when purified and spiritualized, has no Byronic bitterness, no selfish morbidness, no impenetrable gloom, but in his own exquisite lines it is, —

"A shadowy land, where joy and sorrow kiss,
Each still to each corrective and relief,
Where dim delights are brightened into bliss,
And nothing wholly perishes but Grief.

"Ah, me! — not dies — no more than spirit dies;
But in a change like death is clothed with wings;
A serious angel, with entrancèd eyes,
Looking to far off and celestial things."

Again, in all these poems there is a nameless spell of a simplicity, fervid yet tender, and an imagination, strong yet delicate, both in its perception and expression.

His style, "like noble music unto noble words," is elaborate, yet perfectly natural. There is no trace of labor; grace guides and power impels. So perfect is it at times in its natural power that the mind is almost unconscious of the word-symbol in grasping immediately the thought revealed.

There is in the verse a ceaseless melody and perfect finish. At times there is "the easy elegance of Catullus," always his delight, and a metrical translation of whose poems he had completed.

Rare endowment with broad culture is evinced in the high intellectual level always maintained; and the evenness of quality that is always of the mountain top. He always knows his power, and its range. His song is always clear and true.

Moreover, with a universality of poetic feeling, he has struck every chord, and always with a keen sensibility and delicacy of natural instinct. Among the finest poems, how wide is this range and varied this power!

"The Vision of Poesy," his longest work, written in youth, essaying the mission and the philosophy of the poetic art, has some lofty passages, and all the promise of his later power, felicity, and melody.

"A Year's Courtship" is in its glow, and grace, and music the perfection of classic art.

The dainty voluptuousness in a "Serenade" kindles with the luxuriousness of the South.

His "Præceptor Amat" is warm with the breath of rapturous feeling, and rich with the fragrance of flowers.

"Ethnogenesis," "the birth of the nation," is regarded by some his greatest poem. It is prophecy linked with the hope and aspiration of the newborn nation of the South. A permanent image of the Southern nature and character is thus richly portrayed: —

> "But the type
> Whereby we shall be known in every land
> Is that vast gulf which lips our Southern strand,
> And through the cold, untempered ocean pours
> Its genial streams, that far off Arctic shores
> May sometimes catch upon the softened breeze
> Strange tropic warmth and hints of summer seas."

The Cotton Boll," in "the snow of Southern summers," is a forerunner of Lanier's "Corn." It reveals the mystic spell and kingly power of that far-stretching tropic snow, and contains that glowing painting of Carolina from sea to mountain, which closes

> "No fairer land hath fired a poet's lays,
> Or given a home to man!"

"Too Long, O Spirit of Storm," is the fused passion of the poet's heart appalled at the moral death of stagnation. It has all the intensity and subtlety of Shelley.

In "The Lily Confidante," delicate and fanciful as it is, the reply of the Lily "is a simple yet sacred melody," hallowing the purity of passion.

"The Arctic Voyager" suggests Tennyson's "Ulysses" in its high faith, lofty purpose, and sustained power.

"Spring" is the burst of the Southern spring, in its flooding life and glory and beauty. There is "a nameless pathos in the air." A wonderful revelation is going on before our eyes! No miracle could startle in the ever new creation, so strange and rapturous is this joy of sense and spiritual rebirth.

Nor was his genius only reflective, and creative, and playful; his was a trumpet voice also. When the blast of war sounded, his voice rang like a clarion in "Carolina" and "Call to Arms." Beyond their local meaning, which kindles and thrills, now as then, the men of the South, they have an abiding, universal power from the standpoint of art; for there is nothing finer in all the martial strains of the lyric.

Paul Hayne, his brother poet, speaking of "Carolina," as "lines destined perhaps to outlive the political vitality of the State, whose antique fame they celebrate," said: —

"I read them first, and was thrilled by their power and pathos, upon a stormy March evening in Fort Sumter! Walking along the battlements, under the red light of a tempestuous sunset, the wind steadily and loudly blowing from off the bar across the tossing and moaning waste of waters, driven inland; with scores of gulls and white sea-birds flying and shrieking round me, — those wild voices of Nature mingled strangely with the rhythmic roll and beat of the poet's impassioned music. The very spirit, or dark genius, of the troubled scene appeared to take up and to repeat such verses as —

"'I hear a murmur as of waves
That grope their way through sunless caves,
Like bodies struggling in their graves,
Carolina!
And now it deepens; slow and grand
It swells, as rolling to the land,
An ocean broke upon the strand,
Carolina!
Shout! let it reach the startled Huns!
And roar with all thy festal guns!
It is the answer of thy sons,
Carolina!'"

Profoundly appealing as are Timrod's war strains, for they are the heart-cry of a people, still it should be noted that there is scarcely a battle ode that does not close with an invocation to peace, such was the lofty nature of the poet. War to him was only the drawn sword of right, and truth, and justice, which accomplished, the prayer for peace was ever on his lips, as witness the noble invocation to Peace, closing his "Christmas," that has so often stirred and hushed at once the heart of the South.

The Ode, written for Memorial Day, April, 1867, of the Confederate graves at Charleston, was his last production. He had sung in lofty strains each phase of the struggle, its hope, its courage, its fear, its despair; he now sings his latest song, a wreath of flowers upon the unmarked graves of the Southern dead, and has hallowed these sacred mounds to his people in the words, —

> "There is no holier spot of ground
> Than where defeated valor lies,
> By mourning beauty crowned!"

These poems are written in the life-blood of the poet and his generation. The patriotic fire, the devoted sacrifice and splendid achievement, that "Carolina," "Cry to Arms," "Unknown Dead," "Carmen Triumphale," "Charleston," "Storm and Calm," and the other of the war poems celebrate were not only the rushing tide of earnest feeling of a noble people then, but are now a part of the glory and heritage of the State, of the South, and of the American republic. They were the mighty heart-beats of that great epoch. They are now irrevocable history, and make these poems a part of the abiding literature of America.

"A Common Thought" is the poet's premonition of his end; but he sees no vision of the dying glory of sunset, no going out into the dark, no presentiment of a vague and gloomy voyage on a homeless sea; but in the sunshine, in the growing light of ever broadening day, amid the joy and splendor of nature, bright prophecy and intuition of immortality, is to come the sudden, solemn mystery of the whisper, "He is gone!" And so it was. For as the sun broadened into glad day, and the full radiance illumined and animated earth and sea and sky, "as it purpled in the zenith, as it brightened on the lawn," this rich young life, in its own fresh morning of genius and spiritual sunshine, passed, and in his own triumphant words, —

> "not dies, no more than Spirit dies;
> But in a change like death was clothed with wings."

THE LATE JUDGE GEORGE S. BRYAN

IT would not be fitting that this memorial edition of Timrod's Poems should go forth to the world without proper recognition, on the part of the TIMROD MEMORIAL ASSOCIATION, of the relation occupied and the services rendered to the poet in his lifetime by the late Hon. George S. Bryan, of Charleston. During the whole of Timrod's career Judge Bryan was his devoted friend, ever ready to assist him materially, morally, and in every other respect.

His faith in Timrod's genius never wavered, and but for his early assistance, sympathy, and encouragement, much of the fruit of that genius would have been lost or wasted. He helped him in adversity, cheered him in his hours of anxiety and despondency, and from first to last, throughout the literary and spiritual history of the poet, he did more than any other friend to keep alive in his heart the steadfast flame of faith in his poetic destiny; Judge Bryan's name must always be inseparably connected with Henry Timrod's in the literary annals of South Carolina.

January, 1899.

POEMS

SPRING

SPRING, with that nameless pathos in the air
Which dwells with all things fair,
Spring, with her golden suns and silver rain,
Is with us once again.

Out in the lonely woods the jasmine burns
Its fragrant lamps, and turns
Into a royal court with green festoons
The banks of dark lagoons.

In the deep heart of every forest tree
The blood is all aglee,
And there 's a look about the leafless bowers
As if they dreamed of flowers.

Yet still on every side we trace the hand
Of Winter in the land,
Save where the maple reddens on the lawn,
Flushed by the season's dawn;

Or where, like those strange semblances we find
That age to childhood bind,
The elm puts on, as if in Nature's scorn,
The brown of Autumn corn.

As yet the turf is dark, although you know
That, not a span below,
A thousand germs are groping through the gloom,
And soon will burst their tomb.

Already, here and there, on frailest stems
Appear some azure gems,
Small as might deck, upon a gala day,
The forehead of a fay.

In gardens you may note amid the dearth
The crocus breaking earth;
And near the snowdrop's tender white and green,
The violet in its screen.

But many gleams and shadows need must pass
Along the budding grass,
And weeks go by, before the enamored South
Shall kiss the rose's mouth.

Still there 's a sense of blossoms yet unborn
In the sweet airs of morn;
One almost looks to see the very street
Grow purple at his feet.

At times a fragrant breeze comes floating by,
And brings, you know not why,
A feeling as when eager crowds await
Before a palace gate

Some wondrous pageant; and you scarce would
start,
If from a beech's heart,
A blue-eyed Dryad, stepping forth, should say,
"Behold me! I am May!"

Ah! who would couple thoughts of war and crime
With such a blessëd time!
Who in the west wind's aromatic breath
Could hear the call of Death!

Yet not more surely shall the Spring awake
The voice of wood and brake,
Than she shall rouse, for all her tranquil charms,
A million men to arms.

There shall be deeper hues upon her plains
Than all her sunlit rains,
And every gladdening influence around,
Can summon from the ground.

Oh! standing on this desecrated mould,
Methinks that I behold,
Lifting her bloody daisies up to God,
Spring kneeling on the sod,

And calling, with the voice of all her rills,
Upon the ancient hills
To fall and crush the tyrants and the slaves
Who turn her meads to graves.

THE COTTON BOLL

While I recline
At ease beneath
This immemorial pine,
Small sphere!
(By dusky fingers brought this morning here
And shown with boastful smiles),
I turn thy cloven sheath,
Through which the soft white fibres peer,
That, with their gossamer bands,
Unite, like love, the sea-divided lands,
And slowly, thread by thread,
Draw forth the folded strands,
Than which the trembling line,
By whose frail help yon startled spider fled
Down the tall spear-grass from his swinging bed,
Is scarce more fine;
And as the tangled skein
Unravels in my hands,
Betwixt me and the noonday light,
A veil seems lifted, and for miles and miles
The landscape broadens on my sight,
As, in the little boll, there lurked a spell
Like that which, in the ocean shell,
With mystic sound,
Breaks down the narrow walls that hem us round,
And turns some city lane

Into the restless main,
With all his capes and isles!

Yonder bird,
Which floats, as if at rest,
In those blue tracts above the thunder, where
No vapors cloud the stainless air,
And never sound is heard,
Unless at such rare time
When, from the City of the Blest,
Rings down some golden chime,
Sees not from his high place
So vast a cirque of summer space
As widens round me in one mighty field,
Which, rimmed by seas and sands,
Doth hail its earliest daylight in the beams
Of gray Atlantic dawns;
And, broad as realms made up of many lands,
Is lost afar
Behind the crimson hills and purple lawns
Of sunset, among plains which roll their streams
Against the Evening Star!
And lo!
To the remotest point of sight,
Although I gaze upon no waste of snow,
The endless field is white;
And the whole landscape glows,
For many a shining league away,
With such accumulated light

As Polar lands would flash beneath a tropic day!
Nor lack there (for the vision grows,
And the small charm within my hands—
More potent even than the fabled one,
Which oped whatever golden mystery
Lay hid in fairy wood or magic vale,
The curious ointment of the Arabian tale—
Beyond all mortal sense
Doth stretch my sight's horizon, and I see,
Beneath its simple influence,
As if with Uriel's crown,
I stood in some great temple of the Sun,
And looked, as Uriel, down!)
Nor lack there pastures rich and fields all green
With all the common gifts of God,
For temperate airs and torrid sheen
Weave Edens of the sod;
Through lands which look one sea of billowy gold
Broad rivers wind their devious ways;
A hundred isles in their embraces fold
A hundred luminous bays;
And through yon purple haze
Vast mountains lift their plumed peaks cloud-crowned;
And, save where up their sides the ploughman creeps,
An unhewn forest girds them grandly round,
In whose dark shades a future navy sleeps!
Ye Stars, which, though unseen, yet with me gaze

Upon this loveliest fragment of the earth!
Thou Sun, that kindlest all thy gentlest rays
Above it, as to light a favorite hearth!
Ye Clouds, that in your temples in the West
See nothing brighter than its humblest flowers!
And you, ye Winds, that on the ocean's breast
Are kissed to coolness ere ye reach its bowers!
Bear witness with me in my song of praise,
And tell the world that, since the world began,
No fairer land hath fired a poet's lays,
Or given a home to man!

But these are charms already widely blown!
His be the meed whose pencil's trace
Hath touched our very swamps with grace,
And round whose tuneful way
All Southern laurels bloom;
The Poet of "The Woodlands," unto whom
Alike are known
The flute's low breathing and the trumpet's tone,
And the soft west wind's sighs;
But who shall utter all the debt,
O Land wherein all powers are met
That bind a people's heart,
The world doth owe thee at this day,
And which it never can repay,
Yet scarcely deigns to own!
Where sleeps the poet who shall fitly sing
The source wherefrom doth spring

That mighty commerce which, confined
To the mean channels of no selfish mart,
Goes out to every shore
Of this broad earth, and throngs the sea with ships
That bear no thunders; hushes hungry lips
In alien lands;
Joins with a delicate web remotest strands;
And gladdening rich and poor,
Doth gild Parisian domes,
Or feed the cottage-smoke of English homes,
And only bounds its blessings by mankind!
In offices like these, thy mission lies,
My Country! and it shall not end
As long as rain shall fall and Heaven bend
In blue above thee; though thy foes be hard
And cruel as their weapons, it shall guard
Thy hearth-stones as a bulwark; make thee great
In white and bloodless state;
And haply, as the years increase—
Still working through its humbler reach
With that large wisdom which the ages teach—
Revive the half-dead dream of universal peace!
As men who labor in that mine
Of Cornwall, hollowed out beneath the bed
Of ocean, when a storm rolls overhead,
Hear the dull booming of the world of brine
Above them, and a mighty muffled roar
Of winds and waters, yet toil calmly on,
And split the rock, and pile the massive ore,
Or carve a niche, or shape the archëd roof;

So I, as calmly, weave my woof
Of song, chanting the days to come,
Unsilenced, though the quiet summer air
Stirs with the bruit of battles, and each dawn
Wakes from its starry silence to the hum
Of many gathering armies. Still,
In that we sometimes hear,
Upon the Northern winds, the voice of woe
Not wholly drowned in triumph, though I know
The end must crown us, and a few brief years
Dry all our tears,
I may not sing too gladly. To Thy will
Resigned, O Lord! we cannot all forget
That there is much even Victory must regret.
And, therefore, not too long
From the great burthen of our country's wrong
Delay our just release!
And, if it may be, save
These sacred fields of peace
From stain of patriot or of hostile blood!
Oh, help us, Lord! to roll the crimson flood
Back on its course, and, while our banners wing
Northward, strike with us! till the Goth shall cling
To his own blasted altar-stones, and crave
Mercy; and we shall grant it, and dictate
The lenient future of his fate
There, where some rotting ships and crumbling quays
Shall one day mark the Port which ruled the Western seas.

PRÆCEPTOR AMAT

It is time (it was time long ago) I should sever
This chain — why I wear it I know not — forever!
Yet I cling to the bond, e'en while sick of the mask
I must wear, as of one whom his commonplace task
And proof-armor of dullness have steeled to her charms!
Ah! how lovely she looked as she flung from her arms,
In heaps to this table (now starred with the stains
Of her booty yet wet with those yesterday rains),
These roses and lilies, and — what? let me see!
Then was off in a moment, but turned with a glee,
That lit her sweet face as with moonlight, to say,
As 't was almost too late for a lesson to-day,
She meant to usurp, for this morning at least,
My office of Tutor; and instead of a feast
Of such mouthfuls as *poluphloisboio thalasses*,
With which I fed her, I should study the grasses
(Love-grasses she called them), the buds, and the flowers
Of which I know nothing; and if "with *my* powers,"
I did not learn all she could teach in that time,
And thank her, perhaps, in a sweet English rhyme,
If I did not do this, and she flung back her hair,
And shook her bright head with a menacing air,
She 'd be — oh! she 'd be — a real Saracen Omar

To a certain much-valued edition of Homer!
But these flowers! I believe I could number as
soon
The shadowy thoughts of a last summer's noon,
Or recall with their phases, each one after one,
The clouds that came down to the death of the
Sun,
Cirrus, Stratus, or Nimbus, some evening last year,
As unravel the web of one genus! Why, there,
As they lie by my desk in that glistering heap,
All tangled together like dreams in the sleep
Of a bliss-fevered heart, I might turn them and
turn
Till night, in a puzzle of pleasure, and learn
Not a fact, not a secret I prize half so much,
As, how rough is this leaf when I think of her
touch.
There 's one now blown yonder! what can be its
name?
A topaz wine-colored, the wine in a flame;
And another that 's hued like the pulp of a melon,
But sprinkled all o'er as with seed-pearls of Ceylon;
And a third! its white petals just clouded with
pink!
And a fourth, that blue star! and then this, too! I think
If one brought me this moment an amethyst cup,
From which, through a liquor of amber, looked up,
With a glow as of eyes in their elfin-like lustre,

Stones culled from all lands in a sunshiny cluster,
From the ruby that burns in the sands of Mysore
To the beryl of Daunia, with gems from the core
Of the mountains of Persia (I talk like a boy
In the flush of some new, and yet half-tasted joy);
But I think if that cup and its jewels together
Were placed by the side of this child of the weather
(This one which she touched with her mouth, and let slip
From her fingers by chance, as her exquisite lip,
With a music befitting the language divine,
Gave the roll of the Greek's multitudinous line),
I should take — not the gems — but enough! let me shut
In the blossom that woke it, my folly, and put
Both away in my bosom — there, in a heart-niche,
One shall outlive the other — is 't hard to tell which?
In the name of all starry and beautiful things,
What is it? the cross in the centre, these rings,
And the petals that shoot in an intricate maze,
From the disk which is lilac — or purple? like rays
In a blue Aureole!

And so now will she wot,
When I sit by her side with my brows in a knot,
And praise her so calmly, or chide her perhaps,
If her voice falter once in its musical lapse,
As I 've done, I confess, just to gaze at a flush

In the white of her throat, or to watch the quick
    rush
Of the tear she sheds smiling, as, drooping her
    curls
O'er that book I keep shrined like a casket of
    pearls,
She reads on in low tones of such tremulous sweet-
    ness,
That (in spite of some faults) I am forced, in dis-
    creetness,
To silence, lest mine, growing hoarse, should betray
What I must not reveal — will she guess now, I
    say,
How, for all his grave looks, the stern, passionless
    Tutor,
With more than the love of her youthfulest suitor,
Is hiding somewhere in the shroud of his vest,
By a heart that is beating wild wings in its nest,
This flower, thrown aside in the sport of a minute,
And which he holds dear as though folded within it
Lay the germ of the bliss that he dreams of! Ah,
    me!
It is hard to love thus, yet to seem and to be
A thing for indifference, faint praise, or cold blame,
When you long (by the right of deep passion, the
    claim,
On the loved of the loving, at least to be heard)
To take the white hand, and with glance, touch,
    and word,

Burn your way to the heart! That her step on the stair?
Be still thou fond flutterer!

How little I care
For your favorites, see! they are all of them, look!
On the spot where they fell, and — but here is your book!

THE PROBLEM

Not to win thy favor, maiden, not to steal away thy heart,
Have I ever sought thy presence, ever stooped to any art;
Thou wast but a wildering problem, which I aimed to solve, and then
Make it matter for my note-book, or a picture for my pen.
So, I daily conned thee over, thinking it no dangerous task,
Peeping underneath thy lashes, peering underneath thy mask —
For thou wear'st one — no denial! there is much within thine eyes;
But those stars have other secrets than are patent in their skies.
And I read thee, read thee closely, every grace and every sin,

Looked behind the outward seeming to the strange wild world within,
Where thy future self is forming, where I saw — no matter what!
There was something less than angel, there was many an earthly spot;
Yet so beautiful thy errors that I had no heart for blame,
And thy virtues made thee dearer than my dearest hopes of fame;
All so blended, that in wishing one peculiar trait removed,
We indeed might make thee better, but less lovely and less loved.
All my mind was in the study — so two thrilling fortnights passed —
All my mind was in the study — till my heart was touched at last.
Well! and then the book was finished, the absorbing task was done,
I awoke as one who had been dreaming in a noonday sun;
With a fever on my forehead, and a throbbing in my brain,
In my soul delirious wishes, in my heart a lasting pain;
Yet so hopeless, yet so cureless — as in every great despair —
I was very calm and silent, and I never stooped to prayer,

Like a sick man unattended, reckless of the coming death,
Only for he knows it certain, and he feels no sister's breath.
All the while as by an Até, with no pity in her face,
Yet with eyes of witching beauty, and with form of matchless grace,
I was haunted by thy presence, oh! for weary nights and days,
I was haunted by thy spirit, I was troubled by thy gaze,
And the question which to answer I had taxed a subtle brain,
What thou art, and what thou wilt be, came again and yet again;
With its opposite deductions, it recurred a thousand times,
Like a coward's apprehensions, like a madman's favorite rhymes.
But to-night my thoughts flow calmer — in thy room I think I stand,
See a fair white page before thee, and a pen within thy hand;
And thy fingers sweep the paper, and a light is in thine eyes,
Whilst I read thy secret fancies, whilst I hear thy secret sighs.
What they are I will not whisper, those are lovely, these are deep,

But one name is left unwritten, that is only breathed
in sleep.
Is it wonder that my passion bursts at once from
out its nest?
I have bent my knee before thee, and my love is all
confessed;
Though I knew that name unwritten was another
name than mine,
Though I felt those sighs half murmured what I
could but half divine.
Aye! I hear thy haughty answer! Aye! I see thy
proud lip curl!
"What presumption, and what folly!" why, I only
love a girl
With some very winning graces, with some very
noble traits,
But no better than a thousand who have bent to
humbler fates.
That I ask not; I have, maiden, just as haught a
soul as thine;
If thou think'st thy place above me, thou shalt
never stoop to mine.
Yet as long as blood runs redly, yet as long as
mental worth
Is a nobler gift than fortune, is a holier thing than
birth,
I will claim the right to utter, to the high and to
the low,
That I love them, or I hate them, that I am a
friend or foe.

Nor shall any slight unman me; I have yet some little strength,
Yet my song shall sound as sweetly, yet a power be mine at length!
Then, oh, then! but moans are idle — hear me, pitying saints above!
With a chaplet on my forehead, I will justify my love.
And perhaps when thou art leaning on some less devoted breast,
Thou shalt murmur, "He was worthier than my blinded spirit guessed."

A YEAR'S COURTSHIP

I SAW her, Harry, first, in March —
You know the street that leadeth down
By the old bridge's crumbling arch? —
Just where it leaves the dusty town

A lonely house stands grim and dark —
You 've seen it? then I need not say
How quaint the place is — did you mark
An ivied window? Well! one day,

I, chasing some forgotten dream,
And in a poet's idlest mood,
Caught, as I passed, a white hand's gleam —
A shutter opened — there she stood

Training the ivy to its prop.
  Two dark eyes and a brow of snow
Flashed down upon me — did I stop? —
  She says I did — I do not know.

But all that day did something glow
  Just where the heart beats; frail and slight,
A germ had slipped its shell, and now
  Was pushing softly for the light.

And April saw me at her feet,
  Dear month of sunshine and of rain!
My very fears were sometimes sweet,
  And hope was often touched with pain.

For she was frank, and she was coy,
  A willful April in her ways;
And in a dream of doubtful joy
  I passed some truly April days.

May came, and on that arch, sweet mouth,
  The smile was graver in its play,
And, softening with the softening South,
  My April melted into May.

She loved me, yet my heart would doubt,
  And ere I spoke the month was June —
One warm still night we wandered out
  To watch a slowly setting moon.

Something which I saw not — my eyes
  Were not on heaven — a star, perchance,
Or some bright drapery of the skies,
  Had caught her earnest, upper glance.

And as she paused — Hal! we have played
  Upon the very spot — a fir
Just touched me with its dreamy shade,
  But the full moonlight fell on her —

And as she paused — I know not why —
  I longed to speak, yet could not speak;
The bashful are the boldest — I —
  I stooped and gently kissed her cheek.

A murmur (else some fragrant air
  Stirred softly) and the faintest start —
O Hal! we were the happiest pair!
  O Hal! I clasped her heart to heart!

And kissed away some tears that gushed;
  But how she trembled, timid dove,
When my soul broke its silence, flushed
  With a whole burning June of love.

Since then a happy year hath sped
  Through months that seemed all June and May,
And soon a March sun, overhead,
  Will usher in the crowning day.

Twelve blessed moons that seemed to glow
  All summer, Hal! — my peerless Kate!
She is the dearest — "Angel?" — no!
  Thank God! — but you shall see her — wait.

So all is told! I count on thee
  To see the Priest, Hal! Pass the wine!
Here 's to my darling wife to be!
  And here 's to — when thou find'st her — thine!

SERENADE

HIDE, happy damask, from the stars,
  What sleep enfolds behind your veil,
But open to the fairy cars
  On which the dreams of midnight sail;
And let the zephyrs rise and fall
  About her in the curtained gloom,
And then return to tell me all
  The silken secrets of the room.

Ah, dearest! may the elves that sway
  Thy fancies come from emerald plots,
Where they have dozed and dreamed all day
  In hearts of blue forget-me-nots.
And one perhaps shall whisper thus:
  Awake! and light the darkness, Sweet!
While thou art reveling with us,
  He watches in the lonely street.

YOUTH AND MANHOOD

ANOTHER year! a short one, if it flow
  Like that just past,
And I shall stand — if years can make me so —
  A man at last.

Yet, while the hours permit me, I would pause
  And contemplate
The lot whereto unalterable laws
  Have bound my fate.

Yet, from the starry regions of my youth,
  The empyreal height
Where dreams are happiness, and feeling truth,
  And life delight —

From that ethereal and serene abode
  My soul would gaze
Downward upon the wide and winding road,
  Where manhood plays;

Plays with the baubles and the gauds of earth —
  Wealth, power, and fame —
Nor knows that in the twelvemonth after birth
  He did the same.

Where the descent begins, through long defiles
  I see them wind;

And some are looking down with hopeful smiles,
　　And some are — blind.

And farther on a gay and glorious green
　　Dazzles the sight,
While noble forms are moving o'er the scene,
　　Like things of light.

Towers, temples, domes of perfect symmetry
　　Rise broad and high,
With pinnacles among the clouds; ah, me!
　　None touch the sky.

None pierce the pure and lofty atmosphere
　　Which I breathe now,
And the strong spirits that inhabit there,
　　Live — God sees how.

Sick of the very treasure which they heap;
　　Their tearless eyes
Sealed ever in a heaven-forgetting sleep,
　　Whose dreams are lies;

And so, a motley, unattractive throng,
　　They toil and plod,
Dead to the holy ecstasies of song,
　　To love, and God.

Dear God! if that I may not keep through life
　　My trust, my truth,

And that I must, in yonder endless strife,
Lose faith with youth;

If the same toil which indurates the hand
Must steel the heart,
Till, in the wonders of the ideal land,
It have no part;

Oh! take me hence! I would no longer stay
Beneath the sky;
Give me to chant one pure and deathless lay,
And let me die!

HARK TO THE SHOUTING WIND

HARK to the shouting Wind!
Hark to the flying Rain!
And I care not though I never see
A bright blue sky again.

There are thoughts in my breast to-day
That are not for human speech;
But I hear them in the driving storm,
And the roar upon the beach.

And oh, to be with that ship
That I watch through the blinding brine!
O Wind! for thy sweep of land and sea!
O Sea! for a voice like thine!

Shout on, thou pitiless Wind,
To the frightened and flying Rain!
I care not though I never see
A calm blue sky again.

TOO LONG, O SPIRIT OF STORM

Too long, O Spirit of Storm,
Thy lightning sleeps in its sheath!
I am sick to the soul of yon pallid sky,
And the moveless sea beneath.

Come down in thy strength on the deep!
Worse dangers there are in life,
When the waves are still, and the skies look fair,
Than in their wildest strife.

A friend I knew, whose days
Were as calm as this sky overhead;
But one blue morn that was fairest of all,
The heart in his bosom fell dead.

And they thought him alive while he walked
The streets that he walked in youth—
Ah! little they guessed the seeming man
Was a soulless corpse in sooth.

Come down in thy strength, O Storm!
And lash the deep till it raves!

I am sick to the soul of that quiet sea,
Which hides ten thousand graves.

THE LILY CONFIDANTE

Lily! lady of the garden!
Let me press my lip to thine!
Love must tell its story, Lily!
Listen thou to mine.

Two I choose to know the secret —
Thee, and yonder wordless flute;
Dragons watch me, tender Lily,
And thou must be mute.

There 's a maiden, and her name is . . .
Hist! was that a rose-leaf fell?
See, the rose is listening, Lily,
And the rose may tell.

Lily-browed and lily-hearted,
She is very dear to me;
Lovely? yes, if being lovely
Is — resembling thee.

Six to half a score of summers
Make the sweetest of the "teens" —
Not too young to guess, dear Lily,
What a lover means.

Laughing girl, and thoughtful woman,
I am puzzled how to woo —
Shall I praise, or pique her, Lily?
Tell me what to do.

"Silly lover, if thy Lily
Like her sister lilies be,
Thou must woo, if thou wouldst wear her,
With a simple plea.

"Love 's the lover's only magic,
Truth the very subtlest art;
Love that feigns, and lips that flatter,
Win no modest heart.

"Like the dewdrop in my bosom,
Be thy guileless language, youth;
Falsehood buyeth falsehood only,
Truth must purchase truth.

"As thou talkest at the fireside,
With the little children by —
As thou prayest in the darkness,
When thy God is nigh —

"With a speech as chaste and gentle,
And such meanings as become
Ear of child, or ear of angel,
Speak, or be thou dumb.

"Woo her thus, and she shall give thee
Of her heart the sinless whole,
All the girl within her bosom,
And her woman's soul."

THE STREAM IS FLOWING FROM THE WEST

THE stream is flowing from the west;
As if it poured from yonder skies,
It wears upon its rippling breast
The sunset's golden dyes;
And bearing onward to the sea,
'T will clasp the isle that holdeth thee.

I dip my hand within the wave;
Ah! how impressionless and cold!
I touch it with my lip, and lave
My forehead in the gold.
It is a trivial thought, but sweet,
Perhaps the wave will kiss thy feet.

Alas! I leave no trace behind —
As little on the senseless stream
As on thy heart, or on thy mind;
Which was the simpler dream,
To win that warm, wild love of thine,
Or make the water whisper mine?

Dear stream! some moons must wax and wane
  Ere I again shall cross thy tide,
And then, perhaps, a viewless chain
  Will drag me to her side,
To love with all my spirit's scope,
To wish, do everything but—hope.

VOX ET PRÆTEREA NIHIL

I 'VE been haunted all night, I 've been haunted all day,
By the ghost of a song, by the shade of a lay,
That with meaningless words and profusion of rhyme,
To a dreamy and musical rhythm keeps time.
A simple, but still a most magical strain,
Its dim monotones have bewildered my brain
With a specious and cunning appearance of thought,
I seem to be catching but never have caught.

I know it embodies some very sweet things,
And can almost divine the low burden it sings;
But again, and again, and still ever again,
It has died on my ear at the touch of my pen.
And so it keeps courting and shunning my quest,
As a bird that has just been aroused from her nest,
Too fond to depart, and too frightened to stay,
Now circles about you, now flutters away.

Oh! give me fit words for that exquisite song,
And thou couldst not, proud beauty! be obdurate
long;
It would come like the voice of a saint from above,
And win thee to kindness, and melt thee to love.
Not gilded with fancy, nor frigid with art,
But simple as feeling, and warm as the heart,
It would murmur my name with so charming a tone,
As would almost persuade thee to wish it thine own.

MADELINE

O LADY! if, until this hour,
I 've gazed in those bewildering eyes,
Yet never owned their touching power,
But when thou couldst not hear my sighs;
It has not been that love has slept
One single moment in my soul,
Or that on lip or look I kept
A stern and stoical control;
But that I saw, but that I felt,
In every tone and glance of thine,
Whate'er they spoke, where'er they dwelt,
How small, how poor a part was mine;
And that I deeply, dearly knew,
That hidden, hopeless love confessed,
The fatal words would lose me, too,
Even the weak friendship I possessed.

And so, I masked my secret well;
The very love within my breast
Became the strange, but potent spell
By which I forced it into rest.
Yet there were times — I scarce know how
These eager lips refrained to speak, —
Some kindly smile would light thy brow,
And I grew passionate and weak;
The secret sparkled at my eyes,
And love but half repressed its sighs, —
Then had I gazed an instant more,
Or dwelt one moment on that brow,
I might have changed the smile it wore,
To what perhaps it weareth now,
And spite of all I feared to meet,
Confessed that passion at thy feet.
To save my heart, to spare thine own,
There was one remedy alone.
I fled, I shunned thy very touch, —
It cost me much, O God! how much!
But if some burning tears were shed,
Lady! I let them freely flow;
At least, they left unbreathed, unsaid,
A worse and wilder woe.

But now, — *now* that we part indeed,
And that I may not think as then,
That as I wish, or as I need,
I may return again, —

Now that for months, perhaps for years—
I see no limit in my fears —
My home shall be some distant spot,
Where thou — where even thy name is not,
And since I shall not see the frown,
Such wild, mad language must bring down,
Could I — albeit I may not sue
  In hope to bend thy steadfast will —
Could I have breathed this word, adieu,
  And kept my secret still?

Doubtless thou know'st the Hebrew story —
  The tale 's with me a favorite one —
How Raphael left the Courts of Glory,
  And walked with Judah's honored Son;
And how the twain together dwelt,
  And how they talked upon the road,
How often too they must have knelt
  As equals to the same kind God;
And still the mortal never guessed,
How much and deeply he was blessed,
Till when — the Angel's mission done —
  The spell which drew him earthwards, riven —
The lover saved — the maiden won —
  He plumed again his wings for Heaven;
O Madeline! as unaware
Thou hast been followed everywhere,
  And girt and guarded by a love,
As warm, as tender in its care,

As pure, ay, powerful in prayer,
  As any saint above!
Like the bright inmate of the skies,
It only looked with friendly eyes,
And still had worn the illusive guise,
  And thus at least been half concealed;
But at this parting, painful hour,
It spreads its wings, unfolds its power,
  And stands, like Raphael, revealed.

More, Lady! I would wish to speak, —
But it were vain, and words are weak,
And now that I have bared my breast,
Perchance thou wilt infer the rest.
So, so, farewell! I need not say
  I look, I ask for no reply,
The cold and scarcely pitying "nay"
  I read in that unmelted eye;
Yet one dear favor, let me pray!
  Days, months, however slow to me,
Must drag at last their length away,
  And I return — if not to thee —
At least to breathe the same sweet air
That wooes thy lips and waves thy hair.
Oh, then! — these daring lines forgot —
Look, speak, as thou hadst read them not.
So, Lady, may I still retain
A right I would not lose again,
For all that gold or guilt can buy,
Or all that Heaven itself deny,

A right such love may justly claim,
Of seeing thee in friendship's name.
Give me but this, and still at whiles,
A portion of thy faintest smiles,
It were enough to bless;
I may not, dare not ask for more
Than boon so rich, and yet so poor,
But I should die with less.

A DEDICATION

TO K. S. G.

FAIR Saxon, in my lover's creed,
My love were smaller than your meed,
And you might justly deem it slight,
As wanting truth as well as sight,
If, in that image which is shrined
Where thoughts are sacred, you could find
A single charm, or more or less,
Than you to all kind eyes possess.
To me, even in the happiest dreams,
Where, flushed with love's just dawning gleams,
My hopes their radiant wings unfurl,
You 're but a simple English girl,
No fairer, grace for grace arrayed,
Than many a simple Southern maid;
With faults enough to make the good
Seem sweeter far than else it would;

Frank in your anger and your glee,
And true as English natures be,
Yet not without some maiden art
Which hides a loving English heart.
Still there are moments, brief and bright,
When fancy, by a poet's light,
Beholds you clothed with loftier charms
Than love e'er gave to mortal arms.
A spell is woven on the air
From your brown eyes and golden hair,
And all at once you seem to stand
Before me as your native land,
With all her greatness in your guise,
And all her glory in your eyes;
And sometimes, as if angels sung,
I hear her poets on your tongue.
And, therefore, I, who from a boy
Have felt an almost English joy
In England's undecaying might,
And England's love of truth and right,
Next to my own young country's fame
Holding her honor and her name,
I — who, though born where not a vale
Hath ever nursed a nightingale,
Have fed my muse with English song
Until her feeble wing grew strong —
Feel, while with all the reverence meet
I lay this volume at your feet,
As if through your dear self I pay,
For many a deep and deathless lay,

For noble lessons nobly taught,
For tears, for laughter, and for thought,
A portion of the mighty debt
We owe to Shakespeare's England yet!

KATIE

It may be through some foreign grace,
And unfamiliar charm of face;
It may be that across the foam
Which bore her from her childhood's home,
By some strange spell, my Katie brought,
Along with English creeds and thought—
Entangled in her golden hair—
Some English sunshine, warmth, and air!
I cannot tell—but here to-day,
A thousand billowy leagues away
From that green isle whose twilight skies
No darker are than Katie's eyes,
She seems to me, go where she will,
An English girl in England still!

I meet her on the dusty street,
And daisies spring about her feet;
Or, touched to life beneath her tread,
An English cowslip lifts its head;
And, as to do her grace, rise up
The primrose and the buttercup!

I roam with her through fields of cane,
And seem to stroll an English lane,
Which, white with blossoms of the May,
Spreads its green carpet in her way!
As fancy wills, the path beneath
Is golden gorse, or purple heath:
And now we hear in woodlands dim
Their unarticulated hymn,
Now walk through rippling waves of wheat,
Now sink in mats of clover sweet,
Or see before us from the lawn
The lark go up to greet the dawn!
All birds that love the English sky
Throng round my path when she is by:
The blackbird from a neighboring thorn
With music brims the cup of morn,
And in a thick, melodious rain
The mavis pours her mellow strain!
But only when my Katie's voice
Makes all the listening woods rejoice
I hear — with cheeks that flush and pale —
The passion of the nightingale!

Anon the pictures round her change,
And through an ancient town we range,
Whereto the shadowy memory clings
Of one of England's Saxon kings,
And which to shrine his fading fame
Still keeps his ashes and his name.

Quaint houses rise on either hand,
But still the airs are fresh and bland,
As if their gentle wings caressed
Some new-born village of the West.
A moment by the Norman tower
We pause; it is the Sabbath hour!
And o'er the city sinks and swells
The chime of old St. Mary's bells,
Which still resound in Katie's ears
As sweet as when in distant years
She heard them peal with jocund din
A merry English Christmas in!
We pass the abbey's ruined arch,
And statelier grows my Katie's march,
As round her, wearied with the taint
Of Transatlantic pine and paint,
She sees a thousand tokens cast
Of England's venerable Past!
Our reverent footsteps lastly claims
The younger chapel of St. James,
Which, though, as English records run,
Not old, had seen full many a sun,
Ere to the cold December gale
The thoughtful Pilgrim spread his sail.
There Katie in her childish days
Spelt out her prayers and lisped her praise,
And doubtless, as her beauty grew,
Did much as other maidens do—
Across the pews and down the aisle
Sent many a beau-bewildering smile,

And to subserve her spirit's need
Learned other things beside the creed!
There, too, to-day her knee she bows,
And by her one whose darker brows
Betray the Southern heart that burns
Beside her, and which only turns
Its thoughts to Heaven in one request,
Not all unworthy to be blest,
But rising from an earthlier pain
Than might beseem a Christian fane.
Ah! can the guileless maiden share
The wish that lifts that passionate prayer?
Is all at peace that breast within?
Good angels! warn her of the sin!
Alas! what boots it? who can save
A willing victim of the wave?
Who cleanse a soul that loves its guilt?
Or gather wine when wine is spilt?

We quit the holy house and gain
The open air; then, happy twain,
Adown familiar streets we go,
And now and then she turns to show,
With fears that all is changing fast,
Some spot that 's sacred to her Past.
Here by this way, through shadows cool,
A little maid, she tripped to school;
And there each morning used to stop
Before a wonder of a shop

Where, built of apples and of pears,
Rose pyramids of golden spheres;
While, dangling in her dazzled sight,
Ripe cherries cast a crimson light,
And made her think of elfin lamps,
And feast and sport in fairy camps,
Whereat, upon her royal throne
(Most richly carved in cherry-stone),
Titania ruled, in queenly state,
The boisterous revels of the fête!
'T was yonder, with their "horrid" noise,
Dismissed from books, she met the boys,
Who, with a barbarous scorn of girls,
Glanced slightly at her sunny curls,
And laughed and leaped as reckless by
As though no pretty face were nigh!
But — here the maiden grows demure —
Indeed she 's not so *very* sure,
That in a year, or haply twain,
Who looked e'er failed to look again,
And sooth to say, I little doubt
(Some azure day, the truth will out!)
That certain baits in certain eyes
Caught many an unsuspecting prize;
And somewhere underneath these eaves
A budding flirt put forth its leaves!

Has not the sky a deeper blue,
Have not the trees a greener hue,

And bend they not with lordlier grace
And nobler shapes above the place
Where on one cloudless winter morn
My Katie to this life was born?
Ah, folly! long hath fled the hour
When love to sight gave keener power,
And lovers looked for special boons
In brighter flowers and larger moons.
But wave the foliage as it may,
And let the sky be ashen gray,
Thus much at least a manly youth
May hold — and yet not blush — as truth:
If near that blessed spot of earth
Which saw the cherished maiden's birth
No softer dews than usual rise,
And life there keeps its wonted guise,
Yet not the less that spot may seem
As lovely as a poet's dream;
And should a fervid faith incline
To make thereof a sainted shrine,
Who may deny that round us throng
A hundred earthly creeds as wrong,
But meaner far, which yet unblamed
Stalk by us and are not ashamed?
So, therefore, Katie, as our stroll
Ends at this portal, while you roll
Those lustrous eyes to catch each ray
That may recall some vanished day,
I — let them jeer and laugh who will —
Stoop down and kiss the sacred sill!

So strongly sometimes on the sense
These fancies hold their influence,
That in long well-known streets I stray
Like one who fears to lose his way.
The stranger, I, the native, she,
Myself, not Kate, had crossed the sea;
And changing place, and mixing times,
I walk in unfamiliar climes!
These houses, free to every breeze
That blows from warm Floridian seas,
Assume a massive English air,
And close around an English square;
While, if I issue from the town,
An English hill looks greenly down,
Or round me rolls an English park,
And in the Broad I hear the Larke!
Thus when, where woodland violets hide,
I rove with Katie at my side,
It scarce would seem amiss to say:
"Katie! my home lies far away,
Beyond the pathless waste of brine,
In a young land of palm and pine!
There, by the tropic heats, the soul
Is touched as if with living coal,
And glows with such a fire as none
Can feel beneath a Northern sun,
Unless — my Katie's heart attest! —
'T is kindled in an English breast!

Such is the land in which I live,
And, Katie! such the soul I give.
Come! ere another morning beam,
We 'll cleave the sea with wings of steam;
And soon, despite of storm or calm,
Beneath my native groves of palm,
Kind friends shall greet, with joy and pride,
The Southron and his English bride!"

WHY SILENT

WHY am I silent from year to year?
  Needs must I sing on these blue March days?
What will you say, when I tell you here,
  That already, I think, for a little praise,
      I have paid too dear?

For, I know not why, when I tell my thought,
  It seems as though I fling it away;
And the charm wherewith a fancy is fraught,
  When secret, dies with the fleeting lay
      Into which it is wrought.

So my butterfly-dreams their golden wings
  But seldom unfurl from their chrysalis;
And thus I retain my loveliest things,
  While the world, in its worldliness, does not miss
      What a poet sings.

TWO PORTRAITS

I

You say, as one who shapes a life,
That you will never be a wife,

And, laughing lightly, ask my aid
To paint your future as a maid.

This is the portrait; and I take
The softest colors for your sake:

The springtime of your soul is dead,
And forty years have bent your head;

The lines are firmer round your mouth,
But still its smile is like the South.

Your eyes, grown deeper, are not sad,
Yet never more than gravely glad;

And the old charm still lurks within
The cloven dimple of your chin.

Some share, perhaps, of youthful gloss
Your cheek hath shed; but still across

The delicate ear are folded down
Those silken locks of chestnut brown;

Though here and there a thread of gray
Steals through them like a lunar ray.

One might suppose your life had passed
Unvexed by any troubling blast;

And such — for all that I foreknow —
May be the truth! The deeper woe!

A loveless heart is seldom stirred;
And sorrow shuns the mateless bird;

But ah! through cares alone we reach
The happiness which mocketh speech;

In the white courts beyond the stars
The noblest brow is seamed with scars;

And they on earth who 've wept the most
Sit highest of the heavenly host.

Grant that your maiden life hath sped
In music o'er a golden bed,

With rocks, and winds, and storms at truce,
And not without a noble use;

Yet are you happy? In your air
I see a nameless want appear,

And a faint shadow on your cheek
Tells what the lips refuse to speak.

You have had all a maid could hope
In the most cloudless horoscope:

The strength that cometh from above;
A Christian mother's holy love;

And always at your soul's demand
A brother's, sister's heart and hand.

Small need your heart hath had to roam
Beyond the circle of your home;

And yet upon your wish attends
A loving throng of genial friends.

What, in a lot so sweet as this,
Is wanting to complete your bliss?

And to what secret shall I trace
The clouds that sometimes cross your face,

And that sad look which now and then
Comes, disappears, and comes again,

And dies reluctantly away
In those clear eyes of azure gray?

At best, and after all, the place
You fill with such a serious grace,

Hath much to try a woman's heart,
And you but play a painful part.

The world around, with little ruth,
Still laughs at maids who have not youth,

And, right or wrong, the old maid rests
The victim of its paltry jests,

And still is doomed to meet and bear
Its pitying smile or furtive sneer.

These are indeed but petty things,
And yet they touch some hearts like stings.

But I acquit you of the shame
Of being unresisting game;

For you are of such tempered clay
As turns far stronger shafts away,

And all that foes or fools could guide
Would only curl that lip of pride.

How then, O weary one! explain
The sources of that hidden pain?

Alas! you have divined at length
How little you have used your strength,

Which, with who knows what human good,
Lies buried in that maidenhood,

Where, as amid a field of flowers,
You have but played with April showers.

Ah! we would wish the world less fair,
If Spring alone adorned the year,

And Autumn came not with its fruit,
And Autumn hymns were ever mute.

So I remark without surprise
That, as the unvarying season flies,

From day to night and night to day,
You sicken of your endless May.

In this poor life we may not cross
One virtuous instinct without loss,

And the soul grows not to its height
Till love calls forth its utmost might.

Not blind to all you might have been,
And with some consciousness of sin —

Because with love you sometimes played,
And choice, not fate, hath kept you maid —

You feel that you must pass from earth
But half-acquainted with its worth,

And that within your heart are deeps
In which a nobler woman sleeps;

That not the maiden, but the wife
Grasps the whole lesson of a life,

While such as you but sit and dream
Along the surface of its stream.

And doubtless sometimes, all unsought,
There comes upon your hour of thought,

Despite the struggles of your will,
A sense of something absent still;

And then you cannot help but yearn
To love and be beloved in turn,

As they are loved, and love, who live
As love were all that life could give;

And in a transient clasp or kiss
Crowd an eternity of bliss;

They who of every mortal joy
Taste always twice, nor feel them cloy,

Or, if woes come, in Sorrow's hour
Are strengthened by a double power.

II

Here ends my feeble sketch of what
Might, but will never be your lot;

And I foresee how oft these rhymes
Shall make you smile in after-times.

If I have read your nature right,
It only waits a spark of light;

And when that comes, as come it must,
It will not fall on arid dust,

Nor yet on that which breaks to flame
In the first blush of maiden shame;

But on a heart which, even at rest,
Is warmer than an April nest,

Where, settling soft, that spark shall creep
About as gently as a sleep;

Still stealing on with pace so slow
Yourself will scarcely feel the glow,

Till after many and many a day,
Although no gleam its course betray,

It shall attain the inmost shrine,
And wrap it in a fire divine!

I know not when or whence indeed
Shall fall and burst the burning seed,

But oh! once kindled, it will blaze,
I know, forever! By its rays

You will perceive, with subtler eyes,
The meaning in the earth and skies,

Which, with their animated chain
Of grass and flowers, and sun and rain,

Of green below, and blue above,
Are but a type of married love.

You will perceive that in the breast
The germs of many virtues rest,

Which, ere they feel a lover's breath,
Lie in a temporary death;

And till the heart is wooed and won
It is an earth without a sun.

III

But now, stand forth as sweet as life!
And let me paint you as a wife.

I note some changes in your face,
And in your mien a graver grace;

Yet the calm forehead lightly bears
Its weight of twice a score of years;

And that one love which on this earth
Can wake the heart to all its worth,

And to their height can lift and bind
The powers of soul, and sense, and mind,

Hath not allowed a charm to fade —
And the wife 's lovelier than the maid.

An air of still, though bright repose
Tells that a tender hand bestows

All that a generous manhood may
To make your life one bridal day,

While the kind eyes betray no less,
In their blue depths of tenderness,

That you have learned the truths which lie
Behind that holy mystery,

Which, with its blisses and its woes,
Nor man nor maiden ever knows.

If now, as to the eyes of one
Whose glance not even thought can shun,

Your soul lay open to my view,
I, looking all its nature through,

Could see no incompleted part,
For the whole woman warms your heart.

I cannot tell how many dead
You number in the cycles fled,

And you but look the more serene
For all the griefs you may have seen,

As you had gathered from the dust
The flowers of Peace, and Hope, and Trust.

Your smile is even sweeter now
Than when it lit your maiden brow,

And that which wakes this gentler charm
Coos at this moment on your arm.

Your voice was always soft in youth,
And had the very sound of truth,

But never were its tones so mild
Until you blessed your earliest child;

And when to soothe some little wrong
It melts into a mother's song,

The same strange sweetness which in years
Long vanished filled the eyes with tears,

And (even when mirthful) gave always
A pathos to your girlish lays,

Falls, with perchance a deeper thrill,
Upon the breathless listener still.

I cannot guess in what fair spot
The chance of Time hath fixed your lot,

Nor can I name what manly breast
Gives to that head a welcome rest;

I cannot tell if partial Fate
Hath made you poor, or rich, or great;

But oh! whatever be your place,
I never saw a form or face

To which more plainly hath been lent
The blessing of a full content!

LA BELLE JUIVE

Is it because your sable hair
Is folded over brows that wear
At times a too imperial air;

Or is it that the thoughts which rise
In those dark orbs do seek disguise
Beneath the lids of Eastern eyes;

That choose whatever pose or place
May chance to please, in you I trace
The noblest woman of your race?

The crowd is sauntering at its ease,
And humming like a hive of bees —
You take your seat and touch the keys:

I do not hear the giddy throng;
The sea avenges Israel's wrong,
And on the wind floats Miriam's song!

You join me with a stately grace;
Music to Poesy gives place;
Some grand emotion lights your face:

At once I stand by Mizpeh's walls:
With smiles the martyred daughter falls,
And desolate are Mizpeh's halls!

Intrusive babblers come between;
With calm, pale brow and lofty mien,
You thread the circle like a queen!

Then sweeps the royal Esther by;
The deep devotion in her eye
Is looking "If I die, I die!"

You stroll the garden's flowery walks;
The plants to me are grainless stalks,
And Ruth to old Naomi talks.

Adopted child of Judah's creed,
Like Judah's daughters, true at need,
I see you mid the alien seed.

I watch afar the gleaner sweet;
I wake like Boaz in the wheat,
And find you lying at my feet!

My feet! Oh! if the spell that lures
My heart through all these dreams endures,
How soon shall I be stretched at yours!

AN EXOTIC

Not in a climate near the sun
  Did the cloud with its trailing fringes float,
Whence, white as the down of an angel's plume,
  Fell the snow of her brow and throat.

And the ground had been rich for a thousand years
  With the blood of heroes, and sages, and kings,
Where the rose that blooms in her exquisite cheek
  Unfolded the flush of its wings.

On a land where the faces are fair, though pale
  As a moonlit mist when the winds are still,
She breaks like a morning in Paradise
  Through the palms of an orient hill.

Her beauty, perhaps, were all too bright,
  But about her there broods some delicate spell,
Whence the wondrous charm of the girl grows soft
  As the light in an English dell.

There is not a story of faith and truth
  On the starry scroll of her country's fame,

But has helped to shape her stately mien,
  And to touch her soul with flame.

I sometimes forget, as she sweeps me a bow,
  That I gaze on a simple English maid,
And I bend my head, as if to a queen
  Who is courting my lance and blade.

Once, as we read, in a curtained niche,
  A poet who sang of her sea-throned isle,
There was something of Albion's mighty Bess
  In the flash of her haughty smile.

She seemed to gather from every age
  All the greatness of England about her there,
And my fancy wove a royal crown
  Of the dusky gold of her hair.

But it was no queen to whom that day,
  In the dim green shade of a trellised vine,
I whispered a hope that had somewhat to do
  With a small white hand in mine.

The Tudor had vanished, and, as I spoke,
  'T was herself looked out of her frank brown eye,
And an answer was burning upon her face,
  Ere I caught the low reply.

What was it! Nothing the world need know —
  The stars saw our parting! Enough, that then

I walked from the porch with the tread of a king,
  And she was a queen again!

THE ROSEBUDS

Yes, in that dainty ivory shrine,
With those three pallid buds, I twine
And fold away a dream divine!

One night they lay upon a breast
Where Love hath made his fragrant nest,
And throned me as a life-long guest.

Near that chaste heart they seemed to me
Types of far fairer flowers to be —
The rosebuds of a human tree!

Buds that shall bloom beside my hearth,
And there be held of richer worth
Than all the kingliest gems of earth.

Ah me! the pathos of the thought!
I had not deemed she wanted aught;
Yet what a tenderer charm it wrought!

I know not if she marked the flame
That lit my cheek, but not from shame,
When one sweet image dimly came.

There was a murmur soft and low;
White folds of cambric, parted slow;
And little fingers played with snow!

How far my fancy dared to stray,
A lover's reverence needs not say—
Enough — the vision passed away!

Passed in a mist of happy tears,
While something in my trancèd ears
Hummed like the future in a seer's!

A MOTHER'S WAIL

My babe! my tiny babe! my only babe!
My single rose-bud in a crown of thorns!
My lamp that in that narrow hut of life,
Whence I looked forth upon a night of storm!
Burned with the lustre of the moon and stars!

My babe! my tiny babe! my only babe!
Behold the bud is gone! the thorns remain!
My lamp hath fallen from its niche — ah, me!
Earth drinks the fragrant flame, and I am left
Forever and forever in the dark!

My babe! my babe! my own and only babe!
Where art thou now? If somewhere in the sky

An angel hold thee in his radiant arms,
I challenge him to clasp thy tender form
With half the fervor of a mother's love!

Forgive me, Lord! forgive my reckless grief!
Forgive me that this rebel, selfish heart
Would almost make me jealous for my child,
Though thy own lap enthroned him. Lord, thou hast
So many such! I have — ah! had but one!

O yet once more, my babe, to hear thy cry!
O yet once more, my babe, to see thy smile!
O yet once more to feel against my breast
Those cool, soft hands, that warm, wet, eager mouth,
With the sweet sharpness of its budding pearls!

But it must never, never more be mine
To mark the growing meaning in thine eyes,
To watch thy soul unfolding leaf by leaf,
Or catch, with ever fresh surprise and joy,
Thy dawning recognitions of the world.

Three different shadows of thyself, my babe,
Change with each other while I weep. The first,
The sweetest, yet the not least fraught with pain,
Clings like my living boy around my neck,
Or purrs and murmurs softly at my feet!

Another is a little mound of earth;
That comes the oftenest, darling! In my dreams,
I see it beaten by the midnight rain,
Or chilled beneath the moon. Ah! what a couch
For that which I have shielded from a breath
That would not stir the violets on thy grave!

The third, my precious babe! the third, O Lord!
Is a fair cherub face beyond the stars,
Wearing the roses of a mystic bliss,
Yet sometimes not unsaddened by a glance
Turned earthward on a mother in her woe!

This is the vision, Lord, that I would keep
Before me always. But, alas! as yet,
It is the dimmest and the rarest, too!
O touch my sight, or break the cloudy bars
That hide it, lest I madden where I kneel!

OUR WILLIE

'T WAS merry Christmas when he came,
Our little boy beneath the sod;
And brighter burned the Christmas flame,
And merrier sped the Christmas game,
Because within the house there lay
A shape as tiny as a fay—
The Christmas gift of God!

In wreaths and garlands on the walls
The holly hung its ruby balls,
        The mistletoe its pearls;
And a Christmas tree's fantastic fruits
Woke laughter like a choir of flutes
        From happy boys and girls.
For the mirth, which else had swelled as shrill
As a school let loose to its errant will,
        Was softened by the thought,
That in a dim hushed room above
A mother's pains in a mother's love
        Were only just forgot.
The jest, the tale, the toast, the glee,
All took a sober tone;
We spoke of the babe upstairs, as we
Held festival for him alone.
When the bells rang in the Christmas morn,
It scarcely seemed a sin to say
That they rang because that babe was born,
Not less than for the sacred day.
Ah! Christ forgive us for the crime
Which drowned the memories of the time
        In a merely mortal bliss!
We owned the error when the mirth
Of another Christmas lit the hearth
        Of every home but this.
When, in that lonely burial-ground,
With every Christmas sight and sound
Removed or shunned, we kept

A mournful Christmas by the mound
Where little Willie slept!

Ah, hapless mother! darling wife!
I might say nothing more,
And the dull cold world would hold
The story of that precious life
As amply told!
Shall we, shall you and I, before
That world's unsympathetic eyes
Lay other relics from our store
Of tender memories?
What could it know of the joy and love
That throbbed and smiled and wept above
An unresponsive thing?
And who could share the ecstatic thrill
With which we watched the upturned bill
Of our bird at its living spring?
Shall we tell how in the time gone by,
Beneath all changes of the sky,
And in an ordinary home
Amid the city's din,
Life was to us a crystal dome,
Our babe the flame therein?
Ah! this were jargon on the mart;
And though some gentle friend,
And many and many a suffering heart,
Would weep and comprehend,
Yet even these might fail to see

What we saw daily in the child —
Not the mere creature undefiled,
But the winged cherub soon to be.
That wandering hand which seemed to reach
        At angel finger-tips,
And that murmur like a mystic speech
        Upon the rosy lips,
That something in the serious face
Holier than even its infant grace,
And that rapt gaze on empty space,
Which made us, half believing, say,
"Ah, little wide-eyed seer! who knows
But that for you this chamber glows
With stately shapes and solemn shows?"
Which touched us, too, with vague alarms,
Lest in the circle of our arms
We held a being less akin
To his parents in a world of sin
Than to beings not of clay:
How could we speak in human phrase,
Of such scarce earthly traits and ways,
        What would not seem
        A doting dream,
In the creed of these sordid days?
        No! let us keep
        Deep, deep,
In sorrowing heart and aching brain,
This story hidden with the pain,
Which since that blue October night

When Willie vanished from our sight,
Must haunt us even in our sleep.
In the gloom of the chamber where he died,
And by that grave which, through our care,
From Yule to Yule of every year,
Is made like Spring to bloom;
And where, at times, we catch the sigh
As of an angel floating nigh,
Who longs but has not power to tell
That in that violet-shrouded cell
Lies nothing better than the shell
Which he had cast aside —
By that sweet grave, in that dark room,
We may weave at will for each other's ear,
Of that life, and that love, and that early doom,
The tale which is shadowed here:
To us alone it will always be
As fresh as our own misery;
But enough, alas! for the world is said,
In the brief "Here lieth" of the dead!

ADDRESS DELIVERED AT THE OPENING OF THE NEW THEATRE AT RICHMOND

A PRIZE POEM

A FAIRY ring
Drawn in the crimson of a battle-plain —
From whose weird circle every loathsome thing
And sight and sound of pain
Are banished, while about it in the air,
And from the ground, and from the low-hung skies,
Throng, in a vision fair
As ever lit a prophet's dying eyes,
Gleams of that unseen world
That lies about us, rainbow-tinted shapes
With starry wings unfurled,
Poised for a moment on such airy capes
As pierce the golden foam
Of sunset's silent main —
Would image what in this enchanted dome,
Amid the night of war and death
In which the armèd city draws its breath,
We have built up!
For though no wizard wand or magic cup
The spell hath wrought,
Within this charmëd fane, we ope the gates
Of that divinest Fairy-land,
Where under loftier fates
Than rule the vulgar earth on which we stand,

Move the bright creatures of the realm of thought.
Shut for one happy evening from the flood
That roars around us, here you may behold—
    As if a desert way
    Could blossom and unfold
    A garden fresh with May—
Substantialized in breathing flesh and blood,
    Souls that upon the poet's page
    Have lived from age to age,
And yet have never donned this mortal clay.
    A golden strand
Shall sometimes spread before you like the isle
    Where fair Miranda's smile
Met the sweet stranger whom the father's art
    Had led unto her heart,
Which, like a bud that waited for the light,
    Burst into bloom at sight!
Love shall grow softer in each maiden's eyes
As Juliet leans her cheek upon her hand,
    And prattles to the night.
    Anon, a reverend form,
    With tattered robe and forehead bare,
That challenge all the torments of the air,
            Goes by!
And the pent feelings choke in one long sigh,
While, as the mimic thunder rolls, you hear
    The noble wreck of Lear
Reproach like things of life the ancient skies,
    And commune with the storm!

Lo! next a dim and silent chamber where,
Wrapt in glad dreams in which, perchance, the Moor
Tells his strange story o'er,
The gentle Desdemona chastely lies,
Unconscious of the loving murderer nigh.
Then through a hush like death
Stalks Denmark's mailëd ghost!
And Hamlet enters with that thoughtful breath
Which is the trumpet to a countless host
Of reasons, but which wakes no deed from sleep;
For while it calls to strife,
He pauses on the very brink of fact
To toy as with the shadow of an act,
And utter those wise saws that cut so deep
Into the core of life!

Nor shall be wanting many a scene
Where forms of more familiar mien,
Moving through lowlier pathways, shall present
The world of every day,
Such as it whirls along the busy quay,
Or sits beneath a rustic orchard wall,
Or floats about a fashion-freighted hall,
Or toils in attics dark the night away.
Love, hate, grief, joy, gain, glory, shame, shall meet,
As in the round wherein our lives are pent;
Chance for a while shall seem to reign,

While Goodness roves like Guilt about the street,
And Guilt looks innocent.
But all at last shall vindicate the right,
Crime shall be meted with its proper pain,
Motes shall be taken from the doubter's sight,
And Fortune's general justice rendered plain.
Of honest laughter there shall be no dearth,
Wit shall shake hands with humor grave and sweet,
Our wisdom shall not be too wise for mirth,
Nor kindred follies want a fool to greet.
As sometimes from the meanest spot of earth
A sudden beauty unexpected starts,
So you shall find some germs of hidden worth
Within the vilest hearts;
And now and then, when in those moods that turn
To the cold Muse that whips a fault with sneers,
You shall, perchance, be strangely touched to learn
You 've struck a spring of tears!

But while we lead you thus from change to change,
Shall we not find within our ample range
Some type to elevate a people's heart—
Some hero who shall teach a hero's part
In this distracted time?
Rise from thy sleep of ages, noble Tell!
And, with the Alpine thunders of thy voice,
As if across the billows unenthralled
Thy Alps unto the Alleghanies called,
Bid Liberty rejoice!

Proclaim upon this trans-Atlantic strand
The deeds which, more than their own awful mien,
Make every crag of Switzerland sublime!
And say to those whose feeble souls would lean,
Not on themselves, but on some outstretched hand,
That once a single mind sufficed to quell
The malice of a tyrant; let them know
That each may crowd in every well-aimed blow,
Not the poor strength alone of arm and brand,
But the whole spirit of a mighty land!

Bid Liberty rejoice! Aye, though its day
Be far or near, these clouds shall yet be red
With the large promise of the coming ray.
Meanwhile, with that calm courage which can smile
Amid the terrors of the wildest fray,
Let us among the charms of Art awhile
    Fleet the deep gloom away;
Nor yet forget that on each hand and head
Rest the dear rights for which we fight and pray.

A VISION OF POESY

Part I

I

In a far country, and a distant age,
  Ere sprites and fays had bade farewell to earth,
A boy was born of humble parentage;
  The stars that shone upon his lonely birth
Did seem to promise sovereignty and fame—
Yet no tradition hath preserved his name.

II

'T is said that on the night when he was born,
  A beauteous shape swept slowly through the
    room;
Its eyes broke on the infant like a morn,
  And his cheek brightened like a rose in bloom;
But as it passed away there followed after
A sigh of pain, and sounds of elvish laughter.

III

And so his parents deemed him to be blest
  Beyond the lot of mortals; they were poor
As the most timid bird that stored its nest
  With the stray gleanings at their cottage-door:
Yet they contrived to rear their little dove,
And he repaid them with the tenderest love.

IV

The child was very beautiful in sooth,
  And as he waxed in years grew lovelier still;
On his fair brow the aureole of truth
  Beamed, and the purest maidens, with a thrill,
Looked in his eyes, and from their heaven of blue
Saw thoughts like sinless Angels peering through.

V

Need there was none of censure or of praise
  To mould him to the kind parental hand;
Yet there was ever something in his ways,
  Which those about him could not understand;
A self-withdrawn and independent bliss,
Beside the father's love, the mother's kiss.

VI

For oft, when he believed himself alone,
  They caught brief snatches of mysterious rhymes,
Which he would murmur in an undertone,
  Like a pleased bee's in summer; and at times
A strange far look would come into his eyes,
As if he saw a vision in the skies.

VII

And he upon a simple leaf would pore
  As if its very texture unto him
Had some deep meaning; sometimes by the door,
  From noon until a summer-day grew dim,

He lay and watched the clouds; and to his thought
Night with her stars but fitful slumbers brought.

VIII

In the long hours of twilight, when the breeze
Talked in low tones along the woodland rills,
Or the loud North its stormy minstrelsies
Blent with wild noises from the distant hills,
The boy — his rosy hand against his ear
Curved like a sea-shell — hushed as some rapt seer,

IX

Followed the sounds, and ever and again,
As the wind came and went, in storm or play,
He seemed to hearken as to some far strain
Of mingled voices calling him away;
And they who watched him held their breath to trace
The still and fixed attention in his face.

X

Once, on a cold and loud-voiced winter night,
The three were seated by their cottage-fire —
The mother watching by its flickering light
The wakeful urchin, and the dozing sire;
There was a brief, quick motion like a bird's,
And the boy's thought thus rippled into words:

XI

"O mother! thou hast taught me many things,
  But none I think more beautiful than speech —
A nobler power than even those broad wings
  I used to pray for, when I longed to reach
That distant peak which on our vale looks down,
And wears the star of evening for a crown.

XII

"But, mother, while our human words are rife
  To us with meaning, other sounds there be
Which seem, and are, the language of a life
  Around, yet unlike ours: winds talk; the sea
Murmurs articulately, and the sky
Listens, and answers, though inaudibly.

XIII

"By stream and spring, in glades and woodlands
    lone,
  Beside our very cot I 've gathered flowers
Inscribed with signs and characters unknown;
  But the frail scrolls still baffle all my powers:
What is this language and where is the key
That opes its weird and wondrous mystery?

XIV

"The forests know it, and the mountains know,
  And it is written in the sunset's dyes;

A revelation to the world below
  Is daily going on before our eyes;
And, but for sinful thoughts, I do not doubt
That we could spell the thrilling secret out.

XV

"O mother! somewhere on this lovely earth
  I lived, and understood that mystic tongue,
But, for some reason, to my second birth
  Only the dullest memories have clung,
Like that fair tree that even while blossoming
Keeps the dead berries of a former spring.

XVI

"Who shall put life in these? — my nightly dreams
  Some teacher of supernal powers foretell;
A fair and stately shape appears, which seems
  Bright with all truth; and once, in a dark dell
Within the forest, unto me there came
A voice that must be hers, which called my name."

XVII

Puzzled and frightened, wondering more and more,
  The mother heard, but did not comprehend;
"So early dallying with forbidden lore!
  Oh, what will chance, and wherein will it end?
My child! my child!" she caught him to her breast,
"Oh, let me kiss these wildering thoughts to rest!

XVIII

"They cannot come from God, who freely gives
  All that we need to have, or ought to know;
Beware, my son! some evil influence strives
  To grieve thy parents, and to work thee woe;
Alas! the vision I misunderstood!
It could not be an angel fair and good."

XIX

And then, in low and tremulous tones, she told
  The story of his birth-night; the boy's eyes,
As the wild tale went on, were bright and bold,
  With a weird look that did not seem surprise:
"Perhaps," he said, "this lady and her elves
Will one day come, and take me to themselves."

XX

"And wouldst thou leave us?" "Dearest mother, no!
  Hush! I will check these thoughts that give thee pain;
Or, if they flow, as they perchance must flow,
  At least I will not utter them again;
Hark! didst thou hear a voice like many streams?
Mother! it is the spirit of my dreams!"

XXI

Thenceforth, whatever impulse stirred below,
  In the deep heart beneath that childish breast,

Those lips were sealed, and though the eye would glow,
Yet the brow wore an air of perfect rest;
Cheerful, content, with calm though strong control
He shut the temple-portals of his soul.

XXII

And when too restlessly the mighty throng
Of fancies woke within his teeming mind,
All silently they formed in glorious song,
And floated off unheard, and undivined,
Perchance not lost — with many a voiceless prayer
They reached the sky, and found some record there.

XXIII

Softly and swiftly sped the quiet days;
The thoughtful boy has blossomed into youth,
And still no maiden would have feared his gaze,
And still his brow was noble with the truth:
Yet, though he masks the pain with pious art,
There burns a restless fever in his heart.

XXIV

A childish dream is now a deathless need
Which drives him to far hills and distant wilds;
The solemn faith and fervor of his creed
Bold as a martyr's, simple as a child's;
The eagle knew him as she knew the blast,
And the deer did not flee him as he passed.

XXV

But gentle even in his wildest mood,
  Always, and most, he loved the bluest weather,
And in some soft and sunny solitude
  Couched like a milder sunshine on the heather,
He communed with the winds, and with the birds,
As if they might have answered him in words.

XXVI

Deep buried in the forest was a nook
  Remote and quiet as its quiet skies;
He knew it, sought it, loved it as a book
  Full of his own sweet thoughts and memories;
Dark oaks and fluted chestnuts gathering round,
Pillared and greenly domed a sloping mound.

XXVII

Whereof — white, purple, azure, golden, red,
  Confused like hues of sunset — the wild flowers
Wove a rich dais; through crosslights overhead
  Glanced the clear sunshine, fell the fruitful showers,
And here the shyest bird would fold her wings;
Here fled the fairest and the gentlest things.

XXVIII

Thither, one night of mist and moonlight, came
  The youth, with nothing deeper in his thoughts

Than to behold beneath the silver flame
  New aspects of his fair and favorite spot;
A single ray attained the ground, and shed
Just light enough to guide the wanderer's tread.

XXIX

And high and hushed arose the stately trees,
  Yet shut within themselves, like dungeons, where
Lay fettered all the secrets of the breeze;
  Silent, but not as slumbering, all things there
Wore to the youth's aroused imagination
An air of deep and solemn expectation.

XXX

"Hath Heaven," the youth exclaimed, "a sweeter spot,
  Or Earth another like it? — yet even here
The old mystery dwells! and though I read it not,
  Here most I hope — it is, or seems so near;
So many hints come to me, but, alas!
I cannot grasp the shadows as they pass.

XXXI

"Here, from the very turf beneath me, I
  Catch, but just catch, I know not what faint sound,
And darkly guess that from yon silent sky
  Float starry emanations to the ground;
These ears are deaf, these human eyes are blind,
I want a purer heart, a subtler mind.

XXXII

"Sometimes — could it be fancy? — I have felt
The presence of a spirit who might speak;
As down in lowly reverence I knelt,
Its very breath hath kissed my burning cheek;
But I in vain have hushed my own to hear
A wing or whisper stir the silent air!"

XXXIII

Is not the breeze articulate? Hark! Oh, hark!
A distant murmur, like a voice of floods;
And onward sweeping slowly through the dark,
Bursts like a call the night-wind from the woods!
Low bow the flowers, the trees fling loose their dreams,
And through the waving roof a fresher moonlight streams.

XXXIV

"Mortal!" — the word crept slowly round the place
As if that wind had breathed it! From no star
Streams that soft lustre on the dreamer's face.
Again a hushing calm! while faint and far
The breeze goes calling onward through the night.
Dear God! what vision chains that wide-strained sight?

XXXV

Over the grass and flowers, and up the slope
 Glides a white cloud of mist, self-moved and slow,
That, pausing at the hillock's moonlit cope,
 Swayed like a flame of silver; from below
The breathless youth with beating heart beholds
A mystic motion in its argent folds.

XXXVI

Yet his young soul is bold, and hope grows warm,
 As flashing through that cloud of shadowy crape,
With sweep of robes, and then a gleaming arm,
 Slowly developing, at last took shape
A face and form unutterably bright,
That cast a golden glamour on the night.

XXXVII

But for the glory round it it would seem
 Almost a mortal maiden; and the boy,
Unto whom love was yet an innocent dream,
 Shivered and crimsoned with an unknown joy;
As to the young Spring bounds the passionate South,
He could have clasped and kissed her mouth to mouth.

XXXVIII

Yet something checked, that was and was not
dread,
Till in a low sweet voice the maiden spake;
She was the Fairy of his dreams, she said,
And loved him simply for his human sake;
And that in heaven, wherefrom she took her birth,
They called her Poesy, the angel of the earth.

XXXIX

"And ever since that immemorial hour,
When the glad morning-stars together sung,
My task hath been, beneath a mightier Power,
To keep the world forever fresh and young;
I give it not its fruitage and its green,
But clothe it with a glory all unseen.

XL

"I sow the germ which buds in human art,
And, with my sister, Science, I explore
With light the dark recesses of the heart,
And nerve the will, and teach the wish to soar;
I touch with grace the body's meanest clay,
While noble souls are nobler for my sway.

XLI

"Before my power the kings of earth have bowed;
I am the voice of Freedom, and the sword

Leaps from its scabbard when I call aloud;
  Wherever life in sacrifice is poured,
Wherever martyrs die or patriots bleed,
I weave the chaplet and award the meed.

XLII

"Where Passion stoops, or strays, is cold, or dead,
  I lift from error, or to action thrill!
Or if it rage too madly in its bed,
  The tempest hushes at my 'Peace! be still!'
I know how far its tides should sink or swell,
And they obey my sceptre and my spell.

XLIII

"All lovely things, and gentle — the sweet laugh
  Of children, Girlhood's kiss, and Friendship's clasp,
The boy that sporteth with the old man's staff,
  The baby, and the breast its fingers grasp —
All that exalts the grounds of happiness,
All griefs that hallow, and all joys that bless,

XLIV

"To me are sacred; at my holy shrine
  Love breathes its latest dreams, its earliest hints;
I turn life's tasteless waters into wine,
  And flush them through and through with purple tints.
Wherever Earth is fair, and Heaven looks down,
I rear my altars, and I wear my crown.

XLV

"I am the unseen spirit thou hast sought,
  I woke those shadowy questionings that vex
Thy young mind, lost in its own cloud of thought,
  And rouse the soul they trouble and perplex;
I filled thy days with visions, and thy nights
Blessed with all sweetest sounds and fairy sights.

XLVI

"Not here, not in this world, may I disclose
  The mysteries in which this life is hearsed;
Some doubts there be that, with some earthly woes,
  By Death alone shall wholly be dispersed;
Yet on those very doubts from this low sod
Thy soul shall pass beyond the stars to God.

XLVII

"And so to knowledge, climbing grade by grade,
  Thou shalt attain whatever mortals can,
And what thou mayst discover by my aid
  Thou shalt translate unto thy brother man;
And men shall bless the power that flings a ray
Into their night from thy diviner day.

XLVIII

"For, from thy lofty height, thy words shall fall
  Upon their spirits like bright cataracts
That front a sunrise; thou shalt hear them call
  Amid their endless waste of arid facts,

As wearily they plod their way along,
Upon the rhythmic zephyrs of thy song.

XLIX

"All this is in thy reach, but much depends
Upon thyself — thy future I await;
I give the genius, point the proper ends,
But the true bard is his own only Fate;
Into thy soul my soul have I infused;
Take care thy lofty powers be wisely used.

L

"The Poet owes a high and holy debt,
Which, if he feel, he craves not to be heard
For the poor boon of praise, or place, nor yet
Does the mere joy of song, as with the bird
Of many voices, prompt the choral lay
That cheers that gentle pilgrim on his way.

LI

"Nor may he always sweep the passionate lyre,
Which is his heart, only for such relief
As an impatient spirit may desire,
Lest, from the grave which hides a private grief,
The spells of song call up some pallid wraith
To blast or ban a mortal hope or faith.

LII

"Yet over his deep soul, with all its crowd
Of varying hopes and fears, he still must brood;

As from its azure height a tranquil cloud
  Watches its own bright changes in the flood;
Self-reading, not self-loving — they are twain —
And sounding, while he mourns, the depths of pain.

LIII

"Thus shall his songs attain the common breast,
  Dyed in his own life's blood, the sign and seal,
Even as the thorns which are the martyr's crest,
  That do attest his office, and appeal
Unto the universal human heart
In sanction of his mission and his art.

LIV

"Much yet remains unsaid — pure must he be;
  Oh, blessëd are the pure! for they shall hear
Where others hear not, see where others see
  With a dazed vision: who have drawn most near
My shrine, have ever brought a spirit cased
And mailëd in a body clean and chaste.

LV

"The Poet to the whole wide world belongs,
  Even as the teacher is the child's — I said
No selfish aim should ever mar his songs,
  But self wears many guises; men may wed
Self in another, and the soul may be
Self to its centre, all unconsciously.

LVI

" And therefore must the Poet watch, lest he,
  In the dark struggle of this life, should take
Stains which he might not notice; he must flee
  Falsehood, however winsome, and forsake
All for the Truth, assured that Truth alone
Is Beauty, and can make him all my own.

LVII

" And he must be as armèd warrior strong,
  And he must be as gentle as a girl,
And he must front, and sometimes suffer wrong,
  With brow unbent, and lip untaught to curl;
For wrath, and scorn, and pride, however just,
Fill the clear spirit's eyes with earthly dust."

The story came to me — it recks not whence —
In fragments. Oh! if I could tell it all,
If human speech indeed could tell it all,
'T were not a whit less wondrous, than if I
Should find, untouched in leaf and stem, and bright,
As when it bloomed three thousand years ago,
On some Idalian slope, a perfect rose.
Alas! a leaf or two, and they perchance
Scarce worth the hiving, one or two dead leaves
Are the sole harvest of a summer's toil.
There was a moment, ne'er to be recalled,
When to the Poet's hope within my heart,

They wore a tint like life's, but in my hand,
I know not why, they withered. I have heard
Somewhere, of some dead monarch, from the tomb,
Where he had slept a century and more,
Brought forth, that when the coffin was laid bare,
Albeit the body in its mouldering robes
Was fleshless, yet one feature still remained
Perfect, or perfect seemed at least; the eyes
Gleamed for a second on the startled crowd,
And then went out in ashes. Even thus
The story, when I drew it from the grave
Where it had lain so long, did seem, I thought,
Not wholly lifeless; but even while I gazed
To fix its features on my heart, and called
The world to wonder with me, lo! it proved
I looked upon a corpse!

What further fell
In that lone forest nook, how much was taught,
How much was only hinted, what the youth
Promised, if promise were required, to do
Or strive for, what the gifts he bore away—
Or added powers or blessings—how at last,
The vision ended and he sought his home,
How lived there, and how long, and when he passed
Into the busy world to seek his fate,
I know not, and if any ever knew,
The tale hath perished from the earth; for here
The slender thread on which my song is strung

Breaks off, and many after years of life
Are lost to sight, the life to reappear
Only towards its close — as of a dream
We catch the end and opening, but forget
That which had joined them in the dreaming brain;
Or as a mountain with a belt of mist
That shows his base, and far above, a peak
With a blue plume of pines.
But turn the page
And read the only hints that yet remain.

Part II

I

It is not winter yet, but that sweet time
In autumn when the first cool days are past;
A week ago, the leaves were hoar with rime,
And some have dropped before the North wind's blast;
But the mild hours are back, and at mid-noon,
The day hath all the genial warmth of June.

II

What slender form lies stretched along the mound?
Can it be his, the Wanderer's, with that brow
Gray in its prime, those eyes that wander round
Listlessly, with a jaded glance that now
Seems to see nothing where it rests, and then
Pores on each trivial object in its ken?

III

See how a gentle maid's wan fingers clasp
The last fond love-notes of some faithless hand;
Thus, with a transient interest, his weak grasp
Holds a few leaves as when of old he scanned
The meaning in their gold and crimson streaks;
But the sweet dream has vanished! hush! he speaks!

IV

"Once more, once more, after long pain and toil,
And yet not long, if I should count by years,
I breathe my native air, and tread the soil
I trod in childhood; if I shed no tears,
No happy tears, 't is that their fount is dry,
And joy that cannot weep must sigh, must sigh.

V

"These leaves, my boyish books in days of yore,
When, as the weeks sped by, I seemed to stand
Ever upon the brink of some wild lore —
These leaves shall make my bed, and — for the hand
Of God is on me, chilling brain and breath —
I shall not ask a softer couch in death.

VI

"Here was it that I saw, or dreamed I saw,
I know not which, that shape of love and light.

Spirit of Song! have I not owned thy law?
  Have I not taught, or striven to teach the right,
And kept my heart as clean, my life as sweet,
As mortals may, when mortals mortals meet?

VII

"Thou know'st how I went forth, my youthful breast
  On fire with thee, amid the paths of men;
Once in my wanderings, my lone footsteps pressed
  A mountain forest; in a sombre glen,
Down which its thundrous boom a cataract flung,
A little bird, unheeded, built and sung.

VIII

"So fell my voice amid the whirl and rush
  Of human passions; if unto my art
Sorrow hath sometimes owed a gentler gush,
  I know it not; if any Poet-heart
Hath kindled at my songs its light divine,
I know it not; no ray came back to mine.

IX

"Alone in crowds, once more I sought to make
  Of senseless things my friends; the clouds that burn
Above the sunset, and the flowers that shake
  Their odors in the wind — these would not turn
Their faces from me; far from cities, I
Forgot the scornful world that passed me by.

X

"Yet even the world's cold slights I might have borne,
Nor fled, though sorrowing; but I shrank at last
When one sweet face, too sweet, I thought, for scorn,
Looked scornfully upon me; then I passed
From all that youth had dreamed or manhood planned,
Into the self that none would understand.

XI

"She was — I never wronged her womanhood
By crowning it with praises not her own —
She was all earth's, and earth's, too, in that mood
When she brings forth her fairest; I atone
Now, in this fading brow and failing frame,
That such a soul such soul as mine could tame.

XII

"Clay to its kindred clay! I loved, in sooth,
Too deeply and too purely to be blest;
With something more of lust and less of truth
She would have sunk all blushes on my breast;
And — but I must not blame her — in my ear
Death whispers! and the end, thank God! draws near!"

XIII

Hist! on the perfect silence of the place
Comes and dies off a sound like far-off rain
With voices mingled; on the Poet's face
A shadow, where no shadow should have lain,
Falls the next moment: nothing meets his sight,
Yet something moves betwixt him and the light.

XIV

And a voice murmurs, "Wonder not, but hear!
Me to behold again thou need'st not seek;
Yet by the dim-felt influence on the air,
And by the mystic shadow on thy cheek,
Know, though thou mayst not touch with fleshly hands,
The genius of thy life beside thee stands!

XV

"Unto no fault, O weary-hearted one!
Unto no fault of man's thou ow'st thy fate;
All human hearts that beat this earth upon,
All human thoughts and human passions wait
Upon the genuine bard, to him belong,
And help in their own way the Poet's song.

XVI

"How blame the world? for the world hast thou wrought?
Or wast thou but as one who aims to fling

The weight of some unutterable thought
Down like a burden? what from questioning
Too subtly thy own spirit, and to speech
But half subduing themes beyond the reach

XVII

"Of mortal reason; what from living much
In that dark world of shadows, where the soul
Wanders bewildered, striving still to clutch
Yet never clutching once, a shadowy goal,
Which always flies, and while it flies seems near,
Thy songs were riddles hard to mortal ear.

XVIII

"This was the hidden selfishness that marred
Thy teachings ever; this the false key-note
That on such souls as might have loved thee jarred
Like an unearthly language; thou didst float
On a strange water; those who stood on land
Gazed, but they could not leave their beaten strand.

XIX

"Your elements were different, and apart —
The world's and thine — and even in those intense
And watchful broodings o'er thy inmost heart,
It was thy own peculiar difference
That thou didst seek; nor didst thou care to find
Aught that would bring thee nearer to thy kind.

XX

"Not thus the Poet, who in blood and brain
  Would represent his race and speak for all,
Weaves the bright woof of that impassioned strain
  Which drapes, as if for some high festival
Of pure delights — whence few of human birth
May rightly be shut out — the common earth.

XXI

"As the same law that moulds a planet, rounds
  A drop of dew, so the great Poet spheres
Worlds in himself; no selfish limit bounds
  A sympathy that folds all characters,
All ranks, all passions, and all life almost
In its wide circle. Like some noble host,

XXII

"He spreads the riches of his soul, and bids
  Partake who will. Age has its saws of truth,
And love is for the maiden's drooping lids,
  And words of passion for the earnest youth;
Wisdom for all; and when it seeks relief,
Tears, and their solace for the heart of grief.

XXIII

"Nor less on him than thee the mysteries
  Within him and about him ever weigh —
The meanings in the stars, and in the breeze,
  All the weird wonders of the common day,

Truths that the merest point removes from reach,
And thoughts that pause upon the brink of speech;

XXIV

"But on the surface of his song these lie
  As shadows, not as darkness; and alway,
Even though it breathe the secrets of the sky,
  There is a human purpose in the lay;
Thus some tall fir that whispers to the stars
Shields at its base a cotter's lattice-bars.

XXV

"Even such my Poet! for thou still art mine!
  Thou mightst have been, and now have calmly died,
A priest, and not a victim at the shrine;
  Alas! yet was it all thy fault? I chide,
Perchance, myself within thee, and the fate
To which thy power was solely consecrate.

XXVI

"Thy life hath not been wholly without use,
  Albeit that use is partly hidden now;
In thy unmingled scorn of any truce
  With this world's specious falsehoods, often thou
Hast uttered, through some all unworldly song,
Truths that for man might else have slumbered long.

XXVII

"And these not always vainly on the crowd
Have fallen; some are cherished now, and some,
In mystic phrases wrapped as in a shroud,
Wait the diviner, who as yet is dumb
Upon the breast of God — the gate of birth
Closed on a dreamless ignorance of earth.

XXVIII

"And therefore, though thy name shall pass away,
Even as a cloud that hath wept all its showers,
Yet as that cloud shall live again one day
In the glad grass, and in the happy flowers,
So in thy thoughts, though clothed in sweeter rhymes,
Thy life shall bear its flowers in future times."

THE PAST

TO-DAY'S most trivial act may hold the seed
Of future fruitfulness, or future dearth;
Oh, cherish always every word and deed!
The simplest record of thyself hath worth.

If thou hast ever slighted one old thought,
Beware lest Grief enforce the truth at last;
The time must come wherein thou shalt be taught
The value and the beauty of the Past.

Not merely as a warner and a guide,
  "A voice behind thee," sounding to the strife;
But something never to be put aside,
  A part and parcel of thy present life.

Not as a distant and a darkened sky,
  Through which the stars peep, and the moon-
      beams glow;
But a surrounding atmosphere, whereby
  We live and breathe, sustained in pain and woe.

A shadowy land, where joy and sorrow kiss,
  Each still to each corrective and relief,
Where dim delights are brightened into bliss,
  And nothing wholly perishes but Grief.

Ah, me!—not dies—no more than spirit dies;
  But in a change like death is clothed with wings;
A serious angel, with entrancèd eyes,
  Looking to far-off and celestial things.

DREAMS

Who first said "false as dreams"? Not one who
      saw
  Into the wild and wondrous world they sway;
No thinker who hath read their mystic law;
  No Poet who hath weaved them in his lay.

Else had he known that through the human breast
  Cross and recross a thousand fleeting gleams,
That, passed unnoticed in the day's unrest,
  Come out at night, like stars, in shining dreams;

That minds too busy or too dull to mark
  The dim suggestion of the noisier hours,
By dreams in the deep silence of the dark,
  Are roused at midnight with their folded powers.

Like that old fount beneath Dodona's oaks,
  That, dry and voiceless in the garish noon,
When the calm night arose with modest looks,
  Caught with full wave the sparkle of the moon.

If, now and then, a ghastly shape glide in,
  And fright us with its horrid gloom or glee,
It is the ghost of some forgotten sin
  We failed to exorcise on bended knee.

And that sweet face which only yesternight
  Came to thy solace, dreamer (didst thou read
The blessing in its eyes of tearful light?),
  Was but the spirit of some gentle deed.

Each has its lesson; for our dreams in sooth,
  Come they in shape of demons, gods, or elves,
Are allegories with deep hearts of truth
  That tell us solemn secrets of ourselves.

THE ARCTIC VOYAGER

SHALL I desist, twice baffled? Once by land,
And once by sea, I fought and strove with storms,
All shades of danger, tides, and weary calms;
Head-currents, cold and famine, savage beasts,
And men more savage; all the while my face
Looked northward toward the pole; if mortal strength
Could have sustained me, I had never turned
Till I had seen the star which never sets
Freeze in the Arctic zenith. That I failed
To solve the mysteries of the ice-bound world,
Was not because I faltered in the quest.
Witness those pathless forests which conceal
The bones of perished comrades, that long march,
Blood-tracked o'er flint and snow, and one dread night
By Athabasca, when a cherished life
Flowed to give life to others. This, and worse,
I suffered — let it pass — it has not tamed
My spirit nor the faith which was my strength.
Despite of waning years, despite the world
Which doubts, the few who dare, I purpose now —
A purpose long and thoughtfully resolved,
Through all its grounds of reasonable hope —
To seek beyond the ice which guards the Pole,
A sea of open water; for I hold,

Not without proofs, that such a sea exists,
And may be reached, though since this earth was made
No keel hath ploughed it, and to mortal ear
No wind hath told its secrets . . . . With this tide
I sail; if all be well, this very moon
Shall see my ship beyond the southern cape
Of Greenland, and far up the bay through which,
With diamond spire and gorgeous pinnacle,
The fleets of winter pass to warmer seas.
Whether, my hardy shipmates! we shall reach
Our bourne, and come with tales of wonder back,
Or whether we shall lose the precious time,
Locked in thick ice, or whether some strange fate
Shall end us all, I know not; but I know
A lofty hope, if earnestly pursued,
Is its own crown, and never in this life
Is labor wholly fruitless. In this faith
I shall not count the chances — sure that all
A prudent foresight asks we shall not want,
And all that bold and patient hearts can do
Ye will not leave undone. The rest is God's!

DRAMATIC FRAGMENT

Let the boy have his will! I tell thee, brother,
We treat these little ones too much like flowers,
Training them, in blind selfishness, to deck
Sticks of our poor setting, when they might,
If left to clamber where themselves incline,
Find nobler props to cling to, fitter place,
And sweeter air to bloom in. It is wrong —
Thou striv'st to sow with feelings all thine own,
With thoughts and hopes, anxieties and aims,
Born of thine own peculiar self, and fed
Upon a certain round of circumstance,
A soul as different and distinct from thine
As love of goodness is from love of glory,
Or noble poesy from noble prose.
I could forgive thee, if thou wast of them
Who do their fated parts in this world's business,
Scarce knowing how or why — for common minds
See not the difference 'twixt themselves and others —
But thou, thou, with the visions which thy youth did cherish
Substantialized upon thy regal brow,
Shouldst boast a deeper insight. We are born,
It is my faith, in miniature completeness,
And like each other only in our weakness.
Even with our mother's milk upon our lips,

Our smiles have different meanings, and our hands
Press with degrees of softness to her bosom.
It is not change — whatever in the heart
That wears its semblance, we, in looking back,
With gratulation or regret, perceive —
It is not change we undergo, but only
Growth or development. Yes! what is childhood
But after all a sort of golden daylight,
A beautiful and blessed wealth of sunshine,
Wherein the powers and passions of the soul
Sleep starlike but existent, till the night
Of gathering years shall call the slumbers forth,
And they rise up in glory? Early grief,
A shadow like the darkness of eclipse,
Hath sometimes waked them sooner.

THE SUMMER BOWER

It is a place whither I 've often gone
For peace, and found it, secret, hushed, and cool,
A beautiful recess in neighboring woods.
Trees of the soberest hues, thick-leaved and tall,
Arch it o'erhead and column it around,
Framing a covert, natural and wild,
Domelike and dim; though nowhere so enclosed
But that the gentlest breezes reach the spot
Unwearied and unweakened. Sound is here
A transient and unfrequent visitor;

Yet if the day be calm, not often then,
Whilst the high pines in one another's arms
Sleep, you may sometimes with unstartled ear
Catch the far fall of voices, how remote
You know not, and you do not care to know.
The turf is soft and green, but not a flower
Lights the recess, save one, star-shaped and
 bright —
I do not know its name — which here and there
Gleams like a sapphire set in emerald.
A narrow opening in the branchëd roof,
A single one, is large enough to show,
With that half glimpse a dreamer loves so much,
The blue air and the blessing of the sky.
Thither I always bent my idle steps,
When griefs depressed, or joys disturbed my heart,
And found the calm I looked for, or returned
Strong with the quiet rapture in my soul.
 But one day,
One of those July days when winds have fled
One knows not whither, I, most sick in mind
With thoughts that shall be nameless, yet, no doubt,
Wrong, or at least unhealthful, since though dark
With gloom, and touched with discontent, they had
No adequate excuse, nor cause, nor end,
I, with these thoughts, and on this summer day,
Entered the accustomed haunt, and found for once
No medicinal virtue.
 Not a leaf
Stirred with the whispering welcome which I sought,

But in a close and humid atmosphere,
Every fair plant and implicated bough
Hung lax and lifeless. Something in the place,
Its utter stillness, the unusual heat,
And some more secret influence, I thought,
Weighed on the sense like sin. Above I saw,
Though not a cloud was visible in heaven,
The pallid sky look through a glazëd mist
Like a blue eye in death.

The change, perhaps,
Was natural enough; my jaundiced sight,
The weather, and the time explain it all:
Yet have I drawn a lesson from the spot,
And shrined it in these verses for my heart.
Thenceforth those tranquil precincts I have sought
Not less, and in all shades of various moods;
But always shun to desecrate the spot
By vain repinings, sickly sentiments,
Or inconclusive sorrows. Nature, though
Pure as she was in Eden when her breath
Kissed the white brow of Eve, doth not refuse,
In her own way and with a just reserve,
To sympathize with human suffering;
But for the pains, the fever, and the fret
Engendered of a weak, unquiet heart,
She hath no solace; and who seeks her when
These be the troubles over which he moans,
Reads in her unreplying lineaments
Rebukes, that, to the guilty consciousness,
Strike like contempt.

A RHAPSODY OF A SOUTHERN WINTER NIGHT

OH! dost thou flatter falsely, Hope?
The day hath scarcely passed that saw thy birth,
Yet thy white wings are plumed to all their scope,
And hour by hour thine eyes have gathered light,
And grown so large and bright,
That my whole future life unfolds what seems,
Beneath their gentle beams,
A path that leads athwart some guiltless earth,
To which a star is dropping from the night!

Not many moons ago,
But when these leafless beds were all aglow
With summer's dearest treasures, I
Was reading in this lonely garden-nook;
A July noon was cloudless in the sky,
And soon I put my shallow studies by;
Then, sick at heart, and angered by the book,
Which, in good sooth, was but the long-drawn sigh
Of some one who had quarreled with his kind,
Vexed at the very proofs which I had sought,
And all annoyed while all alert to find
A plausible likeness of my own dark thought,
I cast me down beneath yon oak's wide boughs,
And, shielding with both hands my throbbing brows,

Watched lazily the shadows of my brain.
The feeble tide of peevishness went down,
And left a flat dull waste of dreary pain,
Which seemed to clog the blood in every vein;
The world, of course, put on its darkest frown —
In all its realms I saw no mortal crown
Which did not wound or crush some restless head;
And hope, and will, and motive, all were dead.
So, passive as a stone, I felt too low
To claim a kindred with the humblest flower;
Even that would bare its bosom to a shower,
While I henceforth would take no pains to live,
Nor place myself where I might feel or give
A single impulse whence a wish could grow.
There was a tulip scarce a gossamer's throw
Beyond that platanus. A little child,
Most dear to me, looked through the fence and smiled
A hint that I should pluck it for her sake.
Ah, me! I trust I was not well awake —
The voice was very sweet,
Yet a faint languor kept me in my seat.
I saw a pouted lip, a toss, and heard
Some low expostulating tones, but stirred
Not even a leaf's length, till the pretty fay,
Wondering, and half abashed at the wild feat,
Climbed the low pales, and laughed my gloom away.

And here again, but led by other powers,
A morning and a golden afternoon,
These happy stars, and yonder setting moon,
Have seen me speed, unreckoned and untasked,
A round of precious hours.
Oh! here, where in that summer noon I basked,
And strove, with logic frailer than the flowers,
To justify a life of sensuous rest,
A question dear as home or heaven was asked,
And without language answered. I was blest!
Blest with those nameless boons too sweet to trust
Unto the telltale confidence of song.
Love to his own glad self is sometimes coy,
And even thus much doth seem to do him wrong;
While in the fears which chasten mortal joy,
Is one that shuts the lips, lest speech too free,
With the cold touch of hard reality,
Should turn its priceless jewels into dust.
Since that long kiss which closed the morning's talk,
I have not strayed beyond this garden walk.
As yet a vague delight is all I know,
A sense of joy so wild 't is almost pain,
And like a trouble drives me to and fro,
And will not pause to count its own sweet gain.
I am so happy! that is all my thought.
To-morrow I will turn it round and round,
And seek to know its limits and its ground.
To-morrow I will task my heart to learn

The duties which shall spring from such a seed,
And where it must be sown, and how be wrought.
But oh! this reckless bliss is bliss indeed!
And for one day I choose to seal the urn
Wherein is shrined Love's missal and his creed.
Meantime I give my fancy all it craves;
Like him who found the West when first he caught
The light that glittered from the world he sought,
And furled his sails till Dawn should show the land;
While in glad dreams he saw the ambient waves
Go rippling brightly up a golden strand.

Hath there not been a softer breath at play
In the long woodland aisles than often sweeps
At this rough season through their solemn deeps—
A gentle Ariel sent by gentle May,
Who knew it was the morn
On which a hope was born,
To greet the flower e'er it was fully blown,
And nurse it as some lily of her own?
And wherefore, save to grace a happy day,
Did the whole West at blushing sunset glow
With clouds that, floating up in bridal snow,
Passed with the festal eve, rose-crowned, away?
And now, if I may trust my straining sight,
The heavens appear with added stars to-night,
And deeper depths, and more celestial height,
Than hath been reached except in dreams or death.

Hush, sweetest South! I love thy delicate breath;
But hush! methought I felt an angel's kiss!
Oh! all that lives is happy in my bliss.
That lonely fir, which always seems
As though it locked dark secrets in itself,
Hideth a gentle elf,
Whose wand shall send me soon a frolic troop
Of rainbow visions, and of moonlit dreams.
Can joy be weary, that my eyelids droop?
To-night I shall not seek my curtained nest,
But even here find rest.
Who whispered then? And what are they that peep
Betwixt the foliage in the tree-top there?
Come, Fairy Shadows! for the morn is near,
When to your sombre pine ye all must creep;
Come, ye wild pilots of the darkness, ere
My spirit sinks into the gulf of Sleep;
Even now it circles round and round the deep—
Appear! Appear!

FLOWER-LIFE

I THINK that, next to your sweet eyes,
And pleasant books, and starry skies,
I love the world of flowers;
Less for their beauty of a day,
Than for the tender things they say,

And for a creed I 've held alway,
That they are sentient powers.

It may be matter for a smile —
And I laugh secretly the while
I speak the fancy out —
But that they love, and that they woo,
And that they often marry too,
And do as noisier creatures do,
I 've not the faintest doubt.

And so, I cannot deem it right
To take them from the glad sunlight,
As I have sometimes dared;
Though not without an anxious sigh
Lest this should break some gentle tie,
Some covenant of friendship, I
Had better far have spared.

And when, in wild or thoughtless hours,
My hand hath crushed the tiniest flowers,
I ne'er could shut from sight
The corpses of the tender things,
With other drear imaginings,
And little angel-flowers with wings
Would haunt me through the night.

Oh! say you, friend, the creed is fraught
With sad, and even with painful thought,
Nor could you bear to know

That such capacities belong
To creatures helpless against wrong,
At once too weak to fly the strong
Or front the feeblest foe?

So be it always, then, with you;
So be it — whether false or true —
I press my faith on none;
If other fancies please you more,
The flowers shall blossom as before,
Dear as the Sibyl-leaves of yore,
But senseless, every one.

Yet, though I give you no reply,
It were not hard to justify
My creed to partial ears;
But, conscious of the cruel part,
My rhymes would flow with faltering art,
I could not plead against your heart,
Nor reason with your tears.

A SUMMER SHOWER

Welcome, rain or tempest
From yon airy powers,
We have languished for them
Many sultry hours,
And earth is sick and wan, and pines with all her flowers.

What have they been doing
In the burning June?
Riding with the genii?
Visiting the moon?
Or sleeping on the ice amid an arctic noon?

Bring they with them jewels
From the sunset lands?
What are these they scatter
With such lavish hands?
There are no brighter gems in Raolconda's sands.

Pattering on the gravel,
Dropping from the eaves,
Glancing in the grass, and
Tinkling on the leaves,
They flash the liquid pearls as flung from fairy sieves.

Meanwhile, unreluctant,
Earth like Danaë lies;
Listen! is it fancy,
That beneath us sighs,
As that warm lap receives the largesse of the skies?

Jove, it is, descendeth
In those crystal rills;
And this world-wide tremor
Is a pulse that thrills
To a god's life infused through veins of velvet hills.

Wait, thou jealous sunshine,
Break not on their bliss;
Earth will blush in roses
Many a day for this,
And bend a brighter brow beneath thy burning kiss.

BABY'S AGE

SHE came with April blooms and showers;
We count her little life by flowers.
As buds the rose upon her cheek,
We choose a flower for every week.
A week of hyacinths, we say,
And one of heart's-ease, ushered May;
And then because two wishes met
Upon the rose and violet —
I liked the Beauty, Kate, the Nun —
The violet and the rose count one.
A week the apple marked with white;
A week the lily scored in light;
Red poppies closed May's happy moon,
And tulips this blue week in June.
Here end as yet the flowery links;
To-day begins the week of pinks;
But soon — so grave, and deep, and wise
The meaning grows in Baby's eyes,
So *very* deep for Baby's age —
We think to date a week with sage!

THE MESSENGER ROSE

If you have seen a richer glow,
Pray, tell me where your roses blow!
Look! coral-leaved! and — mark these spots
Red staining red in crimson clots,
Like a sweet lip bitten through
In a pique. There, where that hue
Is spilt in drops, some fairy thing
Hath gashed the azure of its wing,
Or thence, perhaps, this very morn,
Plucked the splinters of a thorn.

Rose! I make thy bliss my care!
In my lady's dusky hair
Thou shalt burn this coming night,
With even a richer crimson light.
To requite me thou shalt tell —
What I might not say as well —
How I love her; how, in brief,
On a certain crimson leaf
In my bosom, is a debt
Writ in deeper crimson yet.
If she wonder what it be —
But she 'll guess it, I foresee —
Tell her that I date it, pray,
From the first sweet night in May.

ON PRESSING SOME FLOWERS

So, they are dead! Love! when they passed
From thee to me, our fingers met;
O withered darlings of the May!
I feel those fairy fingers yet.

And for the bliss ye brought me then,
Your faded forms are precious things;
No flowers so fair, no buds so sweet
Shall bloom through all my future springs.

And so, pale ones! with hands as soft
As if I closed a baby's eyes,
I 'll lay you in some favorite book
Made sacred by a poet's sighs.

Your lips shall press the sweetest song,
The sweetest, saddest song I know,
As ye had perished, in your pride,
Of some lone bard's melodious woe.

Oh, Love! hath love no holier shrine!
Oh, heart! could love but lend the power,
I 'd lay thy crimson pages bare,
And every leaf should fold its flower.

1866

ADDRESSED TO THE OLD YEAR

ART thou not glad to close
  Thy wearied eyes, O saddest child of Time,
  Eyes which have looked on every mortal crime,
And swept the piteous round of mortal woes?

In dark Plutonian caves,
  Beneath the lowest deep, go, hide thy head;
  Or earth thee where the blood that thou hast shed
May trickle on thee from thy countless graves!

Take with thee all thy gloom
  And guilt, and all our griefs, save what the breast,
  Without a wrong to some dear shadowy guest,
May not surrender even to the tomb.

No tear shall weep thy fall,
  When, as the midnight bell doth toll thy fate,
  Another lifts the sceptre of thy state,
And sits a monarch in thine ancient hall.

Him all the hours attend,
  With a new hope like morning in their eyes;

Him the fair earth and him these radiant skies
Hail as their sovereign, welcome as their friend.

Him, too, the nations wait;
"O lead us from the shadow of the Past,"
In a long wail like this December blast,
They cry, and, crying, grow less desolate.

How he will shape his sway
They ask not—for old doubts and fears will cling—
And yet they trust that, somehow, he will bring
A sweeter sunshine than thy mildest day.

Beneath his gentle hand
They hope to see no meadow, vale, or hill
Stained with a deeper red than roses spill,
When some too boisterous zephyr sweeps the land.

A time of peaceful prayer,
Of law, love, labor, honest loss and gain—
These are the visions of the coming reign
Now floating to them on this wintry air.

STANZAS

A MOTHER GAZES UPON HER DAUGHTER, ARRAYED FOR AN APPROACHING BRIDAL. WRITTEN IN ILLUSTRATION OF A TABLEAU VIVANT

Is she not lovely! Oh! when, long ago,
  My own dead mother gazed upon my face,
As I stood blushing near in bridal snow,
  I had not half her beauty and her grace.

Yet that fond mother praised, the world caressed,
  And *one* adored me — how shall *he* who soon
Shall wear my gentle flower upon his breast,
  Prize to its utmost worth the priceless boon?

Shall he not gird her, guard her, make her rich,
  (Not as the world is rich, in outward show,)
With all the love and watchful kindness which
  A wise and tender manhood may bestow?

Oh! I shall part from her with many tears,
  My earthly treasure, pure and undefiled!
And not without a weight of anxious fears
  For the new future of my darling child.

And yet — for well I know that virgin heart —
  No wifely duty will she leave undone;

Nor will her love neglect that woman's art
  Which courts and keeps a love already won.

In no light girlish levity she goes
  Unto the altar where they wait her now,
But with a thoughtful, prayerful heart that knows
  The solemn purport of a marriage vow.

And she will keep, with all her soul's deep truth,
  The lightest pledge which binds her love and life;
And she will be — no less in age than youth
  My noble child will be — a noble wife.

And he, her lover! husband! what of him?
  Yes, he will shield, I think, my bud from blight!
Yet griefs will come — enough! my eyes are dim
  With tears I must not shed — at least, to-night.

Bless thee, my daughter! — Oh! she is so fair! —
  Heaven bend above thee with its starriest skies!
And make thee truly all thou dost appear
  Unto a lover's and thy mother's eyes!

HYMN

SUNG AT AN ANNIVERSARY OF THE ASYLUM OF ORPHANS AT CHARLESTON

We scarce, O God! could lisp thy name,
  When those who loved us passed away,
And left us but thy love to claim,
  With but an infant's strength to pray.

Thou gav'st that Refuge and that Shrine,
  At which we learn to know thy ways;
Father! the fatherless are thine!
  Thou wilt not spurn the orphan's praise.

Yet hear a single cry of pain!
  Lord! whilst we dream in quiet beds,
The summer sun and winter rain
  Beat still on many homeless heads.

And o'er this weary earth, we know,
  Young outcasts roam the waste and wave;
And little hands are clasped in woe
  Above some tender mother's grave.

Ye winds! keep every storm aloof,
  And kiss away the tears they weep!
Ye skies, that make their only roof,
  Look gently on their houseless sleep!

And thou, O Friend and Father! find
  A home to shield their helpless youth!
Dear hearts to love — sweet ties to bind —
  And guide and guard them in the truth!

TO A CAPTIVE OWL

I SHOULD be dumb before thee, feathered sage!
  And gaze upon thy phiz with solemn awe,
But for a most audacious wish to gauge
  The hoarded wisdom of thy learned craw.

Art thou, grave bird! so wondrous wise indeed?
  Speak freely, without fear of jest or gibe —
What is thy moral and religious creed?
  And what the metaphysics of thy tribe?

A Poet, curious in birds and brutes,
  I do not question thee in idle play;
What is thy station? What are thy pursuits?
  Doubtless thou hast thy pleasures — what are *they?*

Or is 't thy wont to muse and mouse at once,
  Entice thy prey with airs of meditation,
And with the unvarying habits of a dunce,
  To dine in solemn depths of contemplation?

There may be much — the world at least says so —
Behind that ponderous brow and thoughtful gaze;
Yet such a great philosopher should know,
It is by no means wise to think always.

And, Bird, despite thy meditative air,
I hold thy stock of wit but paltry pelf —
Thou show'st that same grave aspect everywhere,
And wouldst look thoughtful, stuffed, upon a shelf.

I grieve to be so plain, renownëd Bird —
Thy fame 's a flam, and thou an empty fowl;
And what is more, upon a Poet's word
I 'd say as much, wert thou Minerva's owl.

So doff th' imposture of those heavy brows;
They do not serve to hide thy instincts base —
And if thou must be sometimes munching *mouse*,
Munch it, O Owl! with less profound a face.

LOVE'S LOGIC

AND if I ask thee for a kiss,
  I ask no more than this sweet breeze,
With far less title to the bliss,
  Steals every minute at his ease.
And yet how placid is thy brow!
  It seems to woo the bold caress,
While now he takes his kiss, and now
  All sorts of freedoms with thy dress.

Or if I dare thy hand to touch,
  Hath nothing pressed its palm before?
A flower, I 'm sure, hath done as much,
  And ah! some senseless diamond more.
It strikes me, love, the very rings,
  Now sparkling on that hand of thine,
Could tell some truly startling things,
  If they had tongues or touch like mine.

Indeed, indeed, I do not know
  Of all that thou hast power to grant,
A boon for which I could not show
  Some pretty precedent extant.
Suppose, for instance, I should clasp
  Thus,— so, — and thus! — thy slender waist—
I would not hold within my grasp
  More than this loosened zone embraced.

Oh! put the anger from thine eyes,
  Or shut them if they still must frown;
Those lids, despite yon garish skies,
  Can bring a timely darkness down.
Then, if in that convenient night,
  My lips should press thy dewy mouth,
The touch shall be so soft, so light,
  Thou 'lt fancy me — this gentle South.

SECOND LOVE

COULD I reveal the secret joy
  Thy presence always with it brings,
The memories so strangely waked
  Of long forgotten things,

The love, the hope, the fear, the grief,
  Which with that voice come back to me, —
Thou wouldst forgive the impassioned gaze
  So often turned on thee.

It was, indeed, that early love,
  But foretaste of this second one, —
The soft light of the morning star
  Before the morning sun.

The same dark beauty in her eyes,
  The same blonde hair and placid brow,

The same deep-meaning, quiet smile
  Thou bendest on me now,

She might have been, she *was* no more
  Than what a prescient hope could make, —
A dear presentiment of thee
  I loved but for thy sake.

HYMN

SUNG AT THE CONSECRATION OF MAGNOLIA CEMETERY, CHARLESTON, S. C.

WHOSE was the hand that painted thee, O Death!
  In the false aspect of a ruthless foe,
Despair and sorrow waiting on thy breath —
  O gentle Power! who could have wronged thee so?

Thou rather shouldst be crowned with fadeless flowers,
  Of lasting fragrance and celestial hue;
Or be thy couch amid funereal bowers,
  But let the stars and sunlight sparkle through.

So, with these thoughts before us, we have fixed
  And beautified, O Death! thy mansion here,
Where gloom and gladness — grave and garden — mixed,
  Make it a place to love, and not to fear.

Heaven! shed thy most propitious dews around!
Ye holy stars! look down with tender eyes,
And gild and guard and consecrate the ground
Where we may rest, and whence we pray to rise.

HYMN

SUNG AT A SACRED CONCERT AT COLUMBIA, S. C.

I

Faint falls the gentle voice of prayer
In the wild sounds that fill the air,
Yet, Lord, we know that voice is heard,
Not less than if Thy throne it stirred.

II

Thine ear, thou tender One, is caught,
If we but bend the knee in thought;
No choral song that shakes the sky
Floats farther than the Christian's sigh.

III

Not all the darkness of the land
Can hide the lifted eye and hand;
Nor need the clanging conflict cease,
To make Thee hear our cries for peace.

LINES TO R. L.

That which we are and shall be is made up
Of what we have been. On the autumn leaf
The crimson stains bear witness of its spring;
And, on its perfect nodes, the ocean shell
Notches the slow, strange changes of its growth.
Ourselves are our own records; if we looked
Rightly into that blotted crimson page
Within our bosoms, then there were no need
To chronicle our stories; for the heart
Hath, like the earth, its strata, and contains
Its past within its present. Well for us,
And our most cherished secrets, that within
The round of being few there are who read
Beneath the surface. Else our very forms,
The merest gesture of our hands, might tell
Much we would hide forever. Know you not
Those eyes, in whose dark heaven I have gazed
More curiously than on my favorite stars,
Are deeper for such griefs as they have seen,
And brighter for the fancies they have shrined,
And sweeter for the loves which they have talked?
Oh! that I had the power to read their smiles,
Or sound the depth of all their glorious gloom.
So should I learn your history from its birth,
Through all its glad and grave experiences,
Better than if — (your journal in my hand,

Written as only women write, with all
A woman's shades and shapes of feeling, traced
As with the fine touch of a needle's point) —
I followed you from that bright hour when first
I saw you in the garden 'mid the flowers,
To that wherein a letter from your hand
Made me all rich with the dear name of friend.

TO WHOM?

Awake upon a couch of pain,
  I see a star betwixt the trees;
Across yon darkening field of cane,
  Comes slow and soft the evening breeze.
My curtain's folds are faintly stirred;
  And moving lightly in her rest,
I hear the chirrup of a bird,
  That dreameth in some neighboring nest.

Last night I took no note of these —
  How it was passed I scarce can say;
'T was not in prayers to Heaven for ease,
  'T was not in wishes for the day.
Impatient tears, and passionate sighs,
  Touched as with fire the pulse of pain, —
I cursed, and cursed the wildering eyes
  That burned this fever in my brain.

Oh! blessings on the quiet hour!
  My thoughts in calmer current flow;
She is not conscious of her power,
  And hath no knowledge of my woe.
Perhaps, if like yon peaceful star,
  She looked upon my burning brow,
She would not pity from afar,
  But kiss me as the breeze does now.

TO THEE

Draw close the lattice and the door!
  Shut out the very stars above!
No other eyes than mine shall pore
  Upon this thrilling tale of love.
As, since the book was open last,
  Along its dear and sacred text
No other eyes than thine have passed —
  Be mine the eyes that trace it next!

Oh! very nobly is it wrought, —
  This web of love's divinest light, —
But not to feed my soul with thought,
  Hang I upon the book to-night;
I read it only for thy sake,
  To every page my lips I press —
The very leaves appear to make
  A silken rustle like thy dress.

And so, as each blest page I turn,
  I seem, with many a secret thrill,
To touch a soft white hand, and burn
  To clasp and kiss it at my will.
Oh! if a fancy be so sweet,
  These shadowy fingers touching mine —
How wildly would my pulses beat,
  If they *could* feel the beat of thine!

STORM AND CALM

SWEET are these kisses of the South,
As dropped from woman's rosiest mouth,
And tenderer are those azure skies
Than this world's tenderest pair of eyes!

But ah! beneath such influence
Thought is too often lost in Sense;
And Action, faltering as we thrill,
Sinks in the unnerved arms of Will.

Awake, thou stormy North, and blast
The subtle spells around us cast;
Beat from our limbs these flowery chains
With the sharp scourges of thy rains!

Bring with thee from thy Polar cave
All the wild songs of wind and wave,

Of toppling berg and grinding floe,
And the dread avalanche of snow!

Wrap us in Arctic night and clouds!
Yell like a fiend amid the shrouds
Of some slow-sinking vessel, when
He hears the shrieks of drowning men!

Blend in thy mighty voice whate'er
Of danger, terror, and despair
Thou hast encountered in thy sweep
Across the land and o'er the deep.

Pour in our ears all notes of woe,
That, as these very moments flow,
Rise like a harsh discordant psalm,
While we lie here in tropic calm.

Sting our weak hearts with bitter shame,
Bear us along with thee like flame;
And prove that even to destroy
More God-like may be than to toy
And rust or rot in idle joy!

RETIREMENT

My gentle friend! I hold no creed so false
As that which dares to teach that we are born
For battle only, and that in this life
The soul, if it would burn with starlike power,
Must needs forsooth be kindled by the sparks
Struck from the shock of clashing human hearts.
There is a wisdom that grows up in strife,
And one — I like it best — that sits at home
And learns its lessons of a thoughtful ease.
So come! a lonely house awaits thee! — there
Nor praise, nor blame shall reach us, save what love
Of knowledge for itself shall wake at times
In our own bosoms; come! and we will build
A wall of quiet thought, and gentle books,
Betwixt us and the hard and bitter world.
Sometimes — for we need not be anchorites —
A distant friend shall cheer us through the Post,
Or some Gazette — of course no partisan —
Shall bring us pleasant news of pleasant things;
Then, twisted into graceful allumettes,
Each ancient joke shall blaze with genuine flame
To light our pipes and candles; but to wars,
Whether of words or weapons, we shall be
Deaf — so we twain shall pass away the time
Ev'n as a pair of happy lovers, who,

Alone, within some quiet garden-nook,
With a clear night of stars above their heads,
Just hear, betwixt their kisses and their talk,
The tumult of a tempest rolling through
A chain of neighboring mountains; they awhile
Pause to admire a flash that only shows
The smile upon their faces, but, full soon,
Turn with a quick, glad impulse, and perhaps
A conscious wile that brings them closer yet,
To dally with their own fond hearts, and play
With the sweet flowers that blossom at their feet.

A COMMON THOUGHT

Somewhere on this earthly planet
  In the dust of flowers to be,
In the dewdrop, in the sunshine,
  Sleeps a solemn day for me.

At this wakeful hour of midnight
  I behold it dawn in mist,
And I hear a sound of sobbing
  Through the darkness — hist! oh, hist!

In a dim and murky chamber,
  I am breathing life away;
Some one draws a curtain softly,
  And I watch the broadening day.

As it purples in the zenith,
  As it brightens on the lawn,
There 's a hush of death about me,
  And a whisper, "He is gone!"

POEMS WRITTEN IN WAR TIMES

CAROLINA

I

THE despot treads thy sacred sands,
Thy pines give shelter to his bands,
Thy sons stand by with idle hands,
Carolina!
He breathes at ease thy airs of balm,
He scorns the lances of thy palm;
Oh! who shall break thy craven calm,
Carolina!
Thy ancient fame is growing dim,
A spot is on thy garment's rim;
Give to the winds thy battle hymn,
Carolina!

II

Call on thy children of the hill,
Wake swamp and river, coast and rill,
Rouse all thy strength and all thy skill,
Carolina!
Cite wealth and science, trade and art,
Touch with thy fire the cautious mart,
And pour thee through the people's heart,
Carolina!

Till even the coward spurns his fears,
And all thy fields and fens and meres
Shall bristle like thy palm with spears,
Carolina!

III

Hold up the glories of thy dead;
Say how thy elder children bled,
And point to Eutaw's battle-bed,
Carolina!
Tell how the patriot's soul was tried,
And what his dauntless breast defied;
How Rutledge ruled and Laurens died,
Carolina!
Cry! till thy summons, heard at last,
Shall fall like Marion's bugle-blast
Re-echoed from the haunted Past,
Carolina!

IV

I hear a murmur as of waves
That grope their way through sunless caves,
Like bodies struggling in their graves,
Carolina!
And now it deepens; slow and grand
It swells, as, rolling to the land,
An ocean broke upon thy strand,
Carolina!

Shout! let it reach the startled Huns!
And roar with all thy festal guns!
It is the answer of thy sons,
Carolina!

V

They will not wait to hear thee call;
From Sachem's Head to Sumter's wall
Resounds the voice of hut and hall,
Carolina!
No! thou hast not a stain, they say,
Or none save what the battle-day
Shall wash in seas of blood away,
Carolina!
Thy skirts indeed the foe may part,
Thy robe be pierced with sword and dart,
They shall not touch thy noble heart,
Carolina!

VI

Ere thou shalt own the tyrant's thrall
Ten times ten thousand men must fall;
Thy corpse may hearken to his call,
Carolina!
When, by thy bier, in mournful throngs
The women chant thy mortal wrongs,
'T will be their own funereal songs,
Carolina!

From thy dead breast by ruffians trod
No helpless child shall look to God;
All shall be safe beneath thy sod,
Carolina!

VII

Girt with such wills to do and bear,
Assured in right, and mailed in prayer,
Thou wilt not bow thee to despair,
Carolina!
Throw thy bold banner to the breeze!
Front with thy ranks the threatening seas
Like thine own proud armorial trees,
Carolina!
Fling down thy gauntlet to the Huns,
And roar the challenge from thy guns;
Then leave the future to thy sons,
Carolina!

A CRY TO ARMS

Ho! woodsmen of the mountain side!
Ho! dwellers in the vales!
Ho! ye who by the chafing tide
Have roughened in the gales!
Leave barn and byre, leave kin and cot,
Lay by the bloodless spade;
Let desk, and case, and counter rot,
And burn your books of trade.

The despot roves your fairest lands;
  And till he flies or fears,
Your fields must grow but armèd bands,
  Your sheaves be sheaves of spears!
Give up to mildew and to rust
  The useless tools of gain;
And feed your country's sacred dust
  With floods of crimson rain!

Come, with the weapons at your call —
  With musket, pike, or knife;
He wields the deadliest blade of all
  Who lightest holds his life.
The arm that drives its unbought blows
  With all a patriot's scorn,
Might brain a tyrant with a rose,
  Or stab him with a thorn.

Does any falter? let him turn
  To some brave maiden's eyes,
And catch the holy fires that burn
  In those sublunar skies.
Oh! could you like your women feel,
  And in their spirit march,
A day might see your lines of steel
  Beneath the victor's arch.

What hope, O God! would not grow warm
  When thoughts like these give cheer?

The Lily calmly braves the storm,
  And shall the Palm-tree fear?
No! rather let its branches court
  The rack that sweeps the plain;
And from the Lily's regal port
  Learn how to breast the strain!

Ho! woodsmen of the mountain side!
  Ho! dwellers in the vales!
Ho! ye who by the roaring tide
  Have roughened in the gales!
Come! flocking gayly to the fight,
  From forest, hill, and lake;
We battle for our Country's right,
  And for the Lily's sake!

CHARLESTON

Calm as that second summer which precedes
  The first fall of the snow,
In the broad sunlight of heroic deeds,
  The City bides the foe.

As yet, behind their ramparts stern and proud,
  Her bolted thunders sleep —
Dark Sumter, like a battlemented cloud,
  Looms o'er the solemn deep.

No Calpe frowns from lofty cliff or scar
  To guard the holy strand;
But Moultrie holds in leash her dogs of war
  Above the level sand.

And down the dunes a thousand guns lie couched,
  Unseen, beside the flood —
Like tigers in some Orient jungle crouched
  That wait and watch for blood.

Meanwhile, through streets still echoing with trade,
  Walk grave and thoughtful men,
Whose hands may one day wield the patriot's blade
  As lightly as the pen.

And maidens, with such eyes as would grow dim
  Over a bleeding hound,
Seem each one to have caught the strength of him
  Whose sword she sadly bound.

Thus girt without and garrisoned at home,
  Day patient following day,
Old Charleston looks from roof, and spire, and dome,
  Across her tranquil bay.

Ships, through a hundred foes, from Saxon lands
  And spicy Indian ports,

Bring Saxon steel and iron to her hands,
  And Summer to her courts.

But still, along yon dim Atlantic line,
  The only hostile smoke
Creeps like a harmless mist above the brine,
  From some frail, floating oak.

Shall the Spring dawn, and she still clad in smiles,
  And with an unscathed brow,
Rest in the strong arms of her palm-crowned isles,
  As fair and free as now?

We know not; in the temple of the Fates
  God has inscribed her doom;
And, all untroubled in her faith, she waits
  The triumph or the tomb.

RIPLEY

Rich in red honors, that upon him lie
  As lightly as the Summer dews
Fall where he won his fame beneath the sky
  Of tropic Vera Cruz;

Bold scorner of the cant that has its birth
  In feeble or in failing powers;
A lover of all frank and genial mirth
  That wreathes the sword with flowers;

He moves amid the warriors of the day,
  Just such a soldier as the art
That builds its trophies upon human clay
  Moulds of a cheerful heart.

I see him in the battle that shall shake,
  Ere long, old Sumter's haughty crown,
And from their dreams of peaceful traffic wake
  The wharves of yonder town;

As calm as one would greet a pleasant guest,
  And quaff a cup to love and life,
He hurls his deadliest thunders with a jest,
  And laughs amid the strife.

Yet not the gravest soldier of them all
  Surveys a field with broader scope;
And who behind that sea-encircled wall
  Fights with a loftier hope?

Gay Chieftain! on the crimson rolls of Fame
  Thy deeds are written with the sword;
But there are gentler thoughts which, with thy name,
  Thy country's page shall hoard.

A nature of that rare and happy cast
  Which looks, unsteeled, on murder's face;

Through what dark scenes of bloodshed hast thou
passed,
Yet lost no social grace?

So, when the bard depicts thee, thou shalt wield
The weapon of a tyrant's doom,
Round which, inscribed with many a well-fought
field,
The rose of joy shall bloom.

ETHNOGENESIS

WRITTEN DURING THE MEETING OF THE FIRST SOUTHERN CONGRESS, AT MONTGOMERY, FEBRUARY, 1861

I

HATH not the morning dawned with added light?
And shall not evening call another star
Out of the infinite regions of the night,
To mark this day in Heaven? At last, we are
A nation among nations; and the world
Shall soon behold in many a distant port
Another flag unfurled!
Now, come what may, whose favor need we court?
And, under God, whose thunder need we fear?
Thank Him who placed us here
Beneath so kind a sky — the very sun

Takes part with us ; and on our errands run
All breezes of the ocean ; dew and rain
Do noiseless battle for us ; and the Year,
And all the gentle daughters in her train,
March in our ranks, and in our service wield
        Long spears of golden grain !
A yellow blossom as her fairy shield,
June flings her azure banner to the wind,
  While in the order of their birth
Her sisters pass, and many an ample field
Grows white beneath their steps, till now, behold,
        Its endless sheets unfold
THE SNOW OF SOUTHERN SUMMERS ! Let the earth
Rejoice ! beneath those fleeces soft and warm
        Our happy land shall sleep
        In a repose as deep
  As if we lay intrenched behind
Whole leagues of Russian ice and Arctic storm !

II

And what if, mad with wrongs themselves have
    wrought,
        In their own treachery caught,
        By their own fears made bold,
        And leagued with him of old,
Who long since in the limits of the North
Set up his evil throne, and warred with God —
What if, both mad and blinded in their rage,
Our foes should fling us down their mortal gage,

And with a hostile step profane our sod!
We shall not shrink, my brothers, but go forth
To meet them, marshaled by the Lord of Hosts,
And overshadowed by the mighty ghosts
Of Moultrie and of Eutaw — who shall foil
Auxiliars such as these? Nor these alone,
        But every stock and stone
        Shall help us; but the very soil,
And all the generous wealth it gives to toil,
And all for which we love our noble land,
Shall fight beside, and through us; sea and strand,
        The heart of woman, and her hand,
Tree, fruit, and flower, and every influence,
        Gentle, or grave, or grand;
        The winds in our defence
Shall seem to blow; to us the hills shall lend
        Their firmness and their calm;
And in our stiffened sinews we shall blend
        The strength of pine and palm!

III

Nor would we shun the battle-ground,
        Though weak as we are strong;
Call up the clashing elements around,
        And test the right and wrong!
On one side, creeds that dare to teach
What Christ and Paul refrained to preach;
Codes built upon a broken pledge,
And Charity that whets a poniard's edge;

Fair schemes that leave the neighboring poor
To starve and shiver at the schemer's door,
While in the world's most liberal ranks enrolled,
He turns some vast philanthropy to gold;
Religion, taking every mortal form
But that a pure and Christian faith makes warm,
Where not to vile fanatic passion urged,
Or not in vague philosophies submerged,
Repulsive with all Pharisaic leaven,
And making laws to stay the laws of Heaven!
And on the other, scorn of sordid gain,
Unblemished honor, truth without a stain,
Faith, justice, reverence, charitable wealth,
And, for the poor and humble, laws which give,
Not the mean right to buy the right to live,
        But life, and home, and health!
To doubt the end were want of trust in God,
        Who, if he has decreed
    That we must pass a redder sea
Than that which rang to Miriam's holy glee,
        Will surely raise at need
        A Moses with his rod!

IV

But let our fears — if fears we have — be still,
And turn us to the future! Could we climb
Some mighty Alp, and view the coming time,
The rapturous sight would fill
        Our eyes with happy tears!

Not only for the glories which the years
Shall bring us; not for lands from sea to sea,
And wealth, and power, and peace, though these
shall be;
But for the distant peoples we shall bless,
And the hushed murmurs of a world's distress:
For, to give labor to the poor,
The whole sad planet o'er,
And save from want and crime the humblest
door,
Is one among the many ends for which
God makes us great and rich!
The hour perchance is not yet wholly ripe
When all shall own it, but the type
Whereby we shall be known in every land
Is that vast gulf which lips our Southern strand,
And through the cold, untempered ocean pours
Its genial streams, that far off Arctic shores
May sometimes catch upon the softened breeze
Strange tropic warmth and hints of summer seas.

CARMEN TRIUMPHALE

Go forth and bid the land rejoice,
Yet not too gladly, O my song!
Breathe softly, as if mirth would wrong
The solemn rapture of thy voice.

Be nothing lightly done or said
  This happy day! Our joy should flow
  Accordant with the lofty woe
That wails above the noble dead.

Let him whose brow and breast were calm
  While yet the battle lay with God,
  Look down upon the crimson sod
And gravely wear his mournful palm;

And him, whose heart still weak from fear
  Beats all too gayly for the time,
  Know that intemperate glee is crime
While one dead hero claims a tear.

Yet go thou forth, my song! and thrill,
  With sober joy, the troubled days;
  A nation's hymn of grateful praise
May not be hushed for private ill.

Our foes are fallen! Flash, ye wires!
  The mighty tidings far and nigh!
  Ye cities! write them on the sky
In purple and in emerald fires!

They came with many a haughty boast;
  Their threats were heard on every breeze;
  They darkened half the neighboring seas;
And swooped like vultures on the coast.

False recreants in all knightly strife,
  Their way was wet with woman's tears;
  Behind them flamed the toil of years,
And bloodshed stained the sheaves of life.

They fought as tyrants fight, or slaves;
  God gave the dastards to our hands;
  Their bones are bleaching on the sands,
Or mouldering slow in shallow graves.

What though we hear about our path
  The heavens with howls of vengeance rent?
  The venom of their hate is spent;
We need not heed their fangless wrath.

Meantime the stream they strove to chain
  Now drinks a thousand springs, and sweeps
  With broadening breast, and mightier deeps,
And rushes onward to the main;

While down the swelling current glides
  Our Ship of State before the blast,
  With streamers poured from every mast,
Her thunders roaring from her sides.

Lord! bid the frenzied tempest cease,
  Hang out thy rainbow on the sea!
  Laugh round her, waves! in silver glee,
And speed her to the port of peace!

THE UNKNOWN DEAD

THE rain is plashing on my sill,
But all the winds of Heaven are still;
And so it falls with that dull sound
Which thrills us in the church-yard ground,
When the first spadeful drops like lead
Upon the coffin of the dead.
Beyond my streaming window-pane,
I cannot see the neighboring vane,
Yet from its old familiar tower
The bell comes, muffled, through the shower.
What strange and unsuspected link
Of feeling touched, has made me think —
While with a vacant soul and eye
I watch that gray and stony sky —
Of nameless graves on battle-plains
Washed by a single winter's rains,
Where, some beneath Virginian hills,
And some by green Atlantic rills,
Some by the waters of the West,
A myriad unknown heroes rest.
Ah! not the chiefs, who, dying, see
Their flags in front of victory,
Or, at their life-blood's noble cost
Pay for a battle nobly lost,
Claim from their monumental beds
The bitterest tears a nation sheds.

Beneath yon lonely mound — the spot
By all save some fond few forgot —
Lie the true martyrs of the fight
Which strikes for freedom and for right.
Of them, their patriot zeal and pride,
The lofty faith that with them died,
No grateful page shall farther tell
Than that so many bravely fell;
And we can only dimly guess
What worlds of all this world's distress,
What utter woe, despair, and dearth,
Their fate has brought to many a hearth.
Just such a sky as this should weep
Above them, always, where they sleep;
Yet, haply, at this very hour,
Their graves are like a lover's bower;
And Nature's self, with eyes unwet,
Oblivious of the crimson debt
To which she owes her April grace,
Laughs gayly o'er their burial-place.

THE TWO ARMIES

Two armies stand enrolled beneath
The banner with the starry wreath;
One, facing battle, blight and blast,
Through twice a hundred fields has passed;
Its deeds against a ruffian foe,
Stream, valley, hill, and mountain know,

Till every wind that sweeps the land
Goes, glory laden, from the strand.

The other, with a narrower scope,
Yet led by not less grand a hope,
Hath won, perhaps, as proud a place,
And wears its fame with meeker grace.
Wives march beneath its glittering sign,
Fond mothers swell the lovely line,
And many a sweetheart hides her blush
In the young patriot's generous flush.

No breeze of battle ever fanned
The colors of that tender band;
Its office is beside the bed,
Where throbs some sick or wounded head.
It does not court the soldier's tomb,
But plies the needle and the loom;
And, by a thousand peaceful deeds,
Supplies a struggling nation's needs.

Nor is that army's gentle might
Unfelt amid the deadly fight;
It nerves the son's, the husband's hand,
It points the lover's fearless brand;
It thrills the languid, warms the cold,
Gives even new courage to the bold;
And sometimes lifts the veriest clod
To its own lofty trust in God.

When Heaven shall blow the trump of peace,
And bid this weary warfare cease,
Their several missions nobly done,
The triumph grasped, and freedom won,
Both armies, from their toils at rest,
Alike may claim the victor's crest,
But each shall see its dearest prize
Gleam softly from the other's eyes.

CHRISTMAS

How grace this hallowed day?
Shall happy bells, from yonder ancient spire,
Send their glad greetings to each Christmas fire
Round which the children play?

Alas! for many a moon,
That tongueless tower hath cleaved the Sabbath air,
Mute as an obelisk of ice, aglare
Beneath an Arctic noon.

Shame to the foes that drown
Our psalms of worship with their impious drum,
The sweetest chimes in all the land lie dumb
In some far rustic town.

There, let us think, they keep,
Of the dead Yules which here beside the sea

They 've ushered in with old-world, English glee,
Some echoes in their sleep.

How shall we grace the day?
With feast, and song, and dance, and antique sports,
And shout of happy children in the courts,
And tales of ghost and fay?

Is there indeed a door,
Where the old pastimes, with their lawful noise,
And all the merry round of Christmas joys,
Could enter as of yore?

Would not some pallid face
Look in upon the banquet, calling up
Dread shapes of battles in the wassail cup,
And trouble all the place?

How could we bear the mirth,
While some loved reveler of a year ago
Keeps his mute Christmas now beneath the snow,
In cold Virginian earth?

How shall we grace the day?
Ah! let the thought that on this holy morn
The Prince of Peace — the Prince of Peace was born,
Employ us, while we pray!

Pray for the peace which long
Hath left this tortured land, and haply now
Holds its white court on some far mountain's brow,
There hardly safe from wrong!

Let every sacred fane
Call its sad votaries to the shrine of God,
And, with the cloister and the tented sod,
Join in one solemn strain!

With pomp of Roman form,
With the grave ritual brought from England's shore,
And with the simple faith which asks no more
Than that the heart be warm!

He, who, till time shall cease,
Will watch that earth, where once, not all in vain,
He died to give us peace, may not disdain
A prayer whose theme is — peace.

Perhaps ere yet the Spring
Hath died into the Summer, over all
The land, the peace of His vast love shall fall,
Like some protecting wing.

Oh, ponder what it means!
Oh, turn the rapturous thought in every way!
Oh, give the vision and the fancy play,
And shape the coming scenes!

Peace in the quiet dales,
Made rankly fertile by the blood of men,
Peace in the woodland, and the lonely glen,
Peace in the peopled vales!

Peace in the crowded town,
Peace in a thousand fields of waving grain,
Peace in the highway and the flowery lane,
Peace on the wind-swept down!

Peace on the farthest seas,
Peace in our sheltered bays and ample streams,
Peace wheresoe'er our starry garland gleams,
And peace in every breeze!

Peace on the whirring marts,
Peace where the scholar thinks, the hunter roams,
Peace, God of Peace! peace, peace, in all our homes,
And peace in all our hearts!

ODE

SUNG ON THE OCCASION OF DECORATING THE GRAVES OF THE CONFEDERATE DEAD, AT MAGNOLIA CEMETERY, CHARLESTON, S. C., 1867

I

SLEEP sweetly in your humble graves,
Sleep, martyrs of a fallen cause;
Though yet no marble column craves
The pilgrim here to pause.

II

In seeds of laurel in the earth
The blossom of your fame is blown,
And somewhere, waiting for its birth,
The shaft is in the stone!

III

Meanwhile, behalf the tardy years
Which keep in trust your storied tombs,
Behold! your sisters bring their tears,
And these memorial blooms.

IV

Small tributes! but your shades will smile
More proudly on these wreaths to-day,
Than when some cannon-moulded pile
Shall overlook this bay.

V

Stoop, angels, hither from the skies!
  There is no holier spot of ground
Than where defeated valor lies,
  By mourning beauty crowned!

SONNETS

SONNETS

I

POET! if on a lasting fame be bent
Thy unperturbing hopes, thou will not roam
Too far from thine own happy heart and home;
Cling to the lowly earth, and be content!
So shall thy name be dear to many a heart;
So shall the noblest truths by thee be taught;
The flower and fruit of wholesome human thought
Bless the sweet labors of thy gentle art.
The brightest stars are nearest to the earth,
And we may track the mighty sun above,
Even by the shadow of a slender flower.
Always, O bard, humility is power!
And thou mayst draw from matters of the hearth
Truths wide as nations, and as deep as love.

II

MOST men know love but as a part of life;
They hide it in some corner of the breast,
Even from themselves; and only when they rest
In the brief pauses of that daily strife,
Wherewith the world might else be not so rife,
They draw it forth (as one draws forth a toy
To soothe some ardent, kiss-exacting boy)
And hold it up to sister, child, or wife.
Ah me! why may not love and life be one?
Why walk we thus alone, when by our side,
Love, like a visible God, might be our guide?
How would the marts grow noble! and the street,
Worn like a dungeon-floor by weary feet,
Seem then a golden court-way of the Sun!

III

LIFE ever seems as from its present site
It aimed to lure us. Mountains of the past
It melts, with all their crags and caverns vast,
Into a purple cloud! Across the night
Which hides what is to be, it shoots a light
All rosy with the yet unrisen dawn.
Not the near daisies, but yon distant height
Attracts us, lying on this emerald lawn.
And always, be the landscape what it may —
Blue, misty hill or sweep of glimmering plain —
It is the eye's endeavor still to gain
The fine, faint limit of the bounding day.
God, haply, in this mystic mode, would fain
Hint of a happier home, far, far away!

IV

THEY dub thee idler, smiling sneeringly,
And why? because, forsooth, so many moons,
Here dwelling voiceless by the voiceful sea,
Thou hast not set thy thoughts to paltry tunes
In song or sonnet. Them these golden noons
Oppress not with their beauty; they could prate,
Even while a prophet read the solemn runes
On which is hanging some imperial fate.
How know they, these good gossips, what to thee
The ocean and its wanderers may have brought?
How know they, in their busy vacancy,
With what far aim thy spirit may be fraught?
Or that thou dost not bow thee silently
Before some great unutterable thought?

V

SOME truths there be are better left unsaid;
Much is there that we may not speak unblamed.
On words, as wings, how many joys have fled!
The jealous fairies love not to be named.
There is an old-world tale of one whose bed
A genius graced, to all, save him, unknown;
One day the secret passed his lips, and sped
As secrets speed — thenceforth he slept alone.
Too much, oh! far too much is told in books;
Too broad a daylight wraps us all and each.
Ah! it is well that, deeper than our looks,
Some secrets lie beyond conjecture's reach.
Ah! it is well that in the soul are nooks
That will not open to the keys of speech.

VI

I SCARCELY grieve, O Nature! at the lot
That pent my life within a city's bounds,
And shut me from thy sweetest sights and sounds.
Perhaps I had not learned, if some lone cot
Had nursed a dreamy childhood, what the mart
Taught me amid its turmoil; so my youth
Had missed full many a stern but wholesome truth.
Here, too, O Nature! in this haunt of Art,
Thy power is on me, and I own thy thrall.
There is no unimpressive spot on earth!
The beauty of the stars is over all,
And Day and Darkness visit every hearth.
Clouds do not scorn us: yonder factory's smoke
Looked like a golden mist when morning broke.

VII

GRIEF dies like joy; the tears upon my cheek
Will disappear like dew. Dear God! I know
Thy kindly Providence hath made it so,
And thank thee for the law. I am too weak
To make a friend of Sorrow, or to wear,
With that dark angel ever by my side
(Though to thy heaven there be no better guide),
A front of manly calm. Yet, for I hear
How woe hath cleansed, how grief can deify,
So weak a thing it seems that grief should die,
And love and friendship with it, I could pray,
That if it might not gloom upon my brow,
Nor weigh upon my arm as it doth now,
No grief of mine should ever pass away.

VIII

AT last, beloved Nature! I have met
Thee face to face upon thy breezy hills,
And boldly, where thy inmost bowers are set,
Gazed on thee naked in thy mountain rills.
When first I felt thy breath upon my brow,
Tears of strange ecstasy gushed out like rain,
And with a longing, passionate as vain,
I strove to clasp thee. But, I know not how,
Always before me didst thou seem to glide;
And often from one sunny mountain-side,
Upon the next bright peak I saw thee kneel,
And heard thy voice upon the billowy blast;
But, climbing, only reached that shrine to feel
The shadow of a Presence which had passed.

IX

I KNOW not why, but all this weary day,
Suggested by no definite grief or pain,
Sad fancies have been flitting through my brain;
Now it has been a vessel losing way,
Rounding a stormy headland; now a gray
Dull waste of clouds above a wintry main;
And then, a banner, drooping in the rain,
And meadows beaten into bloody clay.
Strolling at random with this shadowy woe
At heart, I chanced to wander hither! Lo!
A league of desolate marsh-land, with its lush,
Hot grasses in a noisome, tide-left bed,
And faint, warm airs, that rustle in the hush,
Like whispers round the body of the dead!

X

(WRITTEN ON A VERY SMALL SHEET OF NOTE-PAPER)

WERE I the poet-laureate of the fairies,
Who in a rose-leaf finds too broad a page ;
Or could I, like your beautiful canaries,
Sing with free heart and happy, in a cage;
Perhaps I might within this little space
(As in some Eastern tale, by magic power,
A giant is imprisoned in a flower)
Have told you something with a poet's grace.
But I need wider limits, ampler scope,
A world of freedom for a world of passion,
And even then, the glory of my hope
Would not be uttered in its stateliest fashion ;
Yet, lady, when fit language shall have told it,
You 'll find one little heart enough to hold it!

XI

WHICH are the clouds, and which the mountains?
See,
They mix and melt together! Yon blue hill
Looks fleeting as the vapors which distill
Their dews upon its summit, while the free
And far-off clouds, now solid, dark, and still,
An aspect wear of calm eternity.
Each seems the other, as our fancies will —
The cloud a mount, the mount a cloud, and we
Gaze doubtfully. So everywhere on earth,
This foothold where we stand with slipping feet,
The unsubstantial and substantial meet,
And we are fooled until made wise by Time.
Is not the obvious lesson something worth,
Lady? or have I wov'n an idle rhyme?

XII

WHAT gossamer lures thee now? What hope, what name
Is on thy lips? What dreams to fruit have grown?
Thou who hast turned *one* Poet-heart to stone,
Is thine yet burning with its seraph flame?
Let me give back a warning of thine own,
That, falling from thee many moons ago,
Sank on my soul like the prophetic moan
Of some young Sibyl shadowing her own woe.
The words are thine, and will not do thee wrong,
I only bind their solemn charge to song.
Thy tread is on a quicksand — oh! be wise!
Nor, in the passionate eagerness of youth,
Mistake thy bosom-serpent's glittering eyes
For the calm lights of Reason and of Truth.

XIII

I THANK you, kind and best belovëd friend,
With the same thanks one murmurs to a sister,
When, for some gentle favor, he hath kissed her,
Less for the gifts than for the love you send,
Less for the flowers than what the flowers convey,
If I, indeed, divine their meaning truly,
And not unto myself ascribe, unduly,
Things which you neither meant nor wished to say,
Oh! tell me, is the hope then all misplaced?
And am I flattered by my own affection?
But in your beauteous gift, methought I traced
Something above a short-lived predilection,
And which, for that I know no dearer name,
I designate as love, without love's flame.

XIV

ARE these wild thoughts, thus fettered in my rhymes,
Indeed the product of my heart and brain?
How strange that on my ear the rhythmic strain
Falls like faint memories of far-off times!
When did I feel the sorrow, act the part,
Which I have striv'n to shadow forth in song?
In what dead century swept that mingled throng
Of mighty pains and pleasures through my heart?
Not in the yesterdays of that still life
Which I have passed so free and far from strife,
But somewhere in this weary world I know,
In some strange land, beneath some orient clime,
I saw or shared a martyrdom sublime,
And felt a deeper grief than any later woe.

XV

IN MEMORIAM — HARRIS SIMONS

TRUE Christian, tender husband, gentle Sire,
A stricken household mourns thee, but its loss
Is Heaven's gain and thine; upon the cross
God hangs the crown, the pinion, and the lyre:
And thou hast won them all. Could we desire
To quench that diadem's celestial light,
To hush thy song and stay thy heavenward flight,
Because we miss thee by this autumn fire?
Ah, no! ah, no! — chant on! — soar on! — Reign on!
For we are better — thou art happier thus;
And haply from the splendor of thy throne,
Or haply from the echoes of thy psalm,
Something may fall upon us, like the calm
To which thou shalt hereafter welcome us!

POEMS NOW FIRST COLLECTED

SONG

COMPOSED FOR WASHINGTON'S BIRTHDAY, AND RESPECTFULLY INSCRIBED TO THE OFFICERS AND MEMBERS OF THE WASHINGTON LIGHT INFANTRY OF CHARLESTON, FEBRUARY 22, 1859

A HUNDRED years and more ago
  A little child was born —
To-day, with pomp of martial show,
  We hail his natal morn.

Who guessed as that poor infant wept
  Upon a woman's knee,
A nation from the centuries stept
  As weak and frail as he?

Who saw the future on his brow
  Upon that happy morn?
We are a mighty nation now
  Because that child was born.

To him, and to his spirit's scope,
  Besides a glorious home,
We owe that what we have and hope
  Are more than Greece and Rome.

A BOUQUET

Take first a Cowslip, then an Asphodel,
  A bridal Rose, some snowy Orange flowers;
A Lily next, and by its spotless bell
  Place the bright Iris, darling of the showers;
Set gold Nasturtiums, Elder blooms between,
  And Heart's-ease to the Orchis marry sweetly;
Then with red Pinks, and slips of Evergreen,
  You will possess — all folded up discreetly —
In one bouquet, that none but you may know,
  The name I love beyond all names below.

LINES

I STOOPED from star-bright regions, where
Thou canst not enter even in prayer;
And thought to light thy heart and hearth
With all the poesy of earth.

Oh, foolish hope! those mystic gleams
To thee were unsubstantial dreams;
The paltry world had made thee blind,
And shut thy heart and dulled thy mind.

I was a vassal at thy feet,
And cringed more meanly than was meet,
And since I dared not to be free,
Was scouted as a slave should be.

I gave thee all — my truth, my trust —
I bowed my spirit in the dust,
I put a crown upon thy brow,
And am its proper victim now.

A TRIFLE

I KNOW not why, but ev'n to me
My songs seem sweet when read to thee.

Perhaps in this the pleasure lies —
I read my thoughts within thine eyes.

And so dare fancy that my art
May sink as deeply as thy heart.

Perhaps I love to make my words
Sing round thee like so many birds,

Or, maybe, they are only sweet
As they seem offerings at thy feet.

Or haply, Lily, when I speak,
I think, perchance, they touch thy cheek,

Or with a yet more precious bliss,
Die on thy red lips in a kiss.

Each reason here — I cannot tell —
Or all perhaps may solve the spell.

But if she watch when I am by,
Lily may deeper see than I.

LINES

I SAW, or dreamed I saw, her sitting lone,
Her neck bent like a swan's, her brown eyes
 thrown
On some sweet poem — his, I think, who sings
Œnone, or the hapless Maud: no rings
Flashed from the dainty fingers, which held back
Her beautiful blonde hair. Ah! would these black
Locks of mine own were mingling with it now,
And these warm lips were pressed against her
 brow!
And, as she turned a page, methought I heard —
Hush! could it be? — a faintly murmured word,
It was so softly dwelt on — such a smile
Played on her brow and wreathed her lip the while
That my heart leaped to hear it, and a flame
Burned on my forehead — Sa'ra! — 't was my
 name.

SONNET

If I have graced no single song of mine
With thy sweet name, they all are full of thee;
Thou art my Muse, my "May," my "Madeline:"
But "Julia"!—ah! that gentle name to me
Is something far too sacred for the throng
Of worldly listeners 'round me. Yet ev'n now
I weave a chaplet for thy sinless brow;—
Wilt thou not wear it? 'T is a fashionable song,—
I will not say of what,—but on it I
Have wreaked heart, mind, my love, my hopes of fame,
Yet after all it hath no nobler aim
Than thy dear praise. Ere many moons pass by,
When the lost gem is set, the crown complete,
I 'll lay a poet's tribute at thy feet.

TO ROSA ——: ACROSTIC

I TOOK a Rosebud from a certain bower,
And by its side placed an Orange flower,
Then with the Speedwell, blended the perfume
And the sweet beauty of an Apple-bloom,
And thus, 't is one of the loveliest feats,
Is spelled a gentle lady's name in sweets.

ELECTROTYPED AND PRINTED
BY H. O. HOUGHTON AND CO.

The Riverside Press

CAMBRIDGE, MASS., U. S. A.

www.ingramcontent.com/pod-product-compliance
Lightning Source LLC
LaVergne TN
LVHW011202110826
845150LV00006B/1291

* 9 7 8 1 4 2 5 5 7 2 4 9 5 *